ACCLAIM FOR *Ric...*

STRAIGHT MAN

"By turns hilarious and compassionate."   —*Chicago Tribune*

"Russo can penetrate to the tender quick of ordinary American lives."   —*Entertainment Weekly*

"A rich, complex novel . . . with sharp language and sharper imagination, [Russo] delivers the most engaging and rewarding cast of characters of any novel in recent memory."   —*Time Out*

"One of our most adept surveyors of the human landscape."   —*Philadelphia Inquirer*

"A delight. . . . [*Straight Man* has] a kind of buoyant sarcasm."   —*Dallas Morning News*

"[Russo] surrounds the tragic awakening of small-town characters with humor while still preserving their poignancy."   —*Milwaukee Journal-Sentinel*

"The humor prompts big belly laughs, and the pathos sets tears to flowing."   —*Houston Chronicle*

"Russo has established himself as a thoughtful, ironic, and gifted comic novelist. With *Straight Man*, he confirms his place as one of the few modern satirists who not only shows the foibles of his characters, but also demonstrates their compassion, humility, and sense of humor."   —*Orlando Sentinel*

Richard Russo

STRAIGHT MAN

Richard Russo lives in coastal Maine with his wife and their two daughters. He has written five novels: *Mohawk, The Risk Pool, Nobody's Fool, Straight Man,* and *Empire Falls,* and a collection of stories, *The Whore's Child.*

STRAIGHT MAN

Richard Russo

STRAIGHT MAN

Vintage Contemporaries

Vintage Books

A Division of Random House, Inc.

New York

FIRST VINTAGE CONTEMPORARIES EDITION, JUNE 1998

Copyright © 1997 by Richard Russo

All rights reserved under International and Pan-American Copyright
Conventions. Published in the United States by Vintage Books, a division of
Random House, Inc., New York, and simultaneously in Canada by Random
House of Canada Limited, Toronto. Originally published in hardcover
in the United States by Random House, Inc., New York, in 1997.

The Prologue to *Straight Man* was originally published,
in slightly different form, as "Dog," in the December 23-30, 1996,
issue of *The New Yorker*.

The Library of Congress has cataloged the Random House
edition as follows:
Russo, Richard.
Straight man : a novel / Richard Russo.
p. cm.
ISBN 0-679-43246-9
I. Title
PS3568.U812S77   1997
813'.54—dc21   96-48578

Vintage ISBN: 0-375-70190-7

Author photograph © Marion Ettlinger
Book design by Caroline Cunningham

Random House Web address: www.randomhouse.com

Printed in the United States of America
30 29 28 27 26 25 24 23 22 21

For Nat and Judith

Special thanks for faith and hard work and good advice to David Rosenthal, Alison Samuel, and Barbara Russo, for technical assistance and/or inspiration to Jean Findlay, Ed Ervin, Toni Katz, Greg and Peggy Johnson, Kjell Meling, and Chris Cokinis.

PROLOGUE

They're nice to have. A dog.

—F. Scott Fitzgerald,
The Great Gatsby

Truth be told, I'm not an easy man. I can be an entertaining one, though it's been my experience that most people don't want to be entertained. They want to be comforted. And, of course, my idea of entertaining might not be yours. I'm in complete agreement with all those people who say, regarding movies, "I just want to be entertained." This populist position is much derided by my academic colleagues as simpleminded and unsophisticated, evidence of questionable analytical and critical acuity. But I agree with the premise, and I too just want to be entertained. That I am almost never entertained by what entertains other people who just want to be entertained doesn't make us philosophically incompatible. It just means we shouldn't go to movies together.

The kind of man I am, according to those who know me best, is exasperating. According to my parents, I was an exasperating child as well. They divorced when I was in junior high school, and they agree on little except that I was an impossible child. The story they tell of young William Henry Devereaux, Jr., and his first dog is eerily similar in its facts, its conclusions, even the style of its telling, no matter which of them is telling it. Here's the story they tell.

I was nine, and the house we were living in, which belonged to the university, was my fourth. My parents were academic nomads, my father, then and now, an academic opportunist, always in the vanguard of whatever was trendy and chic in literary criticism. This was the fifties, and for him, New Criticism was already old. In early middle age he was already a full professor with several published books, all of them "hot," the subject of intense debate at English department cocktail parties. The academic position he favored was the "distinguished visiting professor" variety, usually created for him, duration of visit a year or two at most, perhaps because it's hard to remain distinguished among people who know you. Usually his teaching responsibilities were light, a course or two a year. Otherwise, he was expected to read and think and write and publish and acknowledge in the preface of his next book the generosity of the institution that provided him the academic good life. My mother, also an English professor, was hired as part of the package deal, to teach a full load and thereby help balance the books.

The houses we lived in were elegant, old, high-ceilinged, drafty, either on or close to campus. They had hardwood floors and smoky fireplaces with fires in them only when my father held court, which he did either on Friday afternoons, our large rooms filling up with obsequious junior faculty and nervous grad students, or Saturday evenings, when my mother gave dinner parties for the chair of the department, or the dean, or a visiting poet. In all situations I was the only child, and I must have been a lonely one, because what I wanted more than anything in the world was a dog.

Predictably, my parents did not. Probably the terms of living in these university houses were specific regarding pets. By the time I was nine I'd been lobbying hard for a dog for a year or two. My father and mother were hoping I would outgrow this longing, given enough time. I could see this hope in their eyes and it steeled my resolve, intensified my desire. What did I want for Christmas? A dog. What did I want for my birthday? A dog. What did I want on my ham sandwich? A dog. It was a deeply satisfying look of pure exasperation they shared at such moments, and if I couldn't have a dog, this was the next best thing.

Life continued in this fashion until finally my mother made a mistake, a doozy of a blunder born of emotional exhaustion and despair. She, far more than my father, would have preferred a happy child. One spring day after I'd been badgering her pretty relentlessly she sat me down and said, "You know, a dog is something you earn." My father heard this, got up, and left the room, grim acknowledgment that my mother had just conceded the war. Her idea was to make the dog conditional. The conditions to be imposed would be numerous and severe, and I would be incapable of fulfilling them, so when I didn't get the dog it'd be my own fault. This was her logic, and the fact that she thought such a plan might work illustrates that some people should never be parents and that she was one of them.

I immediately put into practice a plan of my own to wear my mother down. Unlike hers, my plan was simple and flawless. Mornings I woke up talking about dogs and nights I fell asleep talking about them. When my mother and father changed the subject, I changed it back. "Speaking of dogs," I would say, a forkful of my mother's roast poised at my lips, and I'd be off again. Maybe no one had been speaking of dogs, but never mind, we were speaking of them now. At the library I checked out a half dozen books on dogs every two weeks and left them lying open around the house. I pointed out dogs we passed on the street, dogs on television, dogs in the magazines my mother subscribed to. I discussed the relative merits of various breeds at every meal. My father seldom listened to anything I said, but I began to see signs that the underpinnings of my mother's personality were beginning to corrode in the salt water of my tidal persistence, and when I judged that she was nigh to complete collapse, I took every penny of the allowance money I'd been saving and spent it on a dazzling, bejeweled dog collar and leash set at the overpriced pet store around the corner.

During this period when we were constantly "speaking of dogs," I was not a model boy. I was supposed to be "earning a dog," and I was constantly checking with my mother to see how I was doing, just how much of a dog I'd earned, but I doubt my behavior had changed a jot. I wasn't really a bad boy. Just a noisy, busy, constantly needy boy. Mr. In and Out, my mother called me, because I was in and out of rooms, in and out of doors, in and out of the refrigerator. "Henry," my mother would plead with me. "Light somewhere." One of the things I often needed was information, and I constantly interrupted my mother's reading and paper grading to get it. My father, partly to avoid having to answer my questions, spent most of his time in his book-lined office on campus, joining my mother and me only at mealtimes, so that we could speak of dogs as a family. Then he was gone again, blissfully unaware, I thought at the time, that my mother continued to glare homicidally, for long minutes after his departure, at the chair he'd so recently occupied. But he claimed to be close to finishing the book he was working on, and this was a powerful excuse to offer a woman with as much abstract respect for books and learning as my mother possessed.

Gradually, she came to understand that she was fighting a battle she couldn't win and that she was fighting it alone. I now know that this was part of a larger cluster of bitter marital realizations, but at the time I sniffed nothing in the air but victory. In late August, during what people refer to as "the dog days," when she made one last, weak condition, final evidence that I had earned a dog, I relented and truly tried to reform my behavior. It was literally the least I could do.

What my mother wanted of me was to stop slamming the screen door. The house we were living in, it must be said, was an acoustic marvel akin to the Whispering Gallery in St. Paul's, where muted voices travel across a great open space and arrive, clear and intact, at the other side of the great dome. In our house the screen door swung shut on a tight spring, the straight wooden edge of the door encountering the doorframe like a gunshot played through a guitar amplifier set on stun, the crack transmitting perfectly, with equal force and clarity, to every room in the house, upstairs and down. That summer I was in and out that door dozens of times a day, and my mother said it was like living in a shooting gallery. It made her wish the door wasn't shooting blanks. If I could just remember not to slam the door, then she'd see about a dog. Soon.

I did better, remembering about half the time not to let the door slam. When I forgot, I came back in to apologize, sometimes forgetting then too. Still, that I was trying, together with the fact that I carried the expensive dog collar and leash with me everywhere I went, apparently moved my mother, because at the end of that first week of diminished door slamming, my father went somewhere on Saturday morning, refusing to reveal where, and so of course I knew. "What kind?" I pleaded *with my mother when he was gone. But she claimed not to know. "Your father's doing this," she said, and I thought I saw a trace of misgiving in her expression.*

When he returned, I saw why. He'd put it in the backseat, and when my father pulled the car in and parked along the side of the house, I saw from the kitchen window its chin resting on the back of the rear seat. I think it saw me too, but if so it did not react. Neither did it seem to notice that the car had stopped, that my father had gotten out and was holding the front seat forward. He had to reach in, take the dog by the collar, and pull.

As the animal unfolded its long legs and stepped tentatively, arthritically, out of the car, I saw that I had been both betrayed and outsmarted. In all the time we had been "speaking of dogs," what I'd been seeing in my mind's eye was puppies. Collie puppies, beagle puppies, Lab puppies, shepherd puppies, but none of that had been inked anywhere, I now realized. If not a puppy, a young dog. A rascal, full of spirit and possibility, a dog with new tricks to learn. This dog was barely ambulatory. It stood, head down, as if ashamed at something done long ago in its puppydom, and I thought I detected a shiver run through its frame when my father closed the car door behind it.

The animal was, I suppose, what might have been called a handsome dog. A purebred, rust-colored Irish setter, meticulously groomed, wonderfully mannered, the kind of dog you could safely bring into a house owned by the university, the sort of dog that wouldn't really violate the no pets clause, the kind of dog, I saw clearly, you'd get if you really didn't want a dog or to be bothered with a dog. It'd belonged, I later learned, to a professor emeritus of the university who'd been put into a nursing home earlier in the week, leaving the animal an orphan. It was like a painting of a dog, or a dog you'd hire to pose for a portrait, a dog you could be sure wouldn't move.

Both my father and the animal came into the kitchen reluctantly, my father closing the screen door behind them with great care. I like to think that on the way home he'd suffered a misgiving, though I could tell that it was his intention to play the hand out boldly. My mother, who'd taken in my devastation at a glance, studied me for a moment and then my father.

"What?" he said.

My mother just shook her head.

My father looked at me, then back at her. A violent shiver palsied the dog's limbs. The animal seemed to want to lie down on the cool linoleum, but to have forgotten how. It offered a deep sigh that seemed to speak for all of us.

"He's a good dog," my father said, rather pointedly, to my mother. "A little high-strung, but that's the way with purebred setters. They're all nervous."

This was not the sort of thing my father knew. Clearly he was repeating the explanation he'd just been given when he picked up the dog.

"What's his name?" my mother said, apparently for something to say.

My father had neglected to ask. He checked the dog's collar for clues.

"Lord," my mother said. "Lord, lord."

"It's not like we can't name him ourselves," my father said, irritated now. "I think it's something we can manage, don't you?"

"You could name him after a passé school of literary criticism," my mother suggested.

"It's a she," I said, because it was.

It seemed to cheer my father, at least a little, that I'd allowed myself to be drawn into the conversation. "What do you say, Henry?" he wanted to know. "What'll we name him?"

This second faulty pronoun reference was too much for me. "I want to go out and play now," I said, and I bolted for the screen door before an objection could be registered. It slammed behind me, hard, its gunshot report even louder than usual. As I cleared the steps in a single leap, I thought I heard a thud back in the kitchen, a dull, muffled echo of the door, and then I heard my father say, "What the hell?" I went back up the steps, cautiously now, meaning to apologize for the door. Through the screen I could see my mother and father standing together in the middle of the kitchen, looking down at the dog, which seemed to be napping. My father nudged a haunch with the toe of his cordovan loafer.

He dug the grave in the backyard with a shovel borrowed from a neighbor. My father had soft hands and they blistered easily. I offered to help, but he just looked at me. When he was standing, midthigh, in the hole he'd dug, he shook his head one last time in disbelief. "Dead," he said. "Before we could even name him."

I knew better than to correct the pronoun again, so I just stood there thinking about what he'd said while he climbed out of the hole and went over to the back porch to collect the dog where it lay under an old sheet. I could tell by the careful way he tucked that sheet under the animal that he didn't want to touch anything dead, even newly dead. He lowered the dog into the hole by means of the sheet, but he had to drop it the last foot or so. When the animal thudded on the earth and lay still, my father looked over at me and shook his head. Then he picked up the shovel and leaned on it before he started filling in the hole. He seemed to be waiting for me to say something, so I said, "Red."

My father's eyes narrowed, as if I'd spoken in a foreign tongue. "What?" he said.

"We'll name her Red," I explained.

In the years after he left us, my father became even more famous. He is sometimes credited, if credit is the word, with being the Father of American Literary Theory. In addition to his many books of scholarship, he's also written a literary memoir that was short-listed for a major award and that offers insight into the personalities of several major literary figures of the twentieth century, now deceased. His photograph often graces the pages of the literary reviews. He went through a phase where he wore crewneck sweaters and gold chains beneath his tweed coat, but now he's mostly photographed in an oxford button-down shirt, tie, and jacket, in his book-lined office at the university. But to me, his son, William Henry Devereaux, Sr., is most real standing in his ruined cordovan loafers, leaning on the handle of a borrowed shovel, examining his dirty, blistered hands, and receiving my suggestion of what to name a dead dog. I suspect that digging our dog's grave was one of relatively few experiences of his life (excepting carnal ones) that did not originate on the printed page. And when I suggested we name the dead dog Red, he looked at me as if I myself had just stepped from the pages of a book he'd started to read years ago and then put down when something else caught his interest. "What?" he said, letting go of the shovel, so that its handle hit the earth between my feet. "What?"

It's not an easy time for any parent, this moment when the realization dawns that you've given birth to something that will never see things the way you do, despite the fact that it is your living legacy, that it bears your name.

Part One

OCCAM'S RAZOR

What I expected, was

Thunder, fighting

Long struggles with men

And climbing.

—Stephen Spender

CHAPTER

I

When my nose finally stops bleeding and I've disposed of the bloody
paper towels, Teddy Barnes insists on driving me home in his ancient
Honda Civic, a car that refuses to die and that Teddy, cheap as he is,
refuses to trade in. June, his wife, whose sense of self-worth is not easily tilted, drives a new Saab. "That seat goes back," Teddy says, observing that my knees are practically under my chin.

When we stop at an intersection for oncoming traffic, I run my fingers along the side of the seat, looking for the release. "It does, huh?"

"It's supposed to," he says, sounding academic, helpless.

I know it's supposed to, but I give up trying to make it, preferring
the illusion of suffering. I'm not a guilt provoker by nature, but I can
play that role. I release a theatrical sigh intended to convey that this is
nonsense, that my long legs could be stretched out comfortably beneath
the wheel of my own Lincoln, a car as ancient as Teddy's Civic, but built
on a scale more suitable to the long-legged William Henry Devereaux
of the world, two of whom, my father and me, remain above ground.

Teddy is an insanely cautious driver, unwilling to goose his little Civic into a left turn in front of oncoming traffic. "The cars are spaced just wrong. I can't help it," he explains when he sees me grinning at him. Teddy's my age, forty-nine, and though his features are more boyish, he too is beginning to show signs of age. Never robust, his chest seems to have become more concave, which emphasizes his small paunch. His hands are delicate, almost feminine, hairless. His skinny legs appear lost in his trousers. It occurs to me as I study him that Teddy would have a hard time starting over—that is, learning how unfamiliar things work, competing, finding a mate. The business of young men. "Why would I have to start over?" he wants to know, a frightened expression deepening the lines around the corners of his eyes.

Apparently, to judge from the way he's looking at me now, I have spoken my thought out loud, though I wasn't aware of doing so. "Don't you ever wish you could?"

"Could what?" he says, his attention diverted. Having spied a break in the oncoming traffic, he takes his foot off the brake and leans forward, his foot poised over but not touching the gas pedal, only to conclude that the gap between the cars isn't as big as he thought, settling back into his seat with a frustrated sigh.

Something about this gesture causes me to wonder if a rumor I've been hearing about Teddy's wife, June—that she's involved with a junior faculty member in our department—just might be true. I haven't given it much credence until now because Teddy and June have such a perfect symbiotic relationship. In the English department they are known as Fred and Ginger for the grace with which they move together, without a hint of passion, toward a single, shared destination. In an atmosphere of distrust and suspicion and retribution, two people working together represent a power base, and no one has understood this sad academic truth better than Teddy and June. It's hard to imagine either of them risking it. On the other hand, it must be hard to be married to a man like Teddy, who's always leaning forward in anticipation, foot poised above the gas pedal, but too cautious to stomp.

We are on Church Street, which parallels the railyard that divides the city of Railton into two dingy, equally unattractive halves. This is the broadest section of the yard, some twenty sets of tracks wide, and most of those tracks are occupied by a rusty boxcar or two. A century ago the entire yard would have been full, the city of Railton itself thriving, its citizens looking forward to a secure future. No longer. On Church Street, where we remain idling in the left-turn lane, there is no longer a single church, though there were once, I'm told, half a dozen. The last of them, a decrepit red brick affair, long condemned and boarded up, was razed last year after some kids broke in and fell through the floor. The large parcel of land it perched on now sits empty. It's the fact that there are so many empty, littered spaces in Railton, like the windblown expanses between the boxcars in the railyard, that challenges hope. Within sight of where we sit waiting to turn onto Pleasant Street, a man named William Cherry, a lifelong Conrail employee, has recently taken his life by lying down on the track in the middle of the night. At first the speculation was that he was one of the men laid off the previous week, but the opposite turned out to be true. He had in fact just retired with his pension and full benefits. On television his less fortunate neighbors couldn't understand it. He had it made, they said.

When it's safe, when all the oncoming traffic has passed, Teddy turns onto Pleasant, the most unpleasant of Railton streets. Lined on both sides with shabby one- and two-story office fronts, Pleasant Street is too steep to climb in winter when there's snow. Now, in early April, I suspect it may be too steep for Teddy's Civic, which is whirring heroically in its lower gears and going all of fifteen miles an hour. There's a plateau and a traffic light halfway up, and when we stop, I say, "Should I get out and push?"

"It's just cold," Teddy tells me. "Really. We're fine."

No doubt he's right. We will make it. Why this fact should be so discouraging is what I'd like to know. I can't help wondering if William Cherry also feared things would work out if he didn't do something drastic to prevent them.

"I think I can, I think I can, I think I can," I chant, as the light changes and Teddy urges forward the Little Civic That Could. A few months ago I foolishly tried to climb this same hill in a light snow. It was nearly midnight, and I was heading home from the campus and hadn't wanted to go the long way, which added ten minutes. During the long Pennsylvania winters, curbside parking is not allowed at night, so the street had a deserted, ominous feel. Mine was the only car on the five-block incline, and I made it without incident to this very plateau where Teddy and I have now stopped. The office of my insurance agent was on the corner, and I remember wishing he was there to see me do something so reckless in a car he was insuring. When the light changed, my tires spun, then caught, and I labored up the last two blocks. I couldn't have been more than ten yards from the crest of the hill when I felt the tires begin to spin and the rear end to drift. When the car stalled and I realized the brake exerted no meaningful influence, I sat back and became a witness to my own folly. With the engine dead and the snow muffling all other sounds, I found myself in a silent ballet as I slalomed gracefully down the hill, backward as far as the landing where it appeared that I would stop, right in front of my insurance agent's, but then I slipped over the edge and spun down the last three blocks, rebounding off curbs like the cue ball in a game of bumper pool, finally coming to rest at the entrance to the railyard, having suffered a loss of equilibrium but otherwise unscathed. A friend, Bodie Pie, who lives in a second-floor flat near the bottom of the hill and claims to have witnessed my balletic descent, swears she heard me laughing maniacally, but I don't remember that. The only emotion I recall is similar to the one I feel now, with Teddy on this same hill. That is, a certain sense of disappointment about such drama resulting in so little consequence. Teddy is sure we'll make it, and so am I. We have tenure, the two of us.

Once out of town, the rejuvenated Civic rushes along the two-lane blacktop like a cartoon car with a big, loopy smile (I knew I could, I knew I could), the Pennsylvania countryside hurtling by. Most of the trees along the side of the road are budding. Farther back in the deep woods there may still be patches of dirty snow, but spring is definitely in the air, and Teddy has cracked his window to take advantage of it. His thinning hair stirs in the breeze, and I half-expect to see evidence of new leafy growth on his scalp. I know he's been contemplating Rogaine. "You're only taking me home so you can flirt with Lily," I tell him.

This makes Teddy flush. He's had an innocent crush on my wife for over twenty years. If there's such a thing as an innocent crush. If there's such a thing as innocence. Since we built the house in the country, Teddy's had fewer opportunities to see Lily, so he's always on the lookout for an excuse. On those rare Saturday mornings when we still play basketball, he stops by to give me a lift. The court we play on is a few blocks from his house, but he insists the four-mile drive into the country isn't that far out of his way. One drunken night, over a decade ago, he made the mistake of confessing to me his infatuation with Lily. The secret was no sooner out than he tried to extort from me a promise not to reveal it. "If you tell her, so help me . . . ," he kept repeating.

"Don't be an idiot," I assured him. "Of course I'm going to tell her. I'm telling her as soon as I get home."

"What about our friendship?"

"Whose?"

"Ours," he explained. "Yours and mine."

"What about it?" I said. "I'm not the one in love with your wife. Don't talk to me about friendship. I should take you outside."

He grinned at me drunkenly. "You're a pacifist, remember?"

"That doesn't mean I can't threaten you," I told him. "It just means you're not required to take me seriously."

But he was taking me seriously, taking everything seriously. I could tell. "You don't love her as much as you should," he said, real tears in his eyes.

"How would you know?" William Henry Devereaux, Jr., said, dry-eyed.

"You don't," he insisted.

"Would it make you feel better if I promised to ravish her as soon as I get home?"

I mean, the situation was pretty absurd. Two middle-aged men— we were middle-aged even then—sitting in a bar in Railton, Pennsylvania, arguing about how much love was enough, how much more was deserved. The absurdity of it was lost on Teddy, however, and for a second I actually thought he was going to punch me. He had to know I was kidding him, but Teddy belongs to that vast majority who believe that love isn't something you kid about. I don't see how you could *not* kid about love and still claim to have a sense of humor.

Since that night, I'm the only one who makes reference to Teddy's confession. He's never retracted it, but the incident remains embarrassing. "I wish you had some feelings for June," he says now, smiling ruefully. "We could agree to a reciprocal yearning from afar."

"How old are you?" I ask him.

He's quiet for a moment. "Anyhow," he says finally. "The real reason I wanted to drive you home—"

"Oh, Christ," I say. "Here we go."

I know what's coming. For the last few months rumors have been running rampant about an impending purge at the university, one that would reach into the tenured ranks. If such a thing were to happen, virtually everyone in the English department would be vulnerable to dismissal. The news is reportedly being broken to department chairs individually in their year-end conferences with the campus executive officer. According to which rumors you listen to, the chairs are being either asked or required to draw up lists of faculty in their departments who might be considered expendable. Seniority is reportedly not a criterion.

"All right," I tell Teddy. "Give it to me. Who have you been talking to now?"

"Arnie Drenker over in Psychology."

"And you believe Arnie Drenker?" I ask. "He's certifiable."

"He swears he was ordered to make a list."

When I don't immediately respond to this, he takes his eyes off the road for a microsecond to look over at me. My right nostril, which has now swollen to the point where I can see it clearly in my peripheral vision, throbs under his scrutiny. "Why do you refuse to take the situation seriously?"

"Because it's April, Teddy," I explain. This is an old discussion. April is the month of heightened paranoia for academics, not that their normal paranoia is insufficient to ruin a perfectly fine day in any season. But April is always the worst. Whatever dirt will be done to us is always planned in April, then executed over the summer, when we are dispersed. September is always too late to remedy the reduced merit raises, the slashed travel fund, the doubled price of the parking sticker that allows us to park in the Modern Languages lot. Rumors about severe budget cuts that will affect faculty have been rampant every April for the past five years, although this year's have been particularly persistent and virulent. Still, the fact is that every year the legislature has threatened deep cuts in higher education. And every year a high-powered education task force is sent to the capitol to lobby the legislature for increased spending. Every year accusations are leveled, editorials written. Every year the threatened budget cuts are implemented, then at the last fiscal moment money is found and the budget—most of it—restored. And every year I conclude what William of Occam (that first, great modern William, a William for his time and ours, all the William we will ever need, who gave to us his magnificent razor by which to gauge simple truth, who was exiled and relinquished his life that our academic sins might be forgiven) would have concluded—that there will be no faculty purge this year, just as there was none last year, just as there will be none next year. What there will probably be next year is more belt tightening, more denied sabbaticals, an extension of the hiring freeze, a reduced photocopy budget. What there will certainly be next year is another April, and another round of rumors.

Teddy steals another quick glance at me. "Do you have any idea what your colleagues are saying?"

"No," I say, then, "yes. I mean, I know my colleagues, so I can imagine what they're saying."

"They're saying your dismissing the rumors is pretty suspicious. They're wondering if you've made up a list."

I sigh dramatically. "If I did, it'd be a long one. If we ever start cutting the deadwood in our department, we're not going to want to stop at twenty percent."

"That's just the kind of talk that makes people nervous. This is no time to be joking. If you'd trust me, tell me what you know, I could at least reassure our friends."

"What if I don't know anything?"

"Okay, be that way," Teddy says, looking like I've hurt his feelings now. "I didn't tell you everything when I was chair either."

"Yes, you did," I remind him. "I remember because I didn't want to know any of it."

When I see that I've hurt his feelings, I give in a little. "I have my meeting with Dickie later this week," I tell him, trying to remember whether it's tomorrow or Friday.

Teddy doesn't react to this. In fact he doesn't seem to have heard it. Talk about paranoid. He's watching his rearview mirror as if he suspects we're being followed. When I turn around, I see we *are* being followed, tailgated actually, by a red sports car, which jerks into the passing lane dangerously, roars by, darts back in again, forcing Teddy to hit the brakes. It's Paul Rourke's red Camaro, I realize, and when the car pulls over onto the shoulder, Teddy follows, red-faced with impotent fury. Rourke's wife, the second Mrs. R., whose name I can never remember, is at the wheel, but she's clearly acting on her husband's instructions. Though she's normally dreamy-eyed and laconic, something aggressive surfaces when she's behind the wheel. According to Paul, who's been married to the second Mrs. R. long enough to become disenchanted, it's the only time she's ever completely awake. She's always roaring past me on this road to Allegheny Wells, and she always graces me with a long glance before looking away again, apparently disappointed. The bored expression on her face is always the same, unimpeded by recognition.

"If a fight breaks out, she's mine," I tell Teddy, who's still clutching the wheel hard.

"What the—did you see—" he sputters. He's looking over at me to verify events. Anger is one of several emotions Teddy's never sure he's entitled to, and he wants to make certain it's justified in this instance.

Rourke gets out languidly, bends back down, and leans into the car to say something to the second Mrs. R. Probably to stay put. This won't take long. Which it wouldn't, if a fight did break out. Paul Rourke is a big man, and the very idea of getting punched in my already mutilated nose fills me with nausea.

It takes me a while to unfold myself out of Teddy's Civic. Rourke waits patiently, holding the door for me. When I stand up straight, I'm taller than he is, so there's something to be grateful for, even though it's not something of consequence. This is the same man who, several years ago, threw me up against a wall at the department Christmas party, and what worries me today is that there's no wall. If he tosses me now I'm going to end up in the ditch. The good news is he seems content to study my ruined nose and grin at me.

Teddy has gotten out of the car and begun to sputter. "That was almost an accident," he tells Rourke, who, so far, hasn't even honored Teddy with a glance.

"Hello, Reverend," I say, friendly. As a younger man, before converting to atheism, Paul Rourke was a seminarian.

"Does it hurt?" he wants to know, studying my schnoz.

"Sure does, Paul," I assure him, anxious to please.

He nods knowingly. "Good," he says. "I'm glad."

When he raises his hand, I step back, trying not to flinch. In his hand there's a camera, an expensive one, and he gets off about eight automatic clicks before I can offer him my good side.

"This is how I'll remember you when you're gone," he tells me. He nods ever so slightly in Teddy's direction. "Him, I'm just going to forget."

Then he returns to his Camaro, which lurches back onto the pavement, spraying small stones in his wake. "That *does* it," Teddy says, convinced finally, now that it's safe, that anger is indeed an emotion appropriate to this occasion. "I'm filing a grievance."

I laugh all the way up the winding road that leads to the house where Lily and I live. I have to dry my eyes on my coat sleeve. Teddy, I can tell, is sheepish and half angry at me for invalidating his emotions with mirth. "I *mean* it," he assures me, and then I'm lost again.

Lily comes out onto the back deck when she hears a strange car pull up. She's in her jogging clothes and she looks flushed, like she's just finished her run. She gives us a wave, and Teddy can't wait to get out of the car so he can wave back. We're too far away for her to see my ruined nose, but the pose my wife has struck, hands on her slender hips, suggests that she's prepared for lunacy.

"It's not as bad as it looks," Teddy hollers.

As we approach, Lily looks us over critically, trying to discover what Teddy's remark is in reference to. I've been coming home with minor wounds for twenty years, but they are usually below the neck— sprained ankle, swollen knee, stiff lower back, that sort of thing. Our Saturday morning departmental basketball games, back when we all still spoke to each other, frequently resulted in injury. Often courtesy of Paul Rourke, who seemed to keep a different kind of score from the rest of us.

So what Lily is looking for is a limp. A listing to port. A stoop. And of course she can't really see my nose because I'm purposely walking toward her with my head cocked, so as to present her with my good nostril. No easy task, considering the size of the bad one. When we reach the base of the deck, Teddy sees what I'm doing and grabs my chin and rotates it, so that Lily has the full benefit of my mutilation. I wonder if Teddy is as disappointed as I am by her reaction, an arched eyebrow, as if to suggest that even so bizarre an injury was entirely predictable, given my character.

"The man is out of control," Teddy says admiringly.

We go inside because it is still chilly in mid-April and the temperature is dropping with the sun down. I hear Occam whimpering to be let out of the laundry room, to which Lily banishes him when he's been a bad dog. When I open the door, the dog, beside himself with joy, bolts past me and does a frantic lap around the kitchen island, his nails scratching for traction on the tile floor, before he spies Teddy, whose face blanches. Occam is a big dog, a nearly full-grown white German shepherd who'd appeared in our drive almost a year ago. Lily heard him barking, and we went out onto the deck to study the odd spectacle the dog presented. He stood in the middle of the drive as if he'd been instructed to remain there but doubted the wisdom of the command. He seemed to want a second opinion from us. "I think he wants us to follow him," Lily said. "Where do you suppose he came from?"

"If he wants us to follow him, he came from television," I said, but in truth that's what he did look like standing there, barking at us without advancing. Actually, he'd start to come toward us, then appear to remember something horrible, yelp in a completely different register from his bark, retreat a few steps, and start the whole process over again.

We approached cautiously, stopping a few feet from the animal, which was now wagging his tail wildly and grinning at us in a lopsided, rakish manner.

"I've never seen a dog grin like that," Lily observed. "He looks like Gilbert Roland."

I was curious about a glint in the dog's mouth. He looked for all the world like he had a gold tooth.

"Lord, Hank," Lily said. "I think he's snagged."

Which was exactly the animal's problem. What I had perceived as a gold tooth was a treble hook embedded in the dog's lip. He was trailing a long tether of monofilament line, invisible except when the dog strained against it, resulting in that Gilbert Roland smile. Lily held him steady while I bit the line in two. He'd been trailing about a hundred yards of it, apparently all the way up from the lake, two miles away. Back in the house, under Lily's gentle hand and voice, he waited patiently for me to find a pair of wire cutters, nor did he move when I snipped the shaft and removed the hook. "Okay," he seemed to say when the hook was out. "Now what?"

We advertised, put signs up around the neighborhood, but no owner ever came forward, so there was nothing to do but feed the animal and watch him double in size. Since his arrival, we've had few visitors, a fact Occam clearly cannot understand, given how much he enjoys them. He's so elated at seeing this one that he's immune even to the sound of Lily's raised voice, which usually causes him to quake. Teddy, who hasn't seen Occam since his face-licking stage, raises both arms to protect himself. Occam, no longer a face licker, executes his favorite move, the one he uses on all strangers, irrespective of gender. When Teddy's arms go up, Occam burrows his long, pointed snout in Teddy's crotch and lifts, as if he imagines he's got Teddy impaled on the end of his wet nose. In fact, Teddy goes up on tiptoes, furthering the illusion.

"Occam!" Lily bellows, and this time her voice penetrates the animal's canine joy. He lowers Teddy and looks around just in time to catch a rolled-up newspaper on the snout. Yelping pitifully at this reversal of fortune, he slinks across the floor, dragging his haunches in melodramatic humiliation, yelping every step of the way. My own snout throbs in sympathy.

"Good dog!" I tell him, just to confuse things, and Occam's tail comes out from between his legs, darts back and forth, sweeping the floor.

Lily helps Teddy onto one of the stools that ring the kitchen island while I take Occam out onto the deck, where he clatters noisily down the steps. It's his plan to do several furious laps around the house to dispel the humiliation. I know and understand my dog well. We share many deep feelings.

Back inside, the blood is returning to Teddy's face. "Lily taught him that trick," I explain, adding, "I thought he'd never learn it either."

"It's a good thing you're already injured," Lily says, as if she means it. She's both flustered and embarrassed by Teddy's have been groined this way. She's a woman who naturally tends to injuries, and she's trying to think of a way to tend to this one of Teddy's.

"I want you to know that a good-looking woman did this to me," I tell her.

Teddy quickly fills her in. "Gracie," he explains.

"Gracie is no longer a good-looking woman," my wife reminds us. "I'm much better looking than she is since she got fat." She's gone to the counter and returned with a carafe of steaming coffee.

Teddy is considering telling her that she was always better-looking. I can tell by the pitiful, lost look on his face. He actually opens his mouth and then closes it again. In fact, Lily does look wonderful, it occurs to me. Slim, athletic, aglow, she runs a couple miles a day, and if her muscles ache like mine do after a run, she keeps those aches a secret, feeling perhaps, that complaining about aches derived from athletic endeavor is male behavior. She does not have a high opinion of male behavior in general.

"What did she use on you," she says, now that she's had a chance to examine my schnoz close up, "a shrimp fork?"

When Teddy tells her it was the ragged end of Gracie's spiral notebook that she used to gig me, Lily winces, testimony, I'd like to think, to her continued tender feeling for me. Teddy launches into an enthusiastic but imaginatively pedestrian account of the personnel committee meeting that has resulted in my maiming. His entire emphasis is on my goading of Gracie. He misses all the details that even an out-of-practice storyteller like me would not only mention but place in the foreground. He's like a tone-deaf man trying to sing, sliding between notes, tapping his foot arhythmically, hoping his exuberance will make up for not bothering to establish a key. It makes for painful listening, and I privately edit his account—restructuring the elements, making marginal notes, subordinating, joining, cleaving, reemphasizing. I even consider writing up my own version for the *Railton Daily Mirror* (known affectionately to the locals as *The Rear View*). Last year I did a series of op-ed satires under the heading "The Soul of the University," deadpan accounts of academic lunacy under the pseudonym Lucky Hank. A narrative of today's personnel committee meeting might resurrect the series.

Whether it should be resurrected is another issue. Past installments have raised the ire of university administrators and my colleagues, both of whom have accused me of a lack of high seriousness, of undermining what little support there is in the general population for higher education, and of biting the very hand that feeds me. A well-written account of my maiming today would not even require exaggeration to achieve the desired absurdist effect, as Teddy's pedestrian telling proves, but his account lacks something vital. As I tell my students, all good stories begin with character, and Teddy's rendering of the events fails entirely to render what it felt like to be William Henry Devereaux, Jr., as the events were taking place.

William Henry Devereaux, Jr., had, in fact, been suffocating. Phineas (Finny) Coomb, as chair of the personnel committee, had chosen a small, windowless seminar room for us to meet in. Understandable, since there were only six of us. Except that two of the six—Finny himself and Gracie DuBois—were heavily perfumed, and William Henry Devereaux, Jr., had gotten up three times to open a door that was already open. Teddy, his wife, June, and Campbell Wheemer (the only untenured member of our graying department) all seemed to be in complete control of their gag reflexes, but William Henry Devereaux, Jr., was not.

"Are you all right?" Wheemer interrupted the proceedings to inquire. He was only four years out of graduate school at Brown, and he wore what remained of his thinning hair in a ponytail secured by a rubber band. After being hired he had startled his colleagues by announcing at the first department gathering of the year that he had no interest in literature per se. Feminist critical theory and image-oriented culture were his particular academic interests. He taped television sitcoms and introduced them into the curriculum in place of phallocentric, symbol-oriented texts (books). His students were not permitted to write. Their semester projects were to be done with video cameras and handed in on cassette. In department meetings, whenever a masculine pronoun was used, Campbell Wheemer corrected the speaker, saying, "Or she." Even Teddy's wife, June, who'd embraced feminism a decade earlier, about the same time she stopped embracing Teddy, had grown weary of this affectation. Lately, everyone in the department had come to refer to him as Orshee.

"I'm fine," I assured him.

"You were making funny noises," Orshee explained.

"Who?"

"You." Four voices seconding my young colleague's observation: Finny's, Teddy's, June's, Gracie's.

"You were . . . gurgling," Orshee elaborated.

"Oh, that," I said, though I had not been aware of gurgling. Gargling perhaps, on Gracie's cloying, heady perfume, but not gurgling. Was it her proximity in the small, airless room, or had she made a mistake this morning and applied her perfume twice?

Looking at Gracie now, you had a hard time remembering the effect of her hiring twenty years ago. She had been like one of those dancers in black fishnet stockings and tails and a top hat, being passed from hand to sweaty hand over the heads of an otherwise all-male revue. As Jacob Rose, then our chair and now our dean, was fond of observing, every man in the college wanted to fuck her, except Finny, who wanted to *be* her. That was then. I doubt we could hoist her over our heads now. We're not the men we used to be, and Gracie is twice the woman. The sad thing is that anybody has only to look at Gracie (or, in my case, catch a whiff of that perfume) to know she still wants to be that woman. And, hell, we understand. We'd like to be those men.

"Would you quit staring at me?" Gracie turned to face me, alarmed. "And would you quit sniffing like that?"

"Who?" I said.

"You!" Four voices. Finny's, Teddy's, June's, Orshee's.

"Does the chair have anything to report on the status of the search?" Finny inquired. Finny was dressed today as he was dressed every day after spring break, in a white linen suit and pink tie that showed off to great advantage his recently acquired Caribbean tan. Several years ago he'd let his white hair grow bushy, then hung a large color portrait of Mark Twain in his office, which he was fond of standing next to.

"Limbo," I reported. Our search for a new chairperson had gone pretty much as expected. In September we were given permission to search. In October we were reminded that the position had not yet been funded. In December we were grudgingly permitted to come up with a short list and interview at the convention. In January we were denied permission to bring anyone to campus. In February we were reminded of the hiring freeze and that we had no guarantee that an exception would be made for us, even to hire a new chair. By March all but six of the remaining applicants had either accepted other positions or decided they were better off staying where they were than throwing in with people who were running a search as screwed up as this one. In April we were advised by the dean to narrow our list to three and rank the candidates. There was no need to narrow the list. By then only three remained out of the original two hundred.

"Is the dean pushing?" Finny wanted to know. This was the sort of thing I should be able to find out, he was suggesting, since Jacob Rose and I were friends. My not having concrete information to report was evidence to Finny, were any needed, that I was attempting to scuttle the search for a new chair, a search I've not been in favor of from the beginning. My position has been that our department is so deeply divided, that we have grown so contemptuous of each other over the years, that the sole purpose of bringing in a new chair from the outside was to prevent any of us from assuming the reigns of power. We're looking not so much for a chair as for a blood sacrifice. As a result of my stated position, Finny suspects that the dean and I are secretly attempting to subvert both the search and the department's democratic principles.

"I believe it would be accurate to describe the dean as more pushed against than pushing," I reported.

"He's a wimp," June agreed, though she and Teddy are also friends with Jacob.

"Or she," I added, apropos of nothing.

Orshee looked up, confused. This was his line. Had he missed an opportunity to say it?

"Why are we here?" Teddy wondered, not at all philosophically. "Why not wait until the position has been approved before ranking the candidates? This is liable to take hours, and we have no guarantee that the position won't be rescinded tomorrow, in which case we will have wasted our time."

"The dean has requested that we rank the remaining candidates," Finny intoned, "and so rank them we shall."

Common sense efficiently disposed of, endless discussion of the three remaining candidates ensued. Twice I had to be requested to stop gurgling. Three times I beat Campbell Wheemer to his "or she" line. No one seemed able to recall what had attracted us to these three can-

didates to begin with. I doubted, in fact, that we ever *were* attracted to
them. They represented what was left after we'd winnowed out the
applications that were personally threatening. To hire someone distinguished would be to invite comparison with ourselves, who were
undistinguished. Not that this particular logic ever got voiced openly.
Rather, we reminded each other how difficult it was·to retain candidates with excellent qualifications. To make matters worse, we were
suspicious of any good candidate who expressed interest in us. We suspected that he (or she!) might be involved in salary negotiations with
the institution that currently employed him (or her!) and trying to
attract other offers to be used as leverage with their own deans.

Gracie was anxious to whittle the final three applicants down to
two, having discovered something alarming about the third. "Professor Threlkind is an untenable candidate given our present scheme,"
she pointed out. As she spoke, she referred to notes on the untenable
Threlkind that she'd written down in her large spiral notebook. During the course of our personnel committee meetings, she'd worried the
spiral out of its coil, so that its hooked, lethal end was exposed, using it
to chip flecks of lacquer from her raspberry thumbnail. "We're already
overstaffed in Twentieth Century," she reminded us. "Also, we have
no demonstrated need for a second poet," she added, since the candidate had listed several poetry publications in little magazines.

The reason the untenable Threlkind was still part of our deliberations was that Gracie had come down with the flu last November and
missed the meeting at which she might have had him dismissed from
further consideration. Her own field was Twentieth-Century British,
and she'd desktop-published, just last year, a second volume of her
poetry. If the untenable Threlkind were hired, Gracie would have to
share courses in these areas, courses that she had long considered her
own private stock.

"And I'd also like to point out that the candidate is yet another white
male," she concluded, closing her notebook in a gesture of finality.

"Do we already have a poet?" I heard William Henry Devereaux,
Jr., inquire innocently. Teddy and June stared at their hands, traces of
smiles curling their lips. They had a long list of political enemies, and
Gracie was near the top, having been part of the coalition that had
brought Teddy down off his chairmanship.

"That's an out-of-order remark," Finny declared without conviction, and I caught a whiff of his minty breath mixing dangerously with Gracie's perfume.

"I think we should eliminate both male candidates," Orshee offered.

"Are you suggesting that we not consider male candidates?" Teddy wondered. "Simply on the basis of gender?"

"Exactly," Orshee replied.

"That would be illegal," Teddy said, but his voice didn't fall quite right, leaving an implied "wouldn't it?" hanging in the air.

"It'd be moral," Orshee insisted. "It'd be right."

"Still, it's not the procedure we followed when we hired you," Finny reminded him. Finny, who'd come out of the closet several years ago and then gone back in again, had even more reason than the rest of us to be disappointed in our young colleague. He'd been Orshee's most vocal advocate, having apparently concluded on the basis of several remarks made during his interview that Campbell Wheemer was gay, whereas it turned out that all Orshee was trying to imply was that gay people were fine with him, as were black people and Asian people and Latino people and Native American people. In fact, Orshee would have preferred to be one of these people himself, politically and morally speaking, had the choice been his. Bad luck.

"You *should* have hired a woman," Orshee continued. He seemed on the verge of tears, so deep were his convictions in this matter of his having been hired over a qualified woman.."And when I come up for tenure, you should vote against me. If we in the English department don't take a stand against sexism, who will?"

This time even I was aware of my gurgling.

"I'm not in favor of eliminating both male candidates," Gracie clarified her position. "Just Professor Threlkind. Because we don't need another white male. Because we don't need another person in Twentieth Century. Because we don't need another poet. That's three strong reasons, not one."

As she spoke I could see Teddy shaking his head out of the corner of my eye, probably because he knew me, and because he knew Gracie, and because he knew Gracie was going to tee it up for me one more time, and because he knew I'd yank the driver out of the bag and let her rip.

"Who's our first poet?" I asked of no one in particular. "Somebody remind me."

The spiral notebook caught me full in the face with enough force to bring tears to my eyes. Everyone, including Finny, who brought to meetings he chaired the emotional equilibrium of a cork in high seas, looked on, bug-eyed. But what confused me was the fact that the notebook Gracie used remained, unaccountably, right in front of my face. For an irrational moment I actually thought she had written something on the cover that she was inviting me to read. Cross-eyed, I tried to examine what was before my nose. Only when I realized that Gracie was in fact trying to retrieve her notebook, and that each tentative tug sent a sharp pain all the way up into my forehead, only then did I realize that the barbed end of the spiral ring had hooked and punctured my right nostril, that I was gigged like a frog and leaning across the table toward Gracie like a bumbling suitor begging a kiss.

The next moment I was surrounded, though I couldn't see anyone through the tears. "Oh my Gawd," I heard Gracie say, and she let go of the notebook, as if to suggest that by doing so she could end her involvement with me. I could just go ahead and keep her notebook if I wanted.

"This is crazy," Orshee kept repeating, as if he were being forced to witness the sort of thing he would have preferred not to see happen, even to a white male.

Finally, at my own suggestion, Teddy was dispatched in search of a custodian, and by the time the two men returned with a set of needle nose pliers with wire-cutting capabilities, the other members of the personnel committee had all clustered safely behind me because I had sneezed twice, spraying blood the length of the seminar table and flecking Finny's white suit with pink.

All of this Teddy now reports to my wife, and to his credit he doesn't end the story there. He's not an English teacher for nothing, and he understands a thing or two about dramatic movement.

"So here we are, all back in our seats at the table." He grins at Lily. "Your husband is honking blood into a swatch of brown paper towels from the men's room. Gracie is blubbering how sorry she is. Finny is daubing his white suit with his handkerchief. And you'll never guess what your husband does next."

From the look on his face, I can tell that Teddy is confident that nobody in a million years could guess what William Henry Devereaux, Jr., did or said next, but he's forgotten who he's talking to, namely the woman who's been living with William Henry Devereaux, Jr., for thirty years and who claims to know him better than he knows himself.

"I bet he called the question," my wife replies, apparently without having to give the matter much thought, and looking right at me when she speaks, as if challenging me to deny it.

Teddy's face falls. He looks like he's been groined a second time. "Right," he admits, his voice saturated with profound disappointment. "He said, 'Let's vote.' "

My wife looks disappointed as well, as if there's no particular glory to be garnered in predicting what a man like me will do next. "You know how sensitive Gracie is about her poetry. What's wrong with you?"

In truth, I don't know. I had not intended to belittle Gracie. At least not until I got started, after which it felt like the natural thing to do, though I no longer remember why. I don't dislike Gracie. At least I don't dislike her when I think about her. When I'm in one place and she's in another. It's when she's near enough to backhand that backhanding her always seems like a good idea. This is true of several of my colleagues, actually, though they don't bother me in the abstract.

"Anyway," Teddy is saying. "I thought I better bring him home. So far he hasn't even said thank you." Part of Teddy's camaraderie with Lily has always been based on their shared belief that I am an ingrate.

In my view, I am not an ingrate, but I can play that role. "Thank you for what?" I ask him. "Thanks to you my car is still in the faculty lot. Lily will have to take me to campus before she leaves for Philadelphia. All so you can come out here and flirt with her."

Teddy goes so scarlet at this that Lily leans over and gives him a kiss on the cheek, which makes him redder still. "It's nice to be flirted with occasionally," she tells him, though if I'm not mistaken this remark is aimed at me.

"Philadelphia?" it occurs to Teddy to inquire.

"A job interview," she explains.

And now he blanches, all the blood of embarrassment draining out of his face. He looks first at Lily, then at me. "You guys might leave?"

"No." She pats him on the hand. "But keep that to yourself. The principal at the high school is retiring next year. I'm trying to force the school board to name his successor."

You can actually see the relief on Teddy's face.

"Have June give me a call if she wants me to pick anything up."

"She'll want some of that good olive oil," Teddy says sadly, as if he knows his wife's desires and would rather not think about them.

When Teddy slides off his barstool, Lily offers to walk him out to the car, and when they're gone I take the empty coffee cups over to the sink. From the kitchen window I can see the tops of their heads as they stand in the driveway below the deck and hear their muffled voices through the glass. Something about the way they're standing there, some hint of heretofore unthinkable intimacy, causes me to imagine Teddy and Lily as lovers. I place them in our bed, Lily's and mine, and for some reason Lily is on top. Probably because I can't imagine Teddy on top. With Lily, with his own wife, with any woman over the age of eighteen. He's just too apologetic. Even more bizarre, I imagine myself in the room with them, a witness on the brink of several possible but not necessarily compatible, or even valid, emotions—surprise, anger, jealousy, curiosity, excitement. I tell myself that if I'm a little detached from this imaginary betrayal, it's because I know that Teddy and Lily are not lovers. In real life if Teddy's fantasy ever came true, he'd confess it. He'd come to my office, haggard and happy and damned, and tell me what he'd done, then go out and buy a gun and shoot himself in the foot by way of comic penance, and then apologize all over again for lacking the courage to make a stronger statement. He's an academic, after all, like the rest of us.

When they share a quick hug and separate chastely, I'm almost disappointed. I think I hear Lily tell him to give her best to June, whom she hasn't seen since when. Then Teddy asks her something that I can't make out at first. What he wants to know, what I decide it sounds like, is whether Lily thinks I'm going to be okay. It occurs to me rather forcefully that he is not inquiring after my nose. I wish I could make out Lily's response, but I can't.

Across the way, on top of the opposite hill, I can see Paul Rourke's satellite dish partially obscured by tree branches, and it chooses this moment to search out a different satellite. Rourke's dish is constantly

in motion. A compulsive pro basketball watcher, he's always looking
for feeds. I know it's an optical illusion, but this time when the dish
stops, it appears aimed directly at me. In a sci-fi movie, a beam of light
would emit from its dark center and I would be reduced to cinders.
Between the dish and me is my own pale reflection in the glass. I try
to take Teddy's question seriously, but for a man like me it's not easy.
Of course I'm going to be okay. True, this is not a young man's face
looking back at me from my kitchen window, but the nose is its only
gruesome feature.

I'm still engrossed in its purple swelling when Lily's reflection
appears behind mine and she observes sadly, "You can be *such* a jerk."

CHAPTER

2

As a rule I jog before dinner, but Teddy has thrown everything off by coming home with me and drinking coffee and flirting with Lily. By the time my wife and I finish a quiet supper, it's almost dark, but there's a full moon and very little traffic on our country road. I get into my sweats and go out onto the deck to loosen up. From there I can survey the thing we've for so long called our lives.

The house—this house we've lived in since moving out of Railton—is situated at the top of a long, winding, tree-lined incline. Nestled down among the trees are a half dozen other houses, all more expensive than ours, all owned by university people—senior professors, administrators, a coach. In summer, when everything is green, no house on our hill is visible from the others, which creates the impression of solitude, dispelled only by the occasional glint of painted metal as our cars glide among the trees, the yellow window at night winking through the stirring foliage, the distant argument conducted at an open kitchen window and borne along on the breeze. Starting in late autumn, though, and continuing through the long Pennsylvania winter, we are more aware of our neighbors' existence, as we become partially visible to each other among the naked trees. And so during half the year, at least, we wave to one another apologetically, getting into and out of our cars, taking the trash out to the road, shoveling snow off our decks. Now, in April, we are anxiously awaiting our solitude—the reason we all moved to Allegheny Wells to begin with.

Lily and I purchased the first lot in the development nearly twenty years ago, using the advance on my novel to make the necessary down payment to buy the land and begin construction. Unlike those who followed, we cut down the majority of trees on the lot and put in grass. Lily, who grew up in a grim, dark neighborhood in Philly, wanted light and plenty of it, and long, sloping lawns for me to mow. She also wanted decks, front and back, and lots of patio furniture, as if the presence of summery chaise longues possessed the power to ward off Pennsylvania winters. Needless to say, we store the patio furniture in the garage below the front deck seven full months of the year. But our deck is the best one around for sitting. Cutting down so many trees seems to have reduced the insect population, and we are seldom bothered by bugs. Our neighbors farther down the hill and across the road complain that they are driven indoors as soon as the sun gets below the trees. From our deck we listen to the syncopation of their bug zappers.

Summer deck sitting is one of the ways Lily and I are compatible. Once we're done with classes in a few short weeks, the summer evenings will stretch before us, long and languid. We'll bring bottles of chilled white wine out with us and either read or talk until the quiet and the dark and the wine make us sleepy. Years ago, when the house was new, we occasionally made love outdoors on the deck, but it's been a long time since we've done that. There's something to be said for outdoor sex, with its vague danger and attending excitement, but sensible middle-aged people are apt to feel foolish screwing on plastic outdoor furniture. Your skin sticks to it, and the sound it makes when you peel yourself free is the sound of folly. And soon the special excitement associated with the possibility that you will be discovered in the act of passion begins to fade because, of course, you are not discovered. On dark, quiet summer nights in the country you can hear a visitor's car approaching on the county road below from half a mile off, and you know when it turns off onto your access road, and you can track its progress as it labors up the hill toward the house. By the time whoever it is parks and climbs the creaky deck stairs, you could be showered and freshly dressed, a pot of coffee brewing, cookies arranged on a dish. Surprise, at our age?

And is it the secret desire for surprise, I wonder as I do my obligatory deep knee bends on the deck, that has caused me to imagine my wife and friend as lovers tonight? It's not the first such vision I've been visited by lately. Once, several months ago, perhaps because I'd heard he was going through a divorce, it occurred to me that Lily might be involved with a man she worked with at the high school, a man named Vince with whom we'd both been casually friendly for years. Sad, serious, decent, socially awkward, he'd always seemed the sort of man Lily would be attracted to if a frivolous, wisecracking, smooth, long-legged fellow like me weren't in the picture, and for some reason it felt oddly thrilling to contemplate a new love for Lily, the sort of thing a man could almost wish for his wife if it didn't involve a betrayal of himself. For a week or so I'd imagined signs of infatuation in Lily, but finally they were impossible to sustain, though for some reason I tried.

Since then they've been replaced by increasingly ridiculous yet vivid fantasies of Lily and other men in the throes of passion, and I can't help wondering what they mean. Because in a sense, they aren't ridiculous at all. My wife is an attractive woman, and it's not just Teddy's enduring devotion I offer in evidence here. There is, in addition, my own. There's no question of her ability to attract a lover. Is it arrogant of me to assume that, married as she is to William Henry Devereaux, Jr., she's immune to falling in love with another? Well, yes, it is arrogant, and yet for reasons I could not articulate (I know there are times, like tonight, when Lily is not all that pleased with me), I simply know that she loves me and that she loves no other. Which certainty makes the strange, unsought fantasies that much more unsettling. Many of my male colleagues—married and divorced—regularly confess to sexual longings. They all want to get laid. But, to my knowledge, I'm the only one who regularly envisions my *wife* getting laid.

Yet as I survey these wooded houses it occurs to me that they are probably home to stranger imaginings than mine. Disappointment and betrayal and emotional confusion dwell in most of them. Many are for sale and have been since the divorces that spoiled them. Jacob Rose's ex-wife, for instance, still lives in the house nearest ours. Finny's ex lives at the bottom of the hill. The completion of their house had coincided almost to the day with Finny's discovery of his true sexual identity, though he later reneged, returning, he claims, to the heterosexual fold, though not to his wife. I doubt my imaginings are more bizarre than those of Finny's ex, who ventures out of the house they built together only when it's absolutely necessary.

No doubt we all should have been suspicious of what these new houses represented, built as they were at the crossroads of our careers—a year or two after promotion to associate or full professor, in unspoken acknowledgment of the second or third child that made the house in town too small, an admission that promotion in an institution like West Central Pennsylvania University was a little bit like being proclaimed the winner of a shit-eating contest. Certainly such success did not reflect greater worth on the open academic market. To move to a better college, we'd have to give up something—tenure or rank or salary, or some combination of the three. A few did. Lily and I probably should have. After I published "the book" we might have used the advance to move. But we'd quickly learned how much more expensive it was to live in places where people wanted to live. The advance and promotion that got a bulldozer knocking down trees at the top of our hill in Allegheny Wells wouldn't have started a Homelite chain saw in Ithaca or Berkeley or Cambridge.

And who knows? Maybe we were wise to stay put. In a little over a month I will be fifty, and the book I published at twenty-nine remains, as Paul Rourke likes to point out, the collected works of William Henry Devereaux, Jr. The bearded, shaggy-haired author who stares down the camera so piercingly from the jacket of *Off the Road* no longer greatly resembles the clean-shaven, thinning-haired, proboscis-punctured full professor who reflected back at me earlier from my kitchen window. I sometimes tell myself that I might have found another book in me if I'd been in a different, more demanding environment, one with better students, more ambitious colleagues, a shared sense of artistic urgency, the proper reverence for the life of the mind. But then I remember Occam's Razor, which strongly suggests that I am a one-book author. Had I been more, I'd be more. Simple.

And Lily likes to remind me that it wasn't building the house that proved problematic but rather purchasing the two adjacent lots to prevent neighbors. It was this, she argues, that marked the beginning of the English Department Wars that have raged ever since and that show no signs of abating. Lily would argue that when we purchased those lots, we set in motion the events that would inevitably lead to Gracie DuBois snagging my nose with her spiral notebook. And since the long chain of cause and effect can hardly be played out with so many of the players still alive, there's every reason to expect further consequence, even from such an increasingly remote cause. Were it not for Occam's Razor, which always demands simplicity, I'd be tempted to believe that human beings are more influenced by distant causes than immediate ones. This would be especially true of overeducated people, who are capable of thinking past the immediate, of becoming obsessed by the remote. It's the old stuff, the conflicts we've never come to terms with, that sneaks up on us, half forgotten, insisting upon action. Nothing I said in today's meeting could have provoked Gracie's attack, though it might provoke another attack, provided we're both still alive, in another decade or two, after my goading has had a chance to incubate. And if Paul Rourke ever finds a way to murder me and make it look like an accident, it won't be the result of any recent, half-reasonable grievance he has against me but rather because I refused to sell him a lot almost twenty years ago when he wanted me to. Perhaps that's the simplicity of it, the way Occam's Razor might apply to old animosities in general and to Rourke and me in particular—that all things grow from the same seed, planted long ago.

Actually, Rourke's was the first of many offers we received and continue to receive on our two adjacent lots. What happened was that clearing a service road up through the trees on our hill caused a stampede. The man who owned the land had been promoting its development for years, without success. Everybody thought it was a good place to build houses, but nobody wanted to be first. Before the foundation of our place had been completed, three more lots had been sold halfway down the hill. That fall Jacob Rose was made dean, and he purchased the largest of the remaining lots, two full acres, and began construction on a house twice the size of ours, as befit a dean, even a dean of liberal arts. In November Finny and his wife bought a lot at the bottom of the hill. When I heard that, I went to the credit union for a loan. "We came out here to escape these people," I explained to Lily, who hated to go further into debt for such a purpose.

For some reason Lily did not share my sense of impending doom at the Sold signs that kept appearing, nailed to the trees along the service road. I couldn't understand her failure to grasp what was happening. It was my opinion (then and now) that two people who love each other need not necessarily have the same dreams and aspirations, but they damn well ought to share the same nightmares. "Don't you get it?" I told her. "The English department is moving to Allegheny Wells."

She stared at me for a long time, feigning incomprehension, then said my name in that way she has when she wants to suggest that I'm being more than usually unreasonable. "Hank," she said. "Jacob Rose is your friend. There's nothing wrong with Finny and Marie."

"There's nothing wrong with Finny?" I exclaimed, pretending incredulity. Not quite pretending, actually. "My God, where will it end? Today Finny, tomorrow who?"

Paul Rourke was who. He called me that December, three months after we purchased the adjacent lots with credit union money. "Not for sale," I told him.

"Everything's for sale," he said, pissing me off right away. He'd apparently concluded that I was being greedy. The price of the few remaining lots had doubled in the year since I'd purchased the first, and Rourke reminded me that if I sold both adjacent lots at the price he was offering, my own land would have been free. "Don't be a prick," he added. "I hear they're going to start a new development on the other side of the road. Once they do that, who's going to bend over for *you*?"

"You'll always bend over for me," I recall saying. "And don't think I don't appreciate it."

He'd heard right though. Later that week a yellow bulldozer, a grader, and a large earthmover materialized along the shoulder of our county road, and for the next two days the air was thick with dust from falling trees. From our front deck Lily and I had a pretty good view. It was late November and the branches were barren, making the hill on the opposite side of the road visible. Red surveyors' stakes were planted like winter blooms all over the hillside, mapping out lots and marking the twistings and turnings of the new access road.

"I thought Harry told us the state owned all the land on the other side of the road," I said to Lily, who had joined me on the snowy deck to watch.

"Now you don't want people to live across the road," she observed. "You get more misanthropic every day."

"I get older every day," I pointed out. I do not now and did not then consider myself a curmudgeon, but I can play that role. "My experience of human nature gets wider and deeper."

"Actually," she said, "you just get more like your father."

I knew better than to argue when Lily introduces my father into an argument. It signals a willingness on her part to get down and dirty. Further, it's an invitation for me to raise the issue of her own father, and I know where accepting such an invitation will lead. "The difference is that my father enjoys being him," I told her. "Whereas I hate it."

This must have sounded like some kind of concession to her, because she did not pursue her advantage. "Wish now that you'd sold to Rourke?"

"Good lord, no."

"You may, though. He's going to hate you forever."

This did not strike me as a crystal ball type prediction. I reminded her that Rourke had hated me long before I refused to sell him the lot, that he was predestined to hate me, that he was, after all, a demented rationalist, that his field (eighteenth-century English poetry) was the dullest in the long history of literature, that Rourke was a bitter renegade Catholic and failed seminarian, that he couldn't quite eliminate the old theology he'd come to despise, that it gave him Jesuit gas. Had I allowed him to become our neighbor, proximity would have provided him with a dozen more reasons to hate me. And, living right next door, where he could keep an eye on my comings and goings, he might even have found by this time some way of murdering me and making it look like an accident. Whereas, if he wanted to kill me now he'd have to cross the street, pass houses occupied by Jacob Rose's ex-wife, the ex–football coach's ex-wife, and other ex-wives who know me. I consider these ex-wives my last line of defense.

For a while, though, I doubted even they would protect me, because the new development—Allegheny Estates II—was ill-fated from the beginning. Though to the naked eye our hills were identical Siamese twins, joined at a slender blacktop vertebra, the houses on the other side seemed cursed. Over there, when it rained everyone's basement filled with water. Mud slid down the hill and formed an impressive mound at the base of the stone pillars that marked the entrance to the development. Under pressure, the pillars themselves began to lean inward perceptibly. Every wooden deck in the development was warped, and on quiet summer nights, on our side of the road, you could now and then actually hear the sound of a two-by-four snapping across the way.

If all of this weren't enough, a plague of gypsy moths defoliated the entire forest that surrounded Allegheny Wells one summer, giving us a wintry look in July, allowing those of us on the charmed side of the road a good view of life on the doomed side. The following summer the leaves returned to our hill, their green doubly bright and lush, while across the way more serious damage had mysteriously been done. There many trees died and had to be felled, increasing the severity of the mud slides, while the few remaining trees strained to produce anemic-looking foliage, which turned yellow-brown in early August.

For all this—the flooded basement, the fissure in the family room wall, the mud he has to drive through between the tilting pillars at the entrance to Allegheny Estates II, even the gypsy moths—Paul Rourke holds me personally responsible. His protestations to the contrary, I know Rourke to be a profoundly religious man, not at all an atheist as he claims. His truest belief is in an evil deity whose sole purpose is to tax and heap upon him evidence of life's fundamental unfairness, of which I continue to be living proof. It was Rourke who inspired my *Railton Mirror* nom de plume. Lucky Hank, he calls me.

I am not myself a religious man, but I can play that role, and I often have through the years with my disgruntled neighbor. I refer to the blacktop that separates our two developments as the Red Sea. It's Egypt he's living in, I tell him, and ask him what sort of infestation he expects this spring, what further sign of God's displeasure will manifest itself, how many more signs he needs in order to become a believer. I tell him he worries me, living so close. So far, God has respected the macadam road that separates us, but the Old Testament is replete with stories of the sinner's neighbors getting zapped right along with the sinner. I tell him the way I figure it, if I'd sold him the lot he wanted, I'd be zapped already.

I finish up my stretching exercises as quickly as I can. I only do them as a concession to last summer's pulled hamstring, done right at the base of our hill. It pinged like a banjo string, leaving me hobbled for a good part of the summer, requiring me to play first base in our summer softball league, and keeping me out of the NBA (the Noontime Basketball Association for faculty) all first semester. I can still feel the injury, a vague leg ghost. I pamper it in the knowledge that virtue is every now and then rewarded and because I'm determined to reclaim left field this summer, though I fear my injury may have cost me the position for good. Unfortunately, I have proven an excellent first baseman. I'm a tall, rangy target for the other side of the infield to throw at, and I have long arms that aid in the stretch. Phil Watson, who doubles as my doctor and the captain of our team, proclaimed after a single inning that first base was my natural position.

"My natural physical position, you mean," I clarified.

He frowned at this distinction.

"My spiritual position is the outfield," I explained. True, I might be a good target for shortstops to throw at, but I'm most myself ranging in the outfield after fly balls. I no longer have great speed, but I still possess a long, graceful stride. I feel like an outfielder. "Left field is my Zen position," I continued. "You can damage an outfielder by making him play first. No man should be forced to play out of spiritual position."

"What's a spiritual position?" my wife's voice condescends out of thin air. I look up and spot her in the window of her study, from which vantage point she's apparently been studying me.

Have I spoken aloud? When I don't immediately answer her question, she says, "Tell me you aren't going running in the dark."

"All the best relationships are based on honesty," I reply. "I cannot in perfect honesty tell you that I'm not going running. I can promise that I won't run very fast, if that's of interest."

"You've still got your cold."

"I'm all better," I assure her.

"Hank," she says. "You've been eating antihistamines all week."

"Allergies," I explain. "Everything's blooming." I look around for an example of something in bloom.

Lily just shakes her head. Hasn't enough happened to me already today, is her point. My nose is mutilated. Isn't that sufficient? My going running along our dark county highway right now strikes her as perverse, an invitation to further injury. She believes there is a logic to this line of thinking—that my nose makes me especially vulnerable to a traffic accident tonight. I half-expect her to remind me that I've been stalked by mishap all year. Most recently, a couple weeks ago, I climbed a stepladder, lost track of where I was in relation to the garage's cross beams, and rammed my head into a solid oak rafter. Lily found me fifteen minutes later sitting on the concrete floor, dazed, a thin line of blood squiggling from the part in my hair all the way down to the crewneck of my sweatshirt. I can tell by the look on her face that Lily's thinking about bringing this up now, but she doesn't. One of the nice things about our marriage, at least to my way of thinking, is that my wife and I no longer have to argue everything through. We each know what the other will say, and so the saying becomes an unnecessary formality. No doubt some marriage counselor would explain to us that our problem is a failure to communicate, but to my way of thinking we've worked long and hard to achieve this silence, Lily's and mine, so fraught with mutual understanding.

"When you get back, let's talk," she says ominously, as if she's been eavesdropping on my thoughts again.

"Okay," I say, trying to sound eager or, failing that, agreeable.

"I'm thinking maybe I should cancel this trip," she says.

"No," I tell her. "You should go."

"You'll be okay?"

"Sure. Why not?"

But now it's my wife who's located the perfect rhetorical place for silence.

"Left field," I explain, "is my spiritual position. Not first base."

"I know, Hank," she says, as if she'd like me to understand that this isn't all she knows.

CHAPTER

3

At the bottom of our hill, I turn left, as I do most evenings, and head out away from town. Lily turns right and jogs toward Railton, explaining that the run is prettier, also flatter. But it's just like Lily to run toward town and, she would say, just like me to run away from it. My logic is simple. You don't spend a lot of money building a house out in the country and then run back toward the town you just fled. If running in the opposite direction means that you're running away, then so be it.

Lily's logic must be more complex, but then she's no great believer in Occam's Razor. A teacher in the beleaguered public schools' secondary system, she has more reason than I to flee the town but, as the daughter of a Philadelphia cop, also more inclination to turn and fight. Instead of using her tenure, her seniority, her obvious gifts as a teacher to better her position at the high school by teaching the honors students or, like so many of my colleagues' spouses, by wheedling her way into the college and a somewhat lighter teaching load, Lily has plunged into the community's educational nether regions, teaching the low-track kids, "the rocks," as they are referred to by the other teachers. No, our light, airy home in Allegheny Wells is not an escape from town for Lily, just a temporary refuge into which she can retreat and recharge her batteries for the next day's wars. Though she goes slower, she jogs farther than I do, and from the crest of the last hill, before she heads back to Allegheny Wells, she can see Railton, sooty and sprawling and self-satisfied in the valley below, see, as it were, her task. Actually, I don't know this to be true. I don't know how far she runs. It's what I imagine.

My running in the opposite direction acknowledges, I suppose, an even sadder truth—that we should have left Railton altogether, instead of making this coward's march a slender four miles out of town. When the wind is right, wisps of dark, ashy film are borne on the breeze like polluted snow all the way from town. And so I run deeper into the green hills and woods, vaguely aware that these extend, more or less unbroken, all the way to Canada, where, beer commercials tell us, everything is pure and clean.

About a mile up the blacktop is the tiny village of Allegheny Wells proper, a community of some twenty houses, roughly the same size as the two Allegheny Estates developments. Here, the houses are smaller, two-bedroom raised ranches mostly, and they are clustered around, at the village's only intersection, the steepled Presbyterian church, the lights in the belfry of which are coming on just as I lumber into town. Except during services, the church's front door is always padlocked, probably to guard against the temporary conversions of cold, winded joggers like me. I consider doing a victory lap around the building and heading back. After all, that would be a two-mile run, and I only began jogging again a couple of weeks ago. But for some reason I'm energized by my throbbing nose and my visible breath escaping in white, reassuring bursts, so I decide to turn right at the intersection and jog up the half-mile grade to where my daughter Julie and her husband, Russell, have just this autumn built their house. My wife may believe that I run away from unpleasantness, but in my view there's unpleasantness on all points of the compass, including this one.

This house of Julie's is a proscribed topic. When I bring it up, Lily shoots me one of her warning glances and reminds me that we've agreed to butt out of our children's lives. Basically, I agree. I dislike meddling in their affairs, even when it's obvious as hell that somebody

ought to. Still, there wouldn't have been much margin in pointing out
to my daughter Julie that they could not afford this house she and Russell were building.

This simple fact is so manifest that it cannot have escaped even
Julie, who has never understood money—how it comes to you, how
long it's likely to last, where it goes, how long it will be before there's
more, what you'll do until then. More painful than her naivete is the
fact that she doesn't believe herself to *be* naive. Should you make the
mistake of asking her why she's doing something so stupid, she'll
explain it to you. The house, she informed me, would be not just a
home but also a tax shelter. "You're kidding, right?" I asked her, looking for signs that she might be kidding, finding instead evidence of
anger. "Tax shelters are for people who make too *much* money," I
explained, "not too little. The fact that you resent paying taxes on your
earnings doesn't necessarily mean you need a shelter." The effect of
such fiscal wisdom on my daughter was so predictable that even I
might have predicted it. All along it has been her intention not just to
build this house but to build it *anyway*—that is, come hell or high
water, in defiance of reality and sense, both of which represent for Julie
the odds that will just have to be overcome. Julie likes movies, and I
suspect she's seen one too many of the sort where long odds are defied
and faith rewarded. By trying to reason with her, I became part of the
already long odds she'd vowed to beat. My daughter likes television,
too, and I suspect that her thought process has been corrupted by advertising. Like many Americans, she no longer understands the meaning of simple words. She sees nothing absurd about the assertion "you
deserve a break today" when it's applied across the entire spectrum of
society. She believes she's *worth* the extra money she spends on her hair.
Several of her friends have big houses. Doesn't she *deserve* one too? Is
she *worth* less than her friends?

Still, what Lily means when she says that we should butt out of our
children's lives is that it's our duty to put the best possible face upon
their behavior, even in the privacy of our own home. If my wife had
her way, we would never allude to the sometimes insane behavior of
our children, as if merely acknowledging their errors in judgment
might further jinx their doomed schemes. Be fair, Lily is fond of counseling. Give them a chance to fail.

Fine by me. It's the attendant pretense that mangles me. We have to pretend they're being smart when they're being dumb. Such pretenses, I have tried to explain to Lily, fly in the face of Occam's Razor, which demands that entities must not be multiplied beyond what is necessary. Lies and pretenses, I explain, always require more lies and pretenses. "Promise you'll act surprised," is one of Lily's favorite, supposedly harmless pretenses, one I'm required to act out every time somebody does an entirely predictable thing that is supposed to take me unawares. Feigned stupidity never strikes Lily as undignified, but it does me. For one thing, it's always used against you later on. (We thought you might be suspicious when you saw all the cars parked outside on your fortieth birthday. Aren't writers supposed to be observant?) Lily's got her reasons too. Often they have to do with not hurting people's feelings. And so I'm required to act surprised at the announcement of a mutual friend's pregnancy a few short weeks after a hastily arranged wedding. "It hurts *my* feelings to pretend to be this dumb," I tell my wife. "Don't you care what people think of *me?*" But she just smiles. "They won't notice," she always explains. "It'll blend in with all the times you're genuinely slow."

With regard to Julie and Russell's new house, I've been required to pretend that the result will not be disaster. To further the illusion of our confidence in their judgment, we've loaned them money. That I've kept my own counsel on the matter has annoyed Lily and at times made me mildly repentant. If the house bankrupts them now, it will be my fault for having failed them at the level of psychic support.

There's about a fifty-fifty chance it will. Russell has recently quit a good job for what he thought would be a better one, only to discover that several large government loans needed to start up the project he was to direct have not been approved as expected. It could be months, he now admits. A year maybe. In the meantime I don't know how they're living. It can't be on Julie's service manager's salary at a department store at the Railton Mall. Russell, a computer software specialist, does a little freelancing.

The house itself is testimony to their sudden reversal of expectation. From the front it's a dead ringer for our own house, not coincidentally, since they've used our contractor, our plans. And it's true what Lily says. I'm sometimes genuinely slow on the uptake. Seeing their house rise out of the ground was an unsettling experience, but it took many weeks for me to tumble to the reason—that our daughter was building our house. Only when I saw the two decks—one front, one back—did the realization come into clear focus. "How'd they get the plans is what I'd love to know," I told Lily.

"From me, of course," my wife said, as if this were one of life's mysteries that even I should be able to plumb on my own.

"You gave them our house plans?" I said, life's essential sense of mystery undiminished.

"It saved them a lot of money."

There were other benefits too, according to my daughter. "Carl," she explained, in reference to our builder, "says he's going to get the whole thing right this time. He says he remembers all the little ways he fucked up when he built your place. Ours will be perfect."

Mysteries on top of mysteries. How is it that my daughter is on a first-name basis with the same contractor who worked me like one of his own laborers and pocketed my checks without ever encouraging the tiniest intimacy? And when did my younger daughter start using the phrase "fucked up" in my presence? And, most important, why would Julie want a replica (however perfect) of her parents' house?

"Does this mean that if I ever tire of living in my own fucked-up house I can come live with you?" I asked. To which my daughter put her hands on her slender hips, a dead ringer for her mother in this posture, truth be told, and said, "Oh, Daddy, you don't have to get all pissy. You know what I meant."

Pissy?

"Besides," she said with a grin, "the houses won't be identical. Ours is going to have a pool and Jacuzzi."

It doesn't though. At least not yet. They've put off the construction of these for now. Lily has informed me of this, as if to convince me that there's nothing to worry about, that Russell and Julie are more sensible than I've given them credit for being, the house itself notwithstanding.

But when I chug up to the mailbox and survey their house, there are signs of desperation that transcend the shrunken mound of earth alongside the half-dug hole. That they've run out of money and the bank's confidence rather precipitously is everywhere evidenced. The winding driveway remains unpaved, the lot unlandscaped, the windows unshuttered. A piece of bright blue tarp flaps over the chimney hole like a flag. Their house sends a chill through me, the fear rendered more personal by the resemblance of their house to Lily's and mine. I have two thoughts in rapid succession, the second coming before I can dispel the first. The first is: My God, they aren't going to make it. The second thought is that, in some deeper sense, I'm looking not at their house but rather at my own, and this causes me to recall Teddy's question to my wife as I watched from the kitchen window. Did she think I was going to be all right, was what he'd wanted to know. Or at least I think that was what he was asking.

A car that I'm aware has been following me up the long hill catches me here at its crest. I trot into my daughter's drive to let the car pass. But whoever it is has slowed down in what appears to me comic concern for my safety. When whoever stops, blinker blinking, I realize it's Julie, who toots me out of the way and then waves for me to follow her up the drive. The last thing I want is to visit her and Russell, but I'm stuck, so I do as I'm told. Actually, I've run farther than I planned, so maybe resting up before I head back isn't such a bad idea.

"You didn't look like you were going to make that hill," my daughter says when I trot up. She hands me a small sack of groceries from the trunk and slams it.

"I'm going to be fifty this summer," I remind her, panting. "One of these days you're going to find me alongside the road."

Julie usually chides my morbid humor, but she's caught sight of my nose. "Good lord, Daddy!"

I know this girl, so when she raises a delicate index finger with its carefully sculpted and brightly lacquered nail to touch the purple nostril that my run seems to have further expanded in my lower peripheral vision, I'm quick enough to catch her slender wrist. The rapid circulation of my blood has the nose pounding in time with my pulse, and even the gentlest of touches is, at this moment, a pretty terrifying prospect. "Please," I warn her.

She promises not to, but she can't help leaning in close and making me turn so she can inspect the injury more closely under the porch light. "Yuck" is her final word on the subject, and I can tell how much she'd like to probe the wound with her long-nailed pinkie. "What is there about something revolting that makes you want to touch it?" she wonders out loud.

What indeed? What would William of Occam say? There's a simple explanation, surely.

"Where's Russell?" I say, eager for a change of topic, hoping he will not be home, though I like Russell.

Julie takes the bag of groceries from me and puts it on the kitchen table. "He's around somewhere." She bellows his name. We hear a faint reply.

"Upstairs," Julie says.

"Outside," I say. "Back deck." Their house carries sound the same way ours does, even though ours is fucked up. I can tell Russell is out back. What I can't guess is why. It's far too cold to be deck sitting.

"Come on out," Russell's voice, barely audible, finds us.

What I really need, suddenly, urgently, is to pee, for about the tenth time today, I think, and at the thought of what this probably means, my sweat goes cold. No, I tell myself. Don't even think about it.

We go out on the back deck, where Russell is standing on the bottom rung of a stepladder under the eaves a few feet away. He's got a flashlight in one hand, and he's shining it up into a pretty amazing wasps' nest that's attached to the overhang. There've been several warm days this week, and apparently that's been enough. In Russell's other hand is an enormous can of Raid. He looks like he's been standing in just this attitude for a long time.

"You think they're asleep?" he says.

What I think is that this man should not be a homeowner. My daughter, now that she's seen the nest, has backed up near the sliding deck door, through which she clearly plans to duck.

"I'm not sure wasps *do* sleep, Russell," I tell him.

The flashlight locates me. Apparently Russell had not noticed, until I spoke, that his wife was not alone. "Hank," he says, altogether too glad to see me, as if, now that I'm here, he's got a friend.

"Hi, Russell."

"God. What happened to your nose?"

"Stung by a wasp," I tell him.

"No shit?"

"Would I shit you, Russell?" The answer to this rhetorical question is obviously yes, but Russell has been standing too long beneath a wasps' nest, trying to work up the courage to Raid it. There's nothing more real to him at this moment than a wasp sting, and some damn thing has happened to my nose that a wasp sting just might account for. "They always build their nest right in that same spot in our house too," I tell him. "I came over to warn you. I think we may have identical wasps."

When he finally lowers the flashlight, I can see he's caught on. "I'd sure hate for us to have identical noses," he says. "Yours is the ugliest one I ever saw."

The flashlight returns to my face for another look. I hold up my hand this time, tired of the light in my eyes, and of Russell's curiosity. "I bet if I had that flashlight I could find something ugly on you too," I tell him.

"Jules. Come hold the flashlight while I spray," he suggests.

"Be real," Julie tells him.

I go over, take the flashlight, locate the nest.

"Ready?" Russell wants to know, his voice grim, determined, scared.

"You've never been to war, have you," I say.

"Neither have you," he correctly points out. "You were a typist in Vietnam."

This is not precisely true. I was a typist *during* Vietnam. "I teach *The Red Badge of Courage* every year, though," I tell him. "Spray the bastards so we can go inside."

Russell sprays the gray, paperlike cone until it glistens and begins to drip. There's no activity. I begin to suspect it's last year's cone we're dousing. "That's the way I want to go," Russell says, satisfied with the job once he's finished.

"You want someone to asphyxiate you with insecticide?" I say.

"Nope," he says. "I want to die in my sleep."

"Much as you sleep," Julie says, "there's a good chance you will."

We go inside, to the kitchen, their only fully furnished room. Russell and I sit down. Blessedly, my daughter and son-in-law have not tried to copy our interior furnishings. Perhaps our stuff is fucked up.

Perhaps Julie's imagination is functional regarding tables and chairs and sofas. In place of our island, they have an inexpensive kitchen table, half wood, half glass, in a complex geometric design that makes it hard to see whether you got the oatmeal spill with the rag or missed it.

Russell sits down at the table while Julie starts a pot of coffee and I visit their bathroom, where I stand before their commode like a medieval man of faith. The sensation I had a few minutes earlier, of being powerfully backed up, of risking an explosion, is now belied by what might best be described as a slow faucet drip. What I have, I fear, is a stone. My father has been visited by them all his adult life, though he started earlier, in his thirties. His father before him had also been tormented with them, and my great-grandfather actually died of blood poisoning, the result of a bladder stone the size of a mango that blocked his urethra, backing urine all the way to his eyeballs. I've been putting off the appropriate diagnostic measures in the hope that they would not be necessary. Now, I will have to go to the hospital and be X-rayed, the stone identified, surgery recommended.

I'm less afraid of the knife than of the comic dimension of the malady. My colleagues will consider it just like me to have a joke affliction. "This too will pass," they'll assure me. Given today's mutilation, I'm even more adamant about keeping the stone a secret, somehow getting through the rest of the semester. Then having it taken care of when people are away. Maybe I can even get the procedure done in New Haven, where our daughter Karen lives. Surgery may not even be necessary in a big, metropolitan hospital. I've read somewhere that there's a whole new technology for the treatment of stones that involves busting them up with concentrated blasts of ultrasound.

When my undignified dripping finally ceases, some of the pressure seems to have been released. I give myself a final shake and return to the kitchen and the polite society of my daughter and her husband.

As soon as I sit down at the table I'm aware of electricity in the air. Julie and Russell have had quiet words. The scar at the edge of my daughter's eye, where she flew over the handlebars of her first bike and then into the road, is aflame, and seeing this always makes me feel both sad and responsible, a failed parent. It's not a big scar, just a tuck at the corner of her eye, a small reminder that life is capable of far worse things. When my daughter is happy, the scar disappears completely. But anger and frustration and weariness drag at the corner of her eye, causing her at times to look almost sinister, as she does now. If Lily were here, and I wish she were, she'd find a way to touch the scar gently, her signal to Julie, across the long years, to smile, to make herself beautiful, an act of will.

If unkind things have been said in my absence, Julie has said them, not Russell. I can tell this by looking at him. Now that I have the opportunity to examine Russell, he looks a little heavier to me. He's always been trim and athletic-looking, though he's never played sports, but in the month or two since he's been out of work, he appears to have put on about ten pounds. He's looking slightly unkempt too. He wears his hair fashionably short, usually moussed up in bristles. When you catch him just before he and Julie go out somewhere, he always looks wet. By the end of the evening his hair takes on a more human, Tom Sawyer—ish quality. At the moment his hair looks long and limp, and it occurs to me that though we live close by, I've seen neither Russell nor Julie in about a month. I've been kept up to date on their lives by Lily in much the same fashion that I'm informed about what's happening in the life of our other daughter, Karen, who lives sensibly in a second-floor New Haven flat that bears no resemblance to her parents' house. "So," I say to Russell. "What's up? Long time no hear."

"Well, Hank," Russell admits, "we owe you too much money to enjoy casual conversation."

I don't know quite what to say to this, partly because I'm not sure how much money we've loaned them. The right thing to say is probably "don't worry about it," but I'd hate for them to take me literally, especially if Lily has been more generous than I know.

"What's up is mortgage payments," Julie says. "What's down is personal income and savings accounts."

"And the spirits of a certain privileged young woman," Russell says, looking past me to where Julie is gathering cups and saucers. Then he adds, "Sorry, Hank. That sounded like I was criticizing your child rearing, didn't it?"

"Not at all," I assure him. "Lily raised her. I was teaching *The Red Badge of Courage.*"

"While Mom was earning it," Julie says. She's serving the coffee in fancy cups I've never seen before. "Menstruation always was the real red badge of courage."

Russell and I exchange a look. Julie has always been the least thoughtful but the most outspoken of the three Devereaux feminists. "I guess I should have taken more of an interest," I acknowledge. I don't consider myself a chauvinist, but I can play that role.

Julie joins us at the table, spoons three sugars into her own coffee. "Too late now, Pop," she says, patting my hand. What I'd like is for her to pat Russell's hand, the same sort of I'm-just-kidding pat she gives mine. When Russell sees the gesture, he looks away.

We drink our coffee in silence for a minute. I've stopped sweating from my run, and the drumming in my nose is quieter too. Emotional atmospherics notwithstanding, I'm comfortable in their kitchen, perhaps because of its resemblance to our own, Lily's and mine. Lily is precisely what we're missing, it occurs to me. If she were here, the electricity resulting from Russell and Julie's financial problems would disappear. A natural humidifier is Lily, somehow conveying that things cannot seriously go wrong, at least not in her presence. Even as kids Karen and Julie never fought in front of her, as if they considered their mother's emotional equilibrium essential to the general welfare. Lily has, I'm told, the same effect upon her low-track students, her "rocks." They're a tough bunch, many of them, and a fair number end up in jail, whence they write Lily apologetic letters, explaining, "When I knifed Stanley, I never meant no disrespect to you or what you tried to teach us about living good. I know your pretty disappointed because I'm the same." Lily's the kind of woman who loses sleep over ambiguities like the one in that last statement, and her kids seem to understand that, even the ones who couldn't locate the word *ambiguity* in a dictionary for a free trip to the Bahamas.

"So, how did you come by that nose?" Russell finally asks.

Aware that the truth will probably sound more absurd than my previous lie about the wasp, I tell him, "A poet did it to me." And I can't help grinning at the fact that I've acknowledged that Gracie is a poet.

"Mean one," Russell says.

"About average, actually," I say. "They run to meanness."

"Unlike novelists," Julie says, really surprising me this time. After all, my one novel came out the year she was born, and though we've never told her, there's a pretty good chance she was conceived in celebration of its acceptance for publication. Is my daughter stretching a point, as I just did by conceding poet status to Gracie, or does she really think of me, despite my twenty-year silence, as a writer? Maybe to her my newspaper op-ed pieces count. Maybe she can't see much difference between them and novel writing. Truth be told, I seldom think of myself as a writer anymore, though I write all the time—churning out film and book reviews for the *Railton Mirror,* along with my "The Soul of the University" pieces. But I haven't published, or even written, so much as a short story in the long years since the novel was published, given a foolishly positive review in the *Times* (a review instigated, I later learned, by my father, who knew the editor), and then dove precipitously into that unmarked grave of books that cause no significant ripple in the literary pond. Apparently I'm not the only one who no longer considers me a writer. Last Christmas was the first since *Off the Road*'s publication that I did not get a holiday greeting from Wendy, my agent, though my fall from her good graces may have been the result of a note I sent her the previous year. She'd informed all her clients that due to increased costs of doing business in New York she was going to have to go from a 10 to a 15 percent commission. She may not have seen the humor in my sarcastic refusal to pay her an additional 5 percent of nothing. Have I brought this on myself, I wonder, that people who know me refuse to take me seriously, while to virtual strangers my ironic sallies are received with staunch, serious outrage?

Regardless, the fact that my daughter still thinks of me as a novelist cheers me, its further evidence of her unworldliness notwithstanding.

"I noticed the tennis courts are nearly dry," Julie remarks. She and I play hard, competitive tennis throughout the summer and as far into the fall as weather permits. She's got age and talent on her side, along with a sweet, hard, two-handed backstroke, and she would beat me easily if she could keep her concentration. I am the reason she can't keep her concentration. Part of my game—the only good part, according to Julie—is gamesmanship. She hates to be talked to during a match, so I find all sorts of things to discuss with her. I keep this up until she screams, "*Shut up, damn it!*" a sign that her concentration is shot and that it's okay for me to just play. Our games mystify Russell, who's too nice a fellow in general to understand either sport or competition, and far too uncoordinated to benefit from instruction. When he and Julie started dating seriously and he wanted to make a good impression on me, he suggested we play some one-on-one basketball. The contest was so lopsided, with Lily and Julie looking on, that both my wife and daughter were furious with me afterward. "You didn't have to humiliate him," Lily said.

"I never meant to," I assured her. "I tried to keep him in the game."

"You could have let him score one basket." Julie frowned. "One basket. Would that have been so terrible?"

"He kept throwing the ball over the backboard," I reminded her. "Four times I had to go up on the roof."

"You did everything but slam-dunk over him," Lily said.

"And not for lack of opportunity."

Russell joined the conversation then, taking my side. "Hank's right," he admitted sadly. "I suck. I suck bad. I suck the big one. I never should have asked you to play."

"We'll find another game where we're a better match," I suggested.

"I don't know," he grinned sheepishly. "Basketball's always been my best sport."

No, that was our first and last contest.

"Watch out for the old man this year," I warn my daughter. "My hamstring's healed. I'm already up to two miles a day."

"How come you and Mom never jog together?" my daughter asks so seriously that I'm momentarily puzzled. I've heard the words, but the tone of my daughter's voice suggests a different sort of question entirely, something more on the order of "How come you and Mom have separate bedrooms?" Some damn thing seems to have caused a blip on my daughter's psychic radar screen. Unlike her sister, Julie has never excelled in ordered thinking, but from the time she was a child, she's always been capable of chilling intuitive leaps.

Or possibly she's just curious about why Lily and I never jog together. This explanation would satisfy William of Occam, and it ought to satisfy me.

"She hates my pace," I explain, finishing my coffee and sliding the china cup and saucer toward the middle of the table.

Russell is grinning again. "You go too fast or too slow?"

"She won't say," I grin back at him.

"You're supposed to know," Julie explains. "You're supposed to pay attention."

I could be wrong, but I get the feeling that this remark is addressed to Russell more than me, and from the look on his face, I'd say he's come to the same conclusion. There's another long silence, and when the phone rings and Julie gets up to answer it, I'm glad, until I hear her say, "Yeah, he's over here. You want to talk to him?" A moment passes. Apparently not. Julie listens, her face clouding over. "I'll tell him," she says, and hangs up. Russell raises a sympathetic eyebrow at me. He's young, but he's been married long enough to recognize unpleasantness.

"You're to go home," Julie says. "Mom says Mr. Quigley's been trying to reach you. She says you'll understand."

Unfortunately, I do, though if Billy Quigley's trying to reach me, that's a pretty good reason to stay where I am.

"Mom says he refuses to believe you aren't home."

I stand up, slide my chair back. "When Billy's home, he expects other people to be home too," I explain, approximating my drunken colleague's logic. Billy's problem is he's smart enough to know I don't want to talk to him, but he's too drunk to remember that I always talk to him whether I want to or not.

"I'll give you a lift," Russell offers.

"No," Julie says, showing him the keys dangling from her pinkie. "You've had a rough day. Relax."

Russell takes this parting shot like a man, without flinching. I flinch for him. "Hank," he says without getting up, "take care." There's danger everywhere, he seems to imply.

We take Julie's Escort.

I'm about to break one of the few simple rules I live by and ask Julie if everything is okay between her and Russell, when she says, "So what's with this job interview Mom's got in Philadelphia?"

"It's not something she's seriously considering," I explain. "The principal at Railton High is supposed to retire after next year though. The school board could clarify the line of succession if they felt sufficiently motivated."

"What if they won't? Would she take this other job?"

"Aren't you asking the wrong person?"

We've stopped at the Presbyterian church intersection. Its spire is a beacon, and with the surrounding trees so bare, the scene lacks only snow to be straight out of Currier and Ives. Julie's looking at it, without really seeing. We're idling roughly at this literal crossroads, as if we've both lost our sense of direction. Anyone coming up behind us would probably conclude that we've taken a wrong turn and are lost, that we're either hunched over a map or consulting the stars, the full firmament of which are winking above us, suggesting an infinite number of possible directions, when in fact there are only three, two of which are wrong, and we know which two.

"What would *you* do? Leave your job at the campus?" When I don't have an immediate answer, she adds, "Are you the right person to ask that?"

"No, that would be your mother again."

What happens next surprises me. Without warning my daughter, her small hand balled into a fist, pivots in her seat and punches me as hard as she can on my left biceps. No, as it turns out it wasn't as hard as she could. The second punch is harder, and it's hard enough to cause me to catch her by the wrist before she can deliver a third.

"You bastards," she cries. "You *are* getting a divorce."

"What are you talking about, Julie?"

She's glaring at me, like I'm someone she's concluded, over a lifetime, is not to be trusted. I let go of her wrist to show that I trust her, and she punches me again, though not so hard this time. "I want you to tell me what's going on."

"I don't know," I confess. "Have you been talking to your sister?" I no sooner ask this than I can tell I've intuited the truth of the matter. Karen, an otherwise sensible girl, has always been certain that her mother and I were on the verge of divorce. When she was in high school, several of her best friends' parents went through rancorous divorces, leaving her friends shattered and Karen herself shaken and alive to the possibility the same thing could happen to her parents. She was always looking for signs, and most everything she witnessed, from petty bickering to benign conversations she didn't understand or had joined in progress, she construed as omens of the impending dissolution of her parents' union. And of course, being older than Julie, she was able to convince her younger sister to share her anxieties.

"Mom's always telling her things she won't tell me," Julie explains. "It really pisses me off."

"What did she tell Karen?" I ask, genuinely curious.

"Karen won't say. Which also pisses me off. It's like they're a club, and I can't get in."

"You're imagining things. So is your sister. There's nothing wrong between your mother and me."

Julie shoots me a look. "How would you know? You never know when Mom's unhappy."

"When is she unhappy?"

"See?"

A car has come up behind us and is waiting for us to do something.

"I just . . . I don't think I could take it if you guys divorced right now, okay?" Julie says.

I don't know. Is it wrong of me to regret this nearly complete lack of irony in my offspring? Either this is a changeling sitting next to me, or my genes are breaking down at some submolecular level. How is it that a daughter of William Henry Devereaux, Jr., can deliver a line like this straight? If Lily were here she'd say it's sweet that our daughter would take her parents' marriage so personally and want to save it, but I'm not certain.

When the car behind us toots, Julie rolls down her window, sticks her pretty head out, and yells, "*Fuck off!*" To my amazement, the car does a three-point turn and heads back up the road the way it came.

"Listen," I suggest, "if you and Russell need money . . ."

My daughter looks at me in disbelief. "Was someone talking about money?" she wants to know.

"I don't know *what* we're talking about," I confess. "Your mother's got a job interview in Philadelphia. While she's there she's going to look in on your grandfather and see how he's doing. She'll be back next Monday, okay? That's all there is to know. You're up to speed."

She studies me hard. We're still sitting at the intersection. Finally, she puts the car in gear. "I doubt that," she says, surrendering to her old man a grudging half grin. "I'm just up to *your* speed."

CHAPTER

4

The phone is ringing when I return, so I pick it up. "Hello, pecker-head," says a voice I immediately recognize as Billy Quigley's. "I knew you were there."

"I just walked in."

"Bullshit."

"How drunk are you, Billy?"

"Plenty," he admits. "Not that it's any of your business."

Billy Quigley calls me periodically, reads me the riot act, insults me, then begs my forgiveness, which I always grant, because I like Billy and don't blame him for drinking himself into merciful oblivion. He's fifty-seven and all worn out, and the eight years that remain before he can retire must look to him like an eternity. Irish and Catholic, he's put ten kids through private parochial schools and expensive Catholic colleges by teaching summer sessions and taking course overloads during the regular semesters. He and his wife, a local girl he married young, live in the same shabby little house he bought some thirty years ago, before the neighborhood went bad. Their mortgage payments are all of a hundred and fifty dollars a month, and the rest of his salary goes to paying off mountainous loans. Their youngest daughter, Colleen, a senior at Railton's Mount Olive Catholic High School, has just been accepted at Notre Dame on a music scholarship that will pay part of her expenses. Billy will do the rest.

"I hear Gracie cleaned your clock this afternoon," Billy says, clearly hoping that this is true, that what he's heard is not exaggeration.

"She sure did, Billy," I tell him. "Who told you?"

"None of your business, you goddamn sellout, son of a bitch. You'd sell us all out for a nickel, you goddamn Judas peckerwood."

This, I realize, is what the phone call is about. The persistent rumors of an impending purge have spooked Billy. He's called for my reassurance, which he wouldn't believe even if I offered it, and anyway I decide against it. "Not for a nickel, Billy," I tell him. "Ours is a two-bit department. I always get full price." My strategy with Billy is to play along, wait for him to come around. Lily claims my turning Billy's accusations into a running gag is further evidence that to me everything is a joke. But the fact is, jokes often work on Billy. They work on most people. The exception is Paul Rourke, who's proud of never having cracked a smile at anything I've ever said or done, and who vows he never will. Like everyone else, Billy has only a finite amount of meanness in him, and most times he exhausts it quickly.

"I bet you got my name right at the top of that list. Don't tell me you didn't make one, either, because I don't believe it."

"The merit pay list? Of course I made it. I put you in for a bonus this year."

"Good. I'm going to need it. I tell you my kid got accepted at Notre Dame?"

I tell him he sure did and congratulate him again, wondering if he's already shifted gears.

"Fucking Notre Dame," he says proudly. "Your youngest never even went to college, did she? What the hell was her name?"

"Julie," I tell him. I don't bother to correct him, though in fact Julie did go to several colleges. She enrolled. We paid tuition. She moved into the dorm. But in the most important sense, Billy is right. Julie never went to college.

"And you a college professor," he says. "Is that any way to raise a kid, you peckerhead?"

I'm getting a little tired of this. "We all do the best we can, Billy," I say. "You know that."

"You could send her to school at least," he insists. "Even I could do that, and I'm just a drunk."

We're winding down now, I can tell. These conversations with Billy have a rhythm to them. "You aren't just a drunk," I tell him. "You're a drunk all right, but you aren't just a drunk."

The line is quiet for a moment except for some muffled sounds on Billy's end, and I realize he's cupped his hand over the receiver. When he finally speaks again, I can tell he's been crying. "How come you always let me talk to you like that?" he wants to know. "How come you don't just hang up?"

"I don't know," I tell him. Which is true. "In fact, you're beginning to gripe me. I'd really prefer you didn't bring up my kids."

"I know it," he admits. "I shouldn't do that. That's going too god-damn far. I don't know what comes over me. Sometimes I just feel like I'm going to explode. You ever feel like that?"

I tell him no, and in truth anger—if it's anger he's describing—is an emotion that's foreign to me. Which infuriates Lily, who comes from a family of brawlers. She has dreams where, when she tries to pick a fight with me, I laugh at her, and she holds me accountable for this behavior, though I never laugh at her when she's awake.

"That's because you're a peckerwood," Billy says, though there's humor in his voice now. "Anyhow, I gotta go. More papers to grade."

"Right," I say.

"I want that extra section of comp next fall. And a summer session. And make damn sure Meg gets her two sections, too." Another of Billy's daughters. My favorite. This one teaches for the English department in an adjunct capacity.

I tell him what I've *been* telling him—that I'll do my best, that I don't have a budget yet, that nobody has a budget yet, absurd though that is. "You should just do a regular load," I advise, at the risk of getting him angry again. "What good are you going to be if you crack up?"

"Best thing that could happen," he says. "The loans are all insured. Something happens to me, they're all paid off."

"Good strategy," I tell him. "Get some sleep."

"Okay," he agrees. "The bitch didn't hurt you, did she?"

"Hell no."

"I'm glad. Good night, Hank."

Good night, Billy.

When I hang up, Occam slinks over. He's still dragging his haunches a few inches above the carpet, guilty. I make a sound to let him know it's okay. I hate to provoke guilt, even in animals. One of my few parental rules has been to try not to inspire or encourage guilt in our daughters. Of course it's been easy to play good cop, married to Lily, who grew up as Catholic as Billy Quigley. She outgrew its orthodoxy without being able to surrender its methods—a subtle blend of bribery, guilt provoking, and Skinner-esque behaviorism—strategies my wife has used to combat my own encouraged Emersonian self-reliance theory of child rearing, or anarchy, as Lily refers to it. I suspect our daughters survived childhood by cheerfully ignoring both Lily and me rather than trying to reconcile our disparate advice. They seem to have rejected our wisdom as completely as our suggested reading lists, refusing to see the applicability of either *The Scarlet Letter* (Lily) or *Bartleby* (whose title character is, like me, a disciple of William of Occam) to their own lives. This despite the fact that one or the other of these stories, it seems to me, applies to everybody.

I tell this to Occam, who lowers his head to allow for better ear scratching. I have long suspected that some previous owner abused Occam as a pup, and it's taken him a long time to banish the resulting canine mistrust. It's only in the last few months that he's become a joyous, confident dog, sure enough of the fundamental goodness of life to thrust his pointed snout into the crotches of perfect strangers without fear of retribution.

"One of *what* applies to everybody?" Lily wants to know from the doorway. For nearly thirty years she's been sneaking up on me this way. This time she's wet-headed and fresh from the shower, and she's got a snifter of brandy. Occam starts at the sound of her voice, eyes her suspiciously. When he sees she's not holding a rolled-up newspaper, his eyes close again, and he concentrates on the business of getting his ears scratched.

"I'd like to tell you," I say to my wife, "but you know my conversations with Occam are strictly confidential."

"Mmmm," she says, taking a sip of brandy and looking around my den as if it were the room of a stranger. It's been a long time since she's entered here. The den where I work and Lily's third-floor loft have been, by unspoken agreement, off limits. She agrees not to clean so long as I keep the door shut to ensure that the chaos I engender is visible to me alone and does not spill out into the rest of the house. She has to move a pile of books and student essays in order to sit on my beat-up old sofa.

I take a sip of her offered brandy, and its strangely bitter taste suggests to me one of two things. Either somebody is substituting cheap brandy for the stuff I bought or the bitterness has nothing to do with the brandy. What I suspect is that this brandy is intended to brace me for unpleasantness, and that any brandy used for this purpose may be imbued with medicinal bitterness if you suspect the truth. I set the brandy down on a remedial freshman composition entitled "My Neighborhood," a shrewd little piece of sociology that begins, "The reason my neighborhood is unique is because the people are so friendly," an observation it shares with over half the others in the stack, which, taken together, have the amusing effect of invalidating each other.

"What were you and Teddy talking about?" it occurs to me to ask.

"When?" Lily asks, not unreasonably, though I can't help feeling she's stalling.

"When you walked him to the car."

Lily looks sad. "You," she admits. "He's worried about you."

"He shouldn't be," I say, though I'm not sure what I mean. What I feel is an odd combination of "there's no reason for him to worry" and "he shouldn't concern himself."

"He thinks you're committing political suicide by not taking this purge business seriously. He says even your friends are ready to strangle you."

"You think I *should* take the rumors seriously?"

She takes a sip of brandy, studies the murky liquid that remains. "You remember Gladys Cox?"

"Never heard of her."

"You've met her half a dozen times."

"Oh, *that* Gladys Cox."

"She works in the chancellor's office. She says the legislature's not fooling around this year. The cuts in higher education are going to be deep . . ."

When I don't say anything right away, Lily says, "What's that look that just came over your face?"

I can't explain it, of course, and the reason has little to do with the fact that it's unreasonable to ask a man to explain an expression on his own face when he can't see it. What I'm really at a loss to explain is the odd thrill I feel at the possibility that the rumor might be true. But I also remember the look of excitement in Teddy's own eyes when he brought the matter up in the Civic. Could it be that we two middle-aged men are so hungry for *some*thing to happen to us?

"So you haven't been asked to come up with a list?"

"Don't be absurd."

"Promise me you never would?"

"Do I need to?"

She considers this. For too long, in my opinion, but when she speaks, she sounds sincere. "No," she admits. "And for what it's worth, Teddy doesn't believe you would either."

"He just wondered if *you* thought I would?"

Now it's her turn to ignore *my* question. "Billy all right?" she wonders. This is a change of subject, but what's hanging in the air between us is the implied connection that exists, in her mind, and perhaps in my own, that we've just moved from discussing one troubled man to another.

"Billy's never been all right," I tell her. "He's probably no worse tonight than usual though. Worried. He can't afford to lose his job."

"Who could?"

I'm offered and I accept another sip of brandy. This one doesn't taste so bitter, so I venture, "Julie's all upset."

"I know," Lily says.

"You do?"

She shrugs. "Remember how tough things used to be when we were broke all the time?"

In truth, I don't. I remember being broke, but I don't recall things being that tough.

"She's awfully hard on Russell."

"I know. We were hard on each other, too."

"When?"

She doesn't answer right away. "I hated being broke. It never bothered you as much. The only time it ever bothered you was when we had to ask your father for a loan."

"When did we do that?" I ask. I feel an uncomfortable tickle of memory, but I can't place the circumstance.

"When we moved here. The pub date money for *Off the Road* hadn't arrived. We were afraid we'd get here and not be able to pay the movers. Your father wired us fifteen hundred dollars so we could get our stuff."

I begin to remember now. "But then the pub money came just before we left Indiana. We returned his check uncashed."

"And hurt his feelings."

"Whose?" I say, and when Lily doesn't reply, "Why would his feelings have been hurt?"

"You made pretty clear that you were desperate, or you wouldn't have asked."

"We *were* desperate."

"Then you sent the check back Express Mail, as if you didn't even want it in the house overnight. As if by returning it so quickly you could erase the fact that he'd sent it."

"I don't think he took it that way," I tell her, because I don't. But it's an odd thing. About the only time we ever argue is when we talk about our fathers. I persist in liking hers, she in liking mine. Such are the grounds for our ongoing dispute. "He's always been far too self-absorbed to have his feelings hurt. If you don't believe me, ask my mother."

"She called when you were gone. You should stop by and see her tomorrow before she leaves."

"I will," I say.

"Don't tell me, tell her."

"Okay," I give in. "By the way. Julie says I never notice when you're unhappy. Are you? Unhappy?"

"Not often."

"When?"

She rises and comes over to where I'm sitting, kisses me on the forehead. When her robe gaps at the neck, I see that she is naked beneath, and it occurs to me that this kiss, this bewitching view, as well as the rich, beguiling scent of bath oil that I'm being afforded, just might be an invitation. When a man like William Henry Devereaux, Jr., asks his wife if she is ever unhappy, an invitation of this sort is all he wants by way of answer. Such things happen between husbands and wives, even when they've been married for almost thirty years. There is no reason I can think of that it shouldn't happen between my wife and me tonight. "I'm unhappy to be in my period right now," she says, supplying the reason, and then, more seriously, "and I'm unhappy to see you so lost, Hank," she adds, running her fingers through what's left of my thinning hair, stopping at the little scar that remains from my encounter with the garage rafter.

"Ouch," I say, pretending it's more tender there than it is, pretending my wife has hurt me when she has not. Oddly, a split second before embarking on this pretense, I had planned to bury my face in the gap in her robe, inhale the fresh fragrance of her skin deeply into my lungs, tell her I wished she didn't have to run off to Philadelphia this weekend of all weekends. Instead I choose to pretend that I am wounded by her touch, this woman whose touch has been so light and knowing through the years. And so she stands, looks down at me, disappointed, as if she knows full well the choice I've made and why I've made it. If she understands the why, she's ahead of me.

A moment later, when the door closes behind Lily, I am left alone with Occam, who, it now occurs to me, smells.

The next morning we pull into the Modern Languages lot next to my ancient, pale blue Lincoln, which looks, in the most remote corner of the lot, like the kind of car somebody might leave for dead. My own condition isn't much better. I'm bug-eyed from lack of sleep, having stayed up late reading, and when I finally did fall asleep, I had a continuing dream of sliding backward in the Lincoln down snowy Pleasant Street Hill. Also, my cold is back, a fact I'm trying to conceal from Lily, who predicted that it would be, thanks to my run. I've taken an antihistamine, and it's beginning to dry me up, but it's also left me light-headed. Despite relieving myself before leaving the house, I already have to go again. There's a lot I'd like to say to my wife at this moment of her leaving, and I consider telling her that I think I've formed my first stone. Lily would stay if I asked her to, which means I can't ask. Instead I say, "You look great," which is true. "I'd hire you."

"Thanks," she says, and there's genuine gratitude in her voice. The very idea of her going on a job interview fills me with admiration.

Tenured these last fifteen years, I find it hard to imagine being in that position again, of allowing myself to be judged.

"Say hi to Angelo for me. And call before you go over there. He's liable to gun you down on the front porch if you surprise him." Ever since her father quit drinking, he's fallen victim to paranoia, noticing, perhaps for the first time, what's happened to the neighborhood.

"I tried to call him a couple times last night, and again this morning," she tells me. "I kept getting his machine."

"Angelo has an answering machine?"

"I just hope he hasn't started drinking again."

"I always preferred him drunk," I say, though I know it's the wrong thing. "At least he was happy."

"He was also passing blood in his urine, Hank. His drinking was no joke."

"His *not* drinking is no joke either," I point out. Again, the wrong thing, and because I don't want to start an argument, I get out, close the door, come around to her side. She rolls down the window, I think, so she can give me a kiss, but it turns out it's to observe me better. "Take care of yourself, okay? I have this fear. I can't decide where you're going to be when I get home. In the hospital or in jail."

Lily always likes to leave me with a prediction. "Jail?" I ask. When I bend down to kiss her, she says, just before our lips meet, "When's your meeting with Dickie Pope?"

"This afternoon? No, tomorrow." In truth, I can't remember. "Any instructions?"

"Be the man you are. Be the man I married."

Our lips meet. "Which?" I want to know. "Make up your mind."

Overnight, two posters have appeared on the outer doors of Modern Languages, one announcing next week's donkey basketball game pitting administration against faculty, the other announcing that Army ROTC's scheduled Saturday morning M-16 practice has been canceled. Reason? Ammo did not arrive. These two community announcements suggest how much the campus has changed since the arrival of a certain young, bearded, radical English professor named William Henry Devereaux, Jr., over twenty years ago. Back then, such signs would have been unthinkable. Now it's hard to imagine anyone objecting. The CIA recruits on campus, so it's probably appropriate enough for senior faculty to saddle up diaper-clad donkeys for the purpose of mocking sport, our institution of higher learning, the life of the mind, and themselves, the ship of dignity having sailed long ago. I myself am looking forward to the game. The donkeys should negate my age and inability to run the fast break. I'm confident I can shoot from my ass.

"I'm sure you can," says a voice behind me.

When I turn, I see that Mike Law, Gracie's husband, has come up behind me, and that I'm blocking his entrance. It must be true. I'm speaking aloud without knowing it.

"Nice nose," he adds.

Shaggy-bearded and stoop-shouldered, Mike Law is the most morose-looking man on campus, and that's saying something. We stand facing each other, two sheepish, middle-aged men, each of whom fears he owes the other an apology. Silly, when you think about it. Mike is certainly not responsible for the behavior of the woman who is his wife. And if I have come into conflict with Gracie, goaded her to violence against my person, then I owe her, not her husband, an apology. Yet here we stand, the two of us, sharing an invalid emotion. On the other hand, nearly all the emotions of men our age are apparently invalid.

"I'm told I had it coming," I admit.

"I'm told the same thing," Mike informs me. "I'd keep my guard up if I were you. I don't think she's finished."

I nod and we shake hands. Why we should shake hands is probably as unclear to Mike Law as it is to me.

"Stop by some evening and we'll shoot a rack of pool," he urges me, as he does every time we run into each other. Mike has spent the last five years finishing his basement, where he's put a pool table, a dartboard, a jukebox stocked with fifties rock and roll, and a wet bar. He's rumored to have a small keg of beer tapped in the spare refrigerator at all times, and it's a measure of his isolation that despite such enticements very few of his colleagues will provide company for a man so seriously depressed. "I've got my own entrance now," he explains, another sad enticement. I can visit him without running into his wife, is what he wants me to understand. I *should* visit him, I know. I was an usher at his wedding—what—fifteen years ago? Longer? Black Saturday, he calls it.

"How are things downstairs?" I ask him. French, Spanish, German, Italian, and Classics occupy the floor below ours.

"Silly, small, mean-spirited, lame," he explains. "Same as English."

"Have you been over to the Vatican?" it occurs to me to wonder, since Mike is the senior person in Spanish. "Asked to make out a list?"

He shakes his head. "There's just the three of us in Spanish. I heard Sergei had a private meeting, but he denies it, the prick."

Sergei Braja, I remember, chairs Languages, which comprises a single department. "What's your best guess?"

"Wouldn't surprise me," he admits. "Gracie's convinced, of course. She may even know, the way she sucks up to Little Dick."

"Thank God you and I remain pure," I say, holding the door for him.

"We end up stalling in front of doors and talking to ourselves though."

This early, the English department corridor is empty, its offices dark, except for those who have been punished with eight o'clock classes. Those plus Finny, who requests eight o'clock classes, five days a week, every term. These requests are viewed by Teddy and June as further evidence of serious perversity in Finny, but I know they are nothing of the kind. In many ways Finny is the most rational member of our ragtag band, at least if you grant him the one or two assumptions he proceeds from. By requesting early morning and late afternoon classes, by enforcing a strict attendance policy, and by devoting the first three weeks of class to differentiating between restrictive and nonrestrictive noun clauses, Finny halves his teaching load each term. Students start dropping out by the second week of classes, and by the end of the term he has a seminar of seven or eight where once there were the regulation twenty-three. This, he maintains when challenged, is the result of genuine university standards, evenly applied.

Between ten in the morning and four in the afternoon Finny's days stretch out, long and languorous, and he takes a two-hour lunch at the Railton Sheraton on the other side of town in the company of a favored male student or two, it is rumored. I have my doubts about this rumor, just as I have about all academic rumors. Since returning to his medication and the closet, Finny has maintained strict appearances, often arriving at department functions with a female companion, as if she were capable of dispelling the communal recollection of his two-week career as a transvestite.

This occurred during the final days of the Vietnam War. Our bugging out of Southeast Asia may even have influenced Finny to flee his marriage, and his logic apparently was that if he could do without his wife, there was a good chance that he could do without his medication as well. In this latter he was apparently mistaken. The first day off his meds, he became garrulous and good-natured, which was bizarre enough, but he also appeared to be wearing eyeliner and mascara. The second day, residual medication flushed from his system, he appeared in full regalia. Black satin dress. Pearls. High heels. Bellowing down the long hallways of Modern Languages: "Blessings, my good people, on this glorious day that God has made! Throw open your windows!" Teddy, then chair, locked himself in the office I now occupy and refused to come out. Otherwise, Finny managed to visit just about everyone.

Never was a man dressed as a woman more full of joie de vivre than Finny off his meds. "We have to let out the dragon," he insisted to one and all. "Just let him out! Let him fly off and lay waste to other kingdoms. Let him *be gone*!" he thundered, from atop his unsteady high heels, his rapture bringing tears to his eyes and causing his mascara to run. "If you don't get out of my office," Paul Rourke told him, "I'm going to rip your nylons off and strangle you with them." June Barnes merely counseled him against pearls before five. Only Billy Quigley, who normally had no use for Finny, seemed glad to see him. He offered Finny a seat and a generous belt from his flask. "I've drunk with uglier broads than you," he informed his colleague, adding, "Not much uglier though."

But Finny's freedom and happiness were short-lived. By the time the last marine was choppered off the roof of the American embassy in Saigon, his soon-to-be ex-wife had Finny hospitalized and drugged back into disheartened heterosexuality and male attire. After a month-long convalescence he returned to the classroom in Modern Languages with half a dozen new exercises illustrating the difference between restrictive and nonrestrictive clauses, and since then he's caused no problems, unless you considered his arrogant incompetence and brain-scalding classroom tedium problematic.

I stop outside Finny's classroom and peer in through the small window in the door. Finny's soft monotone makes it impossible to hear what he's saying. His students have the grim look of death camp dwellers, and in a sixty-second timed test, six of the eleven consult their watches. Four yawn. One starts violently awake. And they're only fifteen minutes into class. By the time I've completed the timed test, one or two students have noticed my face framed in the small window. Pretty soon, everybody but Finny is aware of me. A couple of these students are also taking a class with me, and these roll their eyes, as if to say, "Can you believe this? Why doesn't somebody *do* something? Why don't *you* do something?" I roll my eyes back at them. Because.

I make what I think is a clean getaway, but then I hear the classroom door open behind me and feel pursuit. "This," Finny hisses at my retreating form, "is harassment."

I turn to face him. Finny is resplendent, as always these days, in a white suit, pink tie, white shoes. "Finny," I say. "Qué pasa?"

His rich tan deepens. "And so is that," he points out, quite rightly. Within the last year Finny, an ABD from Penn, has become the proud recipient of a Ph.D. from American Sonora University, an institution that exists, so far as we've been able to determine, only on letterhead and in the form of a post office box in Del Rio, Texas, the onetime home, if I am not mistaken, of Wolfman Jack.

In truth I shouldn't goad him. I know this. It was my malicious goading of Gracie in yesterday's personnel committee meeting that resulted in my mutilated nose, which is at this very moment throbbing like a guilty conscience.

"I know you don't respect me, or anybody else in the department," he tells me. "But that doesn't mean you get to ridicule me in front of my students."

I hold up my hands in surrender. "Finny—"

"Stay away from my classroom, or I'll file a grievance," he warns me. "I'll get a restraining order if I have to."

"I teach in that room too," I point out, since it's true. "I don't think I can be restrained from a room I teach in."

This stops him momentarily.

"When *I'm* in it," he explains seriously.

"Oh. Well. That. Sure," I agree, as if I couldn't be more delighted to have the whole misunderstanding cleared up. "Just one question."

He pauses at his classroom door, hand on the knob. "What?"

"How did you get the bloodstains out of that?"

"The suit you're referring to is at the dry cleaner's, thanks to you."

Thanks to me? "You have two identical white linen suits?"

"Is there any law against that?"

"Well, there's natural law, of course."

"It's only fair to warn you," he warns me, "that I spent part of last night on the phone. There's considerable sentiment among our colleagues for a recall of the chair."

I can't help but chuckle at this. "Name one time in the last twenty years when that wasn't true."

Rachel, our department secretary, is at her computer terminal when I enter. Like Finny, she dresses up for work. Unlike him, she doesn't wear cologne. Rachel is one of the half dozen women on campus with whom I have to work at not falling in love. The majority of these women are in their midthirties to midforties and married to men who don't deserve them. (I regard these men the way Teddy regards me.) Rachel's husband, from whom she is recently separated, is an enormously self-satisfied local man who is frequently employed by Conrail (and just as frequently laid off), a man whose inner emotional equilibrium is not easily tilted. Only a wife with aspirations of her own could manage it, but unfortunately that's what he had in Rachel, who, in addition to serving as department secretary and raising their son, Jory, has been, for the last ten years of their depressing marriage, quietly writing short stories and working up the courage to show them to me. This year I've been helping her rewrite them, teaching her the little tricks of the craft she needs to know. That's about all I have to teach her, since the requisite heart, voice, vision, and sense of narrative are already there, learned intuitively.

Last fall, buoyed and excited by my enthusiastic response to a new story, she made the mistake of sharing my comments with her husband and inviting him to read one of her stories. It took him most of the evening, she said, sitting there in his armchair, laboring over her sentences, his brow darkening, phrase by phrase, pausing every so often to glance at her. When he finished, he got up, scratched himself thoughtfully, and said I must be trying to get her in the sack. Where literary criticism is concerned, he's a minimalist.

Rachel is surprised to see me so early. It's only eight-twenty, and I'm not due for another two hours by conservative estimate. Rachel's hours are seven-thirty to three-thirty, so she can pick up her son at the elementary school. I had no idea she actually came in so early, but here she is, so she must. When she gets a gander at my nose, which is even uglier this morning than last night, Rachel starts visibly, and the look on her face remains frightened, as if she fears the explanation will only intensify my injury's horrific aspect. "Rachel," I say, pouring myself a cup of coffee, "you're on the job."

She is speechless, looking at me, and her reaction, I realize, is what I'd secretly been hoping for from Lily, who over the years has learned to take me in stride. There's no reason a wife shouldn't take her husband in stride, of course, yet it's disappointing to be so taken, especially for a man like me, so intent on breaking people's gait.

"I stayed up reading a good book last night," I tell her.

"Really?" she says. I can tell she'd like to think I'm alluding to her revised story collection, given to me a couple weeks ago, but she's afraid to presume. The hope in her voice is excruciating.

"Let's have lunch," I suggest. "I'll tell you all about it." I'm not trying to get Rachel in the sack, as her husband, the minimalist, fears, but I did spend the evening with her, in a manner of speaking, so I consider lunch with Rachel a platonic reward.

"You're having lunch with the dean?" she says, holding up a pink message slip. Most of Rachel's statements sound like questions. Her inability to let her voice fall is related to her own terrible insecurity and lack of self-esteem. She's been working in the department for nearly five years now, and it's only recently that she's stopped excusing herself to go to the women's room to vomit when someone is cross with her. According to Rachel, only Paul Rourke causes her gag reflex to kick in anymore, and I assure her that this is perfectly normal.

I take the memo, glance at its scant information. The time noted in the upper-left-hand corner is seven-thirty.

"What's Jacob doing in so early?" I wonder out loud. An academic dean in his office before midmorning cannot be good news. Jacob and I are friends, and I know he never buys lunch except to mitigate bad news. "Anything else?"

Rachel reluctantly hands me two more messages, as if she would have spared me if she could. I take them into my office, close the door. The first memo is from Gracie, who would like me to set aside some time this afternoon to meet with her. Her message contains neither apology nor suggestion of regret at having mutilated her chairman. The second is from the faculty union representative, Herbert Schonberg, who has been begging an audience for weeks, probably in order to discuss my continuing misconduct as interim chair, a position I've been elected to precisely because my lack of administrative skill is legend.

No one for an instant considered the possibility that I would do anything. No one imagined I could locate the necessary forms to do anything. I am regarded throughout the university as a militant procedural incompetent. This is partly due to the fact that I have maintained loudly, publicly, for twenty years that not policy but rather epic failures of imagination and goodwill are the reason for our collective woes. My lack of political acumen, coupled with my perverse inclination to side occasionally with my enemies (much to Teddy's dismay when he was chair, since mine was often a deciding vote), my inattention to the details of political machination, and my failures of short-term memory made me, my colleagues thought, the perfect compromise candidate for the temporary chair of our hopelessly divided department. How much harm could I do in a year?

A good deal, as it's turned out, thanks to Rachel. Nobody imagined what might happen if ever I were aided and abetted by a competent secretary, someone who knew where the forms were and how to fill them out and who to send them to and when. Teddy's fall from grace after six years as chair was occasioned by what was generally and correctly seen to be his abuse of power, this despite his constant and cloying diplomacy. The rules set forth explicitly in the department's operating paper, if taken literally, are egalitarian in nature, and render the chair an impotent facilitator, should he or she be foolish enough to obey them. Teddy hadn't the slightest intention of obeying them, of course, only of appearing to, and the fact that it took six years for this to become manifest was ample testimony to his administrative expertise, as well as to the fact that he desperately wanted to keep the job and its reduced teaching load.

Not wanting the job, on the other hand, has freed me to dispense entirely with subterfuge. Whereas the conventional wisdom had been that a year would be too little time for me to wreak much havoc, I have demonstrated that a great deal of havoc can be wrought in two semesters by anyone so inclined, at least if that person is sufficiently insensitive to ridicule, personal invective, and threat. Who could have guessed that I'd take it upon myself to undermine seriously the very principles of egalitarian democracy that have kept us all in a state of suspended animation for over a decade?

Well, anyone who knew me might have guessed, but no one did, and now, nearly a full academic year after having taken up the reins of abusive power, I am still at large, the subject of vitriolic letters to the dean, the campus executive officer, and the school newspaper, as well as anonymous memos distributed late at night in department mailboxes and the regular appearance of official documents arriving via registered mail, many of which threaten litigation if I do not immediately and with all haste cease and desist. Taken all around, as Huck Finn was fond of saying, it's been fun.

When I hear the phone ring in the outer office, I tell Rachel over the intercom that I have just stepped out, and, to keep her from becoming a liar at my behest, I do just that. There's nobody I want to talk to this early.

That includes Billy Quigley, who finds me in the corridor trying to locate the right key to lock the private door to my office. He's on his way to his office prior to his nine o'clock class. He looks like he sucked the bottle dry about three in the morning and then stayed awake another hour or two to whistle into it. "Are you coming or going?" he inquires.

"I never know anymore," I tell him. "Come join me for a cup of coffee in the student center."

He makes a face. Apparently the idea of coffee offends him. "Am I getting my extra section next fall or what?"

"I'm having lunch with the dean today," I tell him. "Who knows? Maybe I'll get a budget."

"Screw the budget," Billy says, genuinely pissed off that I'd use such a cheap ploy to avoid the issue. "We're talking a crummy three grand, not thirty. Don't give me budget."

I'm on his side, of course. This budgetary danse macabre, a semester-by-semester ritual, is ridiculous. There's no valid reason why we can't be told the semester before if the soft money to cover all necessary sections of freshman composition will in fact be made available. To expect reason is where the fallacy lies.

"Like I told you last night," I explain, "I'll do what I can."

"What do you mean, 'last night'?"

Billy Quigley often doesn't remember that he's called me, and I can tell by the puzzled, belligerent look on his swollen face that he has no recollection of our conversation, or of the fact that we concluded it amicably, indeed sentimentally.

"Billy," I say. "You have a nice day."

"Hank," Billy Quigley says. "You have a rotten one."

CHAPTER

6

The student center is normally a short walk, now a somewhat longer one, thanks to the massive excavation out of which will grow, this summer, the new College of Technical Careers building. Ground-breaking ceremonies were scheduled earlier in the month until one of the dignitaries, our local congressman, waving enthusiastically to imaginary constituents for the benefit of TV cameras, missed the first step getting off his charter plane and broke his ankle on the second, making it necessary to conduct the ground-breaking ceremonies later this afternoon, after the excavation has been dug. They'll have to find a camera angle for that first symbolic shovelful of earth that does not include the enormous pit.

In truth, this hole fills me with misgivings, and not because a Pennsylvania congressman has fallen in the line of duty trying to dedicate it. Perhaps, I tell myself, it's that a surprise—a replica of my own house—grew out of the last such excavation I inspected. Seeing this new hole suggests that more surprises may be in store for me. On the other hand, all logic dictates that I should be reassured by this hole in the ground. It was competed for by the other campuses in the university system and awarded to ours, a sign of favor in these straitened academic times. Soon concrete footers will be poured and walls will climb out of the hole, and the summer air will be full of the sound of jackhammers and drills, the raised voices of men with real, urgent information to communicate ("Watch your fucking head there!") as steel girders swing through the dusty air.

All of this will proceed quite naturally from this still undedicated but undeniable hole in the ground, and what it all suggests is that these rumors about an impending purge of our professorial ranks simply cannot be true. Even university administrators are not foolish enough to spend millions on a new facility in the same year they intend to fire tenured faculty and claim financial hardship as justification. Unless they have no intention of building anything here. Unless the faculty are going to be invited to drink Jim Jones Kool-Aid after the donkey basketball game and then buried in a mass grave. This scenario also accounts for the facts as we know them, and although I can hear William of Occam snickering across the centuries, the sound does not dispel my misgivings. Right this instant, the hole does more closely resemble a mass grave site for dull-witted faculty than a new, state-of-the-art, technical careers center, and I can't help offering up a nervous smile at the idea that the administration might put the lot of us so beyond further grievance with one deft, efficient stroke.

Huddled on the far side of the campus pond, where the tall trees offer better protection from the wind, are thirty or forty ducks and geese. There was a time when these birds migrated, but anymore they're year-round residents, tenured and content, squatting motionless on the bank, like abandoned decoys, subsisting on popcorn and other student junk food, too fat to fly and, as the saying goes, too ugly to love.

They are easily faked out, too, as if they've been too long separated from their better instincts, too often seduced by baser ones. Their heads rotate on their otherwise motionless bodies, and when I take my hands out of my pockets and make a flicking motion, tossing imaginary popcorn along the bank, the birds start toward me, trailing V's on the placid surface of the pond. I'd like to think they know better, that they are capable of perceiving from across the pond that I have nothing for them. I've been told by hunters that ducks are smart, that they have remarkable vision, that from high in the sky they can detect subtle movements on the ground, see the whites of hunters' eyes.

If true, these particular ducks are the village idiots of their species, waddling up out of the water and quacking around on the brown grass in search of what I've pretended to throw them. They can see it isn't there, but they search for it anyway. Their protests reach a remarkable crescendo. Among the mallards are three tough-looking white geese, and the tallest and most elegant of these comes over and hisses at me, its bill wide open, its dark, toothless maw surprisingly menacing. Its white breast is dappled with smatterings of rust color, which remind me of the blood I sneezed the length of the seminar table yesterday afternoon. "Finny," I say to the angry goose. "Qué pasa?"

When the goose hisses again, I take my hands out of my pockets to show the troops I have no popcorn, no stale bread, no candy. Some of the smaller ducks shove off the bank again and begin their slow return, offering a parting, disillusioned quack or two. Eventually the others follow, leaving me with the goose I've dubbed Finny.

"Don't blame me," I tell him. "You knew better."

"Professor Devereaux?" says a voice behind me. It belongs to Leo, a student in my writing workshop. Leo is tall and gangly, with red hair and a long, pimply neck. A couple of months ago he told me, as if he suspected that I alone might understand, that he despises all his other courses, not so much because they are taught by fools as because he laments any time spent not writing. He even regrets the necessity to eat and sleep. He lives to write.

"There are lots of other reasons to live," I assured him. "Especially at your age."

"Not for me," he declared adamantly, as if he suspected that this was what I really wanted to hear, unequivocal testimony to his commitment. "They all say it's a compulsion," he explained, his red face aflame. He subscribed to several magazines for writers, and read all the author interviews. "You write because you have to. Because you have no choice."

"Of course you have a choice," I insisted, not wanting to reinforce such a romantic view of writing for a young man with talent as modest as Leo's.

"Not me," he repeated. "For me it's writing or nothing."

Since we had this conversation back in February, spring has arrived, and everything is in bloom but Leo's talent. In workshop his stories have been routinely eviscerated. He has another up for discussion today, and my guess is he's in for a long afternoon. I'm also afraid he'll ask me now what I thought of his story, though I've forbidden such inquiries prior to workshop. Fortunately, that's not the question he wants to ask at this moment. "Who are you talking to?"

"This goose," I assure him.

And in fact he looks relieved. "I was afraid you were talking to yourself."

The cafeteria of the student center is divided into a large student dining hall and a much smaller room for faculty and staff. The separation is strictly convention. There are no signs to designate it officially, but students steer clear of the faculty/staff area. In the beginning of the fall semester, a disoriented freshman may wander in, see all the tweed, pivot, and beat a hasty retreat, like a clergyman who finds himself in the foyer of a brothel. A couple weeks into the term and everyone knows. The students are great respecters of our space. I, however, am no great respecter of theirs. Often as not, I take a small table in the student section.

In the bookstore across from the cafeteria I've purchased a *Railton Mirror* and also picked up a copy of the student newspaper, fully aware that these have never once cheered me up. I scan *The Rear View,* hoping for a follow-up story on William Cherry, the man who, earlier this month, lay down on the railroad tracks one night and was decapitated. The original story had hinted that there was more to the circumstance than met the eye, but it may be that despair is the simplest of tales. In lieu of what I'm looking for, I'm offered on the opinions page an article written by my mother, who, like her son, is a frequent contributor. Her column today is on the Department of Housing and Urban Development, which maintains and operates the senior citizen tower at which she volunteers, though she is herself older than half of the residents. What she is taking issue with today is HUD's policy of mainstreaming mental patients into HUD facilities that were once exclusively the domain of senior citizens. A boy in Bellemonde, the next town over, is her object lesson on the failure of HUD policy. Two weeks after leaving the institution that had been in charge of his care, the boy took the elevator to the top of the Bellemonde Tower, then the stairs leading up to the roof. From there he climbed onto the wall, surveyed the world, and leapt from it. An eighty-year-old woman sitting on her balcony saw him go by and heard him land on the hood of a car in the parking lot with such force that he set off the horn, which continued to blow for another twenty minutes, until the locked door could be broken into with the Jaws of Life and the horn disconnected. My mother's thesis, if I read her correctly, is that elderly women should not have to bear witness to such tragic events. The mentally ill should have their own building to jump off unless they're over sixty-five.

I should probably have an opinion about this myself, but after reading my mother's column I find myself conflicted by her logic, with which I'm always reluctant to agree, knowing her as I do. And I admit that a moral man wouldn't get sidetracked pondering irrelevant details, like whether the boy also noticed the old woman as he passed her floor, whether seeing her there so unexpectedly provided him a lucid moment before he set off that horn. Back when I was a writer, I might have been able to justify such musings, since odd details and unexpected points of view are the stuff of which vivid stories are made, but now such thoughts seem more like evidence of an unbalanced mind, a warped sensibility.

The student newspaper contains a lot more humor, though most of it is unintentional. Except for the front page (campus news) and the back page (sports), the campus rag contains little but letters to the editor, which I scan first for allusions to myself and next for unusual content, which in the current climate is any subject other than the unholy trinity of insensitivity, sexism, and bigotry, which the self-righteous, though not always literate, letter writers want their readers to know they're against. As a group they seem to believe that high moral indignation offsets and indeed outweighs all deficiencies of punctuation, spelling, grammar, logic, and style. In support of this notion there's only the entire culture.

The front page contains two big stories, one announcing the ground-breaking dedication this afternoon of the Technical Careers Complex, the second informing the community that the yearlong asbestos removal project is near completion, only the Modern Languages Building remaining. There's a picture of one of the asbestos removal workers in his mask and special clothing, which I study for a moment, trying to decide why a man whose appearance has been completely disguised should remind me of my father, William Henry Devereaux, Sr., who begat not only me but American Literary Theory and is about to return to his son's vicinity, if not his life, after a forty-year hiatus.

Rather than contemplate the return of W.H.D., Sr., I pick up and begin to read Leo's latest effort, with which I have to be at least marginally conversant by this afternoon's workshop. His new story appears to be cinematically inspired—that is, uninspired. It's about the ghost of a long dead murderer who returns at twenty-year intervals to terrorize the same small town, graphically executing the descendants of the original townsfolk who hanged him in the previous century. The final scene of the story is climactic merely in the sense that after slaughtering a young woman character whose only crime seems to have been cockteasing, the ghost murderer rapes her corpse. The murder itself is accomplished in a single well-developed paragraph, the rape in the following single-spaced page and a half. In a handwritten note appended to the story and addressed to me, Leo expresses one or two slight misgivings. He wonders if the rape scene is overdone. And he wants to assure me that the narrative is not finished. Originally, he'd thought of it as a short story, but now he suspects it may be a novel. Next to his query concerning the rape scene, I write: "Always understate necrophilia." Then at the bottom of the final page, "Let's talk."

"Okay, let's," says a voice at my shoulder, and when I look up I see it's Billy Quigley's daughter Meg.

"You're a sight for sore eyes," I say, motioning for her to join me. It's true, too. Neither Billy Quigley nor his long-suffering wife would appear to have many genetic gifts to bequeath their offspring, but all of their girls are beautiful. Meg's beauty is almost breathtaking, and, in the manner of most truly beautiful women, she reminds you of no one but herself, whereas her other sisters all resemble each other, like young soap opera actresses. Meg has a face you wouldn't expect to see again this century.

She pulls out the chair opposite mine. She has a steaming cup of tea and a lumpy brown paper sack that looks like it may contain a tennis ball. "I didn't know there were any hard and fast rules governing the aesthetics of necrophilia."

I lean back and study her. What's in the bag is a peach. "I just ran into your old man," I say. "He didn't look so hot."

"I give him a year," Meg says. On the subject of her father, Meg's talk is always hard, casual. The two of them fight tough, cruel battles. Meg's public stance is that her father is a moron. I suspect that her private stance is pretty different. She's been married, once, to a man who didn't measure up to Billy. Now she's playing the field, trying to find a man who might and not having much luck, at least in Railton. Her behavior is one of the things she and her father fight about. Late one afternoon in the middle of the fall semester I got a call at the department from a man looking for her father. Meg had passed out drunk at a pub downtown, and the man wanted Billy to come fetch her. Because Billy was in class and because it was the sort of thing he could live without knowing, I drove over myself, loaded Meg into the backseat of my Lincoln, and took her back to her apartment, depositing her on the sofa in the front room and beating a hasty retreat when she woke up enough to ask me to undress her and put her to bed.

"In that case I'd try to make things up with him," I suggest. "You're his favorite."

Meg shakes her head. "It makes me crazy to go over there. I can't even describe what it's like in that house."

I can imagine though. Over the years the Quigley house has gone into the same serious decline as the rest of the neighborhood, its paint peeling, its porch rotting, its tiny lawn, even its sidewalk, given over to weeds. When Lily and I first moved to Railton, Billy's had been a respectable lower-middle-class neighborhood, home to several junior faculty from the university. Now it's the domain of demoralized Conrail workers who have gone from unemployment to subsistence checks from the government, whose marauding kids roam the streets at night, neglecting the homework my wife has assigned them, marking time until they'll be old enough to acquire the fake ID's that will allow them to climb onto barstools next to their sad parents in seedy neighborhood taverns that sport out-of-date beer signs in their dark windows.

"He could use a little moral support is all I'm saying."

"Couldn't we all," she says, toughness falling away for an instant, then returning almost immediately. "It's not easy knowing you owe your very existence to other people's stupidity."

I know better than to disagree, unless I want to be drawn into a serious quarrel right here in the student center. Meg's feelings on the subject of her parents' strict Catholicism are intense. After delivering the tenth little Quigley (there'd been three miscarriages as well), their family doctor had told Meg's mother that if she had another she'd be risking her life, but even then birth control had been unthinkable until a young parish priest, new in Railton, had taken her aside and told her that she'd done her part, that God expected no more. Meg was the fifth of the ten kids, and she always maintained that if her parents had possessed a brain between them they'd have stopped at four. It's one of the things I like about Meg. Most human beings want the door to swing shut behind them.

Since I've been a good boy and not started an argument, Meg offers me a bite of her peach.

"Do I dare?" I say.

"That's the question all right," she agrees.

In truth, I don't, though the issue may not be the daring. Meg has been flirting with me ever since I declined to undress her and put her to bed, and I've been flirting back, perhaps because we both seem to understand that it's just flirting. My cowardice is always understood to be the only impediment to our becoming lovers. Which will make a man my age curious. Almost curious enough to find out for sure, if it weren't for the suspicion that Meg enjoys watching me squirm more than she'd enjoy the sex. Squirming, I think I'd enjoy the sex more.

"Nope," she says after a moment. "It took you too long to decide."

When she finishes the peach, she hands me the pit. "See?" she grins. "All gone."

"There are other peaches," I can't help pointing out.

"Not like that one," she insists. "That was the best one ever."

Regrets, I have a few.

She gets up. "I've got a class. Will I be teaching in the fall?"

"I hope so," I tell her, as I told her father. "I'll try."

"You should let us adjuncts into your union."

"You have my vote."

She smirks, as if my promises are not something she places a lot of stock in. She may even know something about my standing in the union. "You know what my moron father wants me to do now?"

"No, what?"

"Go back for my Ph.D.," she says. "He's offered to pay for it."

"What a jerk," I say, deciding to play along.

Her face clouds over. "Watch yourself, bozo. This is my old man we're talking about."

CHAPTER

7

The campus is on the outskirts of town, five or ten minutes from the business district, depending on whether you catch the two traffic lights or miss them. I'm to meet Jacob Rose at Keglers, downtown, at noon. The food on campus is unworthy of a dean. Therefore, we will dine at a bowling alley. Keglers is on the other side of the tracks which divide the town neatly in half. There is no bad side of the tracks in Railton. Also no good side. The rule is, the closer you get to the tracks, the worse. Back in the town's heyday, when all the trains passed through on their way to Chicago and points west, one right after the other, the only way to escape the dirt and soot was to live up the slope, above where the ash settled. Houses in the lower elevations grew epidermal layers of gray film. Now, though the railroad is all but dead, what remains of the business district is so sooty and gray that a month of rains couldn't cleanse it, and the town is such a blight that local and state politicians have been working overtime to locate funds to complete a spur of north-south four-lane divided highway that will bypass it. The construction will mean jobs for Railton's chronically unemployed railroad workers and will make life easier on the truckers who now clog the narrow streets of downtown Railton. In this way the highway is being touted as an economic boon for the region, but when it's completed, the four-lane will be the final step in Railton's ostracism, officially excusing travelers from stopping, or even slowing down.

I arrive early, but Jacob Rose is already there. In fact, he's halfway through his corned beef sandwich. "Sorry," he says when I pull out a chair. "I had to wedge in an appointment at twelve-thirty, which means I've got to eat and run. Try the corned beef."

The lounge overlooks the bowling alley below, only two of its twenty-two lanes in use. A sloppy, slow-moving fellow in low-slung, baggy jeans leaves an ugly split and bellows, "You cocksucker!"

"Is it the corned beef that you like here or the ambience?" I ask Jacob Rose.

"There's no such thing as ambience in Railton," he says. "Nice nose."

"Thanks."

"I hear Gracie did it," he says. "You must have been protecting your groin."

In fact, the corned beef looks pretty good. I check around for a waitress. There's apparently only one, and she's across the room flirting with the bartender.

"Not a bad strategy," the dean admits. "With Gracie you're always wise to guard against the low blow." An observation born of personal experience, I know.

"Leaves the rest pretty wide open, though."

"Fortunately, leaving himself wide open is Hank Devereaux's trademark," Jacob reminds me.

I wave at the waitress, who is still unaware of my presence. She pivots on an ample hip and settles onto a stool at the bar.

"I hate to add to your difficulties . . . ," the dean continues.

"Then don't, for Christ's sake," I tell him, stealing one of his fries.

"This might not be such bad news, actually," he says, wiping his mouth on a paper napkin, pushing his chair back an inch or so from the table. "The English department's review has been moved up. Internal will begin its part in September. External will follow in October. If you're owed any favors at other institutions, now's the time to call in the markers."

I run my fingers through my hair. "That's crazy," I tell him. "We're in transition. We're hiring a new chair."

"Strictly a money decision," Jacob says. "The external team is doing Eastern and Northern also. This way all three get reviewed at once and the boys at the main campus get to promote the idea that we're all one university, geographically dispersed, as they're so fond of saying."

"Ideologically dispersed, you mean. Philosophically. Demographically. Economically."

"Be that as it may. And don't worry about being in transition. Because the funding isn't going to come through for your chair search. That's strictly between us. It'll be next week before you're told officially."

"Would it do any good to ask why?"

Jacob shrugs. "You could ask. I could tell you. But it would just piss you off. You wouldn't enjoy your lunch. Why don't you order something?" He glances over his shoulder and effortlessly catches the eye of the waitress who's been ignoring me. She slides off her stool and comes over. "How's everything?" she wants to know.

"Terrific," he assures her. "I'd like some coffee though."

When the girl makes to depart, he adds, "Don't you want anything, Hank?"

The girl stares at me in surprise, as if I've just materialized at the table. "Oh!" she exclaims. "Hi there!"

I order a corned beef sandwich. She writes this down, gets the dean's coffee, then returns to her barstool.

"Off the record, nobody's convinced that bringing in someone from outside will cure the English department's ailments," Jacob says.

"That was my original position, if you recall."

"Well then, you got your way, for once," Jacob grins. "Which reminds me. Finny asked me for a ruling on procedure. He doesn't want you to conduct the on-campus interviews. He says since you weren't in favor of an outside search in the first place, you shouldn't be in charge. Since there won't be any on-campus interviews anyway, I'm going to rule in his favor. Let him feel good about something."

"I bet you can trace your lineage all the way back to Solomon."

"He's also threatening litigation if you don't stop harassing him about his degree from the Ventura Boulevard Burrito Palace and School for the Arts. According to university counsel, there isn't much we can do. If Finny wants to embarrass himself by listing a degree from an unaccredited institution, it's his business. We can't humiliate him without embarrassing ourselves in the process. If he ever goes up for full professor, we can chop his biscuits, but until then . . ."

"That's fine," I assure him. "I don't want him fired. I'd just like to control the damage he does."

"That's where we're different," Jacob says, his voice full of good-natured resignation, pushing his coffee cup toward the center of the table. "I'd like to fire the bastard. Anyway, I gotta go."

"Listen," I say. "Before you do your vanishing act, tell me when I'm going to get my soft money."

He gives me a look that says I know better than to ask this. Which I do. "When I get mine."

"Not good enough," I tell him.

"I know. What can I say?"

"Make me a promise. Let me make a few promises. The money always comes through. Why not give our adjunct faculty a little peace of mind? Call it an early Christmas present."

"You're forgetting your audience."

"Okay, call it a Yom Kippur present."

"Call it Ramadan, for all I care. I can't give you money I don't have. If I promise and the appropriation doesn't come through, who benefits? We go through this shit every year. The troops all know the drill."

"Knowing the drill doesn't make it a good drill," I point out uselessly. "You could make an issue of this if you were properly motivated. You could do the right thing for once, just for the hell of it."

Jacob now assumes the weary expression he dons when I've gone too far, traded on the fact that we were both once mortal, played ball together, were even denied tenure. "Don't you ever get nosebleeds up there on the high moral ground?"

I smile innocently. "This nose?"

"Right. I lost my head."

"I'm serious about this, Jacob," I tell him, and I'm surprised to discover that I am. When difficult things can't get done, it's too bad. When easy things can't get done, and there's no good reason, it's more than too bad. It makes everything seem deep down mean and petty. "I've got department stationery, you know. And I'm pretty sure you'd be responsible for any promises I make. Piss me off and I'll not only hire them, I'll promise them raises."

"That would be your last official act though."

"No threats please," I say. "There can't be more than two or three people in the whole university who would take a Jacob Rose threat seriously, and I'm not one of them."

As soon as I say this, I'm sorry, because of course it's cruel, and its cruelty resides in its truth. Jacob is neither respected nor heeded in the university's upper echelons. This is partly because the liberal arts are not themselves respected, partly because, for all his tough talk, Jacob has never been very good in the clinches, where most of the interesting administrative blows are struck. He's known to be a nice, decent guy, the result of which is that he's frequently told to bend over, assume the position. To let me know I've hurt his feelings, he drops his hail-fellow mask and says, "I'll do what I can."

Having already used this line twice today, I'm not all that thrilled to hear it coming back at me. I don't doubt Jacob's good intentions, now that I've stung them into declarative life, but there's the question of his follow-through, his priorities, which will realign themselves once the sting has worn off. I know this danger firsthand, having witnessed my own intentions soften, my own priorities reconfigure without much conscious aid from William Henry Devereaux, Jr.

The dean pushes back his chair and stands. Our waitress reappears with the check. "I'll get this," Jacob grins.

"It seems only fair," I point out.

"Oops," the waitress says, startled by the unexpected sound of my voice. "I forgot to turn your ticket in to the kitchen."

I tell her to never mind.

"Get the tip, will you?" Jacob says, enjoying himself again.

I leave a pretty generous tip, considering. What I'm after is irony.

The girl smiles at me brightly. "You'ns hurry back," she says. So much for irony.

When we're out in the parking lot, Jacob says, "How come where women are concerned, they either don't notice you at all or they want to rip your nose off?"

"Let's do this again soon," I tell him.

"How's Lily?"

"Good," I tell him, adding, "How's Jane?" in reference to his wife of eighteen years, who gave him the boot a decade ago.

"Screw you," he says.

I decide, what the hell, why not send up a trial balloon? "Interesting rumors making the rounds these days," I say, watching for a reaction.

There is none, and that itself is a reaction. "You gotta love academe," Jacob says. "Rumors are the manna of our particular desert."

"Hypothetical question," I venture further. "Suppose an academic dean—say, of liberal arts—actually knew something for once. Would he share what he knew with an old friend?"

"Is this an old friend who insults the dean and questions his integrity? Who can be counted on to be a pain in the testicles?" Jacob continues, for clarification. "Probably the dean would, at the right time."

"Would the right time be soon?"

"Soon? I suppose *soon* is a good word."

"It's true, isn't it," I tell him. "The job makes the man."

"What's this I hear about your old man moving to Railton?"

This stops me cold. I haven't told anyone but Lily. "Where did you hear that?"

"Your mother. She was wondering about the possibility of an honorary chair on campus. For William Henry Devereaux, she said. At first I thought she meant you. Which was why I laughed. Then it occurred to me she was talking about your father."

I smile and nod to acknowledge the insult, but otherwise ignore it. "And you said?"

"I told her she should approach the chancellor. She said she already had his number."

"She's got just about everybody's number, believe me. Even my father's. Not that it ever did her any good. Tennis Saturday?" I suggest, shifting gears.

"Can't," he says. "I'm going out of town. In the meantime, you're in charge. Just don't do anything."

"Let me know if you get the job," I say.

To judge from Jacob's reaction, this is a shrewd guess. He puts his index finger to his lips. "If I do, I'll take you with me."

"No thanks," I say. "I'm having too much fun right here."

I follow him out of the parking lot, and we get to the tracks just as the red lights begin to blink and the guardrail descends. Jacob guns his Regal and swings under the first rail and around the second. The last thing I see before the freight train comes between us is the dean gleefully giving me the finger.

CHAPTER

8

My mother's flat is in a section of Railton that was, once upon a distant time, monied. In the heyday of the railroad there were large public gardens, and the neighborhoods surrounding these gardens were full of stately Victorian and Edwardian homes—mansions, some of them—of which only a few remain, most of those in disrepair, on the street where my mother lives. The public gardens themselves no longer exist, having been converted back in the thirties to an amusement park, which itself flourished and then died in the late sixties. All that remains of it now is a condemned, rickety Ferris wheel, a vacant shell of a building that once housed the carousel, and the huge open-air pavilion where summer dances and concerts were held overlooking what was once a manmade lake and is now a muddy declivity. Despite its decay, the former public gardens/amusement park remains the most valuable real estate in the city, though for several decades it has been mired in litigation, a battle of greedy but otherwise disinterested out-of-state heirs.

The houses on my mother's street have all been divided into large, high-ceilinged, drafty, impossible-to-heat rental flats, most of which are owned by the same man, my mother's landlord, Charles Purty, who has purchased them one by one, at fire sale prices, over a period of thirty years. The only house on the street he doesn't own is a decrepit old brownstone purchased by the diocese for an all but extinct order of nuns—the Sisters of the Divine Heart.

When I pull up in front of my mother's flat, I notice that Mr. Purty, who lives next door, is setting up his monthly yard sale, which always runs from late Thursday afternoon to midday Sunday. He's got about a dozen large, folding metal tables, and his tilting porch is stacked with cardboard boxes full of the junk he will set out on them. Mr. Purty is a world-class scavenger, and since he retired a couple years ago from selling discount furniture and appliances, turning the business over to a son who no longer allows him to set foot in the store, he's divided his time between scouting garage and estate sales in remote corners of central Pennsylvania and courting my mother, who, at seventy-three (several years Mr. Purty's senior), must remind him of all these elegant, impractical old houses he's purchased over the years. My mother is proving more difficult to acquire. She gives him the time of day only when she needs to go somewhere (she no longer drives) and I'm unavailable to take her. Then she graciously allows Mr. Purty to chauffeur her about in his full-size pickup truck, a vehicle she despises because it's hard for a small, modest woman like my mother to climb up into and because the seat is always lumpy with junk Mr. Purty's bought at yard sales. My mother, a woman who never looks before she sits, hates being goosed, even by inanimate objects.

But Mr. Purty is a patient man, and even now, with my father's return imminent, he's apparently content to wait for my mother to become available. He figures he'll outlast her stubborn reservations about him. He thinks of them as reservations. I doubt that Mr. Purty, whom my mother suspects of being illiterate, knows the word *aversion,* which more precisely describes my mother's feelings for her landlord.

"Henry," Mr. Purty hollers over when I get out of the car and wave. Henry is what my mother calls me, so of course it's how Mr. Purty refers to me as well, though I've encouraged him to call me

Hank. "You look like you could use a pair of these," he says when I've climbed his porch steps and we've shaken hands.

He offers for my inspection a fake plastic nose, glasses, and a mustache. He's right, too. I can imagine half a dozen uses. "How much do you want for them?" I ask.

He waves off my offer of money. "Take 'em."

I put the nose and glasses in my pocket.

"Aren't you going to try them on?"

I just grin at him.

"I see your ma's on the pop-ed page again," Mr. Purty observes. He's a man of few words, a startling percentage of them malapropisms. Lately, having amassed more money than he knows what to do with, he's begun dabbling in stocks and mutual funds, a subject he imagines I, a professor, must know something about. He shares with me his misgivings about the market's "fuctuations." Mr. Purty wears a hearing aid, and the conclusion I've come to is that he's been mishearing words and phrases all his life. My mother's take is predictably less generous. She insists he's never read a book in his life and therefore had no opportunity to compare the words he's hearing with their representations on the printed page. She may be right. One thing is certain. Mr. Purty doesn't understand that his verbal miscues are a serious matter to my mother, that she could never take seriously the affections of a verbally clumsy man. Even his awe of her own verbal dexterity she holds against him. For Mr. Purty, listening to my mother talk is not unlike watching a bear dance. It's just the damndest thing. There's nothing and no one my mother won't pass judgment on, and this nonplusses Mr. Purty, who, if he has opinions, keeps them to himself. That my mother has so many and writes them down for publication in the newspaper strikes Mr. Purty as unaccountable behavior. If he were ever to have an opinion, the last thing he'd think to do with it is write it down.

I myself have only one consistent reaction to my mother's columns in the *Railton Mirror* and that is dread. A relatively small portion of that dread is occasioned by contemplating what she'll say. No, it's actually her byline that causes my heart to plummet. Mrs. William Henry Devereaux is the name she's remained faithful to in the face of common sense all these years since being abandoned by William Henry Devereaux, Sr., my father. Her stated rationale is that she fears, given the remarkable independence and originality of her intellect, that she might be thought a feminist. But what this is really about is that she has always considered herself the wife of William Henry Devereaux, Sr., for worse, not for better, till death do them part, as agreed in public, never mind what the divorce papers say. As a result, there are God knows how many readers of the *Railton Mirror* who believe my mother to be my wife. Often I am called upon in social situations to defend her positions, which would be tedious enough even if I were able to ignore the Oedipal implications of being linked, journalistically, by marriage to my own mother. Lily, that other Mrs. William Henry Devereaux, is pressed even harder to defend opinions she has never voiced and does not share.

"So, how's business?" I ask. The table Mr. Purty just set out is crowded with an assortment of knickknacks, priced to sell. The most expensive item appears to be two dollars. Most are fifty cents. So, for mere pennies you can choose among fifty or so figurines, sacred and profane. Plastic Jesuses and plaster Marys mingle happily with grinning, big-bellied gargoyles. Most puzzling, since I have no reason to suspect that Mr. Purty is capable of an artistic design, much less a blasphemous one.

"I put the good stuff out later in the weekend," he explains. He showed me around his house once. That is, we weaved among the narrow pathways of stuff piled floor to ceiling in every room. "I always offer to give your ma a preview, maybe let her choose something. But she don't seem too interested."

"She's not sure you're a gentleman, Mr. Purty," I say. "She probably thinks you've got other reasons for luring her into your house."

"I do," he admits. "But I'd be a gentleman with her. She's a real aristocat, your ma."

I try not to smile, but I can't help myself. I'd like to explain to Mr. Purty that my mother is not an "aristocat," as he imagines. She's simply imperious, an old scholar-teacher descended from intellectual nobility perhaps, but that's about it.

"You must be excited about your dad coming here to live," he says.

I decide on understatement. "It'll be different having him around, all right."

"Your ma says he's been pretty sick."

"He's suffered a kind of breakdown, I guess," I explain. "They say he's improving."

"Your ma will make him better."

"You think so?"

"Sure."

"Hold that thought, Mr. Purty. And thanks for the nose."

My mother meets me at the door to her downstairs flat, and we exchange pecks on the cheek. "Henry," she says, looking me over briefly, registering my mutilated nostril the way you notice the passing of a bright city bus you're not trying to catch. Both she and my father were the most detached of parents. When I was a child, they would examine me from time to time, as if to make certain that I was still equipped with the standard factory equipment, after which they would return to whatever conversation they'd been engaged in. Neither could understand my attachment to sports, and both were impatient with athletic injuries, small or large, which they perceived as willful. My mother seemed to be of the opinion that serious sprains could be mended with a washcloth. Once I was scrubbed, she pronounced me good as new.

Lately, every time I see my mother, she reminds me of Norma Desmond. It's not physical, really. My mother is a slight woman, but in recent years, as her eyesight has begun to fail, her use of makeup has become less subtle, and the effect is more severe. Her eyebrows seem plucked into a permanent arch, emphasizing that severity. Her clothes are old and out of fashion, though expensive and obsessively cared for. She's the only woman I know who routinely wears lots of jewelry. She applies lipstick before leaving the house, regardless of her destination, and again at the table after meals in public. I can never decide whether she looks as if she's about to go somewhere or as if she's expecting important company. Either way, she's ready for her close-up. I'm no Cecil B. DeMille, but I can play that role. I tell my mother she looks wonderful.

Which she ignores. "I see you were conversing with my ubiquitous landlord," she remarks. "I've had to install new shades. The old ones kept inching up, and that man has more excuses for walking past my windows. He's nosier than an old woman."

"He's looking after you, Mom," I suggest.

"No, he's looking *at* me. Keeping track of my comings and goings. He's afraid I might be seeing someone."

"Well," I concede. "That too." My mother has lived here for four or five years now, since she retired from teaching, and Mr. Purty's attentions have been a more or less constant complaint. A couple months after she moved in, she came home one afternoon and found him in the basement working on the relic of a furnace. When he left, she called a locksmith, and the next time Mr. Purty found it necessary to enter he discovered he was without a valid key to his own house. "What if I need to get in?" he asked, not unreasonably. "You can knock, like everyone else," my mother informed him. "What if you ain't here?" he wanted to know. "If I'm not here, you don't need to get in," he was informed.

"If you'd married him like I told you to, you wouldn't have him lurking around all the time," I remind her. "You know how devoted he is. By now you'd have convinced him to take you to live in Europe."

"True," my mother concedes. She's very aware of the spell she's cast on her landlord. "But then I'd be in Europe with Charles Purty. What if I met someone I liked there?"

"Suit yourself, Mother."

"I will," she assures me. "It's lunchtime. Have you eaten? Would you like a sandwich?"

This is not an easy decision. My stomach is indeed growling, having been teased into expectation by the dean's corned beef. Still, I know what to expect from my mother. Always an austere woman, she's become positively spartan in old age. I don't know what kind of sandwich she has in mind, but I know it will be thin, elegant, mostly bread. On the other hand, this may be my last opportunity for any sort of lunch today. I tell her a sandwich sounds good.

Actually, the worst of my mother's austerity manifested itself after my father left her for the first of his graduate students. I suspect my mother saw in this new circumstance very few attractive choices. Apparently the most appealing was the opportunity for theater. Instead of beggaring my father in the divorce settlement like a sensible woman, she let him off the hook and began to live in what she referred to as the straitened circumstances of an abandoned woman. Her plan, I imagine, was to humiliate my father, which shows how little she understood him if she thought, even for an instant, that such a tactic was likely to succeed. If she wanted to pretend that the dissolution of their marriage had left her destitute, that was fine with him, provided he himself was not made destitute for real.

The simple truth was this. They were both professors at a good midwestern university when my father left, and my mother was well respected and kept her position when my father and Trophy Wife Number One left for the East and life in the academic fast lane. She wasn't then and hasn't been since, so far as I know, strapped for money, though she chose to live far below her means in a shabby genteel university house while she continued to teach, and here in Charles Purty's flat since she retired and moved to Railton.

The sandwich my mother serves me is two slices of white bread into which she has massaged the thinnest possible layer of pimento cheese spread. "I do wish he'd get over his ridiculous crush," she says, sitting down opposite me at the kitchen table. She's made herself a sandwich identical to my own. "I mean, it's absurd. What can he want from a seventy-three-year-old woman?"

Despite this reasonable protest, there's something about the way my mother registers it that suggests she doesn't find it entirely absurd, as if she's got a strong inkling what Mr. Purty has in mind and objects less to the principle of the thing than to the man in question. Perhaps she even wants me to weigh in on the matter, assure her I don't think it's ridiculous for Charles Purty to lust after a woman her age. But I know a son's duties and I know this isn't one of them. True, my mother is a remarkably well-preserved woman, who looks about Mr. Purty's age, though he's several years her junior. Still. I chew my bread and try to look thoughtful and abstractly sympathetic. My nostril begins to pulse with this complex effort.

"He was impressed by your last column," I say, to shift emphasis. A sound strategy. My mother is vain about her writing. Of my father's numerous books of literary criticism, all of which created a stir, only one, his first, is now considered a classic. It's my mother's unwavering position that the reason for this is that the first was the only one she edited. It's her opinion that by abandoning the true companion of his life (herself) for a series of academic bimbos, my father forsook his truest self. Whereas he used to be a powerful and original thinker, now he just jumps on bandwagons. My own take is that my father is simply a careerist, that this is what he would have been regardless.

"It *was* one of my better efforts," she admits. "I'm told the piece may be widely reprinted." When I don't immediately respond to this, she continues, "Speaking of journalistic efforts, may I suggest you avoid autobiography in the future?"

This request is in reference to a recent column of mine, written shortly after I was informed that William Henry Devereaux, Sr., would be returning to the bosom of his family, an event that my mother told me to expect, any day, for nearly a year after he left us and that now, forty years later, has apparently earned her the right to say I told you so. In the essay I recounted the events leading up to the acquisition, naming, and burial of the Irish setter my father brought home when I was a boy.

"Humor is a poor substitute for accuracy," my mother reminds me. "And a poorer proxy for truth."

I've got a wad of pimento-flavored bread lodged in my throat, and I discover the impossibility of swallowing both it and my mother's criticisms at the same time. I focus on the wad of bread first, and only when it is safely disposed of do I say, "What struck you as untrue?"

My mother, who knows me as well as I know her, is prepared for this question. "Mind you, I don't care how I myself am portrayed in your writings, but I do wish you wouldn't give the impression that your father was a fool. I just pray no one sends it to him."

"*I* haven't," I assure her. "So if you don't, I guess no one will."

"It could conceivably be reprinted," she reminds me. "Has that occurred to you? The piece was well enough written. You have always been talented. I just wish you wouldn't employ your talents in defense of falsehood. Often your subjects are trivial, and even then . . . you lack high seriousness, Henry. Weight, for want of a better word. There, I've said it. I don't mean to hurt your feelings, but the truth is that there's nothing more shallow than cleverness. You've become a clever man."

"I do it for the money," I respond cleverly. My mother knows well what the *Railton Mirror* pays its contributors. But as she gathers up my plate and coffee cup, I see that she is seriously annoyed with me. My mother has always been the sort of woman whose emotional state can be

intuited from the volume at which she rattles kitchen utensils. I appreciate this. I would not, believe me, wish my wife to be more like my
mother, except that there is something reassuring about dealing with a
woman whose emotional barometer can be read so easily. Lily, I sometimes regret, lacks my mother's sense of drama. In Lily's opinion rattling
the china not only dramatizes anger but reduces anger to melodrama.
My wife considers overtly dramatic behavior of the sort my mother has
always relished undignified. And Lily is right, no doubt about it. But a
man like me, who's easily confused by women, prefers signposts with
large lettering. My mother contains her own share of depths, but she's
willing to simplify, to offer unambiguous directions: GO . . . STOP . . .
YIELD. William of Occam could follow such road signs, and so can I.

"Are you still miffed that I'm not going with you to New York?" I
venture.

My mother turns from the sink where she's rinsing our plates and
saucers to study me. "No, Henry, I'm not *still* miffed that you're not
going to New York. I never was miffed about that, so I can't very well
still be miffed."

"Oh," I smile at her, since she's obviously miffed at something.

"If you had a truck, or a reliable vehicle of any sort, it would be
another matter, but you and that monstrosity you drive would be of no
use to us. Instead of towing, we'd end up towed. No, your friend
Charles Purty and I will do famously without your assistance. It's time
he got out of Railton, and you know how I love New York. True, I
could wish for a more sophisticated escort. I've never entered the Russian Tea Room in the company of a man wearing cowboy boots and a
shirt with metal buttons, but that can't be helped . . ." Her voice trails
off as she contemplates the scene she's just conjured.

"Call before you go," I suggest, getting to my feet. "I read somewhere that it closed."

"The Russian Tea Room? Don't be absurd." But then, suddenly,
she's serious. Or a different kind of serious. "What worries me is that
you are in no way prepared for your father's return."

This is such a puzzling thing to say that I can't help but stare at her.

"What I was in no way prepared for, Mother, was his departure," I
remind her. "These days, thank God, I could care less what he does and
doesn't do."

The expression she offers me now is my least favorite of all those in her vast arsenal of annoyingly superior looks, the one that says, "Who are you trying to kid, buddy-boy?"

"What?" I say, feeling myself become more than a little heated.

"Have it your way," my mother says, and I see that I was wrong about her last expression being her most annoying. This sad, wry one she's replaced it with is even worse.

I consult my watch. "I have to go teach a class," I remind her. In the Devereaux family, this obligation has always been the ace of trumps, and I can see how much my mother hates to see me play it now.

"Oh, yes," she recalls. "The one where everybody talks but you. I always forget what you call those." My mother hasn't forgotten what workshops are called, or that she disapproves of them. "Before you illuminate all those young minds with your eloquent silence, would you mind going down into the cellar and bringing up the smaller of my two suitcases?"

I follow her to the cellar door, and when she flips the light switch, there's a brief flash, followed by a distinct pop from the dark, nether regions of Charles Purty's cellar. "Oh, phooey," my mother says. "And I'm out of lightbulbs."

"Just leave the door open," I suggest, since I'm pretty sure I can see the suitcase in question from the top of the stairs. "And step out of the light."

My mother does as she's told, for once. "Be careful, Hank," she says, touching my elbow and favoring me with the name she has always despised. "The stairs are in a frightful condition."

And I do as I'm told, for once, recalling, as I start to descend, my wife's premonition that I may end up in the hospital while she's gone, a prophecy I'm determined to thwart. The problem is that once I enter the stairwell I am blocking my own light, and everything below swims into darkness. I feel for the next step cautiously, like a man without much faith that there will be a next step, or that it will be where reason would place it. At first I can feel the walls on each side, but as I descend these fall away, and there is no handrail. "There," I hear my mother say, "you're on the bottom," though how she can see this when I can't is beyond me. She is right, though, I have reached the stone floor, and in another moment or two my eyes adjust. Feeling my way in the dark, I locate the handle of what feels like a suitcase, then another. I set what feels like the smaller of the two on the stair for my mother to inspect. "This one?"

"Yes," she says. "And while you're there? Right next to the suitcases there should be two cardboard boxes marked 'Memorabilia.' "

"Step back out of the light," I suggest, though I can see better now. The ceiling, not very far above my head, is a web of pipes, and I negotiate these carefully as I move around. There appear to be a dozen or so cardboard boxes in the vicinity, all of them labeled "Memorabilia" in my mother's elegant hand.

"Open the top one," she suggests.

I cart the top one over to the foot of the stairs so the light falls on it and open it up. "Photo albums," I call up, though, wedged along the side of the box, something brightly colored catches my eye.

"That's the one," my mother says. "Hand the suitcase up, then bring the box, if you will."

The brightly colored thing, once I've tugged it out, I recognize as the dog collar I purchased as a boy in the hope of convincing my parents to get me a dog to attach it to. I toss it up, so that it lands at my mother's feet. "Ah, Red," I say. "How I loved that dog."

"God, what a little pill you were," my mother recalls nostalgically.

"Here's the suitcase." I duck my head, go partway up the stairs, and hand it up. When my mother comes into view to receive it, backlit, a dark silhouette, something old washes over me so powerfully that I start to back away at the moment of transfer, and for a second I wonder if I'm going to pull my mother down the stairs after me. I lose track of how many steps up I've taken, and suddenly I'm lost, completely lost. Reaching up, I grab one of the pipes, the hot water one as luck would have it, and it's this pipe that keeps me from going down.

"Careful," I hear my mother's voice. "Are you all right?"

It's a good question. I seem to be. Was it dizziness or nausea that passed over me? Did I actually black out for a second? Now it's my own voice I hear. "I just lost my equilibrium for a moment. I'm fine."

"Leave the box. Come on up," she suggests.

A moment later, I'm seated at the kitchen table. My mother is holding out a glass of Railton tap water, which no one was ever healthier for drinking. "You're pale as a ghost," she would have me know.

"How old was that cheese spread?" I ask her.

"Don't go blaming my cheese spread," I'm told. "I ate it too, and there's nothing wrong with me."

"I really have to go teach," I tell her, consulting my watch again. In fact, now that I'm out of the dank cellar and in the light, I feel fine.

"Look at me," she says.

When I do, when I meet her puzzled eyes, I feel a slight aftershock, the trace effects of whatever it was that visited me in the cellar, and then it's all gone and I'm myself again. My mother must agree, because she doesn't argue.

"You must be coming down with something," she concludes on the porch, putting her hand on my chest when I lean forward to kiss her good-bye. Mr. Purty observes this from his own porch across the driveway. I wave at him on my way down the steps, and he waves back understandingly. He knows what it feels like not to be kissed.

CHAPTER

9

Often, imagination isn't everything it's cracked up to be. I have imagined, for instance, how badly my afternoon seminar will go, and it's gone that badly and then some. What occurs to me is this: if I've been smart enough to predict this disaster, I should have been able to prevent it. But imagination without energy remains inert, and my visit to my mother's has left me strangely disoriented, made a disinterested observer of me. Normally I'm an amused observer, but there's nothing all that amusing in today's class. I wonder if my inability to see any humor represents progress of some sort. I am, after all, frequently accused of a lack of high seriousness. But this class can't be progress toward anything. Apparently my students agree. They're looking at each other as if they're trying to remember what they were thinking back in January when they enrolled.

Of course the trouble began before I arrived, provoked by the unfortunate Leo's unwillingness to understate necrophilia. By the time I entered the classroom, the situation was already out of hand. A virulent young woman named Solange, who has coal black hair with an angry streak of white—her mean streak, as I've come to think of it— was in the process of observing that the reason Leo always writes about pussy is that he is one. He pretends to be some kind of Hemingway, but the truth is he's a wimp, a wanna-be, a case of arrested development. Trouble has been brewing between these two all semester. For the last couple weeks she's been saying things under her breath, and I've made the mistake of ignoring them. But there was no way to ignore this. When I asked Solange if she was finished, if we could begin our work- shop of Leo's story, she replied that she would be happy to begin it her- self. The story, in her view, was more of this author's incessant, sexist nonsense. Trash, without a single redeeming feature. She could see no use for it beyond kindling.

Such remarks seldom stimulate discussion, and they have not done so here. Leo, his cheeks aflame, tried to summon his usual smug grin but failed. As the semester has progressed, it's become more and more difficult for Leo to maintain his public posture, which is that he and I are, after a fashion, team-teaching the course. He's the only student taking the workshop a second time, and he's intimated to his class- mates that, of course, I hold him to a higher standard and that we have an unspoken understanding. Since he's the only student on campus who's properly obsessed with becoming a writer, I see it as my duty to push him harder than the others, to make sure he's not ruined by too much praise. From the author interviews Leo devours, he has learned that about the worst thing that can happen to a talented young writer is to be given too much praise, so Leo is grateful to me for protecting him. I don't know whether he's grateful to the other students in the workshop, who have been even more determined than their instructor not to ruin him with too much praise. Or any praise.

Right now, with the exception of Solange, they are all looking to me for guidance, aware that I don't, as a rule, encourage the kind of in-your- face dismissal of someone's labors that Solange has accorded Leo. There are two rules in my workshop, and most of the time these head off trou- ble. The first rule is that all comments and criticisms are to be directed at the manuscript and not its author. In return for this consideration, the author is not permitted to speak in defense of the manuscript.

These are excellent, though fundamentally flawed, rules. The problem with the first is that what's wrong with any given manuscript is often easily located in the personality or character of its author, as is the case with Leo's story. Leo needs more than aesthetic and technical advice in short story writing. Leo needs, among other things, to get laid. His grim young face bears eloquent testimony to the fact that no young woman has ever been kind to him. His stories are a revenge on the lot of them. At this particular moment, having been branded a wimp, he's a study in scarlet. In addition to his red hair and flushed face and long, pimply neck, two of the fingers of his right hand are bleeding at the cuticles. Throughout the winter his raw fingers have been full of hangnails. The tiny deltas of skin are always peeled back, like tomato skins, revealing the tender pulp beneath. I see that today it's the index finger of his right hand he's been excavating, and there are several bright pinpoints of blood at the cuticle for him to suck at, then examine secretly, as if he suspects the truth of his nature—that he's red to the core.

Although they have been chafing each other all semester, Leo and Solange are not so different. Both are friendless, so far as I can tell. Neither seems to have discovered a way to exist in the world. Solange fancies herself a poet, and to her this has less to do with writing poetry than it does with adopting a superior attitude. She dresses in black, eschews makeup, smokes dope, feigns a kind of exhausted boredom. She'd like to think she's smart (she is) but fears she isn't, at least not smart enough to justify her superiority. She's pale-skinned and bony, and this, I suspect, is partly why she objects so strongly to Leo's lurid adolescent fantasies. In his stories girls like Solange don't rate notice, much less ravishing. To attract the attention of one of Leo's vengeful ghosts, a girl has to have big breasts, not a protruding breastbone. Last fall, Solange fled Gracie's poetry seminar, I suspect, because Gracie herself is all womanly excess, and not above conveying to young women like Solange that their hips may be too narrow for childbearing, their breasts too flat to satisfy infant or lover, their lips too dry to inspire passion, their eyes too cold to welcome.

Of course such things cannot be said to students like Leo and Solange (or, for that matter, to Gracie). And since the only things that might be helpful are the things that cannot be said, I am without a strategy for the present circumstance. I should tell Solange she's out of order. Clearly, that's what everyone expects me to do. They all know my view that tough, rigorous criticism is predicated on good, not ill, will. And so they are confused by my reluctance to take Solange to task in this instance. Is it because her personal assault took place before the official beginning of class? Or am I suggesting that in this instance the attack is justified, that Leo has brought it on himself over the last several months, aggressively exhausting our charity by assaulting us with one bloody pussy story after another?

The truth of why I do nothing is that imaginatively I'm still back in my mother's basement, still feeling the lingering effects of whatever it was that washed over me there. For some reason the tips of my fingers are tingling, and I can't shake the feeling that I should have examined the contents of all the cardboard boxes stacked up against the wall, that one of them contained something of importance to me, something I've forgotten. I flex the palm of my hand where I grabbed the hot water pipe. The skin there has that smooth, shiny, burned look, like it might split open. If I am right that Leo is red to his very core, what color is William Henry Devereaux, Jr., at his center? I wonder.

So, instead of earning my pay with this group of expectant students, I exercise the prerogative of all bad teachers by conveying that I'm disappointed in the lot of them, that they have proven unworthy of my guidance, that they will now have to earn their way back into my good graces. I tell the class that I don't intend to say a word until somebody locates an issue worth discussing. Something specific and objective, not general and subjective. Sorting out these terms, I rationalize, will give everyone time to simmer down. I take off my watch and set it on the table beside me, watch its hands move, study my chastened students. Solange, having had her say, takes out a Penguin *Macbeth* and pretends to read it. Leo has become catatonic except for throwing the occasional murderous glance in my direction. I know what he's thinking. I have allowed this bitch to unman him. Whatever.

When, by my watch, there are only two minutes left in class, I rouse myself from my lethargy and summon the muse of melodrama by allowing my forehead to clunk heavily down on the metal seminar table that happens at this moment to be the only thing we all have in common. When I raise it again, everyone is looking at me, wide-eyed, fearful. Even Solange, who's dropped *Macbeth* like a bloody knife.

"I know *you,* Tiffany," I say.

Everyone groans. I'm returning them to the beginning, to a character exercise from their intro class. It's called "I know you, Al. You're (not) the kind of man who—" The exercise is designed to test the writer's understanding of his characters by challenging him to complete the sentence in an interesting and revealing way. I know you, Al. You're the kind of man who still opens doors for women. I know you, Susie. You're not the kind of girl who forgets an insult. In advanced workshops, "I know you, Al" has become shorthand for suggesting the story's characters are not sharply defined.

"Are the victims in this story characters?"

A general shaking of heads, Leo alone abstaining.

"What do we know of the murderer beyond what was done to him?"

"Nothing." Grudging grumbles. This is old, insulting stuff.

"There," I say. "If someone had been astute enough to observe that this story has no characters an hour ago, we could have all gone home."

"Tiffany is very real to me," Leo insists. He looks like he would like to slaughter us all. "Very real."

"The only thing real to you"—Solange puts *Macbeth* in her bag—"is her bloody snatch. Grow up."

Since this should not be the last word, I say, "Class dismissed," just as the bell rings.

Everyone files out. Except Leo, who wants to escort me to my office. He can't believe I've actually said there are no characters in his story. He reads part of the rape scene aloud as we walk, just to show me how wrong I am. By the time we arrive at my office, my good spirits are restored.

CHAPTER

10

Rachel has several messages for me.

Herbert Schonberg, the union rep, is very disappointed I've chosen not to return his calls. To me, his choice of the word *disappointed* suggests insincerity. June Barnes, Teddy's wife, wants me to call her at home at my first convenience, never mind why, just do it. Mysterious and intriguing. Orshee wants to consult me about a real estate matter. Mysterious without being intriguing. Gracie still begs an audience. Neither mysterious nor intriguing, but possibly dangerous. Tony Coniglia wants me to know he's booked a racquetball court for four-thirty and asks if I could be on time for once. Vaguely insulting. And Rachel says there's another message for me on my desk, which there is. In the center of my blotter sit five peach pits, a dark, wet spot radiating outward. As I study these, it occurs to me that a lot of people are taking liberties with my excellent disposition. After all, I *am* the chair of a large academic department, however temporarily.

There's no reason I should be treated as if I were wearing a Kick Me sign.

Rachel buzzes and says she's going home.

"Already?" I say. "You're going to leave me all alone?"

"It's three-fifteen?" she says, her intercom voice full of all too real guilt. "I have to pick up Jory?"

"I'm kidding," I tell her. "Go."

"You really liked the stories?"

"I sent them to Wendy, my agent," I tell her. "At least I think she's still my agent."

I wait to see how Rachel will react to what I've done without her permission. Last fall she started submitting her stories for publication but then quit when her husband began saying I told you so about the rejections and complaining about the cost of postage. I've told her to use the department mail so it won't cost her anything, but she's far too ethical. Besides, she suspects that her moron husband is right about her not being good enough. She may even believe he's right about my trying to get her into bed.

Rachel doesn't say anything for a minute, and in the silence I consider whether I just might be trying to get Rachel into bed. I can almost picture it, but not quite, probably because I'm still staring at the peach pits soaking my blotter. Can Meg Quigley have eaten all these peaches? And what is she trying to say? Is she extending Eliot's metaphor by suggesting that, unlike timid Prufrock, she dares to eat a half a dozen peaches? What would that mean, in purely sexual terms? Or does she just want me to understand I'm the pits?

Imaginatively, I appear to be in bed with both of these women at once, unequal to either task. I go through the batch of memos again, hoping there's a message from Lily that I missed—she ought to have arrived in Philly by now—but there isn't.

"Thanks?" Rachel finally says. "When?"

"Last week. I made a copy."

Another silence. "Promise that if she hates them you won't tell me?"

"Why?" I ask her. "What makes her the final arbiter?"

Silence, for a moment. "Who is?"

"I am," I say. "How many times do I have to tell you?"

"I really have to go?" she says.

Me too. All this imagination is not without consequence. I have to pee again. My last visit was on my way to class, what, an hour ago? Now I have to go again.

The intercom crackles, and Rachel is on again. "Professor DuBois would like to see you."

"Okay," I say, directly into the intercom, loud enough so that I'm sure Gracie will hear. "Frisk her and send her in."

Gracie enters. She's dressed beautifully, expensively, in a beige dress that looks like it could be cashmere. As her always lush body has gotten bigger, so has her hair, as if it's her intention to keep her general bodily proportions the same. She looks, frankly, heroic and quite wonderful, a brave woman intent on one last sexual conquest before menopause. I can understand Mike Law's having become dispirited. If ever a man was unequal to a task presented by a woman, Mike is that man. As always, Gracie's perfume precedes her, and I remember that it was the sensation I had of asphyxiating in Gracie's perfume yesterday that got me started on her.

"I don't suppose there's any chance we could conduct this meeting like adult professionals?" she says, not unreasonably, given the fact that I have slipped on the false nose and glasses I got from Mr. Purty. I've detached the mustache on the theory that it doesn't contribute to the effect I'm after, which is slight exaggeration, not broad parody. The black plastic glasses to which the fake nose is attached are not unlike my own reading glasses, just as the plastic schnoz is only slightly more ridiculous that my own ruined proboscis.

However, Gracie's reaction is disappointing. I was counting on a double take at least. If I had done to Gracie's person what she has done to mine, I'd have had a bad moment. I'd have concluded, however briefly, that I'd injured her worse than I thought. Guilt would have made the comic nose look momentarily real in the cruel light of moral imagination. Either Gracie has no moral imagination or she knows who she's dealing with.

"Gracie . . . ," I begin.

"Dr. DuBois," she corrects me, waits. I myself don't have a Ph.D., is her point, and she doesn't want me taking liberties.

We both wait.

"Fine," she continues. "Well, I only have a few minutes, but I wanted to see you before I left town."

My wife, the dean, my mother and Charles Purty, now Gracie. That makes five.

"Actually, I've come to apologize, Professor Devereaux. I never intended—"

"Hank," I correct her, with a magnanimous gesture. When I take off the fake nose, Gracie, to her credit, does wince.

"I've thought about the whole thing," she says, "and I've come to the conclusion that the only thing to do is separate the personal issues from the professional."

Though I have no idea what this means, I tell her I think that's an excellent idea.

"I've decided to file a grievance against you," she continues.

"Is that the professional part or the personal?" I interrupt.

Gracie ignores this. "That way my position as a senior faculty member will be clear. And that I have no intention of being pushed aside."

Here Gracie pauses so that I may digest this.

"I know you think this is small of me, but I must protect my turf. If we were hiring another fiction writer, you'd do the same."

I consider telling Gracie that we're arguing a moot point since the funding isn't going to come through and no one's turf is going to be invaded, but I have promised Jacob Rose that this will remain our secret, and, besides, most academic arguments end up moot, so there's no particular reason to surrender this one, which has already cost me a nostril. "Gracie—" I begin.

She holds up her hand. "Maybe you're more secure than I am. I admit you're a successful writer. I just think it's cruel of y'all to want to show me up. I've given fifteen years to this institution. I won't be moved aside."

If this weren't so pitiful, it would be funny. Not just Gracie's feelings of inadequacy, which are real enough. But as a tenured full professor in our egalitarian, unionized, colonial outpost, Gracie couldn't be moved aside with a backhoe. I open my mouth to tell her this when it occurs to me that she'll take the comment as a cruel reference to her having gained weight. The other thing that shuts me up is incredulity. Gracie's concession—that I am a successful writer—illustrates how little we have in the way of expectation around here. My slender book, published twenty years ago, and forgotten the year after, is the cause of Gracie's insecurity. The last thousand copies of the eight thousand print run were purchased by the campus bookstore at remainder price and have been sold there for full jacket price for the last fifteen years. Last I checked, there were still a couple hundred left. Who but Gracie would be jealous of such success?

"Anyway," she continues. "The grievance is only part of what I want to talk to you about. You may not believe me, but I've always liked you, Hank. You're like a character in a good book. Almost real, you know? Not like professors. I know I'm one of them. I wasn't always, but I am now."

Of all the odd things Gracie has ever said to me, this is surely the oddest and the most touching. No less absurd, of course, this professed admiration for the fact that I'm almost real.

"You should know," she says, her voice lowered now, "that Finny is sounding people out on the idea of a recall. I think he plans to introduce the motion at the next department meeting. The way things stand, I'm afraid I know the way I'd have to vote."

Gracie's wrong about herself, it occurs to me. She's more real than she knows. But she's right about what she's become.

"Do we understand each other?" Gracie wants to know. Her smile has a suggestion of the lewd about the edges.

"Better than we understand ourselves," I tell her, putting the false nose and glasses back on to illustrate my point. "By the way," I say. "I expect to file a grievance against you as well."

A flicker of fear, closely followed by surprise. The latter is probably because I am the only member of our department who's never filed or even threatened to file a grievance against a colleague.

"And I should warn you that a charge of sexual harassment is a serious matter," I tell her, deadpan.

"*Sexual* harassment?" Gracie knows better than to ask this question. I can tell she senses a trap, but she just can't help herself. In English departments the most serious competition is for the role of straight man.

"You weren't turned on yesterday?" I say, mock incredulous. "I mean, *I* was turned on."

When she's gone, I quickly remove my disguise and, like Clark Kent, hasten to the men's washroom down the hall, where I stand in front of the unforgiving mirror awaiting my water. While I'm standing there, three students come in, unzip, pee, zip, and leave without washing their hands, and I'm still right where I was, contemplating the things in life that youth takes for granted. I have all the classic symptoms of age, however—sleeplessness, creaking bones, inflexibility (physical and other). I know a great many older men who admit to silent, lonely vigils, sitting like old women on their commodes at three in the morning, waiting, waiting, falling asleep finally with their heads in their hands, only to be startled awake by the sound of their own tinkle. William Henry Devereaux, Sr., I suspect, is one, and though I am still some months shy of fifty, I am apparently to be another.

Like today's theoretical physicists, and like William of Occam, my six-centuries-dead spiritual guide, who sought to reconcile Faith with rational inquiry, I'm seeking a unifying theory. Twenty-four hours ago I stood in front of this same mirror filling rough brown paper towels with blood from my punctured nostril. Today, I'm back, dick in hand. Yesterday, my blood flowed more freely than my urine does today. What I'd like to know is whether this is funny or tragic.

I have my suspicions.

Here's the kind of twice a week racquetball game Tony Coniglia and I play. Tony, who's fifty-eight and built like a fire hydrant, stands in the center of the court and serves. It's what he does best. His thick, compact body generates considerable power, and on the serve he can blister the ball low and hard down either side of the court. His mechanics never vary, which means his opponent can't go into the point with any preconceived ideas. The rest of his game is similarly sneaky. He can pass, dink, and kill off the same motion, which means he can make you look silly, and there's nothing he likes more than making you look silly.

What Tony can't do is run. He's had heart trouble on and off for the last five years, and his doctor allows him only mild exercise. This is where the most beguiling feature of our contests comes in. Tony has decided that it's all right for him to play racquetball if he takes no more than one step in any direction from center court, which means it's my job to hit the ball back to him within this radius. Otherwise he deems the ball unplayable and takes the point. I'm allowed to kill the ball directly in front of him if I'm able, but I can't use angles. Since rac-quetball is a game of angles, my handicap is so huge that he has to give *me* points, usually six to eight a game, and even then I seldom win. When he gets too far ahead, he turns and glowers at me, his bushy eye-brows knitted, and tells me to bear down.

"Bear down," he says now with the score 14–7, his favor. "I'm awfully tough today. You're going to have to play harder."

Tony's most ironic statements are always delivered deadpan. Either that or he doesn't consider them ironic. Maybe he really thinks he's tough today. I suspect there are times when he forgets the handi-cap that allows him to compete in the first place. He loves to compete and to wager. He'd bet money on our games if I would go along. I might go along except that I never know who's won the point until he tells me. So we make other, nonracquetball wagers, though I never understand these either. Tony has a sister in Tampa, and therefore he follows the Tampa Bay Buccaneers football team, and every season he comes up with some crazy scheme that will allow him to bet on them. Last year he told me to pick any team I wanted, and he'd take the Bucs. For twenty dollars. Whichever team had the best record at the end of the season. "Okay," I said, "I'll take the Oakland Raiders."

"You can't have them," Tony explained. "It has to be a comparable team."

"Comparable to Tampa Bay?" I said, already confused.

"Any comparable team."

It turned out I could have any team without much talent. I could take the Jets or the Rams or the Seahawks, for instance. "I still don't understand. What are we betting on?"

"On which is the better team, of course," Tony explained, as if he suspected I was being intentionally dense.

"What if they don't play each other?"

"Overall record," he said. "Playing each other doesn't count."

"How can it not count if they play each other?" I objected, attempt-ing to apply Occam's Razor. "Wouldn't that game settle the issue right there?"

But he wouldn't hear of it. The more he thought about it, the more wrinkles he wanted to throw in. If the Bucs made the play-offs and my team didn't, I'd have to pay double (and vice versa, he added reluctantly).

"And you promise to tell me if I win?" I said when he was finished explaining.

"It's simple. Pay attention," he said, and then he explained the wager again, this time adding another wrinkle or two. So I picked the Chargers, who lost in the first round of the play-offs. Tampa Bay finished in the cellar. He paid up, too, though he was pretty pissed off that I wouldn't go double or nothing next season. Again I could take any team I wanted (except the Chargers were now on the list of teams I couldn't choose) and he'd take the Bucs. I took his money and put it in my pocket.

"Bear down," Tony advises now. "There's not much point to this if you aren't going to try."

In fact he's been running me all over the court, and I'm exhausted, frustrated, ready to concede. Also, I have to pee again.

"Game point," Tony reminds me, then serves. I return the ball hard, and it whistles off the front wall, the perfect passing shot I'm not allowed, well out of Tony's reach.

"Game," he says. "Mine."

I throw up my hands in defeat. "Thank God," I say. I've grown used to losing on my best shots.

"Let's go one more," Tony suggests.

"No," I tell him.

"One more," he says.

We play one more. If anything, my play improves, which means that I lose by an even greater margin. He terms this final defeat of mine a humiliation. Myself, I'm not sure how to feel about it.

Tony always knows how to feel. In the shower he sings *Rigoletto* full bore. He never cares who's in there with us. The operatic urge that accompanies victory is too strong to be denied, no matter who stares. Today, we're alone, so it's just me staring in my customary disbelief.

"I've been thinking a lot about women lately," Tony says, when we're toweling off. He enjoys the effect of omitted transition. "Of fornicating with them, actually."

I know there's no need to respond to Tony when he introduces subjects in this fashion, so I work on my lock, which is tricky and usually requires two or three correct applications of the combination.

"Do you realize that I'm far better at fornication now than I was at eighteen?"

I tell him I'm glad to hear it.

"It's true," he says, still deadpan. "I have a lot more stamina, more desire, more technique. I have a lot to offer women."

Indeed, Tony has something of a reputation in this regard. In addition to a few faculty wives, his conquests include not a few undergraduate students, though he never dates or beds them, he assures me, until after his final grades are in. Such professional scruples notwithstanding, Tony's indiscretions have cost him a final promotion to full professor, a penalty he accepts with great good grace.

"More than any other human activity," he says, stepping into his Jockey shorts, adjusting himself carefully in them, "the act of fornication defines us. That's a known fact. All the evidence suggests that I've got a lot of good years left."

On the fifth try my lock finally opens.

"Fornication is more spiritual than physical," Tony continues. "Most women know that, but not so many men. Which is why men like me are in demand. You laugh," he adds.

It's true. I am laughing, though not so much at Tony's genial boasting as at the fact that he doesn't consider it boasting. Having introduced this subject, he sees no reason why he shouldn't explore it fully, as if his interest were purely analytical, scientific. "You're the only man I know who claims to know what women want," I explain.

"There's nothing mysterious about what women want," Tony informs me. "They want everything. Just like us. What's interesting is what they'll settle for. What's interesting is that often they'll settle for me." He pauses to let me contemplate this mystery. "I don't know if they'd settle for you," he adds.

"Well—" I begin.

"The intensity of the orgasm isn't there anymore," Tony concedes, as if he's anticipated that I'm about to register this objection. "My first time was when I was thirteen, in Brooklyn. There was a woman who lived in our building. She invited me up one afternoon. I had this incredible orgasm standing in the middle of her living room before she could get out of her brassiere."

"I'm not sure that qualifies as fornication."

"That was my brother's position," Tony says. "When I told him about it, he set me straight. I even went back to the woman and apologized."

"Did she accept it?"

"Accept what?" Tony says. "If you're going to be careless with pronouns, we're going to have to talk about something else. Fornication requires precision."

"Not to mention patience," I add.

"Not to mention skill and stamina and affection," Tony continues. "Not to mention other things you're too young to understand. But in answer to your question, she did accept it, all of it, quite graciously."

When we finish dressing, we dry what's left of our hair under wall-mounted dryers. Tony's is black and steely gray, my own sandy and baby-fine. To look at the two of us, you'd never guess what we've been talking about.

"In fact," Tony says, slipping his comb into his back pocket, "I wouldn't object to a little fornication this evening after I've had my supper. Except that I've got a lot of other things I've been putting off. And our friend Jacob has asked me to chair the internal review of the English department."

Tony is watching me in the mirror, one eyebrow arched significantly. I do what I can to disappoint him, as Gracie disappointed me earlier by not reacting to my fake nose.

"I was asked if I thought I could be objective, since you and I are friends."

"And you said?"

"I said sure. I said I didn't consider you to be my friend. I said I've never been friends with you."

I can't help grinning at this. I can hear Tony delivering the line to Jacob Rose, who knows better.

"You should have refused," I tell him. "It's a thankless job."

"I would have," Tony says, "except that I've heard that the word has come down from above to fornicate you people."

"Why would anyone want to fornicate us?" I say, feeling more than a little silly about having slipped into Tony's metaphor. "We've pretty thoroughly fornicated ourselves, I should have thought."

We grab our gym bags and head outside, where it's still light out. The days are growing longer. Most of the students have adjourned to their dorm rooms and dining halls, but across the pond, in the VIP visitors' lot, there's a van that bears the logo of the local Railton television station. The dedication of the new Technical Careers Complex, I remember.

"It's all these grievances and litigation," Tony is saying. "The English department has fifteen grievances pending—against you, the dean, the campus executive officer. That's more than all other faculty grievances put together. What I hear is that since you people can't get along, they're going to fornicate the lot of you."

"I don't know," I tell Tony. "These grievances are the only sign of life we've had from some of these folks in years. Do we want them to return to their slumbers?"

Tony shrugs. "Consider the market. All us old farts could be replaced with young guys at half our salaries. There's a bull market in young scholars."

"We're tenured though," I remind him. "Where do you think we found the courage to fall asleep in the first place and then to wake up pissed off?"

"Enrollments are down," he says cryptically, and if it weren't Tony I'm talking to, I'd suspect he knows more than he's saying. Maybe he's stumbled across an old copy of the *Chronicle of Higher Education* in his dentist's office. On the other hand, Tony's a pretty shrewd observer of local campus politics, even though he doesn't participate in its machinations. I consider seriously for the first time that maybe something *is* brewing. This very day Jacob Rose has told me in almost the same breath that we aren't going to get the new department chair we've been promised and that he himself is interviewing for another job. These might well augur a sea change. Dickie Pope's hiring two years ago as our campus executive officer also occasioned a wave of paranoia. His strengths were in the areas of budget and fund-raising, not academics, so a rumor quickly began to circulate that he'd been hired to preside over budget cuts and executions, though so far he's done little more than absorb into his own budget academic positions freed up by retirements, a practice my colleagues in other institutions seem to regard as standard. As I'm considering these things, I'm conscious of something like a thrill, and I realize that my heart is racing faster than when Tony and I were playing racquetball. Also, I have neglected to pee after our match. I feel like I could arc my stream all the way into the campus pond, fifty yards away.

When we arrive at the water's edge, the ducks and geese are gathered along the bank, squawking loudly. A couple of guys from the TV station are tossing them popcorn. A camera with the station's logo has been mounted on a tripod.

A young woman I recognize from the eleven o'clock news is speaking into a microphone. Tony and I stop to watch, along with a handful of students getting out of late afternoon classes. "I'm standing on the future site of the new multimillion-dollar Technical Careers Complex here on the campus of Shit Bird State University . . ." The young woman repeats this same incomplete sentence four more times, switching the microphone from one hand to the other as she inspects the bottoms of her shoes for duck guano. It's not the words, apparently, that matter. Her sound guy is watching arrows dance on a meter. "Okay?" she says, impatient, tired of her practiced lead-in.

"I wonder if she would enjoy some fornication a little later in the evening," Tony speculates.

With anybody else I'd say, "Why don't you ask her?" But in fact I'm distracted by another drama. The goose I dubbed Finny earlier in the day is angry. The popcorn is gone, a fact he holds against the man who's been feeding it to him. He hisses first at the empty bag that the man has dropped to the ground and then at the hand that was holding it.

"I can't get a level with all this noise," the soundman complains.

When someone stamps a foot near the flock, several frightened mallards take crippled, awkward flight, but Finny holds his ground, hissing and honking with even greater vehemence.

"Somebody want to lose the duck?" the young woman reporter says to no one in particular.

"Goose," Tony tells her. "The little black ones are ducks."

"I hate coming here," the reporter says to her cameraman. Then to the boy who'd been feeding the ducks, "Jerry, go buy another bag of popcorn and lead the noisy bastards across the lake someplace."

"Pond," Tony tells her. "The big ones are lakes. The little ones are ponds."

The young woman raises the microphone to her·lips and speaks into it. "We're here on the campus of Podunk College speaking with an authority on every goddamn thing. And what *is* your name, sir?"

She holds the microphone out in our direction, and the camera swings around. I notice that the rolling light is on. Tony, to complete the jest, is hiding behind me, and when I turn around to locate him, Finny (the goose) is there. His long neck thrusts forward like a snake, nipping my pinkie, as if to say that he remembers me perfectly well from this morning. When I shove my hand into my jacket pocket to prevent a second attack, Finny follows suit, trying to get his bill into the pocket where my hand has disappeared and where he may imagine I'm stingily hoarding food. In truth, all that's in my pocket, except for my hand, is the fake nose and glasses I got from Mr. Purty. Finny latches onto these and yanks them out. A tug-of-war ensues, and it takes all my strength to wrest them away. Losing the prize he has no use for makes Finny frantically angry, and he begins to trumpet and hiss and flap his enormous wings with renewed vigor. "This is better than what we came here for," I hear the camera guy say.

But here's the crazy part. I'm suddenly angry too, and the thrill I felt a few moments before as Tony was hinting at the perhaps malicious designs of the university administration toward my department has not diminished one jot, and these three elements—my anger, the thrill I can't explain, a sudden tidal wave of righteousness—dovetail together sweetly, dangerously, and before I have a chance to consider the wisdom of doing so, I have grabbed the trumpeting Finny by his long, graceful neck and raised him aloft. He's much heavier than I imagined, as if he's full of sand. The rolling light is still on the camera, which I turn to face. I hear myself speaking with a remarkably steady voice. I have slipped on the fake nose and eyeglasses. First, I identify myself as a department chair at the college who wishes to remain anonymous, then I explain that I do not, even at this late spring date, have a budget for next year that will allow me to hire the adjunct staff

I need to cover freshman composition courses next fall. Despite the fact that the university has committed millions to a new building project, it can't seem to commit to the additional dozen or so comp sections we'll need, even though these will cost a paltry three grand per section. I state all of this very succinctly, aware as I am of television time constraints. I am eloquent and ironic concerning the values of our educational system. I am only vaguely aware that as I've been talking, the crowd has grown and that I'm being encouraged with applause. Also I see in my peripheral vision that a limo has pulled up in the parking lot.

"So here's the deal," I shout. I need to shout if I'm going to be heard over Finny's strangled trumpeting and the crowd's applause. "Starting Monday, I kill a duck a day until I get a budget. This is a nonnegotiable demand. I want the money on my desk in unmarked bills by Monday morning, or this guy will be soaking in orange sauce and full of cornbread stuffing by Monday night."

For emphasis, I give the now wild-eyed Finny a quick shake, so that he squawks even more horribly and renews his useless attempts at flight.

Among the men who have gotten out of the limo, I recognize Dickie Pope, the campus executive officer, and Jack Proctor, our state representative, on crutches still, who's here to take credit for the new building project. These are not men of great imagination, but one can hardly blame them for not being prepared for this particular contingency, the sight of a tweed-jacketed, tenured, middle-aged senior professor and department chair in a fake nose and glasses, brandishing a live, terrified goose.

The crowd and the camera crew are now cheering me wildly, not the least interested in the scheduled dedication, but I am not without sympathy for the guys in the suits.

CHAPTER

II

It's almost time for the eleven o'clock news, and I'm in a downtown Railton bar called The Tracks, a favorite watering hole of the local news media—the TV station and the newspaper, the *Railton Mirror.* It's an amazingly noisy place. In addition to several televisions and loud music, half a dozen model trains circumnavigate the bar, clacking and whistling along a shelf that's been specially constructed about eight feet off the floor.

I have an entourage. We've pulled together half a dozen tables so everyone can crowd around, and nobody's going easy. The booze is arriving in pitchers, two at a time, one beer, one margaritas. I can't make out who's ordering them, and nobody seems to be paying either. I'm drinking the margaritas, and so is Tony, whom I have talked into joining the party. I myself have been talked into joining the party by the newswoman, who claims I have made her day, her week, her year. Just when she thought she was going to die of boredom on "The People

Beat," a feature that locates colorful rural people with bizarre hobbies like carving soap figurines. "Travels in Six-Finger-Land," she calls it.

Her name is Missy Blaylock, which I remember as soon as she tells me. I've been almost watching her on the tube for a year. Her segment, usually the last on the eleven o'clock news, after even the weather and sports, represents a signal to Lily and me, should either of us still be awake, to turn off the bedroom television, the overhead light, and go to sleep. Now, in the dim light of The Tracks, I'm seeing Missy Blaylock anew. She's been to the station to deliver the tape and stopped off somewhere to change, having exacted a promise from Tony and me to wait for her. The idea is that we'll watch the news together on the bar's big-screen TV. "You've got tenure, I hope," she says.

In the four hours we've been here, I've accomplished a good deal besides getting drunk. I've made half a dozen phone calls and another half a dozen trips to the sour men's room. I've called all three of the women that four hours' worth of tequila guzzling have convinced me I'm in love with. First Lily, who, I tell myself, is really the only woman I'm in love with. She's told me that she's staying with her father, and I've called his number, once from home and again from the pay phone here at The Tracks. Since I spoke to him last, Angelo has gotten himself a message machine. Why is something I'd like to ask him if somebody would pick up. He never leaves the house and has no known friends or associates. All his police force pals are either dead or living in Florida. What use has a friendless man who never leaves the house for an answering machine? The message is pure Angelo though. "You got Angelo's place. I'm not saying I'm here. I'm not saying I'm not here. You got something to say to me? Now's the time." When I called from home I left a message for Lily to call me and let me know she got in safely, but then I left, so I don't know if she's called. There's a way, I'm sure, to get my messages off my own machine from here at The Tracks, but it involves a secret code number I forgot thirty seconds after inventing it.

"Pick up, Angelo, if you're there," I tell him this time, my second call. "It's Hank Devereaux." My voice sounds strange, though, and it occurs to me that Angelo might not believe me. Tequila lowers my voice and adds gravel. To Angelo, I may sound now more like the sort of man he wished his only daughter had married. I've always been fond of Angelo despite his not having much use for me. I don't take it personally. I try to remember he doesn't have much use for anyone who goes through life unarmed. When this same man arms himself with words Angelo doesn't understand, he likes him even less.

I should be glad nobody's home. By threatening on camera to kill a duck a day until I get my budget, I've become a hero to the members of my entourage, but I know my wife would not be among my admirers if she were here. Which raises the question of why I'm so anxious to tell her about it, why I'm so disappointed she won't be around to catch me on the local news. The other person I wish were around is Jacob Rose, who also would not be pleased to learn what I've gone and done. I recall that he not only left me in charge (a joke, granted) but instructed me to do nothing (another joke) in his absence. When it occurs to me that the two people I'd like most to tell about my misbehavior are by coincidence both out of town, I'm visited by a disturbing yet strangely exhilarating thought. That it may not be a coincidence. No sooner does this possibility occur to me, shooting its small, tender roots into the fertile soil of my long disused creative imagination, than I'm visited by a powerful image of the two of them, my friend and my wife, together in a hotel room in Philadelphia. The picture is at once more focused and believable than the vision I had yesterday of Lily and Teddy, perhaps because Jacob and Lily have always been such good friends. She counseled him through his disastrous affair with Gracie, through his divorce from Jane, through the disappointment of Gracie's sudden decision to marry Mike Law. For the last decade Jacob has been the loneliest man I know (with the possible exception of Mike Law), and such loneliness has been known to weaken scruples. Is it because I like my narratives to hang together that I'm encouraged by the plausibility of this scenario? But it takes two to tango, and the other dancer in the scenario is my wife, a woman I know.

My next call is to Meg Quigley, who answers on the first ring. "Call your father and get him to watch the local news," I suggest, telling her which channel. "You might watch it yourself, actually."

"Where are you?"

"Some dive," I tell her.

"It sounds like The Tracks," she says. "All those model trains."

"How does a nice Catholic girl like you know such places?" I ask her, though I remember quite well the dive I fetched her from last year, the afternoon she wanted me to undress her and put her to bed.

She ignores my question. "Why don't you call him yourself?"

"He behaves badly this time of night. He calls me names."

"You sound drunk."

"By the way," I tell her, "you ruined my blotter."

"Good," she says.

"I'm flattered, Meg, really," I tell her. "It's just that . . ."

But she's hung up.

Finally I call Rachel. I decide to make this one short. The phone I'm calling from is next to the men's room, the door of which keeps swinging open and shut, like desire, offering up the stale odor of over-matched urinal cakes. It's a boy's voice that answers. Confused, I try to remember Rachel's kid's name.

"Shouldn't you be in bed?" I say. It's ten-thirty, after all. Jory. Suddenly his name is there.

"Who the fuck is this?"

I've about made up my mind to mention this kid's mouth to his mother when it dawns on me that I must be talking to the boy's father. Has he moved back in? Have he and Rachel reconciled? I feel a deep, melodramatic loss at this possibility, similar to the loss of Meg Quigley. "Cal?" I say. "Hank Devereaux, Cal. I'm sorry to bother you. Department business," I add, like a guilty man.

Silence. Then a distant door opening, a room or two away. Then the boylike voice, muffled but clear enough to make out. "Hey. Telephone. Your fan club."

Another silence. Longer. Then Rachel's voice on the line, incredulous. "Hello?"

"Rachel," I say to this dodo's wife. "I'm a swine for calling so late. Tell Cal I'm sorry."

"No, it's okay? I was in the tub?"

I'm visited by a vivid mental picture of this, which is banished by the opening of the men's room door and a fresh blast of urinal cakes. "Listen," I say. "Take tomorrow off."

"Tomorrow?"

"Off," I say. "Right."

"Why?"

"I have this feeling it's going to be a bad day."

"I can't afford to?"

"I'll see you're paid," I assure her. "Watch the news at eleven." I tell her which channel.

"Okay?" she says, sounding genuinely frightened. In fact, I'm not sure I know anybody who's as frightened all the time as Rachel.

"Tell Cal I'm sorry I called so late."

"Okay?"

And then it comes over me. "You and he back together? None of my business, I know, but . . ."

"No?"

"Good. In fact, tell him to go screw himself. Tell him I don't like him even a little."

Now that I'm out of women to be in love with, I visit the men's room, where, standing before the long trough, limp dick in hand, my dribbling is hot and painful. Here I have the leisure to consider life's fundamental injustice. As the result of merely contemplating adultery, my father's most conspicuous sin, I'm being visited by my father's malady. For most of my adult life I've considered his periodic battles with kidney stones a kind of karmic justice. What more appropriate judgment on a man who can't keep his dick in his pants, his seed in his dick? But this logic, taken in conjunction with my own predicament, I now realize, can only lead me in a direction I don't wish to go. Am I to genuflect before that odd New Testament notion that to think a sin is to commit it? Am I no different from my father because I *think* to do what he did? A hateful and perverse philosophy, surely, and one that makes the world needlessly complex. Against such lunacy William of Occam became a reluctant heretic. No. Simplicity and justice require that thought and deed not be carelessly elided.

Still, thoughts are not nothing. I recall the way Rachel's voice did not fall when she said good night to me. Of course this may mean only that she doesn't know what to call me in front of her idiot husband. Or perhaps she doesn't know what to call me at this time of night, when neither of us is at the office. Or she just doesn't know what to call me, period, which means she doesn't know what to call our relationship.

And who can blame her? "Hank," I tell her, I tell Rachel, who again stands before me in the mirror above the urinal, fresh from her bath, wearing nothing but a towel, which is about to drop when another voice intrudes.

"No, *you're* Hank," says the man who's joined me at the trough. "I'm Dave. The sound guy, remember?"

And his urine explodes against the porcelain with a force that makes me weak in the knees with envy.

"What are you trying to do?" he wants to know. "Pass a stone?"

I may have saved Missy from the deadly boredom of "The People Beat," but it's Tony Coniglia who has her complete attention now. Having discovered that the bar serves raw clams, he's ordered several dozen, which arrive on crushed ice with cocktail sauce and lemon wedges. When Missy takes a clam, spears it with a cocktail fork, and dips it into the red cocktail sauce, Tony refuses to let her eat it that way. He is adamant, as if some article of his personal credo has been affronted. He wants to show Missy how it's done, and she looks interested to learn. Holding up a clamshell between thumb and index finger, he squeezes two measured drops of lemon from the wedge. Spurning the cocktail fork, he raises the clam as if it were a communion wafer and allows it to slide off the shell and onto his waiting tongue.

"Ooooh," Missy coos.

"The sea," Tony says, having chewed twice and swallowed.

"*All right!*" Missy exclaims, reaching for a clam.

Tony cannot allow this. "Don't rush," he tells her gravely, as if dangerous, unforeseen consequences may be lurking. He will do one for her. She watches him dress the clam and then, eyes closed, offers her tongue, which quivers in anticipation. Tony takes his time delivering the clam, and Missy shivers when it finally arrives, crossing her arms over her ample bosom, hugging herself. Already I have to pee again.

"The sea," Tony says, by way of benediction, when she swallows.

"Ooooh," Missy repeats. "That's good!"

I spoon about a tablespoon of cocktail sauce onto a clam and eat it.

"Pay no attention to that man," Tony warns her seriously. "He can be mildly amusing upon occasion, but in his deepest heart, he is unrefined. He is a cretin."

Missy looks me over to see if this can be so. I eat another clam, the same way, not wanting to confuse her. She's wearing too much makeup, it seems to me, though this may have to do with her work before the camera. Or maybe she has bad skin.

Tony fixes her another clam, feeds her so that she must hug herself again. "I love your friend," she confides to me in a stage whisper. Tony grins at me, one eyebrow arched, as if to suggest that he can't help having this effect on young, large-breasted professional women. "He reminds me of my father," she says.

"Is your father alive?" I ask.

She confesses that he died several years ago.

"Then I see the resemblance."

When a shout goes up, I see myself on the big-screen TV, holding Finny aloft by his slender neck. It's quick, then I'm gone again, and I realize this is a promo. First, there will be a commercial, then the story.

"Turn it up!" Missy bellows.

It takes a minute, but by the time the commercial is over, we have sound. For some reason I don't look right, standing there, and it's not the fact that I'm gripping a goose by the neck. Only when the camera pulls in close do I remember that I conducted this interview wearing the fake nose and glasses. I had imagined these to be a more obvious exaggeration of my features, but on television at least they aren't. The black plastic rims of the glasses don't look obviously toylike, and the flesh-colored plastic nose just looks big. In close-up, on a large-screen TV, you can see that it's a fake nose, but I wonder how many people at home watching regular TV's will conclude that this is the way I look.

To my surprise, the film editor at the station has cut very little of my unprepared text, and now, sitting here in The Tracks, I deeply wish that he had cut it all. I begin to suspect, for the first time, that the sight of a fiftyish English professor with a stranglehold on a startled, terrified goose may not be funny. When I hear myself repeat my threat to kill a duck a day until I get my budget, the camera zooms in on Finny, whose bulging eyes and flapping wings convey to the folks at home that this wacko means business. But the crowd at The Tracks is howling and applauding, and Missy makes me stand up and take a bow. She locates my spare nose and glasses and makes me put these on so everyone can see it's the same guy.

When Dickie Pope, the campus executive officer, and Jack Proctor, our local representative, come on, neither looks amused, but whatever they are saying is drowned out by a chorus of boos. They are only on for about ten seconds, before the producer cuts to the studio news team, dissolved in laughter before they go to another commercial, and another cheer goes up in the bar. I am a hero, it seems.

To celebrate, I make another trip to the men's room.

When I return, the clams are gone and Tony Coniglia, salt-and-pepper hair astir, is dancing with Missy to a hard-driving rock and roll song, the refrain of which goes, "Gimme gimme some lovin'." They appear to be shouting this at each other, though they can't hear above the pounding music. Tony, I can't help noticing, has more range on the dance floor than he does on the racquetball court. In fact, to look at him now, you'd never guess he requires a handicap to be competitive. You'd think he'd be giving *me* points.

I see that Teddy and June have joined the revelers at our table, which strikes me as unaccountable until I remember phoning and telling them to watch the news. I don't recall telling them where I was calling from, but I must have, because here they are. They receive me as a hail-fellow, slapping me on the back. "I always knew you had it in you," Teddy says, his expression a mix of fear and admiration. Like most academics, he is fascinated by childish, unprofessional conduct. It's been a long time since he's behaved outrageously, and he's half jealous and half glad it's me and not him. June too seems to be looking at me differently, as though she's suspected for some time that my reputation as a semi-outrageous and unpredictable character, at least by modest academic standards, was undeserved. "It was great," she admits. "The look on that duck's face was priceless."

Any new respect I may have gained in June's eyes, however, is lost when Tony Coniglia arrives from the dance floor with a pretty young woman. Tony and June go way back, and June doesn't bother to conceal her contempt. This fall, the student magazine she advises printed a strong, unsigned editorial accusing several professors, identified by department, not name, of being sexual predators. One biology professor, it claimed, had a history of treating his classes as "a pool of potential sexual partners."

"*Goose's* face," Tony corrects her good-humoredly. He never responded, publicly or privately, to the magazine article, and there's something in the tone of his voice now that suggests that he might have corrected every statement in the piece just as effortlessly. With a gallant flourish, he pulls out Missy Blaylock's chair for her, as if to suggest that his most egregious human flaw may be an excess of charm. Missy's upper lip is dewy from exertion, and there're the beginnings of dark circles beneath her arms.

"It was a goose," Tony continues. "Who but an English professor would threaten to kill a duck a day and hold up a goose as an example?"

"Duck, goose," Missy says. "Same idea."

Tony throws up his hands.

"Well, it is," Missy insists.

"How come nobody cares about facts anymore?" Tony wonders. "Whatever happened to accuracy? That used to be considered a virtue. Along with fair play."

Missy apparently concludes that Tony is making these observations to her, which is understandable, since he's making eyes at her as he speaks. "I don't know how to be fair to a goose," she confesses.

"By not calling it a duck," Tony explains, as if to a child.

Teddy must think it's a good idea to change the subject, because he says, "Too bad Lily's not here."

We all look at him.

"What?" he insists, mostly to me, since I'm chuckling.

"I don't get it," Missy Blaylock says.

"Teddy's got a crush on Hank's wife, Lily," Tony Coniglia explains happily. "He wishes she were here."

In the time it takes to say these few words, all the blood in Teddy's body locates in his face.

"Isn't *she* his wife?" Missy says, indicating June with her thumb.

Tony shrugs, admits this is true. "For some reason, he prefers Hank's."

Missy leans forward to examine June, but without Lily for comparison, she can't resolve the conundrum. She examines each one of us at the table. "Am I missing something?" she wants to know.

"Volumes," June says.

Missy ignores this, turning back to Tony. "I mean, it's really, like, weird that you'd just say that in front of her," she explains, again using her thumb as a pronoun reference.

"It's not true," Teddy tries to explain. "It's a joke. He just likes to cause trouble."

Missy's eyes first narrow as she considers this possibility, then widen with a recollection. "It's true!" she says. "*You*'re the one who started everything back at the lake!"

When Tony looks over at me, I warn him, "If you say pond, I'm going to club you over the head with this pitcher."

Seeing the margarita pitcher reminds Tony that his glass is empty. He fills it, then Missy's, then tops off the rest of our glasses. The margaritas run out just before they get to June, though Tony seems not to notice.

My threat to brain Tony Coniglia stirs a memory in Teddy, who says enthusiastically, "You should have been with Hank and me yesterday afternoon," unaware that June is switching glasses with him. Then he recounts, Teddy-style, how we were forced off the road by Paul Rourke's Camaro, how there was almost a fistfight right there on the shoulder of the road. I can tell that in the twenty-four hours since the event, Teddy has come to think of this melodramatic account as true. I can also tell he'd like me to back him up.

"Were *you* there?" I ask innocently, just to see the look on his face. I mean, he's known me for twenty years and knows better than to involve me in one of his stories. "Oh, right," I say. "I remember now."

"Thanks a lot," Teddy says, wounded, bleeding. And he's lost his margarita to boot, he notices. Now we need another pitcher, and if he acknowledges this need, he'll have to pay for it, something he'd rather not do. Only when June offers him a thin smile, draining the last of his drink, do I feel regret.

"Can we get some more of those clams?" Missy wants to know.

"Ah!" Tony says. "The sea." As if what he means by this phrase is something very different from what the words denote.

When Missy Blaylock gets up and heads for the women's room, Tony watches her full, round hips. "I'm not easy," he reminds us, "but I can be had."

"No," June says, unpleasantly. "You're easy."

"It's true," Tony sighs ruefully before catching a waitress and ordering more clams and another pitcher of margaritas.

CHAPTER

12

It's later than it should be, and I'm farther gone than I should be, and the moment when I might have exerted my free will, held up my hands, and shouted "No más!" to the cheering crowd is long past. I seem to recall trying to say "No más" at one point, only to discover that this turned the cheering crowd into a jeering crowd. And so, I've decided that it is the will of the people that I remain part of the festivities.

That was then. Now we're heading to Tony's house, and "we" are Tony and Missy Blaylock and William Henry Devereaux, Jr. We three are wedged into the front seat of Tony's Nissan Stanza. Tony and Missy would not hear of my reclining quietly in the backseat. No, I must be Porthos to their Athos and Aramis. We must be all for one in the front seat as the Stanza climbs dutifully up the dark, deserted streets toward Tony's house, which abuts the woods high in the Railton hills, beyond which the slope becomes too severe to clear and build on. Missy is stroking the inside of my thigh, but I attach no significance to this, because she's stroking the inside of Tony's more meaningfully, and cooing at him too, nibbling his earlobe. I suspect that Missy is wired in parallel, so that her right hand does whatever her left is doing. Apparently she can't rub the inside of Tony's thigh with her left hand without doing the same to mine with her right. The front seat of the Nissan, designed for two, not three, makes it difficult to keep affection discreet.

"Green," I announce, when the traffic light we've been stalled at changes.

"Envy," Missy coos. She and Tony have been playing a word association game, and Missy must have concluded that I want to play too.

"Green light," I explain.

"*The Great Gatsby*," Tony answers confidently. "That's an easy one."

I see no way out of this, except to point at the traffic signal above us, which turns yellow as Tony looks up.

"Moon," Missy says, locating the moon. "Green moon. The moon is made of green cheese."

I shake my head.

"Sounds like moon?" Missy wants to know.

The light turns red. Tony puts the Stanza in gear. We proceed through the red light.

"I give up," Missy says.

"Me too," I tell her.

"You can't give up," she objects. "It's your clue."

"Here we are," Tony says, pulling into his driveway.

"Jeez," Missy says. "Do I have to pee."

We all get out. Missy trips along the slate path and up the steps, stamping her feet impatiently until Tony locates the right key. There's only one bathroom in Tony's house, and since waiting is out of the question, I go around the corner and drip on his hydrangeas.

When I'm finished I follow them inside and find Tony in a small room off the kitchen toward the back of the house. I suspect he's gone there so he'll not have to listen to Missy tinkle in the preternatural quiet of the empty house. Against one wall is an expensive computer, monitor, laser printer, all set up on designer computer furniture. Tony purchased the whole rig from a remainder catalog at what he described enthusiastically as incredible savings. The problem is that the various components cannot be induced to work together, and all of the university's so-called computer experts have failed to bring his system on-line. Each has a different explanation of what's wrong, what's needed to fix the mess. When I see that Tony has wheeled his old Smith-Corona electric typewriter into the corner, a sad admission of defeat, I wonder if Russell, my son-in-law, might be able to help out.

"It's like visiting the room of a dead child," he admits so seriously that I am almost moved.

"You were fornicated," I agree.

We hear a distant flush, and Tony arches an eyebrow. "Do you ever wish you were single and good-looking?" he wants to know.

He's grinning at me in the dark, and I can't help grinning back.

"I'm on-line and ready to interface," he says proudly. "I bet it's been a long time since you've even booted up."

Since it's close enough to touch, I hit the ON switch of Tony's computer, which goes directly into high gear, whirring away with great urgency. What appears on the monitor is wonderful. Every symbol on the keyboard is represented, and they fill the screen from margin to margin, the entire nonsense text scrolling upward. Every line that disappears at the top is replaced by another at the bottom, all of it total gibberish. I'm grateful that William of Occam didn't live to see this.

"You call this interfacing?" I say.

He sighs. "It casts into serious doubt the old theory that an infinite number of monkeys at an infinite number of typewriters would eventually write the Great American Novel, doesn't it?"

We watch for a while until Tony turns the machine off, and in the silence we hear Missy, somewhere distant, squeal with delight. She has discovered, it turns out, the hot tub on Tony's back deck. At the kitchen window we watch Missy undress, which she does with remarkable drunken efficiency. When she's completely naked, she spies us at the window, two middle-aged men, and puts her hands on her ample hips and cocks her head as if to say, "Well?"

Tony waves at her. "Pay attention," he nudges me. "You're never too old to learn."

CHAPTER

13

When I say I'm going home, I'm persuaded to stay for one beer. This persuasion takes place at several levels. At the basest of these I'm persuaded because there's a pretty, naked young woman in the Jacuzzi, even if the effect of her beauty is marred somewhat by the fact that the rich steam rising off the surface of the hot tub is uncaking and separating her television makeup. Her face now resembles a low-budget horror movie mask, the idea of which is to suggest skin peeling away from bone. I'm also persuaded to stay where I am in the hot tub by the fact that since we've all climbed in it's begun to rain. Sleet, really. I hunker down. Below the water I'm feeling relief. The water temperature seems to have alleviated some of the pressure in my urinary tract.

Having agreed to keep them company for one beer only, I don't seem to be making much headway on that one beer. It takes me far too long to realize that the reason for this is that it's sleeting at about the same rate I'm drinking, so the glass is filling at the same rate I'm emptying it.

Twice since we've climbed into the tub, the phone has rung and Tony has left Missy and me alone in the burbling water. It's a pretty noisy hot tub, and that, together with the drumming of the freezing rain on the deck, has discouraged conversation. Tony has been equal to the challenge and regaled us with all kinds of stories and the sorts of unrelated arcane bits of knowledge that enchant his students, but when the phone rings a third time, he leaves behind a silence that Missy and I don't even attempt to fill. It's only the third call that causes me to be curious about who's calling Tony at two-thirty in the morning. I can see his head and thick shoulders through the kitchen window. He's turned his back to us, as if he suspects that Missy or I possess lip-reading capabilities. If it's Missy he's worried about, there's no need, for I note that she's snoring peacefully, her head back on the tile, her lips parted slightly, her chest rising and falling to the beat of her respiration. Sleet is actually dancing off her forehead.

Inside, Tony hangs up the phone, stares at it for a second, then takes the receiver off the wall-mounted hook. I wait for him to punch in a number, but instead he opens a kitchen cabinet and places the receiver inside. "Problem?" I inquire when he returns, since, under the circumstances, not asking would seem more unusual than asking.

He waves away my suggestion that there's a problem, though clearly there is something. Still, the sight of Missy Blaylock, naked and fast asleep in his hot tub, is enough to restore his good spirits. "What a picture," he says, surveying Missy, her breasts buoyant on the surface of the water.

Actually, it occurs to me that there are two pictures. The other is Tony, who is himself no more self-conscious than he'd be stepping out of the shower in the men's locker room. He appears to feel neither misgiving nor regret over his tenured paunch and dark, sagging genitals.

"Stay put," he says, prancing impishly back into the house. When he returns he's got a Polaroid camera. Missy, true to her profession, wakes up when she hears the shutter click. Tony takes several pictures, keeping the snapshots dry beneath a towel until they can develop. We huddle together in the tub then and wait for Missy to emerge from photographic darkness. She seems pleased with the result.

"Are these great boobs or what?" she says, handing me one of the Polaroids. "Jugs like these are just plain wasted in the Railton market."

When the rain lets up, I tell Tony and Missy that it's been great fun, but . . .

"It was just one . . . ," Tony sings.

"Of those things," Missy finishes, surprising me that she knows a song lyric of that vintage. Maybe she's older than she looks. In truth, I don't care how old she is, and I feel no regret about leaving her with Tony. I locate my clothes, putting the Polaroid that Missy has pressed upon me as a memento of the occasion in my pocket, and dress in the warm kitchen, feeling full of my own virtue.

It's only when I get outside that I remember my car is downtown, that for the second time in as many days I've been chauffeured some-where against my will. It's about a ten-block walk down the hill. When I've gone about halfway I realize that I'm full of something all right, but it's not virtue. There's a patch of woods on my left, so I duck into the shadow of these to pee. I drip at about the same rate as the branches above, a leisurely process that allows for contemplation. Now that I'm not rubbing haunches with Missy in Tony's hot tub, I can't help rumi-nating on her lament that breasts like hers are wasted in a small media market like Railton, a remark that struck me as funny when she said it but sad upon further reflection. It's Jacob Rose's and Gracie's and Rourke's and Teddy's and June's and perhaps my own position in a nutshell. We have believed, all of us, like Scuffy the Tugboat, that we were made for better things. If anyone had told us twenty years ago that we would spend our academic careers at West Central Pennsylva-nia University in Railton, we'd have laughed.

We aren't laughing now though, and the thought of growing old together is not pleasant, though there's nothing else for us to do. We might manage to be happy, even here, if the faces around us were new, but we have to look at each other every day, and this reminds us of our-selves and all the opportunities we found compelling reasons not to seize. Finny could have finished his dissertation and didn't. June, on the strength of a good, well-placed article, had a job offer at a decent university over a dozen years ago, but Teddy had just gotten tenure and the other university couldn't be talked into taking him as part of a package deal. Later, Teddy got an opportunity to move into adminis-tration, which would have been doing both himself and his students a favor, but June, perhaps out of revenge, talked him out of it. Even Gracie's poetry once showed promise.

We hadn't, any of us, intended to allow the pettiness of committee work, departmental politics, daily lesson plans, and the increasingly militant ignorance of our students let so many years slip by. And now in advancing middle age we've chosen, wisely perhaps, to be angry with each other rather than with ourselves. We've preferred not to face the distinct possibility that if we'd been made for better things, we'd have done those things. Tony is one of the few contented men I know, and at the present moment he's reaping the benefit of being so sensible. He is no doubt fondling the very breasts that Missy Blaylock believes are wasted in Railton. That she allows him to do so will deepen his conviction that he has a lot to offer women, and he's far too intelligent to waste time wondering whether, when Missy's eyes close and she begins to purr, it's his tequila-marinated affection or her dream of a more upscale market that's causing her nipples to harden.

But these are the thoughts of a dripping man in the dark, dripping woods, and when I finish thinking them I punctuate the process with a good, confident zip of my fly. When I emerge from the shadows, I come face to face with a young woman who's laboring on foot up the steep, slick sidewalk. She appears to be in her middle twenties, maybe younger. She has a full, pretty face, which seems almost to apologize for the fact that beneath her heavy, quilted winter coat she's huge. Unaccountably, she's wearing only rubber flip-flops on her bare feet. Her expression is so open, so unguarded that it reminds me of a begging dog that fully expects to get booted but can't help licking you anyway.

"I know you," this girl says, though she's not quite looking at me, or at least not at my eyes. "What's your name?"

She doesn't know me, I'm certain, nor do I know her. The only thing I know for sure is that I'm not going to tell her my name. I've come out of the woods at three o'clock in the morning, and this girl is no more frightened of me than a wet kitten, and that, oddly enough, makes me frightened of her.

"What's your name?" she says again. She pronounces the word *name* so that it rhymes with *mime*. And then she repeats the question twice more, barely allowing her voice to drop before beginning again.

She's moving toward me now, as if she'd like to reach out and touch my face, and I take an instinctive step backward. "Are you all right?" I ask her, not sure what I mean by the question.

It's the sound of my voice, not my question, I think, that stops her. "You're not him," she exclaims, her voice full of calm wonder. "You're not him at all." *All,* pronounced *owl.*

"No," I agree. "I'm not."

"You're not him at all," she repeats, and turns away.

"Are you okay?" I ask again, rather stupidly, but she has resumed her course up the hill. When her flips-flops skid on a slick patch of smooth concrete, she says, "Oooooh. Slip . . . er . . . eee."

My father, William Henry Devereaux, Sr., whose return to the bosom of his family my mother enigmatically claims I am unprepared for, was always a frighteningly reasonable man, and like most reasonable men, he preferred day to night. Unless he's changed, he's still an early riser, usually up, bathed, and dressed by six-thirty. As a boy, I'd frequently find him in his study reading, idly sipping tea in his wing-back reading chair. No matter how early I got up, no matter how late he and my mother had been out the night before, there he'd be. According to my mother, he possessed an uncanny internal chronometer that allowed him to wake and turn off the alarm clock mere moments before it would have gone off.

Anyway, here's my theory. All men are assailed by doubts. Even those like my father who don't seem to be. And we are all, I think, more receptive to doubts and fears (and perhaps even guilt) in the dark than we are in the light of day. I don't think my father cared for these sensations. When I was a boy, of course, I had no way of knowing that the man I found clean shaven and cologned in the book-lined den of the big, old house my parents rented a few blocks from the university might be subject to doubt or fear or guilt. A child's life is full of these, and I may even have concluded that adulthood represented triumph over them. There were probably mornings when I found him there in his reading chair, sweet-smelling and intent upon the printed page, that he was fresh from some illicit encounter with a young female graduate student mere hours before. Apparently he'd had a number of relationships with young women before he settled on the one in his D. H. Lawrence seminar that he preferred to my mother. I'm sure I took his early rising as a sign of virtue, and probably even understood my mother's remaining in bed, her eyes defiantly clenched against the new day, as a character defect, especially given the mood she was in when she finally came downstairs around midmorning and peered in at my father and me with an expression that verged upon menace.

It was my habit on Saturday and Sunday mornings to stretch out on the floor at my father's feet and pore over the encyclopedia. I knew not to interrupt my father's reading, risk one of his monumental scowls, so by the time my mother appeared, I was usually starved. "When's break-fast?" was always my first question to my bathrobed mother, whose already threatening expression always darkened dangerously. I suspect it was those weekend mornings that first led my mother to conclude that I was my father's son, a conviction she still adheres to. My "when's breakfast?" by way of hello must have unhinged her, knowing as she did that I'd just spent two or three hours quietly in my father's company without asking for so much as a glass of water. Who could blame her for not sharing my father's deep appreciation of the new day?

Lily is also a morning person, and I often overheard her tell our daughters, when they were growing up and full of adolescent self-doubt, that things would look different in the morning, and of course this is wise counsel. Not only do things look different in the morning, they look better, which is not, of course, the same as to say that they *are* better. Still, if things look more manageable in the sunlight, we are wise, like my father, to greet the new day early, and I suspect now that there were very few moonlit indiscretions he was not able to banish from his thoughts at six in the morning with the aid of a virtuous book of literary criticism and his own sweet child stretched out at his feet, soaking up Britannica by osmosis.

I am neither a morning person nor, I maintain, my father's son. After a night of misbehavior I cannot tell when my alarm clock is about to go off. I often don't immediately recognize the sound of the alarm even *after* it's gone off. Neither tea nor literary criticism banishes guilty memory in William Henry Devereaux, Jr., who has dreamed, powerfully and variously, all this night long. Only when the ringing continues after I switch off the alarm do I realize it's the telephone I'm hearing. By the time I pick up, the line's dead.

It occurs to me that Lily has been trying to call. She probably tried to reach me last night until it got too late, and now she's begun again. Missing me now may even have convinced her that I didn't come home at all last night, that her prediction has already come true. I'm either in the hospital or in jail.

I wish she'd call back now, because I'd like to share with her the last of my dreams, in which the new College of Technical Careers building has turned out to be yet another replica of my own house, like Julie's, this one on a Brobdingnagian scale. It's the size of the Modern Languages Building, which houses the English department, but it's my house, Lily's and mine, monstrously swollen. Same number of rooms, same floor plan, except built for giants. Inside it, I am a little dollhouse person. To go upstairs I have to stand on a chair, hoist myself up the step, pull the chair up behind me with a rope, then repeat the process. The reason I'm mountain-climbing my way upstairs is that Lily has been calling down to me. She wants to explain to me why she thinks I'm so unhappy. Odder still, I can't wait to hear her explanation, because in the dream I *am* unhappy. In fact, I'm weeping pitifully as I leap, latch on to, and chin my way up the stairs. Of course, you should have seen those stairs. They were enough to make anyone weep. But now, sitting up in bed, safe in my own human-scale house, the clear light of the guiltless new day streaming in the window, I wish I had not conceded my unhappiness to Lily, even in a dream.

Occam is whining pitifully at the bedroom door, as if he too has been troubled by dreams, so I invite him in, something I would never do were my wife in residence. He takes in which side of the bed I'm on, comes around to this side, rests his chin on the bed, and sighs meaning-fully, as if to suggest what I already know, that this does not promise to be a good day. To delay imagining its details, I turn on the television by remote to a morning news-talk show and scratch Occam's ears idly, hoping that Lily will call again. Perhaps because I've got the sound muted, I don't immediately comprehend when I see myself brandishing wild-eyed Finny. Adding sound only deepens my confusion. Occam, as a rule not one to be distracted during an ear scratch, perks up at the sound of his master's voice, looks at the television, then at me. When I don't have an explanation, he trots over to the television and sniffs it. The big shock comes, at least to me, when the short segment (I've been edited more severely this time) concludes and I realize that this isn't the local news that occurs when the network cuts away. No, it's the regular *Good Morning America* crew that's laughing, almost out of control, before heading into the weather.

The telephone is ringing again when I step out of the shower. I'm no longer anxious to pick it up, but I do.

"It's June," Teddy's wife informs me.

"Hi, June."

"How can you associate with that man?" she wants to know.

"What man?" I say, though I know she's referring to Tony Coniglia.

"He's a debauched old rummy," she continues, still fuming about last night. "That thing with the clams was sickening. I bet that reporter with the tits is having second and third thoughts."

"I wouldn't know, June. I don't even know why you've called me."

"Rachel asked me to," she admits. "I'm in your office, actually. All the lines in the outer office are tied up. Rachel must have a crush on you, the grief she's taking on your behalf."

"Who from?" I wonder out loud while pausing to consider the pleasant possibility that a woman I'm half in love with might be half in love with me.

"It's a long list. She's even caught hell from the CEO for refusing to give him your home phone."

"Tell her to go ahead and give it to him. I'm about to leave here anyway."

"She says to remind you about your meeting with Dickie this after-noon. And I'd be prepared for a world of shit when you get here."

"Tell Rachel I have to visit the high school, but I'll be in after that. In fact, tell her I said to take the rest of the day off."

"Seriously?"

"Absolutely," I say. I don't want Rachel taking abuse on my account. "Tell her to go home. Tell her I'm putting her in for a raise."

"I'll tell her, but Vegas odds are four to five you won't last the day."

"Then you all get raises."

Downstairs, I notice what failed to attract my attention last night, that the message light on the answering machine is blinking. Thanks, I suspect, to my television appearance last night, there are twenty-five messages, a new record. That's the bad news. The good news is that twenty of them are hang-ups. There's also one from Billy Quigley, who's apparently gotten impatient and started talking before the sound of the beep. As a result, his message is one slurred word, "Peckerwood." My wife's voice is the only one I care to hear, and it comes late, number 17, in the scheme of things, though I've no idea what time that would make it, whether I was standing in front of the urinal at The Tracks, or on the pay phone flirting with Meg Quigley, or eating raw clams, or sitting in Tony's hot tub with a naked young woman when she called.

There's a flatness to Lily's voice on the tape that suggests she's intuited all of my misbehavior. Her message is brief, leaving the number and name of the hotel she's checked into, which explains why she wasn't at her father's last night when I tried to reach her there. I try to remember why I thought she'd be staying with her father. Was it something she told me? Something I concluded on my own? The former, I'm pretty sure, but my brain is still marinating in tequila, and it hurts to access my memory function. "Don't forget you're visiting my class," Lily reminds me, last thing before saying good night, as if she's anticipated, somehow, the state I'll be in this morning.

I call the number she's left, but when the switchboard puts me through to her room, she doesn't answer. Either she's already left or she's in the shower. Consulting my watch, I try to access the part of the brain that handles analytical functions, but it doesn't seem to be on-line either. When the hotel operator comes back on, I'm visited by an oddly encouraging thought. Maybe the flatness, the regret I've detected in my wife's voice is the result of misbehavior not on my part but rather on hers. I ask the operator to connect me to Jacob Rose's room, which suggests something about the way the human brain prioritizes duties. I've been denied access to memory and analysis, but whatever department handles jealousy and suspicion (intuition?) is offering its services without being asked. After a long moment the operator tells me there's no Jacob Rose registered in the hotel, but there's something in her voice. "There's a Jack Rosen," she offers.

"That's what I said. Jack Rosen," I explain, and a moment later Jack Rosen's room is ringing, and the phone is picked up before I can figure the odds that Jacob would use this alias. A man answers. He sounds a little like Jacob Rose. Or a little Jewish, anyway, which is not surprising, given his name, whether or not he's Jacob Rose. "Jacob," I say. "Thank God I tracked you down."

After a beat, "Who is this?"

"Hank," I tell whoever I'm talking to. "Who do you think? Put Lily on."

"Lily who?"

All right, so it's not Jacob Rose, I conclude, hanging up, half disappointed, half puzzled. I don't think I would have been pleased to discover evidence of my wife's unfaithfulness, but there would have been something exciting about having made a chilling intuitive leap and had it turn out to be correct. It would have spoken far better of the leaper than to have made the same leap and been wrong, which is what I've been.

Motor functions I have, so I drive into town and stop at my favorite lunch counter for breakfast and the morning newspaper. My appearance on the eleven o'clock news was apparently too late to make the morning edition, but I note that there is a short, one-column article on page seven, below the fold, about the suicide of William Cherry, who lay down on the railroad tracks two weeks ago. Neither his wife nor his children apparently observed any symptoms of discouragement or despair, though they acknowledged that he had grown more remote of late. Other than this he seemed upbeat and full of plans for his retirement.

The best thing for tequila poisoning is pancakes, so I eat a plate of these, smothered in syrup, then adjourn to the men's, where I find a private stall with a door that latches, and deposit in the toilet the pancakes, last night's raw clams, the tequila, and my deep conviction that when William Cherry's severed head was borne up the tracks by a train in the direction of Bellemonde, no one, not even his loved ones, suspected what was in it.

Outside, the morning sky is a brilliant blue, and, taking a deep breath, I feel something of my father's optimism. There's no denying the beauty of this brisk spring day in Pennsylvania, no denying that I now feel much, much better.

I arrive at the high school just as the bell between periods rings. I duck into a doorway to avoid being trampled by hordes of young Goths and Visigoths and Vandals, who are running, shoving, slamming into lockers, hurling vicious profanities at each other in the most casual manner, insults which seem not to register. When I was in school such language would have resulted in fistfights and a trip to the principal's office.

I spy Harold Brownlow, one of Lily's colleagues, down the hall. Harold seems to have prevented a mugging, and he's got a huge black boy pinned up against a bulletin board by means of nothing more lethal than Harold's own gnarled index finger. "Give the boy back his lunch money, Guido," Harold warns the big kid solemnly. Guido hangs his head and hands a small white kid a couple bills.

"I didn't mean to take his lunch money, Mr. Brownlow," Guido says. "It was an accident."

"I understand, Guido," Harold says, as the white kid scampers off. "But I don't want any more accidents, understand?"

"Okay, Mr. Brownlow," Guido says, and he lumbers off, looking oddly innocent, as if he himself believes in the concept of accidental extortion.

When Harold sees me, he grins and comes over.

"Guido?" I say, watching the big black kid until he disappears through the double doors.

"Go figure," Harold says, extending a hand. "I think I speak for the entire staff here at the penitentiary when I say how damn proud of you we all are. Who says there's nothing good on television?"

"Too much violence though," I admit.

"I thought it was tasteful, but then that's me," Harold says. "You heard from Lily?"

"She called last night, but I was out."

"Tell her not to do anything rash," Harold advises. "My sources inform me there's been some movement on the school board. People really do want her to stay."

"I'll tell her."

"Of course, if she wanted to start something new, I'd understand," Harold admits sadly. "Time's winged chariot and all that. When I was her age, I got it into my head somehow I was going to die. I played golf every day all summer, convinced every round would be my last. Cost a fortune."

"And here you are."

He nods. "Cured my slice, though. You should come out with Marjory and me sometime." His wife, by coincidence, is Jacob Rose's secretary.

"Maybe this summer."

"All in your head, golf," Harold muses. "A thousand and one contingencies."

"I'm looking for a game with just one contingency," I tell him. "Two at the most."

"Mind if I ask you kind of a personal question?"

"Go head, Harold," I say, though I wish to hell he wouldn't. Still, nothing is more personal to Harold than golf, and having shared with me his most intimate thoughts on this subject, he may feel I owe him something.

"Is that vomit on your collar?" he wants to know.

He shows me where, but it's beneath my chin, and I can't see it.

"Stop at the men's," he suggests. "I don't do so hot when Marge is gone either," he adds, in an attempt to comfort me, surely. Throwing up on yourself is the kind of thing that can happen to married men our age when our wives are gone, is his logic.

In the men's room I address the business of my soiled collar with paper towels and tap water. I also try to think of something to say to Lily's "rocks." About the only people to visit the low-track kids, she says, are reformed drug abusers and promoters of safe sex. Kids like these are told what to avoid, not what to aspire to. And she warned me to be prepared for straightforward, unsophisticated questions. Give them honest answers, she advised, though she may not have anticipated that they'll be asking me about the spot on my collar.

Her rocks are rumbling nervously when I enter the classroom. I see Lily has found a couple copies of *Off the Road,* which are making the rounds without sparking much interest, though one tough-looking young girl in the front row squints at me suspiciously, turns the book over, and studies the author photo, then me again. What the hell happened to you? is what she'd like to ask, I can tell.

"Hey," says a skinny black kid, "you the dude from TV."

At this they look me over with renewed interest. "The duck guy," somebody says.

"We done that shit, you know what'd happen to us?" somebody else wants to know.

And they're off. I can see why Lily likes these kids. In two seconds flat they've got their own conversation going. Everybody's talking but me. I'm the Rosetta stone they're trying to translate, and they don't want any help just yet. After a while though they remember their manners. Lily probably reminded them, last thing, that I'm their guest, that they're supposed to behave, that they're not to hurt me.

"So," says Guido, the accidental extortionist, from the back row. "How much money you *make* on this book?"

When I pass Orshee's office on the way to my own, his door is open, and he invites me in. His office, one of the worst on the English department floor, overlooks the parking lot, and no doubt he has seen me coming. He's dressed in jeans, sneakers, a T-shirt, and a thrift shop sport coat, sort of academic grunge. The look isn't all that different from the one sported by people like Jacob Rose and William Henry Devereaux, Jr., back when we were ourselves young campus radicals. The resemblance, I'm always relieved to note, ends there. There are very few books in my young colleague's office, but he's rigged up a small TV with a built-in VCR. His bookshelves are stacked with videotapes, each one full of recorded, decade-old sitcoms, which he plays throughout the day, even when he's consulting with students. His research on these same shows he publishes, for environmental reasons, in electronic magazines, thereby sparing himself the criticism that his essays are not worth the paper they're printed on. At the moment he's researching an episode of a sitcom that, if I remember correctly, was called *Diff'rent Strokes*. I angle the chair I've been offered so that my back is to the screen.

"This was a seminal show," Orshee informs me, with what appears to be genuine excitement.

"A seminal sitcom?" I say. "High praise."

If he knows I'm tweaking him, he doesn't rise to the bait.

"Conservative white America's great race fantasy. Young black males, nonthreatening and loving. Old white guys who care about the black community. It's great stuff."

As I listen to him, it occurs to me that Orshee was probably the kid who got his lunch money extorted in high school by some demographic relative of Guido's. Here at the college he's safe at last. Nobody's even allowed to make fun of his ponytail.

"I'm thinking about doing a special topics course next year, maybe compare a couple of episodes of *Diff'rent Strokes* with *Huckleberry Finn*. You know, like, the great American racist novel? Show how white attitudes haven't changed, how the basic fantasy's still intact today? June thinks it's a good idea."

Something about the sound of June Barnes's name in Orshee's mouth reminds me of the rumor I keep hearing about my young colleague and Teddy's wife.

"I thought you didn't want them reading books," I say. "Writing being a phallocentric activity and all that."

He locates a remote among his papers and presses pause, freeze-framing the cherublike face of the little black kid who starred in the show. "I'm not against books. You can get in a rut with them though."

"I know. I've been in that rut since I was thirteen."

He blinks. "You didn't learn to read till you were thirteen?"

"I didn't love to read until about then. It's the love that makes the rut."

"Right," he nods seriously. "Hey, what's it like living out in Allegheny Wells?"

"There's cable," I assure him. "Some people have satellite dishes."

"Paul's got one," he says. "Professor Rourke?" he adds, so I'll know who he's talking about.

I decide there must be no significance to his having mentioned June a moment ago. He's just dropping names. He's up for tenure next year and wants me to understand, in case I'm still chair, how well he's fitting in. He's on a first-name basis with all factions. I nod to show I'm with him. "Big guy. Surly."

Orshee ignores this. "I like his house, except I think it may be sliding down the hill."

I suppress a grin.

"June thinks so too."

The article they've been working on all year, I recall, is on clitoral imagery in Emily Dickinson. The way Teddy explained it to me, June, being herself in possession of a clitoris and therefore more sensitive to its encoded appearances in the Dickinson poems, was going to draft the article, which she and Orshee would then revise, making use of his up-to-date critical theory vocabulary. "It's weird," Teddy confessed to me one day back in the fall semester when June's notes were strewn all over the house. "Back when I was fifteen, I was obsessed with pussy. Now I'm fifty and *my wife's* the one obsessed with it."

"We've looked at a couple houses out there, but I don't know," Orshee says. I must look puzzled, because he quickly clarifies his meaning. "Sally and I."

"Right," I say. Sally is the seldom seen young woman who accompanied him to Railton four years ago who has reportedly been "finishing her dissertation."

"I mean, it's really nice out there, and I wouldn't mind being among the trees. But we'd, like, have to give up our dream of living in an integrated neighborhood."

"Right," I say, indicating the television screen over my shoulder with my thumb.

"We shouldn't even be looking at places until I find out about my tenure next year," he concedes. "Except it's a buyer's market right now. According to our realtor, now's the time. Next year, who knows?"

"Tomorrow, who knows?" I agree.

"That's the other thing," he says, studying me carefully now. "All this talk about layoffs this year. If it's last hired, first fired . . ."

"April is the cruelest month, rumor-wise," I remind him.

"Well, if you hear anything, I hope you'll let me know, because we really are considering taking the plunge. June thinks Allegheny Wells is a good investment."

"Sally, you mean."

"No, June. She's been trying to get Teddy to buy out there."

Actually, she's been trying to get Teddy to do this for over a decade, but Teddy can't bring himself to spend that kind of money.

"I just hate to see you give up your dream," I tell Orshee.

He looks blank.

"Of living in an integrated neighborhood," I remind him.

"Oh, right," he says. "Well, we're looking at other places, too."

"And there's always the chance that it will *become* integrated," I remind him, getting up from my chair. "I understand Coach Green is looking to build out there."

"And it's not like we'll be here in Railton forever," he adds.

At this I can't help smiling. "That's what we all thought, kid."

Paul Rourke is collecting his mail in the English department office when I enter. He studies me over the rim of his reading glasses, and it occurs to me to wonder how long he's had these. Also I note that there's more gray in his hair and flesh in his cheeks than the last time I observed him carefully, which was maybe a decade ago. He has a dissipated look about him now, and I can't help wondering if he's become, like Billy Quigley, a solitary drinker. He looks like he could be taken in a fight. Not by me, but by somebody. Not anybody in Humanities, probably. Maybe someone over in P.E.

"Morning, Reverend," I say. "Another beautiful day, praise God."

"Hello, dipwad," he says, returning his attention to his mail, most of which he's tossing directly into the wastebasket at his feet, unopened. "I caught your act last night," he continues without looking up from his task. "It needs work."

Rourke's position regarding me never varies. Despite the fact that I try to make everything into a joke, I'm never funny. Rachel stops typing at her word processor and watches us fearfully. To show her that everything is fine, that an outbreak of hostilities is unlikely between us two old former combatants, I give her a wink. She remembers, as everyone does, that Rourke once threw me up against a wall at the department Christmas party, and she hates to see the two of us in the same room. Maybe, if she's half in love with me, she doesn't want to see me injured.

"Look up *dipwad* for me," I tell her, spelling it. "I think I've been insulted, but I'm not sure."

To my surprise, Rachel clicks onto her dictionary program and actually consults it, out of curiosity, it must be, since she seldom follows my orders. If she did follow my orders, she wouldn't even be here today.

"I hear we may have a new neighbor," I tell Rourke.

He's finished going through his mail now, and there's only one piece he's deemed worth opening. He reads the first paragraph of a document that's at least three pages long, then drops the whole thing into the wastebasket. There must be things about me and my behavior that strike Paul Rourke as being as admirable as the way he's just dispatched his mail strikes me. If so, he keeps his admiration to himself.

"Our obsequious junior colleague? Has he told you about his dream of living in an integrated neighborhood?"

"Just now," I admit. "He thought he might have to give it up."

"What did you advise, being privy to all our academic futures?"

I decide not to ask what he means by this. "I advised him to buy on the good side of the road."

"Does that mean he's not on your list? Or do you want to see him not just fired but totally fucked?"

"List?" I say.

"You want the truth?" he says. "I half-hope you put my name on it."

I'm about to say "what list?" again when Rachel double-clicks out of her dictionary. "It's not in here?" she informs us. "Dipwad?"

Rourke looks at me first, then Rachel. "Of course it isn't," he tells her. "It's out *here*."

Not a bad exit line, I have to admit. "Hey," I say to Rachel when he's gone. "You're *my* secretary, remember? I'm the one you feed the straight lines to."

"Sorry?"

"How should I know if you're sorry?"

This confuses her. I can tell. "Let your voice fall," I remind her on the way into my office. Meg has apparently paid me another visit, because in the middle of my ruined blotter sits a single ripe peach. I study this for a moment, then a note in Rachel's hand that my friend Bodie Pie in Women's Studies has been trying to reach me. I hit the intercom and ask Rachel to join me.

"I'm sorry about last night," I tell her when she closes the door behind her. "I mean, if you and Cal are getting back together, that's great." When she doesn't say something quick enough, I chatter on. "I never should have called the house so late, and I certainly never should have said I didn't like him. That was way out of line."

Rachel is studying her hands as I say all this. I wonder if she's as fond of them as I am. They are not the hands of a young woman. They've endured dishwater and paper cuts and burns on the oven door, but they are fine and graceful, and I would like to take them in my own.

"We're not?" she says, and now I'm the one confused. "Getting back together?"

How absurd that I should feel a powerful wave of relief. I try to tell myself it's nothing but decent affection I feel for her, but the truth is, it doesn't feel entirely decent. She's too lovely a woman for this to be decent affection, though it's probably not exactly indecent either. Is there a state more or less halfway between decency and indecency? Is there a name for such a realm? The Kingdom of Cowardice? The Fiefdom of Altruism? The Grove of Academe?

In the real world Rachel is talking to me. "Sometimes when he's drinking, he remembers he's got a son? Also he likes to drop by at night, to make sure I'm not seeing anyone?"

"I didn't mean to intrude . . . ," I say, a lie.

"He ends up falling asleep?" she explains, adding, "on the couch?" But her eyes are full.

"You want to take the rest of the day off?" I suggest. "I mean it. I've seen days like this before. They don't improve."

She shrugs, wipes the corner of one eye on a sleeve. "He might still be there?"

"Then stay here," I say, trying for a grin. "Okay, I'm off to the Vatican." Since Dickie Pope became CEO four years ago, that's what the old Administration Building has come to be called. I see by my watch that there's just about time to make the walk across campus to Administration Row.

"Don't let them fire you?"

"Never," I assure her. "I'd quit first. See what you can do about getting me a new blotter," I say, slipping the new peach into my jacket pocket. I've been to Administration Row many times and often regretted not having something to throw. I hand Rachel the old, soiled blotter with considerable embarrassment. It looks more like a sexual act has taken place upon it than an oblique invitation extended. "You need to find a new place to hide your master key."

"They all get mad at me when they can't find it?"

"I know. It's just that I'm the only one who's supposed to know where it is, and I'm the only one who doesn't."

"I've told you? You keep forgetting?"

"Rachel," I tell her. "You're right. The problem is me. If Lily calls . . . ," I begin, but then I can't think of what message to leave. What I would say to my wife depends upon a number of variables. Like whether she's seen me on *Good Morning America*. Like whether I am the cause of the flatness I heard in her voice this morning on the answering machine.

"You love her more than life itself?" Rachel suggests.

"Okay," I concede. "Why not? Coming from you she just might buy it."

I notice that Billy Quigley's door is open and try to sneak by, but he catches me, insists that I come inside and close the door behind me.

"I'm in kind of a hurry," I explain, taking a reluctant seat. Billy's office is an all-Irish motif. On the walls, pictures of Yeats, Joyce, O'Casey. And a bottle of good Irish whiskey in the lower drawer of his desk. He wants to pour me one, but I beg him not to. Sometimes I'll share a short one with Billy, but not in the morning. Not after a night like last night. "I'm on my way to my own execution."

"Be late then," he says. "What can they do? Kill you twice?"

"Yes," I say. "That's the beauty of academic life. You get to die over and over."

Billy downs a short shot of Irish whiskey. "I want to talk to you about Meg," he says.

I study him. Billy looks completely sober, for him an unnatural state. I shove my hands in my jacket pockets, find in one of them a tender peach, quickly remove them again. The spasm of guilt I feel suggests that my father was right. You may as well eat the peach if you're going to feel guilty anyway. According to the signals my cross-wired conscience is sending me, by flirting with Billy's beloved daughter, I've betrayed him and my wife and my secretary.

"I want you to do me a favor," he says. He's got me fixed with a liquid, bloodshot eye, and I can't look away. "Tell her you can't rehire her for the fall."

"That's a hell of a favor, Billy," I tell him.

"Hank," he says, his voice low now, embarrassed. "I always try to do what I can for my kids. The rest of them . . . I wouldn't say this to anybody but you . . . the rest of them take the money and run. They're not bad kids. It's not that. But Meg, she's the one that's got the best shot. I talked to a guy I know at Marquette, and he can get her an assistantship next fall."

"And how much will the assistantship cover?"

"A big part."

"And you'll pay for the other big part?"

"I gotta get her away from here."

"They've got bars in Milwaukee, too," I point out, since I know Billy's concerned that Meg spends too much time in Railton dives.

But I don't think he even hears me. "If I can just get her out of this town."

When his voice falls, I let silence fall with it. But in the end, he's more comfortable with the silence than I am. "Look," I say, "why not cross the bridge when we come to it? You know I don't have a budget anyway."

"You will," he smiles crookedly, showing me his bad teeth, teeth he might have fixed if he were willing to spend money on anything but tuition, room, and board. "You'll kill a duck, like the good terrorist you are, and they'll give it to you."

I can't help but smile at him. "It doesn't work that way," I remind him. "You can't humiliate these people. Not really. You can embarrass them momentarily, but that's about it."

"Well, let me put it this way," Billy says, his eyes turning mean. "If you don't do this for me, I'll never forgive you. Finny and that damn Jesuit are planning to recall you, and I'll vote with them. I don't give a shit."

That's the first lie he's told me, though. His voice leaks conviction as plainly as Gracie's leaks insincerity. Billy, I'd like to tell him, if you didn't give a shit you could throw away the bottle, skip town, head south with Finny, and sink your ass in butter.

Finny the man, not Finny the goose.

CHAPTER

15

Thanks to Billy Quigley, I'm ten minutes late for my appointment with the campus executive officer, and thanks again to Billy, this means that I have only fifteen minutes to cool my heels in the outer office instead of the twenty-five I'd have had to wait if I'd been on time. Dickie Pope—he wants us all to call him Dickie, and most of us come pretty close—provides no reading matter in his waiting room, the walls of which are turquoise fabric upholstered. But then they don't provide Catholics with magazines outside the confessional either, and those who visit Dickie's Vatican are either penitents or supplicants. Apparently we're to use the time contemplating our sins and desires.

Still, I'm not without entertainment. I've got a perfectly good peach in my pocket, so I take a seat on the sofa and see how close to the ceiling I can toss it without its actually touching the acoustic tiles. I'm doing pretty well until I have to lunge for one and brush a lamp. The door to Dickie's office opens just as I grab the lamp by its shade and the peach plops onto the rug. Three men emerge, and they all stare first at the lamp, then at me, then finally at the peach. What's wrong with this picture?

There with Dickie Pope is Lou Steinmetz, chief of campus security, who's taken a dim view of me since I came to the university over twenty years ago, in the seventies. At that time I had longish hair and a beard, and while the campus had had no significant protests against the war, Lou watched the news every evening, saw what was happening elsewhere, and mapped out an entire strategy for when the trouble started at the Railton Campus. Years later, after the disappointment wore off, he showed me the chart he'd worked up illustrating various contingencies. It showed several entrances to the campus blocked off. The ball fields and tennis courts at the southern edge of the campus would be used to assemble the National Guard. Then, on Lou's command, the troops would proceed along designated avenues, forcing the rioting throng westward toward the track and grandstand area, which would be used as a makeshift holding pen. It was the early eighties when Lou showed me all of this, and I could see that his eyes were still alive with the scheme.

Just to piss him off, I said, "But there were no riots."

"Good thing, huh?" Lou said, eyebrow raised significantly, and something told me that the reason he'd wanted me to see his chart was not that he thought I'd be interested but rather because in his mind's eye he'd imagined me leading a throng of militant students fresh from the burning of Old Main. He wanted me to see how close I'd come.

It takes me a moment to place the third member of this unholy trinity. Terence Watters is the university's chief legal counsel. I've never seen him except on television trying to obscure some fact or situation embarrassing to the university. He's tall and well groomed, and he has the kind of face that reveals nothing. Behind such expressions convictions go to die.

"Anyway," Dickie says after a beat, "discretion, gentlemen," adding, "Lou, I'm counting on you," as if to hint at what is common knowledge—discretion is not Lou Steinmetz's strong suit. Lou likes to make up a good chart and put a plan in motion with live ammo.

I pick up the peach from the carpet and say, "Hello, girls."

Lou Steinmetz, immediately offended, scowls and actually clenches his fists. Terence Watters, on the other hand, looks as if he's listening to a tape recording of ambient sound on a headset.

"Terry, I don't think you know Hank Devereaux," Dickie says, which starts us all shaking hands. I offer to shake Lou's first, and when he grudgingly extends his hand I put the peach in it. Instead of just setting it down, he tries to get me to take it back, but I've moved on to Dickie Pope and Terence Watters, and for some darn reason Lou can't recapture my attention. I feel for him. It's not an easy thing to be left holding a piece of fruit during introductions. This is the first time it's ever happened to Lou Steinmetz, I can tell.

"Hank's not just the chair of the English department. He's also a local television personality," Dickie explains to his chief counsel.

Which makes me wonder whether he knows about *Good Morning America,* if Dickie thinks I'm just local. The lawyer's hand is cool and dry, my own slightly sticky from the peach, which appears to have ruptured when it fell.

"Hank, why don't you go on in and make yourself comfortable. I want to walk these fellas to the door."

Dickie's office is lavish. Much nicer than Jacob Rose's. My father always managed to secure such an office for his visiting scholar gigs back when I was a boy. When I go over to Dickie's high windows to take in the view, I'm in time to see the three men emerge below, where they continue their conversation on the steps, Lou Steinmetz gesturing off in the direction of the main gate. Lou's campus security cruiser is parked at the curb, and the three men stroll toward it. They're seeing Lou off, I presume, trying again to impress upon him the need for the very discretion he lacks. But when they get to the cruiser, to my surprise, all three men climb into the front seat and drive off. If this is a joke on me, I can't help but admire it. In fact, I make a mental note to employ a version of it myself, soon. Maybe, if I'm to be fired today, I'll convene some sort of emergency meeting, inviting Gracie, and Paul Rourke, and Finny, and Orshee, and one or two other pebbles from my shoe. I'll call the meeting to order, then step outside on some pretext or other, and simply go home. Get Rachel to time them and report back to me on how long it takes them to figure it out. Maybe even get some sort of pool going.

I indulge this pleasant fantasy for a few minutes and then browse Dickie's tall bookshelves for further diversion. Actually, I've heard a story about these books from Jacob Rose, though I discounted it at the time. Few men tell a better story than Jacob, but then, too, few have less regard for the truth. Jacob isn't particularly malicious, at least by the rather liberal standards of academe, but he loves to embellish and is willing to do almost anything to improve a tale in the telling.

As Jacob tells this particular story, during the early summer of his hiring, Dickie Pope arrived in Railton with a large moving van crammed with everything but books. Apparently these built-in book-cases in the CEO's office can accommodate about a thousand, and the fact that he didn't have any caused Dickie some slight embarrassment. He sensed that it wouldn't be a good idea to fill the shelves with family photos and ceramic knickknacks. It occurred to him that Gracie DuBois might be of service, perhaps because she'd been utterly obse-quious ("If there's anything y'all need . . . anything a-tall . . .") to both Dickie and his pale wife. And so Dickie commissioned her to find him some books at local auctions and the secondhand bookstores in State College and make sure they were all delivered to his office sometime in August, before the fall semester started. Which they were, late one afternoon, a physical plant minivan backing up to a rear entrance of the Administration Building, where two custodians off-loaded fifty boxes of books onto hand trucks, scooting them inside as quickly as possible, like a shipment of stolen VCRs. By the time the semester began, Dickie's office was book-lined, floor to ceiling, as befitted the chief executive offi-cer of an institution of higher learning. Even better, Jacob always con-cluded, unlike the books in Gatsby's library, the pages of Dickie's books had been not only cut but read, their margins full of sophomoric scrib-bling in a thousand undergraduate hands.

I've not given much credence to this story until now. But in fact there seems to be no common denominator, no single intelligence that emerges from an examination of the books on these shelves, which seem not to have been organized, except perhaps by size and color. There are two copies of some books, including one by my father, which I take down and examine. It's his first book of criticism, the one that put him on the map, the only really good one, according to my mother, who served as reader, sounding board, and editor, largely unrecognized, except in the fine print of the acknowledgments page, which lists her name among his other debts—to the university that awarded him release time to do the research, the Guggenheim Foundation, which funded its writing, and the writers' colony that gave him (and not my mother) living space for a month one summer.

In truth, the William Henry Devereaux, Sr., of the author photo doesn't look like the type of fellow who'd require a lot of assistance, and that may be one of my father's great gifts—his ability to suggest through a pose, a gesture, that he was himself all he needed. This appearance of self-sufficiency may even have been responsible for his success with young women in the various graduate programs in which he taught. Without being a strikingly handsome man, I suspect he managed to convey to them that whether they did or they didn't was a matter of more concern to them than to him, and so of course they did. I understood why, having courted him too. This same self-sufficiency tormented me as a boy. If he was going somewhere, he made it clear that I could go along or not, as I chose, so I always chose to be near him, rather than my mother, whose company I preferred, because she paid attention to me. The fact that she seemed actually to like having me around, however, made her a less desirable companion when I had a choice between her and my father. I don't recall how old I was before it dawned on me that my efforts to be close to my father were pointless for the simple reason that there *was* no getting close to him, not really. I probably would have come to this simple understanding sooner were it not for my mother, who hadn't, I began to suspect, arrived at it herself.

When I set William Henry Devereaux, Sr., down on the coffee table, another volume, farther down the shelf, attracts my attention. Its dust jacket—indeed the entire volume—is in pristine condition, and when I turn it over to examine the back panel, a serious-looking young man stares up at me with an intense, Rasputin-like gaze, suggestive of intolerance, superiority, and high seriousness. Had I tried, I now wonder, to strike a pose like my father's on the jacket of his own first book? I seem to recall imagining that by dressing in jeans and a collarless shirt, and by having the long hair of the times, I'd offer a striking contrast to my betweeded scholar father, but my posture and attitude now strike me as his, donned, unlike the clothes, without thought. The caption below the author photo reads, "Henry Devereaux at home in Railton, PA." The photo itself seems calculated to suggest that such a man would never be at home in Railton, PA. On the title page I encounter an inscription in my own hand. "For Finny," it says. "With affection and admiration. Good luck."

I require a minute to remember why I might have wished Finny luck (the admiration and affection I take to be license). Then I remember we'd both come up for tenure and promotion to associate professor the same year, and everyone knew that Finny stood no chance. In the six years he'd been at the Railton Campus, he hadn't finished the dissertation begun at the University of Pennsylvania, and about the only thing in his file was a letter from his dissertation director which said that he hadn't given up on Finny and he hoped we wouldn't either. I, on the other hand, with an authored book to my credit, was thought to be a shoo-in, even though I had brashly put myself up for promotion after just a year in residence. Predictably, though no one predicted it, Finny got his promotion that year and I was turned down, a circumstance that had so enraged me that, with Jacob Rose's help (he'd become chair the next year), I put myself up for full professor, an act of such unprecedented and unmitigated arrogance that the committee approved it, thus effectively rooting me to the scene of the crime, too weighed down by tenure, rank, and salary to be marketable ever again.

My own errors in judgment I can forgive, but Finny, the rat, has sold my book, a book I now vividly remember giving him in what I considered at the time to be a sweet, parting gesture, since no man was ever less tenurable than Finny.

Oddly, my outrage at Finny is the only emotion I feel holding the book. *The* book. Without exactly putting me on the map, as my father's first book did him, this modest little volume of mine did a good deal, deciding, to some degree, the destiny of both its author and its author's family. Its acceptance brought us to Railton, and its advance started knocking down those first trees out in Allegheny Wells and bought the adjacent two lots I've since refused to sell and thus given impetus to the various petty English department feuds that have served as our substitute for genuine conflict. Not this actual volume I'm holding in my hand, of course, which has had about as ignominious a life as can befall a book. It's been owned first by a man who apparently wouldn't have it as a gift and then by a man who views it as interior decoration. Like Oliver Twist, it's gone from a bad home to a worse one. When I hear Dickie's voice in the outer office, giving instructions to his secretary, I slip the volume into my coat pocket.

When he comes in, we shake hands again, rather too vigorously for the occasion, it seems to me, though it's true I'm not sure, now that I'm here, what the occasion is. Is this my regularly scheduled, state-of-the-department annual meeting with the campus administration, or is it the meeting I've been warned about, where I will be apprized of the impending purge? Or will both these agenda items be put aside in order to discuss my recent television appearance and the embarrassment I've caused those who pay my salary?

Dickie Pope seldom wears a jacket and tie, and he's not wearing these now. His blue oxford button-down shirt is rolled into an artful three-quarter sleeve. His gray slacks are a miracle of pleating, and his cordovan loafers look like he bought them on the way to the campus this morning. He's a studied regular guy, this Dickie, and as diminutive as his name.

Collapsing onto one end of the sofa along the wall facing the bookshelves, he indicates that I'm free to occupy the other. "Lawyers and cops. Cops and lawyers. And I thought I was going to be an educator," he moans theatrically, studying me as he does so. Surely this is a calculated tactic. I'm from the English department, and he's probably concluded I don't have much use for cops and lawyers. So, for the moment, neither does Dickie. Having established a common value system, maybe we can be friends. Maybe even do business. Who knows? In another ten or twenty minutes, maybe we'll be all cuddly down at his end of the sofa. Either this is his thinking or he really doesn't like cops and lawyers. "Who knew academic life would be so crazy?"

"I had a pretty good idea," I confess. "Both my parents were academics."

This simple intelligence bowls Dickie over. "No *kidding*? I didn't *know* that." He's one stunned little CEO.

"You've got one of my father's books right here," I say, picking up Devereaux Senior from the coffee table where I set him and handing him to Dickie.

"I've got your novel up there too," he says, giving Senior the once-over. "Did you notice?"

He only thinks he does, actually. Devereaux Junior is resting comfortably in my coat pocket, his hard spine under my rib. I feel only a little disappointed to discover that Dickie apparently does have some knowledge of the books that reside upon his shelves, which means that Jacob Rose's account of their acquisition is an exaggeration, if not an outright lie.

"Tell me something," Dickie says, tossing Senior back onto the coffee table, a little cavalierly it seems to me, at least for a man who has not himself authored a book, and therefore runs no risk of being himself tossed. "What's your opinion of Lou Steinmetz?"

I consider how to answer this.

"Be honest," Dickie urges. "It's just us here."

"Well, he's found a line of work that suits him," I tell my new pal Dickie, who's already moved us into the realm of confidentiality. "And he's probably done less harm here than he'd have done someplace where they issue real bullets."

"Oh, the bullets are real enough," Dickie assures me.

"No *kidding*?" I say, my turn now to be bowled over. "Wow. And to think how I've been ragging him all these years. I better quit."

"Nah," Dickie says, crossing one pleated leg over the other at the ankle. "From what I hear, you goad everybody."

I make what I hope is a smooth transition from bowled over to innocent, though my audience appears not to notice.

"Between us?" he continues. We're moving forward rapidly now, forging across the border of confidentiality and into intimacy. "When I watched you on television last night, I thought maybe you were goading *me*."

"But then you realized I wasn't," I add. For some reason I feel the need to supply the ending to his story.

He recrosses his legs thoughtfully. "In fact, I asked my wife. I said, 'Is this guy goading me?' "

"Ah," I say. "*She* was the one who realized?"

"Anyway," he continues, waving the whole goading issue away with the back of his hand. "Guess who I got a call from at seven o'clock this morning?"

I can't imagine he really wants me to guess. When I don't, he doesn't volunteer the information, however, and he's grinning at me like I should know, so I take a flyer. "The chancellor?"

"You got it," he says, clearly gratified. "Guess what he wanted?"

I take another flyer. "To know if there's any way to fire a tenured full professor?"

Dickie makes a hurt face. I've disappointed him. After first displaying prescience, I've now exhibited a surprising lack of imagination. "He wanted to apologize and assure me that I'll have my budget soon. He wanted me to convey to you the complexity of our situation. You don't have your budget because Jacob doesn't have his budget because I don't have my budget all the way up to the chancellor, who doesn't have a budget because the legislature is dragging its feet. As per usual. The chancellor's been promised a budget early next week, and he wanted to assure me that I'll have mine by the end of that same week."

"That's good news," I say. "At a duck a day that means I only have to kill four or five ducks, and we've got close to thirty."

Dickie thinks this is pretty funny and laughs immoderately. I remain immoderately sober. If he's at all disconcerted to be the only one laughing, he shows no sign. "No, seriously," he says. "You did us all a favor, Hank. Last night—I admit it—I could have stabbed you through the throat with an ice pick, but the more I thought about it, the more I thought, we can *use* this."

"The throat?" I say. "With an ice pick?" I mean, after all, we're sitting here on Dickie's leather couch in the office of the chief executive officer of an institution of higher learning, as close to the heart of civilization as you can get without going to a better school.

Dickie ignores me. "I mean I called you every name in the book at first. I said, 'What's that hmm-hmm-hmm-hmm-hmm' trying to do to me?" He pauses, as if to allow me the opportunity to count the *hmm*'s and substitute expletives in the blanks so I'll know what he called me. "But the more I thought about it, the more I thought, 'This is *funny*.'"

Since Dickie Pope has never given any indication of a sense of humor, I can only conclude that he does not think any of this is funny. Unless it's funny in the same way that stabbing me through the throat with an ice pick would be funny. Beneath this performance, Dickie, I realize, is still in a black rage.

"And then suddenly I'm laughing my ass off, this is so hmm-hmm funny. What am I worried about? I say to myself. A little humiliation? A little embarrassment with a state legislator? I mean, we're all adults here, right?"

I consider this to be another rhetorical question, but apparently it isn't.

"Am I right?" Dickie wants to know.

"Absolutely," I assure him.

"So, I say, make use of it. Every problem contains its own solution. That's the first rule every administrator learns."

"How many rules are there altogether?" I ask. I'm not an innocent, but I can play that role.

He ignores me. "Ignore all smart-ass questions" may be one of the other rules. "And it's not like we don't have more serious problems to attend to," he says.

"No," I agree. "It's not like that."

"Speaking of which," Dickie says, as if this digression has just occurred to him. "This rowdy department of yours. How many griev-ances do you have pending right now?"

"Just against me," I ask, "or against Teddy when he was chair?"

He shrugs, generous. "The two of you."

"I've lost count," I admit. "Fifteen? Twenty? Most of them are nui-sance grievances."

"Nuisance," Dickie says, leaning forward to stab my tweedy shoul-der with an elegant index finger. "That's the word. That's the right hmm-hmm word for them. And so's the union that nurtures them, though you may not agree with me."

No doubt about it. Now we're getting somewhere. Because Dickie would not have made such an observation without having done some research. Sometime last night it's occurred to him to wonder just who I am, this guy he wants to stab through the throat with an ice pick. I must be somebody, so who the hell am I? He's made a call or two, and he's learned that I was not in favor of union representation when the vote was taken over a decade ago. He may even know that I've been an outspoken critic of the kind of egalitarian spirit that has pervaded the institution since the union's arrival. Or it could be he's known these things about me for some time. Maybe last fall he wondered just who the hell this "Lucky Hank" guy was who was writing academic satires for the newspaper. Maybe he wanted to put an ice pick in the throat of this Lucky Hank character too. Regardless, if he's taken the trouble to find out about my attitude toward the union, he's also learned that I'm unpredictable, a genuine loose cannon. What he'd like to know now is just how loose. Can he afford me as a friend?

"These things go in cycles," I decide to say. "Every academic union should be tossed out after five years." Then, before Dickie's grin can spread too far, I add, "Then at the end of the next five years, all the university administrators should be booted out and another union voted in."

"That's pretty cynical," Dickie says, as if cynicism were a character trait he'd never have suspected in me until this moment. "Now, I believe in continuity and vision."

"Vision's good," I agree.

"Take this place. You may be right about things moving in cycles," he concedes. "This nuisance union, as you call it, has had our institution by the hmm-hmm for a long time. But anybody with vision"—he pauses here to point to his own right eye, which has narrowed with significance—"can see that things are changing. Forces of nature, Hank, pure and simple. We're fresh out of baby boomers. The colleges that survive the decade are going to be lean and mean. Efficient."

"Efficient?" I say. "Education?"

"You bet."

"Higher education?"

"Lean and mean."

"Well, it's always been mean," I concede.

"And it's gonna get lean. Soon."

I try not to show how little I like the sound of this.

"Nobody can stop what's going to happen," Dickie assures me. "You can't stop a tidal wave. All you can do is find high ground and take your friends with you."

Here it is again. I can be Dickie's friend if I want to be.

"You're saying I get to save my friends? Watch my enemies drown?"

Dickie contemplates my question. "Here's what I'm saying. I know there have been lots of rumors, so I'll tell you what I can. The sad truth is that the chancellor has given me a mandate. Not just me. I wish it were. But it's systemwide. All the campus executive officers. Every one. I have to come up with a plan to reduce staff and costs, across the curriculum, by twenty percent. There's no guarantee that such a plan will have to be implemented. But it has to be drawn up. Twenty percent."

I can't help smiling at this. "If we're going to save Hank Devereaux's friends and drown his enemies, we can cut a lot more than twenty percent."

"Don't sell yourself short," Dickie advises, apparently concerned for my self-esteem. "You're widely respected on this campus. You're a gifted and popular teacher and a well-published author. You may think that those of us on this side of the pond don't know who our good people are, but we do, believe me. I in particular keep my ear to the tracks."

When Dickie says this, I can't help thinking of William Cherry, who apparently did exactly this and had his head borne away and deposited in Bellemonde. For a moment I picture this happening to Dickie.

"Did I say something funny?" he wants to know.

"Not at all," I assure him. "Let me see if I understand. I tell you who to fire and you just do it. You think that's something we can get away with?"

Dickie leans back on the arm of the sofa, locks his fingers behind his head. His armpits, I notice, are not even damp. I, on the other hand, am sweating, and this may be one of the things that Dickie is enjoying. Because he clearly *is* enjoying himself. "I don't think you fully comprehend. It's *not* doing it that we can't get away with," he says, pausing to let this sink in. "Because if we don't do it, somebody else will. Somebody who may be less discriminating than we are."

"I get it," I say. "It can be done well or badly. That's our choice."

"And you wouldn't tell me who to fire, Hank. I wouldn't burden you that way. You wouldn't want such a thing on your conscience. Besides, that's not what you're paid for. If such a thing has to be done, it'll be effected by people whose job it is. No, you'd simply suggest a set of criteria. On the basis of those criteria, I'd be advised who is indispensable to your department, so I don't compromise your mission. After consulting with the academic deans, I would make recommendations based on your advice. The president of the university would act on *my* recommendations. The chancellor on his."

"All of which would be based on mine?"

He shrugs a concession. "Why would I want to ignore your recommendations? You're the expert. If I went off on my own, I could find my hmm-hmm in a sling."

"I see how that could happen."

He nods, rocking gently, hands still behind his head. "Hank, I'll be honest. I know a little about you. Heck. I know a lot about you. I know you're on record as saying your department is full of burnouts. Now's your chance to fashion the kind of department we could all be proud of."

"*I* said the English department was full of burnouts?" I ask. It's true I've thought it often enough, but I can't think of who I've said it to that would have repeated it to Dickie Pope.

"Never mind." He waves this off. "You did, and you were right. Remember. This is just us. Just you and me. Nobody knows what gets said here. But I'd be remiss if I didn't point something out to you, because I know you're a man of integrity and this might not occur to you. You want to know the best part, from *your* standpoint? Number one. There's no guarantee any of this will come to pass. This particular legislature's not enamored of higher education, it's true, but in the eleventh hour, they may see the light. But if they don't, there's still no way you're going to be seen as the bad guy. There'll be some bellyaching at first, no mistake, but it's going to be clear that this was mandated from the top, not the bottom. You'll catch some flack from a small handful of people, but not like the flack I'm going to catch. And what I'm going to catch isn't going to be anything like what the chancellor's going to catch. We're the bad guys, not you. We do the deed, we eat the hmm-hmm, you come out in good shape. Which is fine. We eat a little hmm-hmm, but everybody wins. The institution wins. The students win. And, if a little deadwood gets whittled away, the taxpayers win."

"We get trim," I say thoughtfully. "Lean and mean."

"The idea appeals to you, Hank, I can tell," Dickie says. "And it should, considering the alternative."

"Ah, the alternative. The alternative doesn't look nearly as good," I admit. "And I don't even know what the alternative is."

"Sure you do," Dickie assures me. "A smart guy like you knows that if you don't assist me in these serious deliberations, I'll have to go elsewhere for the advice I need. And somebody else's criteria might not be yours. If I were to ask, say, Phineas Coomb, who's always in here busting me about what a hmm-hmm-hmm you are, who knows? He might advise me to require the Ph.D. for all professorial ranks. Such criteria, evenly applied, would not benefit you, Hank. What's that screwball degree you've got?"

"A master of fine arts?"

He nods. "Not a Ph.D. What if I'm advised everybody should have one? It wouldn't be a good thing. Not for you. Not for Lila. Not for our students. Hell. Not even for me. *I* wouldn't want that, Hank."

"But if you *had* to . . . ," I continue.

His face clouds over. He's finally had enough. Apparently he doesn't like me stepping on his lines. I note with satisfaction that a spot of perspiration darkens one pit before he can put his arms down. "You can't help yourself, can you?" he says. "This goading thing."

Every muscle in his face confronts the task of what the hell to do with a man like me. He finally knows exactly what to make of me, but he can't seem to act on what he knows.

"Well," he says, rising, under control again. "Maybe I'm asking too much here. This is a lot to digest. Heck, I felt the same way back in February when I got the news. Imagine my situation for a minute, if that's not too much to ask. I came here from an institution that just went through the same dramatic downsizing that's being discussed here, the result of the same financial exigencies. You think *I* ever want to go through such a thing again?"

I have to admit, Dickie is pretty good. His carefully calculated sincerity is almost indistinguishable from the real thing. By asking me to consider his situation, he's asked for sympathy even as he's reminded me that he's done this once already, lest I doubt his resolve.

As I'm ushered to the door, Dickie's book-lined wall again attracts his attention, and he goes over to it, scanning the shelves, his hand raised, in the general area where my book was located, where he apparently remembers seeing it last. "I know I've got your book here," he says.

The fact that he's wrong about it is oddly heartening.

Finally he gives up, turns back to me, to the book's author, who stands before him, poor substitute for the book, the object he's hoped to put his hands on, to use, who knows, for flattery? for kindling? I force myself not to look down at my coat pocket. Dickie's got a strange look on his face, like maybe he knows what's happened to this book he's looking for. Or maybe he's reconsidering the possibility that occurred to him this morning and was too hastily rejected—that he could just stab me in the throat with an ice pick. "I hear you don't write anymore," he says, which is, in truth, about the last thing I expect him to say.

"Not true," I inform him. "You should see the margins of my student papers."

"Not the same as writing a book though, right?"

"Almost identical," I assure him. "Both go largely unread."

"If it weren't for lawyers and cops, I'd have time to read," he tells me. "I started that book of yours and liked it. Anyway, take the weekend to think things over. Talk it over with Lila."

Better and better. I can feel my grin spreading, buoyed by the fact that he's gotten my wife's name wrong a second time. He's taken the trouble to research me, but even so he's making mistakes.

"I always discuss everything with Lila," I tell him. "Lila's one shrewd cookie. You think *I'm* smart? You should meet my Lila. In fact, I don't know where I'd be without Lila. If I ever do write another book and make a lot of money, I'm going to buy a yacht and name her the *Lila.*"

Dickie Pope is staring at me, bewildered now, perhaps even convinced I'm insane. When we shake, he doesn't let go of my hand right away. "I'm not sure I've done a good job of convincing you of the gravity of the situation, Hank. And I do want you to understand that there *is* a storm coming. A real gully washer."

Since we're right by the window, which affords a sweeping view of the campus all the way to the duck pond, I offer him our entire tenured academic landscape with a sweeping gesture. "Not a hmm-hmm cloud in the sky," I observe.

CHAPTER

16

On my way back across campus, I see Bodie Pie slip into Social Sciences via the back door and remember she wanted to talk to me, so I follow, risking the possibility that I'll get lost in the building's legendary labyrinths. Social Sciences, the newest building on campus, was built in the midseventies, when there was money for both buildings and faculty. According to myth, the structure was designed to prevent student takeovers, and this may be true. A series of pods, it's all zigzagging corridors and abrupt mezzanines that make it impossible to walk from one end of the building to another. At one point, if you're on the first floor, either you have to go up two floors, over, and down again or you have to go outside the building and then in again in order to arrive at an office you can see from where you're standing. The campus joke is that Lou Steinmetz has an office in the building but no one knows where.

If I'm the most embattled program chair on campus, Bodie Pie, of Women's Studies, runs a close second, and Bodie takes her troubles to heart, which makes her situation far worse than mine. She can usually use some cheering up.

"I don't think I could work in these conditions," I say when I arrive at the open doorway of her dismal office. Women's Studies is in the basement, almost entirely below ground. There's a long, horizontal window in Bodie's office that affords a narrow view of the sidewalk outside, as well as the feet and ankles of people who pass by on it. "Don't you have a secretary, at least?"

I've caught Bodie smoking a cigarette, which she quickly stubs out, guilty. "Girls don't need secretaries. They *are* secretaries."

"Would you feel better if I got you a cup of coffee?" I say, since there's a pot made and I could use a cup myself. I touch the glass, which is hot. It doesn't look like it's been sitting there too long.

"No, I wouldn't feel better," she says. "I saw you come out of the Vatican. I thought I'd ducked in here in time."

"Now you've gone and hurt my feelings, Bodie," I tell her, pouring coffee into two Styrofoam cups. "Besides. I thought you wanted to talk to me."

"Talk to you, not see you. There's a difference." When I don't know what to say to this, she continues. "You ever have one of those days where you hope you won't run into anybody you even remotely like? So you won't have to be civil even?"

I study her. Bodie and I have been friends for a long time, and she's another of the women on campus that I'd be a little in love with if I were not in love with my wife, Bodie's being a lesbian notwithstanding. She is always falling in what she calls romantic courtly love. Sometimes she tells me about it.

"I see you got my present, anyhow," I say, noting the sign I had printed and framed, which is hanging on the wall behind her desk: Welcome to Bitch Gulch. I'm not a misogynist, but I can play that role. I've also had some special stationery printed up for her. Underneath the university seal, I've added a motto: "Where Women are Womyn and Men are Males."

Bodie swivels and studies the sign. "Some of my sisters say it's in bad taste."

"*That's* their objection?"

"They're very serious. Earnest, you'd almost say."

We're grinning at each other now. "Somebody told me that English department floozy gigged you," she says, studying my nose. "Everybody's been telling me, in fact."

I try to imagine what kind of spin the story would have down here in Women's Studies, where I'm a suspected chauvinist and Gracie is thought to be an aging, pitiful tramp, one of the very few female faculty members in the college not encouraged to teach a course in Bodie's interdisciplinary program.

"I've been much in the news lately," I admit, then remember that Bodie, on principle, doesn't own a television and therefore has probably seen neither the local news nor *Good Morning America*. Since nobody's told her yet about my threat to start executing ducks, I give her the short version of these events while we drink our coffee. Bodie's reaction to my account is annoyingly similar to Lily's. This is exactly the sort of thing she's come to expect from me, her tired acceptance seems to suggest. It was also Bodie who witnessed my descent of snowy Pleasant Street Hill last winter.

As I tell her my story, she starts to light two more cigarettes, catches herself, and stops. "So," she says, when I finish. "You've been to see Little Dick. Did you get the 'big storm brewing' speech?"

"Tidal wave," I inform her.

"It's a tidal wave now?"

"Can't be stopped," I tell her. "Only thing we can do is move to high ground. Take our friends with us. You want to come with me? I may have room for one more."

"I hope his pee-pee falls off."

"Don't perpetuate the stereotype," I suggest.

"So? How did you respond?" she wants to know, and I sense that the barometric pressure in the room has changed.

"I said we're too far inland to be affected by tidal waves. He insisted I take the weekend to rethink my position. He said I should talk the whole thing over with Lila."

Normally, this would get a chuckle out of Bodie, but today, nothing. "And you said there was no reason to think it over. You said it'd be a long, cold day in hell before you'd betray your colleagues. You told the little prick he could go fuck himself." The way she's looking at me, I get the impression that this same advice could well be coming my direction, depending upon my answer.

"I'd have to rewind the tape," I tell her.

She ignores this completely. "Because that's what the people who are loyal to the union are all telling him. That's what *I* told him."

"I'm not sure I'm all that loyal to the union," I confess, preparing as I admit this to go fuck myself.

Bodie looks around her office, as if for someplace to spit. "I can't believe you'd even consider siding with the administration."

"A plague on both their houses, is my feeling," I tell her.

This appeases Bodie somewhat, without exactly endearing me to her. "You may be called upon to testify though," she warns. "In the fundamentalist sense. You won't be allowed ironic distance. That I can guarantee."

I turn my empty Styrofoam cup upside down on her desk. "I have to tell you, Bodie. Once again you have failed to make me feel better about the world and my place in it."

Suddenly the tension is gone, and we're friends again. "I'm a pretty constant source of disappointment to men," she concedes, adding sadly, "and not a few women."

"Want to tell me about it?" She usually does.

She studies me, as if she might be seriously contemplating whether to confide this latest heartbreak to me. And perhaps because in the past she always has, I'm surprised when she waves the issue away. "Just somebody," she says. "Somebody who's not supposed to be on my side of the fence even."

And she's no sooner said it than the image has leapt, full blown, up onto my imaginative wide screen—in Technicolor and Dolby stereo—Bodie and Lily, wrestling, naked and sweaty, on top of Bodie's desk. It's happening right here, right now. The picture I've conjured up is so dramatically vivid that it's not undermined even by its absurdity. I mean, after all. To be believable, the scene requires Lily, a woman I know, to become a woman I don't know, a character violation of the sort I'm always warning my fiction writers against. True, I tell them, people have secrets. They have complex inner lives that resist simple interpretation, but what we do know about them cannot be ignored, forgotten, or profaned, and this new role in which I have cast my wife is a clear violation of narrative rules. And this isn't the only violation. In a good story Bodie Pie cannot be *both* having sweaty sex with my wife *and* sitting before me, fully clothed, smoking a cigarette, which she is, though I don't remember her lighting one, and here it is half smoked. When I focus on the burning tip of her cigarette, the lovers are suddenly gone, and once again Bodie's small office contains just us two old friends, talking. Actually, Bodie's the one talking, explaining, I realize, why she left a message for me to call her. "Anyway," she's saying. "Tell him to be on guard."

Clearly, I've missed some damn thing. A small chunk of time, of the life of William Henry Devereaux, Jr., has slipped into some kind of void. "Who?" I say.

"Tony," she says, studying me suspiciously now. "Tony Coniglia. The person we've been talking about."

"Right." I nod demonstratively, as if this has clarified everything.

But she must suspect I'm still not up to speed because she says, "Where did you go just then?"

"What do you mean?" I ask, though I know what she means.

She exhales a long, deep, thoughtful lungful of smoke. "You should have seen your face."

To get back to my office, I must go by the student center and the duck pond. On my way I pass half a dozen students I know, most of whom seem to be looking everywhere but at me. Unless I'm getting paranoid, one student actually changes direction in order to avoid running into me. Is this the result of my television celebrity, I wonder, or am I still wearing the expression alluded to by Bodie Pie? A third explanation occurs to me, and I check to make sure I've zipped up after my last vigil at the urinal. I spend a lot of time with my dick outside my fly these days. Maybe it's begun to feel natural there. But everything seems to be in order.

When I come around the corner of the student center, I see why so many students are embarrassed to meet my eye. On the very spot where I faced the cameras last night, a large group of protesters have gathered. They're carrying placards and chanting something I can't quite make out, because the ducks have joined in quacking and the geese honking and trumpeting, a hell of a din. The TV crew has returned, just pulled up in fact. To my amazement, Missy Blaylock is among them. She climbs out of the van like an arthritic, closes the door softly, leans her broad forehead against its cool metal surface. The sound guy, the same one who last night wanted to know if I was trying to pass a stone, sees me coming and grins. "You're in a world of shit now, son," he says. "These animal rights assholes play for keeps."

"That's who they are?"

"That's who they are. And they want nothing less than your balls," he assures me. "And, hey, I've gotta ask. What'd you guys do to her last night?"

We turn and study Missy, who looked up briefly when she heard my voice, groaned once, and went back to cleaving unto the van.

"I *really* hate coming here," she says. "Did I mention that?"

"I don't think coming to campus was your mistake," I point out.

"Tell me about it," she agrees. "I've got to talk to you about that guy." She says all of this with her forehead still melded to the van.

"Okay," I tell her, "but you know him better than I do."

She straightens up, gives me a narrow-eyed look. "And I believe you have a photograph of me that I would like returned."

"Okay," I agree reluctantly. "But I've spent the whole morning trying to find just the right frame."

When the crew starts carrying equipment over to the pond, I volunteer to help, in the hope that this way I won't be noticed. When we get closer, I can read the placards the protesters are carrying. The most popular seems to be STOP THE SLAUGHTER, and that's what the group is chanting. Some of the placards have my grainy, blown-up photograph on them in the center of the now ubiquitous symbol: ⃠

I don't know who any of these people are, but I have to admire their efficiency, their ability to mobilize so quickly. After all, they've only had about fourteen hours to organize this protest, locate a photograph of the villain they intend to symbolize (it's the photo from my book jacket, I realize), blow it up, nail the poster board to the sticks. And there are probably other organizational difficulties I've not imagined.

As I'm surveying the protesters, it occurs to me that they aren't all strangers. I recognize one thin, balding young fellow from faculty meetings, though I have no idea what department he's in. He notices me at the very moment I notice him, and he points me out to two youngish women at his elbow. They observe me through narrowed eyes, pass the information along to the others. You can actually trace the progress of dubious knowledge among their ranks. Some have to be convinced that I'm the same man as the more youthful one pictured on their signs.

"The jig's up," the sound man warns. "You better split."

Missy, with no cool truck to lean on here, is massaging her temples with the ball end of her microphone. "Could someone ask them to chant more softly?"

"Quit fucking with the mike," her sound guy says. "How can I get a level with you doing that?"

Missy turns toward him, rubs the microphone vigorously on the seat of her tweed skirt, causing the man to remove his headset hastily.

I point to one of the protesters who's carrying a STOP THE SLAUGH-TER sign. "You're too young to remember," I tell Missy, "but I used to carry a sign like that during Vietnam."

"Some things never change," she says. She actually thinks she's agreeing with me.

Her comment, more than any fear for my personal safety, convinces me that it is probably time for me to leave. The protesters have begun to link arms, forming a semicircle around the ducks and geese, daring evil to approach. They've altered their chant, and now they're shouting directly at me: STOP DEVEREAUX. STOP THE SLAUGHTER. Finny (the goose, not the man), perhaps made claustrophobic by so much protection, breaks through the line of defense and trumpets loudly and off key.

"There," the sound man says, confident he's got his level. "We're ready."

At the far edge of the crowd, which has now swelled to about a hundred and fifty people, I spot Dickie Pope and Lou Steinmetz. Lou looks grim but prepared for action if things get out of hand. Dickie is grinning at me, for some reason. In fact, he's pointing with his index finger at the sky. When I look up, I half-expect to see buzzards, but it's not that. In the forty-five minutes since I left his office, the sky has darkened. The clouds directly overhead look positively ominous.

.   .   .

Alone in the men's room down the hall from my office, I have a lot to think about and plenty of time. Picture it, a fifty-year-old man with a purple nose, his heavy, limp dick in hand, and, it must be confessed, a rather heavy heart as well. What's he thinking there at the urinal? He is thinking, in truth, about himself. About William Henry Devereaux, Jr. There are other things a man like me might think about, but at this moment I am unavoidably the subject of my own dubious contemplation, and I've got my reasons. I have myself in hand, as it were. And yet here, I'm also surrounded by me in the numerous, merciless men's room mirrors. The drawn and settled William Henry Devereaux, Jr., who looks back at me invites comparison with the light, bouncing Prince Hal nailed to sticks outside and waved angrily at the duck pond. If all this me weren't enough, I am also in my own pocket, in the sense that my book is there, the one I stole from Dickie Pope's office. Me, me, and more me. So much me. And so little.

Standing here, I become aware of a low, droning sound, like a far-off vacuum cleaner, and I feel a distant tingling in the extremities. I can't help wondering if the brief temporal ellipses I've been suffering these past few days are a sign of approaching illness, but I remind myself that they aren't all that different from the sort of thing that used to happen all the time when I was working on the book that now occupies my jacket pocket. Lily, whenever she noticed that I'd disappeared during a conversation at the dinner table, used to chide me for being physically present but emotionally absent without leave. And my daughter Karen told me years later that she could always tell by looking at me whether I was really there or off in some other world, revising fictional reality. If it's not illness, could it be that there's another book nagging at me? Would I even recognize one now, after so long? If a new book *were* clamoring for attention, what should I do? I am no longer, if indeed I ever was, a romantic with respect to authorship. Bad books call to authors with the same haunting siren song as good ones, and there's no law that says you have to listen, not when there's an ample supply of cotton for the ears. On that note I zip.

Outside, the hall is empty, so I slip into my office through my private door, close it quietly, turn on my small Tensor desk lamp rather than the overhead, hoping for a few moments of peace. Here, the low, droning sound I kept hearing in the men's room is more pronounced. Then, all of a sudden, it's gone. I shake my head but can't bring it back. I see that Rachel has found me a new blotter, so I take young Hal out of my jacket pocket and, instead of shelving him as intended, I open to the first page and begin to read. I'm only a few sentences into the text when Rachel's voice crackles over the intercom, causing me to jump about a foot. "Are you in there?" she wants to know. Which me? I wonder. Young Hal, the wide-ranging outfielder? Or the tenured first baseman with warning-track power? Rachel sounds worried, like it's the door of Dr. Jekyll's laboratory she's been listening at.

"I'm thinking about writing another book, Rachel," I tell her.

"Really? That's great?"

The droning is back, as if triggered by my assertion. It sounds like distant thunder now. Rolling. Rumbling. The storm Dickie pointed to in the sky seems to have arrived.

"You have some messages?" Rachel informs me.

I sigh. These messages, it occurs to me, are the cotton for my ears that I thought to make use of back in the men's room. The academic memo, the voice message, the e-mail (which I don't receive) taken together are the cotton plugs that drown out the siren's song. At first resentful, we scholar-sailors come to be grateful for them.

"Sing them out, Rachel," I tell her bravely, though I see jagged rocks ahead. "And don't spare my feelings. Give them to me straight, kid. I can take it."

"Herbert Schonberg called twice?" The union rep I've been evading for days. "He says he intends to see you this afternoon if he has to track you with bloodhounds?" It occurs to me now that I've been dodging him for the wrong reason. I've assumed he wanted to bust my chops about the various grievances filed against me, including the most recent one, Gracie's, but now I realize it's about Dickie's tidal wave.

"Boring stuff, Rachel. You can do better."

"The dean called again? Long distance? He said thanks a lot? He said you'd understand?"

And I do. My shenanigans, their timing, are not a good advertisement for Jacob. I've disobeyed his strict orders to do nothing in his absence. I may have knocked him clean off the short list. Jacob and I go back a long way, and if I've botched his escape from Railton, I'll deserve to lose his friendship.

"What do you say we go back to the boring ones, Rachel?" I suggest.

Rumble rumble rumble. I lean back in my swivel chair and study the ceiling tiles, which actually appear to be vibrating. "Your daughter called?"

"Julie?"

"She wanted to know if you could come out to the house this afternoon?"

"No," I tell Rachel, the wrong person. "Out of the question."

"She sounded like she was crying?"

"Do you have her number?"

Rachel says she does.

"Call her back. Ask her if she was crying."

Silence.

"Okay, I agree. Bad idea. Bad boss. Call her back and let me talk to her."

I close young Hal. Just as well.

"I'm getting their machine?" Rachel's back on the intercom.

"I'll pick up," I tell her.

I listen to Russell's voice message, and at the beep, say, "It's me, darlin'. Pick up if you're there." I wait several beats. "Okay, it's almost noon. I'll try to come by later."

Suddenly, she's on the line. "Okay," she says, sounding remarkably like her mother, and then just as suddenly she's hung up. I call again, get the machine, wait, tell her to pick up, listen to dead air until the machine clicks off. What the hell is this about? Melodrama, knowing Julie.

I get back on the intercom with Rachel, a sensible woman. "Let's take a long lunch," I suggest. "We'll drive out to the Railton Sheraton. If we're together there won't be anybody to take these messages."

"Sorry? Today's my sexual harassment lunch?"

Sexual harassment lunch? "Okay, I'll bite."

"It's for all the department secretaries?" she explains. "Sort of a workshop?"

"What sort of food do they serve at a sexual harassment lunch?" it occurs to me to ask.

"Nouvelle cuisine?" she suggests. Near as I can remember, this is the first joke Rachel's ever made around me.

"It's come to this," I tell her. "Now I'm playing straight man to my own secretary."

"You're really going to write another book?"

The idea seems to have completely dissipated. "Probably not," I admit, adding, before she can object, "Is that thunder we're hearing?"

"Asbestos removal."

Relieved to discover that my external reality matches Rachel's, at least in this one respect, I study the ceiling tiles, which *are* vibrating, damn them.

"It's our turn? They're detoxing the whole building?"

"God," I say. "Animal rights thugs guarding the pond, sexual harassment lunches, the detoxing of Modern Languages. Something's happening here. What it is ain't exactly clear."

Ambient crackling from the intercom. Indicating what? Puzzlement at my Buffalo Springfield allusion? It's true what they say. Ours is a fragmented culture. If I wrote another book, who would read it?

In the outer office, I hear the phone ring, hear Rachel answer. Then she returns to the intercom. "Professor Schonberg's on his way up?" she says. "I'd hurry? I'd take the south stairs?"

I do as I'm instructed, but only after I've made a place for young Hal on my crowded bookcase. There isn't much room, even for such a slender fellow, so I have to wedge him in pretty tight. Speaking of tight, I just make it through the double doors at the south end of the corridor when I hear the doors at the north end clang open. I don't hear my name. I don't look back.

CHAPTER

17

The Railton Campus has a rear entrance that's seldom used because the road is treacherous in winter, winding and full of potholes in all seasons, and because it doesn't go much of anywhere but Allegheny Wells, the hard way, over the mountain. The only other reason to head out that direction is to go to the county's one notorious bar, a roadhouse called The Circle, which sits just outside the city limits and the short arm of Railton law. The Circle offers free pool on Tuesdays, free darts on Wednesdays, wet T-shirt contests on Thursdays, and dances with live country-western bands on Friday and Saturday nights, during which half a dozen fights usually break out in its huge dirt parking lot. If *The Rear View* is to be believed, the occasional knife is pulled out there in the dark, but weapons more lethal than the pointed toe of a cowboy boot are frowned upon. Lose a fight outside The Circle on a weekend night and chances are you've been stomped, not knifed or shot. Saturday morning finds you in the hospital with cracked ribs and mashed cheekbones. You're probably coughing up blood, but you aren't dead. The Circle is one of the Railton area bars that Billy Quigley wishes his daughter Meg would spend less time in, the one I fetched her from earlier in the year.

I'm nearing The Circle when I become aware that I'm being tailgated by a big, shiny, red pickup truck whose driver is honking his horn and making a gesture which, seen in my rearview mirror, may or may not be obscene. My first thought is that the driver of this vehicle is Rachel's husband, Cal, who's found a way to eavesdrop on our intercom conversations and become confused by our conversational intimacy, her sexual harassment lunch. But this is a far better-looking truck than I suspect Cal drives. And besides, it can't very well be Rachel's husband if it's Mr. Purty, and that's who it is, now that I have a chance to look twice. I'm only mildly disappointed. Had I been pulled out of my car and beaten up by a jealous husband who has nothing to be jealous about, I'd be pretty much in the right. Even Bodie Pie's Bitch Gulch crew would be on my side. Maybe even the majority of my own department would sympathize.

I pull into The Circle's lot and park beneath the big sign that announces Friday night's dance, music to be provided by Waylon's Country Cousins. Mr. Purty, a small man, gives an agile hop down from the cab of the truck, adjusts his hearing aid, and flashes me a grin. "What do you think?" he wants to know.

I whistle. "New?"

"Practically. Fifteen thousand miles, is all. Cherry. The dee-lux model. Three-fifty engine. Tow a U-Haul easy. Room for three in the front seat," Mr. Purty explains, "and I didn't pay what's on that sticker either."

"I'm glad to hear it, Mr. Purty," I tell him, noting the price on the sticker. I didn't know used pickups could cost this much. Or new ones, for that matter.

"I chewed him way down from there," he says, unself-consciously.

"You what?"

"Got him to come way down," Mr. Purty explains. "Young kid. Twenties. Played him for two weeks. Every afternoon I come in and look it over, ask him a new question, then leave. Every afternoon, a different question. How many miles to the gallon? You sure it ain't been in an accident? How firm's that price? Then I leave. Next afternoon,

I'm back. Same thing. Finally, he don't know whether to eat shit, chase rabbits, or bark at the moon. He didn't want to give it to me for my price, but he finally had to. Put brand-new tires on it too. Radials, not them recraps."

I study Mr. Purty for a sign that he's made a joke, but nothing. When I'm with him, I often feel like I'm the one who should be wearing a hearing aid. "It's a beauty," I tell him, though I know this isn't the response Mr. Purty is really after. What he really wants is for me to ask him how much below sticker he got the kid to go. Previous conversations with Mr. Purty have revealed that he's a man obsessed with deals, the kind of man who'd rather have something he doesn't really want at a heavy discount than the thing he yearns for at full price. Cheap, is the way my mother sums him up.

"Get in," he says after a beat. "Have a listen to the stereo."

I start to say no, to tell him I'm in kind of a hurry. Despite Julie's propensity for melodrama, her phone call, the more I think about it, has me worried. But I also realize that this means a lot to Mr. Purty, so I go around the passenger side and climb up and in. I'm a tall man with long legs, and even for me it's a pretty good step up. I can't help smiling when I think of my mother, "the aristocat," who will require a helpful hand under her fanny.

Mr. Purty turns the key in the ignition to its auxiliary position and slips a tape into the stereo. Patsy Cline's voice thunders forth from the speakers at a decibel level loud enough to wake Patsy Cline. Mr. Purty lets it stay that way for a few seconds, until he's sure I've had the full benefit of the system. "Good speakers," he says when he's turned the music down so that we can converse. "You're like me, though, I can tell. You don't like your music loud."

I admit that this is true.

"How 'bout your ma?" he wants to know. "I bet she don't like it loud either."

"You do that to her, she'll have you arrested."

I can tell that Mr. Purty takes this warning seriously. Like most of our conversations, the purpose of this one is to allow me the opportunity to give him tips on how to handle my mother. I know her better than he does, is his thinking. What he doesn't quite grasp is the size of the gap between my knowledge and his own. Even if he managed to get the phrase "chewed him down" correct, he'd be surprised to discover that anyone would object to it. He imagines that what his own approach needs is a little fine-tuning. I don't even know how to begin to tell him how wrong he is.

He punches Patsy out of the tape deck, inters her in the special compartment behind the gearshift, slips in another tape. It's Willie Nelson this time, and Willie can't see nothin' but blue skies. "I picked up Patsy for your ma," Mr. Purty explains. "Me, I like Willie. What about your pa?"

"Unless he's changed, he prefers silence."

Mr. Purty shrugs, as if to acknowledge there's no middle ground between those who like music and those who prefer silence.

I smooth my hand over the dash, admire the interior of this truck that Mr. Purty, poor bastard, has purchased to impress my mother. "Pretty spiffy," I say, hoping one more compliment may release me from the cab. Fat chance.

"It's got antibrakes," he explains, pointing at the floor, as if you could tell antilock brakes by looking at the pedal. "Extracab."

I admire the space between the seat and the back of the cab.

"That tark's usually extra," he explains, "but I made the kid give it to me for no charge."

I myself have no idea what a tark might cost because I don't know what a tark is, until I follow Mr. Purty's gaze out the back window and into the bed of the pickup truck, which is covered with a slate gray tarp.

"You think your ma will like it?"

With a tark and antibrakes? How can she not?

"Let's eat breakfast," he suggests, indicating The Circle, which I never would have guessed served food.

"I ate breakfast about four hours ago, Mr. Purty," I tell him, though it occurs to me that I also lost it shortly thereafter. Perhaps because of this, I'm hungry again, and in truth Mr. Purty has cheered me up. The task he has chosen for himself, of wooing my mother with a bright red pickup truck, a Patsy Cline tape, and a string of malapropisms, is ample justification to me for not taking the world too seriously, its relentless heartbreak notwithstanding.

"I like breakfast," Mr. Purty says. "Lots of times I eat it for lunch. Sometimes even dinner. Your ma like breakfast, does she?"

"I've never known her to eat it," I say truthfully.

He nods morosely. Figures. "This place here's got the best scrapple in Pennsylvania," he assures me. "I bet you never even ate scrapple."

"Never," I have to admit.

"Well, come on then," he says wearily, as if he doubts I'll care for the taste, but at least I'll be glad for the experience.

It turns out that scrapple is like a lot of food that's conceptually challenging. That is, better than you might expect. We chew our intestines in silence until Mr. Purty sees me grinning and reads my thought. "I'd never ask your mother to eat scrapple," he assures me.

CHAPTER

18

If possible, Julie and Russell's house looks even more forlorn in the daytime, its incompleteness more pronounced, its windows more darkly vacant, Julie's little Escort more of a contrast, sitting in the double garage large enough to accommodate a couple of minivans and a riding mower. Since the Escort is sitting there by itself, however, I can rule out one of the scrapple-induced scenarios that occurred to me as I drove over the mountain from The Circle and down into the village of Allegheny Wells. I half-expected to see the long drive full of familiar vehicles, including Lily's. Inside, they'd all—friends, relatives, loved ones—be waiting for me, ready to intervene on my behalf. My wife has already done one such intervention with her father, and she may have decided it's time to try one with me. The possibility struck me with such force at the top of the mountain that I pulled off at a scenic overlook to think it through. Up in the cold, rarefied air, it had almost seemed as if Occam's Razor might be applied. An intervention might have explained, sort of, Julie's strange telephone call. And Lily has been insisting for some time that she's not the only one worried about me. Maybe they've all gotten together, I thought. Maybe the duck episode has convinced my loved ones that I need to be reined in.

The trouble with scenic overlooks is that you can't see the details on the ground below, and when I open the car door now and hear last autumn's brittle leaves stirring in the breeze, the sound might be that of William of Occam having a quiet chuckle at my expense. The point of an intervention, after all, is to modify a specific behavior. In Lily's father's case, for instance, his children and grandchildren were trying to prevent him from drinking himself to death, a fairly unambiguous intention he'd all but announced. The charges leveled against him so relentlessly by the gathered clan were all variations on a single theme. Here's how your drinking has affected me, hurt me, humiliated me, angered me. An intervention on behalf of William Henry Devereaux, Jr., would lack this sort of focus. Teddy Barnes would remind me that I don't love Lily enough. My mother would express her disappointment that I've become a clever man. Billy Quigley would regret that I'm a peckerwood, his daughter Meg that I lack the courage to eat a peach. Finny (the man) and Paul Rourke would accuse me of being unprincipled, Dickie Pope of being too idealistic. In other words, I'm a rather vague pain in the collective ass.

I enter my daughter's house through the kitchen, knocking but not waiting for my knock to be acknowledged, the prerogative of a man entering a house that so minutely resembles his own. Once inside I hear Johnny Mathis on the stereo, strong evidence that Julie is the only one home. Russell is a blues man, not the sort of fellow who'd listen willingly to a lyric that included a phrase like "the twelfth of Never," reinforced by weeping violins.

She's in the living room, my daughter, sitting at one end of the long sofa, staring out the patio door in the general direction of the wasps' nest, which, I note, is still attached to the eave. Surely she's heard me come in, but she doesn't get up, or say hello, or even turn. From the doorway I can see that she's still in her bathrobe, though it's now early afternoon. Seen from the shoulders up, with her slender, graceful neck, she could be her mother sitting there.

I go around the sofa and over to the patio door, my eye attracted by movement in the air. And there, under the eave, unbelievably, half a dozen black wasps are hovering about the cone, darting toward the dry, gray parchment, then veering away, as if repelled by an invisible shield.

"They don't learn," Julie says, and when I turn to answer her, I see her left eye, the same one she injured as a child, is swollen almost shut. The eyeball itself, the small part that's visible, is a web of broken blood vessels.

"Julie," I say helplessly, standing there.

"I want him out of the house," she says.

"Russell did this?"

"I've packed a couple suitcases . . ."

"Julie," I say. "Stop a minute. Russell did this?" Am I wrong that the words need to be spoken?

She reacts to my simple question thoughtfully, as if it contains a philosophical dimension I'm unaware of.

"Did Russell hit you, Julie?"

Again, it takes her a long time to formulate a response. "I fell," she says finally.

"You fell."

"He shoved me," she tells me carefully, "and I fell."

Throughout this exchange, Julie has made no move to get up from the sofa, and I have not taken so much as a step toward her. What we're missing, of course, what we need most, is Lily, not so much so we'll know what to do as so we'll know how to feel, to be sure which emotions are valid. There are times when I can read my wife's soul in her face, and in such moments I can almost read my own.

"Where is he now?" it occurs to me to ask.

"I don't know," she says. "Why? Do you want to check out my story?"

I study my daughter, her accusation. In truth, I do not want to believe this about Russell, whom I have always liked and whose part I have occasionally taken, on those rare occasions when I'm permitted to take a part. And in truth I would like to ask more questions, keep asking them, in fact, until I've ruled out the possibility that this is some kind of accident, some misunderstanding. No doubt Julie has intuited this wish and interpreted it as an act of disloyalty, which perhaps it is.

She looks down at her hands. "I want him gone. Out of my house."

I note the pronoun, let it go. We seem to have gotten through some initial stage and arrived at a point where action is called for, the point where I am thought to excel. "Okay," I tell her, "you'd better come over to our place for a day or two, until . . ." I can't quite finish my thought, it seems, because I'm not quite sure what we'll be waiting for. Russell's return? Lily's return? God on a machine? "Why don't you get dressed and pack a suitcase?"

To my surprise, Julie offers no objection, and when she gets to her feet she's suddenly in my arms and sobbing, "Oh, Daddy," over and over. This all happens so quickly that I don't know whether she's come to me or I've gone to her, not that it matters.

While she throws some things in a suitcase, I study the wasps outside the patio door. Julie's right. They don't learn. If this flimsy parchment death trap isn't home, then what the hell is?

There are two cars parked in my drive when Julie and I pull in. One's an anonymous midsize, the other is Paul Rourke's red Camaro. Seated on the top step of my deck, barefoot and wiggling her toes, is a young woman I recognize, after a moment's hesitation, as the second Mrs. R. Julie studies her, then sends an accusing glance my way. At least I assume that's what's going on behind the dark glasses. "Quit," I tell her. "That's a good way to get another black eye."

I again count the cars blocking the entrance to my garage, arriving at the same total—two. Unless the second Mrs. Rourke drove them both, we're short at least one person. Her husband, it occurs to me, may be off in the trees, bringing me into focus in his crosshairs. This thought makes the skin along the back of my neck prickle, even though I know that Occam's Razor cannot be applied to this dramatic scenario. If Paul Rourke is going to shoot me from the woods behind my own house, he doesn't require even one car, much less two, and presumably he wouldn't want to establish the second Mrs. R. at the scene, unless he's got a third Mrs. Rourke in mind, some pretty twenty-year-old in his English lit survey course, perhaps. The second Mrs. R., who's eating a yogurt on my top step, looks like she's got some good miles left on her, though. She's licking her plastic spoon suggestively, it seems to me.

"They're around back," she calls down when Julie and I get out. "Planning their strategy."

"Good for them," I say, confident that no strategy that isn't grounded in chaos theory is likely to work against a man like me. I reach back inside the car and hit the garage door opener so Julie can go inside with her suitcase.

It turns out that "they" is Paul Rourke and Herbert Schonberg, who apparently meant it about tracking me down this afternoon. They come sauntering around the corner of the house, their heads down, their hands in their pockets. Herbert seems to be urgently impressing some point upon his companion, who's neither buying nor selling. They're a pretty odd couple. Normally Herbert and Rourke wouldn't have much use for each other, but these are not normal times.

It's Herbert who makes a show of being glad to see me, hurrying forward, hand extended. "We took a walk in your woods, Hank," he admits. "I hope you don't mind." He's puffing heroically, a small man with a large belly, unused to physical exertion. Rourke, I note, is not breathing hard.

"You're a hard man to corner," Herbert continues, after we've shaken hands. His tone is jovial—no hard feelings about my being so slippery, he seems to be saying.

"I'm not cornered yet, Herbert," I remind him. "You're not parked behind me, I'm parked behind you."

Paul Rourke, who knows me far better than Herbert, and therefore knows that I'm not cornered, doesn't pretend he's glad to see me. When Herbert and I shook hands, he didn't even take his own out of his pockets. Instead he follows Julie into the garage with his eyes. He does not appear to be trying to figure out what's behind the sunglasses, or why my daughter has a suitcase. His gaze is noted by not only the young woman's father but the second Mrs. R., who drops her plastic spoon into her empty yogurt container. "What?" Rourke wants to know, glancing up at her.

"Nothing."

Rourke snorts, as if he's not surprised it's nothing, given the source.

So far he hasn't acknowledged my presence with eye contact, which is fine by me. For years, since the day he threw me up against the wall at the English Christmas party, we've avoided open conflict by not taking each other on directly. If our arena of conflict were a boxing ring, he'd have conceded to me the entire perimeter. I can dance and run and play on the ropes with impunity, like the lightweight coward I am. He has no desire, he lets on, to chase me, an activity that would be undignified for a heavyweight like himself. But if I'm ever foolish enough to venture into the center of the ring, he'll make short work of me, as he has before. This is his public posture, maintained with sly insults and knowing sneers, the occasional taunt. I suspect that his leering after my daughter is a taunt of sorts.

I'm not a coward, but I can play that role. I turn my attention to Herbert, and grin at him all friendly-like. I can take Herbert. One arm tied behind my back.

"We're hoping you'll give us a half hour of your time, Hank. Paulie here has offered the use of his place if that's more convenient."

"Nah," I say. "It's nicer over here."

Rourke's jaw works a little, but that's his only reaction. It's a nice long jab I've got. Sometimes I can nail him from the corner of the ring, sitting atop the turnbuckle.

"Is Lily home?" Herbert wants to know.

My wife's name must have been part of his briefing out there in the woods. "You mean Lila?" I ask.

Herbert, alarmed, glances over at Rourke, who sighs.

"Just kidding," I say. "Some people call her that."

"'Cause this has got to be strictly private," Herbert says, regaining his equilibrium.

"Can I come in?" the second Mrs. R. wants to know, her voice following us inside.

"Maybe she could chat with your daughter awhile?" Herbert suggests.

"They could have a pajama party," Rourke offers.

"Actually, Julie isn't feeling so hot," I tell them.

Occam is waiting impatiently at the kitchen door, beside himself with delight at the prospect of company. If I could be sure it would be Rourke he'd groin, I'd let him go, but I'm not sure, so I grab his collar until we're all inside and let him out to do laps. Then I let the second Mrs. R. in before Occam can charge up the steps and groin her. She immediately settles onto the couch, puts her feet up on the coffee table, and locates the TV remote. "You're right," she says without looking at me, settling in. "It *is* nicer over here."

I direct Herbert and Paul Rourke to the room I use as a study, close the door behind us, and clear off a couple surfaces so they'll have a place to sit.

"Marriage," Rourke remarks, probably in reference to the second Mrs. R.'s comment, "is essentially a ball-busting experience."

"You only say that because my wife isn't around to hear you," I tell him.

"You think that's it?" he wants to know.

"You're tough," I tell him. "But you aren't *that* tough."

Herbert, I can tell, has had enough banter. "Hank," he says, "you're a pretty sharp fella, so my guess is you've figured out we've got a major shit storm brewing. . . ."

He pauses, perhaps to let this sink in, perhaps to see if I'll betray a reaction. I'm not sure what William of Occam would make of this prologue. There's the obvious attempt to flatter, of course. Herbert's willing to concede I'm "sharp," or at least "pretty sharp," on his own scale of dullness. He also knows that my intellectual acuity is hardly the issue, since stupid people are fully capable of listening to rumors.

"I *have* been hearing there's a storm on the way," I admit, intrigued and amused by the fact that both Dickie Pope and the union he's trying to bust have apparently arrived, independently, at the same metaphor. "You're the first to identify the type of precipitation."

Rourke surrenders another of his nasty smirks at this. Having gone on record as saying that I'm never funny, he can't allow himself the luxury of a real smile.

Herbert is also serious, though he hasn't, to my knowledge, weighed in on the subject of whether or not I'm amusing. "What I hope you realize is that this is not a local phenomenon. These aren't isolated showers we're looking at here. It's gonna rain like a son of a bitch, Hank. Forty days and forty nights. That sort of thing."

"You sound like a man that has half ownership of an ark, Herbert," I say.

"I wish to hell I did, Hank. I do wish it. Before this is over, a lot of people are going to wish they had one. You too, maybe."

Rourke is looking out the window like a man who's already found the high ground and has only an academic interest in those below.

"I'm not here to pressure you, Hank," Herbert continues. "It's true I've got a favor to ask you, but it's a small one, and I think you'll agree it's reasonable."

He pauses again here, and if I didn't know better I'd swear he wants me to agree that the favor is reasonable before I've heard what it is.

"We know you've had your meeting with Dickie," Herbert continues significantly.

"Next you'll be telling me the room was bugged."

Herbert looks genuinely pained by this remark. "We don't have to bug anything, Hank. The bastards are advertising what's going on in these meetings. They're letting on that it's all hush-hush, but the thing is, they don't care. That's the scary part. They're that confident. They're watching us scurry around like bugs. Getting a big kick out of it."

"That's a mighty paranoid view," I say.

Rourke gets to his feet. "Herbert," he says. "I told you before. You're wasting your time. This guy's a rogue. He doesn't give a shit. You're asking him to take something seriously, and it's not in him. If he does anything, he'll write the whole thing up as a satire for the Sunday edition. Guess who'll play the part of the fool."

"I'm trying to convince him it's his ass too," Herbert says.

"Don't bother," Rourke says. "When you're gone and I'm gone and Dickie Pope is gone, Hank Devereaux will be the last one left on the payroll. He isn't called Lucky Hank for nothing."

When Herbert looks at me, as if to ascertain whether this could be true, it occurs to me that maybe they're playing good cop–bad cop. Maybe this was the strategy they were working out in the woods.

"Paulie," Herbert says, weighing his words carefully, "I disagree. And if you don't mind, I'd like to finish this conversation with Hank alone."

"I didn't want to come over here to begin with," Rourke reminds him, his hand on the doorknob.

"Help yourself to whatever's in the fridge," I call to him when the door closes behind him. "Mi casa, su casa."

"That man truly loathes you," Herbert says, when he's sure Rourke isn't coming back.

"I don't think so." I smile. "I just give his life focus, that's all." In truth, it's more likely that Herbert loathes me, but I don't say that.

"Look," Herbert says, "I see no reason why the cards shouldn't be faceup on the table. We both know you've had your differences with the union over the years. Pretty much right from the beginning. Is this a fair assessment? Is this a fair thing to say?"

"I've had a few differences with the other guys too," I remind him. "You're not the only ones who think I'm a prick."

He ignores all this. "And I'm not just talking about all these grievances against you," he adds. "I know it runs deeper than that. You think we defend incompetence, promote mediocrity."

"I wish you *would* promote mediocrity," I assure him. "Mediocrity is a reasonable goal for our institution."

Herbert makes a gesture that suggests he doesn't necessarily agree but won't dispute the matter now. "Here's my point, Hank. It's this. There are a number of people who agree with you, but they're on *our* side on this one. Your buddy Paulie is one of them. He also voted no on the union, if you recall."

"The vote was over a decade ago," I remind Herbert. "And I don't recall how he voted because it was a secret ballot."

"He voted no," Herbert says. "So did you. Trust me."

I do trust him on this one matter, though it's a little disconcerting for both of us to remember so clearly what only one of us is supposed to know for sure.

"What I'm saying is, nobody expects you to become a union man. We win this thing and you can go right back to the way you were before. Be a rogue, like Paulie says, if that's what you enjoy. I don't blame you. It's nice to be courted, not to be taken for granted. I understand that."

"Herbert," I start to demur, but he holds up a hand to stop me, as if to suggest that he knows my motives better than I do, so there's no point.

"We'd like you to be on our side because it's the right side and because we could use you. The way you handle yourself on TV, I can see you being our point man on this if you wanted to be. At the very least you could rally your own troops. English has more votes than any other department."

"They never go anywhere in a block, though, Herbert," I assure him.

"This time they might. Hell, I just talked with Teddy and June. When was the last time they ever sided with Paulie and Finny?"

He's watching me carefully now, waiting to see how I'll absorb this news. I realize that the subtext of this discussion is very different from its text. On the surface Herbert wants me to know that I'm indispensable to the cause. Below it, I'm to know that my department and my friends have already aligned themselves against me. I can be point man, or I can cease to exist. It's testimony to Herbert's rhetorical sophistication that text and subtext do not appear to contradict each other. It makes no difference.

But even if I'm not sure how, I suspect it makes a difference. To Herbert. To Dickie Pope. To me. "You said something about a favor, Herbert," I remind him.

He nods slowly. "We'd like to know your intentions, Hank. You decide you'd like to fight the good fight with your friends, we'd love to have you. You decide you want to make friends with Dickie, go. We just need to know who we can count on. Don't be coy, Hank, is what I'm saying."

"What if I say a plague on both your houses?"

This makes Herbert thoughtful again. "A rogue right to the bitter end, eh? You could try that, I suppose. Me? I wouldn't want to be a friendless man right now, but maybe you're different. Personally, I'd think of neutrality as a death wish."

I can't help laughing at this, though apparently I'm the only one who sees the humor. Herbert is wearing an injured expression. "Just tell me one thing, and then I'll go away," he says, struggling to his feet. "What have we done that's so wrong? Could you explain that to me, because I'd like to understand it. What's wrong with decent pay raises every year? What's wrong with demanding a decent standard of living? What's wrong with good faith negotiation? What's wrong with a little security in life? Do you really want those heartless bastards to run roughshod?"

"That's not one thing, Herbert," I remind him. "That's a lot of things."

"I agree," he says, like he's made his point. And maybe he has. "Could I ask you to think about all those things?"

"Sure, Herbert," I tell him, also getting to my feet.

"And could I ask you not to think too long?"

"You could ask."

And that's where we leave it. When we quit the study, there's nobody in the living room. Rourke and the second Mrs. R. are back out on the deck. Occam, the traitor, is lounging happily between them, allowing himself to be scratched by the second Mrs. R. We go out through the sliding glass door and join them. The sun has come out again, and it's a warm spring afternoon.

"The trees have leaves over here," the second Mrs. R. observes, and she's right, there's more green today than yesterday. In another three or four days, the foliage will be full blown.

"Not over on your side?" I ask in mock surprise.

"Lucky Hank," her husband says.

Herbert says he'll be along presently, so Rourke and the second Mrs. R. plod down the steps and get into Rourke's Camaro. When both car doors close, Herbert says, "I'm hopeful, Hank. I mean it. I just don't see you playing ball with the likes of Dickie Pope. I don't think you see it either."

I don't know what makes me concede even this much to Herbert, but I do. "It's true I'm not fond of Dickie."

Herbert offers to shake hands on that note, and while there may be reasons not to, they don't seem sufficient at this moment in time.

"Me?" Herbert says. "I got a year and a half till retirement. The worst they can do to me isn't all that bad."

He sounds oddly sincere in this, sincere perhaps for the first time today.

"This hasn't been such a bad place for me," he admits. "I've been decently paid. I've been treated well, all things considered. I wouldn't mind giving something back to the institution. If I could piss on that little prick's grave, I'd consider it my gift to higher education."

I can sympathize with this sentiment too, on several levels. I'd dearly love to take a good piss on someone's grave, and I don't really care whose. My groin is throbbing with pent-up desire.

"You realize, don't you, that all these grievances against you could just disappear?" Herbert says. Like his cynical blood brother, Dickie Pope, he has to offer an incentive. He knows better, but he can't help himself.

I can't help myself either. I look him right in the eye. "What griev-ances?" I say.

Herbert, who does not have a great sense of humor, laughs all the way down the steps. His car door closes on the sound, but I can see he's still chuckling as he turns the key in the ignition and backs out around my car. He's wedged in pretty good, so it takes him half a dozen tries before he's able to extract himself. I offer to move the Lincoln, but Herbert declines. He wants to show me he can do this without my help. The symbolism is not lost on me. Even Occam, who watches nervously from the deck, where I've got him by the collar, seems to understand it.

When Herbert and Paul Rourke and the second Mrs. R. have all disappeared among the trees, I feel pretty good. I know what they came for, and I know they left without it. Which means I'm still at large, still slippery.

But for pure joy I can't hold a candle to my dog, and when I let him go he does a dozen victory laps around the perimeter of the deck, the world's smallest dog track, his nails clicking on the wood. It's imagina-tion, I know, that propels him. In Occam's imagination he's not the only dog doing laps on our deck. He's just the fastest dog, the smartest dog, the bravest dog.

"I know you are," I assure him when his race is run and he sits panting before me, exhausted, pleased, optimistic about the future, about other races he will win.

I am about to confide a few other things to my dog when I remem-ber that Julie is inside. In fact, it may be her gaze upon me that causes my daughter to return so forcefully to my consciousness. When I look up at the window of the room Lily uses as her study, I see Julie framed there under the eaves. I give her an embarrassed wave and point to my car to let her know I'm leaving again. When she doesn't respond, I realize she's on the phone, perhaps not looking at me at all. Her expres-sion is complex, not easily read, but in it I can imagine Lucky Hank's luck heading south.

When I stop by the office on my way to class, I discover that Lily has called just minutes before and left a number for me to call her back. According to Rachel, who's handed me a sheaf of pink message slips, half a dozen other people want to talk to me too. "And that red-haired boy's been lurking outside your office again?" she informs me. In general, students are not encouraged to loiter inside the English department office, where they are likely to overhear things that will reveal how much their professors dislike each other, but Leo is the only student strictly prohibited from doing so. His intense presence particularly unnerves Rachel. "Every time I look up, he's watching me with this look on his face? Like he's got X-ray vision?" she confessed to me back in January. "I feel like I'm sitting here in my underwear?" "I'd be very surprised if you were wearing even that much in Leo's imagination."

"Also, Finny's been coming in every fifteen minutes to see if you've returned?"

"This is the true nature of power in academe," I tell Rachel sadly, having taken her warnings to heart and preparing to duck out again. "Those who have any at all have to use the back stairs."

It's only ten minutes until my class, but I take the elevator down to the basement, where there's a recreation room lit by a regiment of soda and juice machines lined up against the far wall. There's also an old-fashioned telephone booth, the kind you can enter and close the folding door behind you. This I do, despite the robust bouquet of undergraduate urine inside. I use my calling card. Lily picks up on the first ring.

"Hank," she says, sounding so weary and melancholy that I wonder if her interview has gone badly, until it occurs to me that it must have been Lily that I saw Julie talking on the phone with as I left. "It feels like a week."

"My thought exactly," I confess, and that's not all I'm thinking. Because it's both wonderful and oddly sad to hear the familiar voice of this woman who shares my life, to feel how much I've missed it. By what magic does she softly say my name and in so doing restore me to myself? More important, why am I so often ungrateful for this gift? Is it because her magic also dispels magic? Is it because her voice, even disembodied as it is now, renders lunatic the fantasies that have been visiting me of late? "Lily . . . ," I say, allowing my voice to trail off and wondering if, when I say her name, it has for my wife any of these same magical properties.

"Where on earth are you?" Lily wants to know, apparently puzzling over a different vocal mystery altogether. "Your voice sounds funny."

I explain that I'm hiding from Finny in a phone booth in the basement of Modern Languages. It's a measure of how long she's been married to an academic that Lily sees nothing unusual about this.

"Your cold is back," she remarks.

"Nah," I say, though of course it is, as predicted, even though I took another twelve-hour antihistamine before leaving the house this morning.

"I talked to Julie earlier," she says. "I guess I picked a bad time to leave, didn't I?"

"I don't know what to make of it yet," I tell her. "I haven't seen Russell."

"It's been brewing for some time," she says.

"It has?"

"Yes, Hank, it has," she says, the remark trailing accusation.

"Why didn't I know it?"

A pause. "I don't know, Hank. Why *don't* you know these things?"

"Because I don't want to? Is that what you're saying?"

"No," my wife says gently, perhaps even affectionately. "Just that you depend on me to know them. Anyway. I'm less worried about Julie than about her father."

"I gather you saw me on television."

"Yes, this morning."

"I've become a hero in certain quarters," I tell her. "Not to Dickie Pope. And of course Rourke still insists my whole act needs work."

"I wish . . . ," she says, but now it's her turn to let her voice trail away.

"What?" I say. "Go ahead."

"I wish you'd just request a leave of absence. Or even resign, if that's what you want. You'll have to do something worse before they'll fire you, and I don't want you to do anything worse."

"You think I'm trying to get myself fired?"

"Aren't you?"

I consider the possibility. "What I want may be a moot point. Dickie told me this morning there's likely to be a twenty percent reduction in staff in the fall."

"Then the rumors are true."

"My colleagues are eager to believe I've sold them out."

"Have you reassured them you didn't?"

"You know the English department. They'll believe what they want."

"No, Hank. The majority will believe *you,* if you tell them. If you tell them straight."

"I promised Dickie I wouldn't decide anything until I'd talked the whole thing over with you. He insisted. The last thing he said to me was, 'Talk it over with Lila.' So tell me, Lila, when are you coming back?"

"Tuesday, I think."

"I thought Monday."

"Me too. I had to postpone the interview."

"How come?"

"Look, Hank, there's . . . a problem here in Philly," she says. And as soon as she says this, I know that it's something real and serious, something she's been sitting on while we talked about academic matters. "How about if we talk tonight?" she suggests. "Aren't you supposed to be in class?"

I consult my watch and see that class is, at this moment, starting without me.

"Angelo?" I say, remembering that I've not been able to reach her father when I've called.

"Yes."

"Is he okay?" Dumb question. It's been a long time since Angelo could be described as okay. Most likely he's tumbled hard off the wagon.

"Yes and no." Her voice is flat now. I'm to understand that it will do me no good to ask further questions. "Did you remember to visit my class this morning?"

I tell her I did. "Guido wanted to know how much money I made from *Off the Road*."

"Poor Guido."

"Poor Guido extorts lunch money off skinny white kids," I tell her, adding, for good measure, "Your husband *was* a skinny white kid once. Bullies used to take *my* lunch money, you know."

"God, I wish you were here, Hank. You just made me smile for the first time in twenty-four hours."

"I used to make you laugh," I recall. "Out loud. Uncontrollably."

"Not uncontrollably," she corrects me.

"Well," I concede. "Maybe not uncontrollably."

"We had more energy then," my wife reminds me. "For laughter. For most things. Plus everything was newer."

"Do you ever wish things were new again?"

"Sometimes," she admits. "Not often."

"Sweet-talker."

When I hang up, I notice a shadowy human movement on the glass of the phone booth door. I see it's Leo, who's apparently observed me sneaking out of the department and followed me into the basement. For all I know he's been standing next to the phone booth for the whole conversation. Right now, he's so close that he has to step back when I open the door. I study him and wonder if it can really be youth I've been regretting the loss of. Leo's got a manuscript in hand, and there's a tremor in his voice that's part excitement and, more strangely, part rage. He can't quite keep his hands still. The way he's holding the pages out to me suggests that one end is on fire, the end he wants me to grab. What I'd like to grab and ring is Leo's long, gooselike neck.

"Great news," he tells me, and I half-expect him to report that Solange, the young woman who eviscerated him in workshop, has been hit by a truck. But the truth, as always, is even stranger. "I've had a story accepted," he says. "For publication."

CHAPTER

20

Attendance is always sparse on Friday afternoons, especially so near the end of the term when the topic is persuasion. So far, I haven't persuaded my freshmen that the ability to persuade is an important skill. Even Blair, my best student, a pale young woman I've been trying all term to coax into confident utterance, seems to doubt the whole enterprise. This particular group of students, like so many these days, seems divided, unequally, between the vocal clueless and the quietly pensive. Somehow, Blair and others like her have concluded that what's most important in all educational settings is to avoid the ridicule of the less gifted. Silence is one way of avoiding it. If I could teach Blair how to become invisible, she'd be interested, but she doesn't want to argue with anybody, and who can blame her? Students like Blair have learned from their professors that persuasion—reasoned argument— no longer holds a favored position in university life. If their professors—feminists, Marxists, historicists, assorted other theorists—belong to suspicious, gated intellectual communities that are less interested in talking to each other than in staking out territory and furthering agendas, then why learn to debate? Despite having endured endless faculty meetings, I can't remember the last time anyone changed his (or her!) mind as a result of reasoned discourse. Anyone who observed us would conclude the purpose of all academic discussion was to provide the grounds for becoming further entrenched in our original positions.

Or perhaps I'm just the wrong person for the job of teaching persuasive techniques. After all, the list of people I myself have failed to persuade recently is pretty impressive. It contains Dickie Pope, Herbert Schonberg, Paul Rourke, Gracie, and Finny (both the man and the goose). I haven't even been able to persuade Leo to temper his excitement at having had a story accepted for publication by a "prestigious anthology" of new American student writing. It's an old scam. Accept the student story or poem for publication, convince the writer to pay production costs, then sell the anthology to proud relatives at extortionary cost. Leo's eyes narrowed suspiciously when I explained how the scam worked, his angry validation morphing to indignant suspicion. Of me. Neither have I been able to convince Leo that he should write a story with no violence in it, a suggestion that's got him plotting, I suspect, the next chapter of his novel, the one where his murderous ghost pays a visit to his old writing teacher. I've read this chapter before, though Leo hasn't written it yet.

With ten minutes left in class, which (thanks to Leo) started fifteen minutes late, my worst student, who's only present today because I threatened to flunk him for the term if he missed another class, leans back in his chair and says, apropos of nothing, "So. Like, are you going to kill a duck, or what?"

Bad students are almost always inspiring students. Most often they inspire despair, but occasionally they'll inspire an assignment. "You tell me, Bobo," I say. Bobo is not the student's name but rather my name for him. "By Monday, in fact. I want from each of you a cogent, persuasive essay. There are two possible theses. Either I should or I should not kill a duck. Don't straddle the fence by suggesting that I maim a duck or pluck a duck."

As I explain the assignment, there's a communal groan, but I'm cheered by the fact that more hostile glances are thrown in Bobo's direction than in my own. Bobo has assumed the posture of a man who should have known better, who *did* know better, in fact, and was the victim of a spasm. His fellow students all seem to understand that they were minutes away from a rare weekend without a writing assignment.

"By *Monday*?" Bobo says, incredulous.

"I've threatened to kill a duck by Monday, Bobo," I remind him. "By Tuesday I won't need your advice."

"Typed?" someone wants to know.

On the way back to the office I skirt the pond, which has returned to its placid aspect, the demonstrators who earlier linked arms against me having all gone home with the TV crews, leaving the fowl unguarded for the weekend. A single STOP THE SLAUGHTER placard has been planted in the bank to ward off evil. Ineffectually, for here I am, able if not ready to wreak mayhem. I notice Finny (the goose, not the man) some fifty yards farther along the bank, and something about his appearance strikes me as curious. When I get a little closer I see what it is. Finny has been fitted with a foam neck brace, like a whiplash victim. He eyes me curiously as I approach, as if he fears I'll make a bad joke at his expense. Animals, I am convinced, are as adamant as humans about maintaining their dignity, and Finny seems to be struggling to maintain his. A cartoon goose in a turtleneck, he cannot quite meet my eye. "Finny," I say, checking to make sure Leo isn't lurking nearby to hear this second conversation with a goose. "Qué pasa?"

A noise issues forth from deep inside Finny, not a sound I've come to associate with this particular goose. It's higher and thinner, a lament. Isn't this a fine state of affairs? he seems to say. Who am I to disagree? There's a bench nearby, so I sit for a few minutes and listen to Finny elaborate until I'm visited by a sneezing fit, the suddenness and violence of which frightens us both.

When I return to the office, Teddy and June Barnes are hanging around the department, pretending to have business, an act I'm not buying this late on a Friday afternoon. Apparently I look suspicious too, at least to Teddy and June and Rachel, who are staring at me with alarm. "Have you been crying?" June wants to know.

"Don't be absurd," I tell her. "I've been talking to a goose."

"Your eyes are slits," Teddy says.

"Maybe I'm allergic," I say. The worst of my cold symptoms have, as predicted, come crashing down on me like Dickie's tidal wave. It's not an easy thing for a man like me to live for twenty-five years with a woman who unerringly predicts illness, whose favorite observation is that she knows me better than I know myself, and who never seems to want for ready evidence. A man like me, who gravitates so naturally to omniscient storytelling, probably should not be married to an oracle. He'll spend all his time trying to prove the oracle wrong, an uphill battle. Ask Oedipus. Ask Macbeth. Ask Thurber. And this role can't have been all that pleasant for Lily either. Oracles must grow tired of talking to people who never listen (Ask Cassandra. Ask Oprah), especially the ones who flirt with omniscience.

When I let myself into my inner office, Teddy and June follow before I can close the door behind me. "We have to talk," Teddy says when I finish blowing my nose and wiping my eyes. He takes a seat in the only chair, other than my own, that I keep in my office.

"Monday," I tell him. I can feel my eyes closing, blindness coming on. Oedipus at Colonus. Thurber in Manhattan. Already I'm watching Teddy and June in letterbox format.

When Teddy notices that June has nowhere to sit, he leaps to his feet to offer her his chair. His reward for this anachronistic gesture is predictable contempt. How long have you been married to this woman? I'd like to ask him. I may be blind, but even I know better. I put my feet up.

"This won't wait till Monday," June says. "You may not have noticed, but we're in full-blown crisis mode here. Everybody knows about your conference with Herbert. Finny's telling people you've cut a deal with the administration. By Monday, you'll be recalled as chair."

There's a knock, and Rachel pokes her head in. "Sorry?" she says, this lovely woman whose sense of timing could bring a man like me to dramatic climax. "Can I interrupt?"

"Rachel?" I say, as if I can't be sure it's her I'm seeing through my slits. "Is that you?"

"I just wanted to tell you I'm heading home?"

"Already?" I say, my usual line. I consult my watch and see that she should have left half an hour ago. "Come sit on my lap. I want to hear all about your sexual harassment lunch."

This proves too much for June, as I hoped it would. "Talk to this asshole," she tells her husband. "Tell him how few friends he has left."

Rachel, alarmed by the use of the word *asshole* among people who boast so many advanced degrees, steps back from the doorway to let June pass and jumps again when the outer door to the English department slams hard enough to rattle the glass.

"I *really* have to go?" she pleads, placing mail and messages before me, apologetically.

"I'm not worthy of you, Rachel," I tell her, and halfway into a joke I find I haven't the heart to finish.

"I'll see you Monday?" she says, glancing warily at Teddy and then back at me. "Could we have lunch, maybe? Talk about my stories?"

"Make a reservation," I tell her. "Someplace nice. There's about a hundred dollars left in the department's general fund. We'll see if we can spend it."

When she's gone, Teddy says, "You're *trying* to get recalled, aren't you?"

"I've been trying all year, pal," I say, thumbing through my mail. "It's about time somebody noticed."

When I suffer another sneezing fit, Teddy takes pity on me. "Okay," he says. "Sunday afternoon. Council of war. And we're going to be way behind. Finny's been on the phone all afternoon. He's got everybody all worked up."

"They believe Finny?" I say. It's a silly question, of course. My colleagues are academics. They indulge paranoid fantasies for the same reason dogs lick their own testicles. "They believe a man who'd kill a duck for them would turn around and sell them out?"

"They don't believe you'd kill a duck, Hank," Teddy says. "You're going to have to get on the phone and convince the few that will listen. The department operating paper requires a two-thirds majority, and Finny thinks he's got several votes to spare. June thinks he's right."

"Then he is," I concede. After all, nobody in the department counts better than June, who predicted her own husband's fall from grace by one vote a year ago. "Let's save ourselves the effort."

"This is crazy," Teddy says. "We've come up with eleventh-hour strategies before. We've made careers out of thwarting Finny."

"True, but it's not much of an ambition," I feel compelled to point out.

"Losing to him would be better?"

"The sad, fucking truth, Teddy, is that it probably matters far less than either of us imagines."

Even as I say this, however, I know it makes a difference. If Finny can manage my ouster as chair, he could well end up advising Dickie Pope, as Dickie himself warned me. And I know I'd be on Finny's list.

I glance around my office to ascertain whether there is anything within these walls that I might miss. The man sitting across from me has missed this office, is missing it still, even though it's now occupied by a friend, so I suppose it's possible that I could miss it too, especially if it were occupied by an enemy. In truth I have enjoyed making mischief from this chair, and while I remain confident of my ability to stir things up from any position on the game board, I'm not sure I'd be able to goad Gracie into mutilating me on a more level playing field. No, if I lose this chair, I will have peaked. My short tenure as chair—I smile to think of it—will be remembered as rule by exasperation. A decade from now, our young colleagues yet to be hired will be stunned to learn that William Henry Devereaux, Jr., was ever chair, however briefly. Teddy, who can't tell a story, will be the historian who tells mine. Remember the day Hank Devereaux got Gracie to gig him through the nose with her spiral notebook ring? Or. Remember the day Hank went on TV and threatened to kill a duck a day until he got a budget? Ineptly as he'll tell these stories, everyone will laugh except Paul Rourke, true to his promise. And me. If I'm still unlucky enough to be wandering these halls, I suspect I won't be laughing.

Back home, I find Julie is asleep on the bed in the guest room, and I'm glad, because in truth I look like hell, both eyes swollen almost completely shut. In the kitchen I take a couple antihistamines and decide to go to bed myself. I'm too exhausted even to stop in the bathroom to pee. The message light on the answering machine is blinking. I'm pretty sure I don't want my messages, but I hit play anyway and am rewarded by a split-second rewind, probably a hang-up. But then I hear a voice I recognize as Billy Quigley's. "You Judas Peckerwood" is his message in its entirety.

Upstairs, I lie down, allow my eyes to close. Judas Peckerwood, I say aloud. In my head I've been composing mental lists ever since I left

Dickie Pope's office, so maybe it's not unfair for Billy Quigley and the others to have leapt to the conclusion that I have betrayed them. Getting rid of the worst of our teachers isn't such a bad idea. There's no excuse for Finny, and his name belongs right at the top of the first mental list I composed. The trouble is that using bad teaching as a criterion would require that I follow Finny's name on the list rather closely with Teddy Barnes's and those of one or two other people I'm fond of. Other criteria are similarly problematic. We could ax those people who have never published a word or given a paper or attended a conference. Who have, as it were, no academic pulse. Such a net would again gather up Finny but also Billy Quigley and several other exhausted ex–high school teachers with M.A.'s, recruited thirty years ago, when the campus expanded. Try as I might, I can't come up with a single criterion, or even a cluster of two or three criteria, that would sacrifice the right people.

Which no doubt suggests something about the task itself. That I've allowed myself to engage in the exercise, even as an exercise, must mean something, though I'm too tired and sick to feel guilty. So here's the question. If it's not guilt, why does the name Judas Peckerwood keep appearing on list after mental list?

Part Two

JUDAS PECKERWOOD

What I had not foreseen

Was the gradual day

Weakening the will

Leaking the brightness away

—Stephen Spender

Since this newspaper printed the story of Lucky Hank's first dog some weeks ago, its author has received three or four times the usual amount of mail (the exact numbers I leave to the reader's imagination), most of it wanting to know more about my father, William Henry Devereaux, Sr., whom I left with blistered hands, standing knee deep in a just-dug grave, wearing ruined chinos and loafers, about to bury a dog I'd managed to kill about two minutes after my father brought him home. My mother, who is well-known to readers of this newspaper (her columns generate far more mail than mine), objected to the story as I told it, claiming that the portrait of my father was unflattering, unfair, and unkind, but the response of other readers suggests the opposite. Their hearts went out instinctively to the father in the story. Several readers shared with me stories of their own valiant attempts to please their own stubborn, ungrateful children. They felt bad for my father and wondered if there was any news of him. They wondered if I had any more stories I could tell about William Henry Devereaux, Sr., stories that

*would be more about him and less about me. And so, I pick up my
father's story where I left off.*

Not long after the dog was buried, my father was made two attractive offers. The first was a full professorship from Columbia University,
which he accepted. As I mentioned before, by this time my father was
already a very famous scholar, and he was apparently weary of all the distinguished visiting professor gigs that were the texture of my childhood
and early adolescence. He may have felt it was time to settle down, as my
mother had for some time been suggesting. The second attractive offer
came from a young woman graduate student from his D. H. Lawrence
seminar, and it was with her that he settled down in New York.

The Columbia deal was sweet. The university offered him a luxuri-
ous apartment within easy walking distance of the campus and partially
subsidized it for him. His salary, for the late sixties, was unheard of, and
in return for it, he was required to do relatively little in the classroom.
He was the nominal editor of a prestigious scholarly magazine, as well as
director of a special collection in the library, but he was also assigned a
research assistant, who attended to many of his duties, including the
grading of papers in the one undergraduate class he taught each year.
Papers from the tiny graduate seminar he graded himself. That is, he
placed a letter grade on them and for all anyone knew may even have
read them. He had written five distinguished books of literary criticism,
one of which, dealing with politics and the novel, had become wildly
popular in the way that an occasional scholarly book on a fashionable
subject will catch on. Everyone buys it, displays it, discusses it, without
finding the time to actually read it. His real job at Columbia was to continue writing such books, to thank the university profusely for its encouragement, and to ensure that all subsequent editions of books he had
written elsewhere would make mention of the fact that he now held a
prestigious named chair at Columbia.

Still, even though teaching was not a significant part of his responsibilities in his new position, the university must have been surprised, given
its modest expectations, to learn upon his arrival that my father was
unable to perform. I know my father was surprised. What befell him was
unprecedented. He arrived at his first class in September, read the names
of his students off his roster, opened his mouth to begin a lecture he had
delivered half a dozen times before, only to discover that his mind was

completely blank, that he was unable to speak so much as a pertinent syllable. He was not confused about what he wanted to say, nor had he forgotten how he'd meant to begin, or the lecture's key details. His mind was simply voided, as if the thoughts in his head were composed of iron filings and he was standing too close to a magnet. He scanned the expectant faces before him and felt complete panic descend upon him. He had all he could do to find the words to excuse himself for a moment and duck out into the hall for a drink at the water fountain, his throat having become a valley of cinders. There in the dark hallway my father's entire lecture returned to him intact, but the panic did not dissipate, so he found a nearby men's room and drew a brown paper towel from the wall dispenser. On this dubious parchment he wrote out in longhand the first two sentences of his lecture as a hedge against repetition of the strangest event of his life, and then he returned to his classroom, not without misgivings for all his sensible precaution. There behind the lectern he unfolded his paper towel and opened his mouth to begin, only to discover that the words, the very letters the words were composed of, had become scrambled. They swam before him merrily, rearranging themselves for his entertainment. This quickly, all understanding had fled. He couldn't have identified the letter B *for a free trip to* Sesame Street, *this despite the fact that he had written a long chapter on that program for his book on pop culture. A new wave of panic crashed over him, and he knew there was nothing to do but plead illness, cancel class, tell students to return on Thursday, at which time he hoped to be himself.*

Word of this incident traveled, as academic gossip always does, at warp speed. It had been an early afternoon class, and by late afternoon everyone on the faculty seemed to have heard of William Henry Devereaux's strange paralysis at the lectern. And, as is the case with most academic gossip, most of the facts had gotten skewed. My father's colleagues seemed confused by the fact that he was able to communicate with them in the hallways. At a department cocktail party that evening they were amazed to find him not only present but charming and eloquent on the subject of his bizarre dysfunction, turning his still fresh humiliation into a comic set piece in which he described everything swimming before his eyes, words suddenly devoid of meaning, letters of phonic significance. It was as if, he explained, he had been transported back through time to a point before the invention of written language. He had a memory of what it was and how it worked, but it all seemed rather foolish. My father's colleagues laughed appreciatively at his recounting of the event, but he could tell that they were horrified, that what he was detailing for them was their worst nightmare come to life. Unable to talk? A failure of discourse? A confession of sexual impotence could not have struck them more forcefully, and the fact that my father was able to make light of such a circumstance elevated him, if possible, in their estimation. To be so brilliant, and yet be unable to speak. This was the stuff of classical tragedy. How wonderful that he was able to come back from hell and tell them about it. What good luck it was that his affliction was confined, apparently, to the classroom, that it did not bleed over into faculty cocktail parties.

Of course, the reason that my father was able to be glib and entertaining regarding his affliction was that he was convinced he'd seen the last of it. In truth he had been terrified to attend the cocktail party, afraid that he would be struck dumb there as well. What a relief to discover that his verbal acuity had not deserted him in the company of his colleagues. He had feared that his paralysis might be a manifestation of stage fright associated with the fact that he had a new job, his first in over a decade where he was expected to stay on for more than a year or two. The cocktail party suggested this was not the case, since this was the more difficult venue, and his performance here was more demanding, a poor performance judged more harshly than a botched lecture in an undergraduate classroom. Actually, he hadn't even botched the lecture. He'd simply been unable to deliver it. No matter. He would deliver it Thursday. For the experience he was richer by one story, not poorer.

Except that when Thursday arrived and my father returned to class and took roll, he felt, as soon as his voice fell on the last syllable of Miss Wainwright's name, the blind panic descend, and once again the words and letters began to rearrange themselves playfully on the page before him. Abandoning his lecture notes, he returned to the roster of his students' names. There, moments before, the letters had made sense, but now these too were scrambled. He knew that the last name in the column was the name of Miss Wainwright, and with difficulty he located the bottom of the column. Did these letters spell Wainwright? How were you supposed to tell? He looked up and located Miss Wainwright without difficulty. He studied her nose first, then an ear. This last thing—this ear—was it too a letter of the alphabet? He couldn't remember. If you put it together with *a nose, did it make a word? Did it spell* Wainwright? *Couldn't be. In that case every student in the class would be named Wainwright. It was all too much. He felt his knees buckle, and he had to be helped from the lectern to an empty chair next to Miss Wainwright. He couldn't stop looking at her nose. "Wainwright," he cooed at it.*

After this second occurrence, his affliction was no joke. My father wrote out all his lectures in advance and came to class prepared to deliver them, but once he'd read the roll, the same thing happened, and when it did he turned the lectern over to his research assistant, who then read the lecture while my father waited in the hall, sick with fear and humiliation. Out there by the door he could hear the manner in which the lecture was read, the vacillating timbre and skewed emphasis of the words as they came out of his assistant's throat, and he understood more poignantly than ever before the difference between delivering information and teaching. Worse, separated from his authoritative personality, his observations— even the ones he was most proud of—seemed not . . . terribly profound.

This circumstance could not go on, and he knew it. He'd have to resign. He'd have to explain the whole humiliating mess to the dean. The worst part of it was that he'd be able to. He had no trouble talking to deans. It was students he couldn't talk to.

This continued through the rest of September and most of October, until one day my father made a discovery that astonished him. Entering the classroom from the hallway, he started talking. Actually, he started in the hallway, where things always made sense. He began his sentence out there with his hand on the doorknob, then just continued as he entered. The class was on Dickens, a writer my father particularly despised for his sentimentality and lack of dramatic subtlety, and never did a scholar lay more complete waste to a dead writer than my father to Charles Dickens that day. Never was intellectual contempt more coolly disguised behind a thin veneer of urbane wit than that afternoon. As he talked, my father gained confidence from his own strong voice. He had given the same lecture before, but never like this. In a fit of unplanned dramatic ecstasy, he read Jo's death scene from Bleak House *to such devastating comic effect that by the time he'd finished the entire class was on the floor. Then they got up off the floor and gave him a standing ovation. This was what they'd paid their money for. Finally, they felt themselves to be in the presence of greatness, as they slammed* Bleak House *shut with contempt.*

*News that my father had at last spoken in the classroom and received
a standing ovation swept through the department, whose patience with
him, truth be told, was beginning to wear a little thin. They'd hired what
they imagined to be a cleanup hitter, only to discover that he lacked even
the warning-track power of all their other hitters. Why hadn't somebody
demanded a physical? It was one thing to be an uninspiring teacher, even
a downright piss poor teacher, but you couldn't be a mute, even if you
were William Henry Devereaux, Sr.*

*A few members of the department were secretly disappointed to learn
that their distinguished colleague had hit the long ball at last, and envious too, because the Dickens lecture was being discussed everywhere, as
if it were the only one that mattered, as if no one else had given an important lecture at Columbia in the last decade. And they were disappointed
as well that they would no longer be able to raise a skeptical eyebrow at
each other when my father appeared in the office to gather his mail. (My
father required two large boxes to accommodate the volume of corre-
spondence he received from readers and other scholars seeking his advice.) You could tell just by observing my father's stride that William
Henry Devereaux, Sr., was back. After the Dickens lecture he looked like
a new man. He looked like a man who'd just gotten laid by twins.*

*His altered appearance notwithstanding, my father was not con-
vinced his trials were over, and the next class after the famous* Bleak
House *lecture proved they weren't. Halfway through the roll call he felt
the now familiar creeping dread coming on, and so he excused himself in
the middle of the* M*'s, went outside into the hall, and spoke the first few
words of his lecture out there, reentering when he had made his beginning. Today's lecture was on* David Copperfield. *Out in the hall, his
hand on the knob, my father said, "Dickens didn't care, you see . . . ," and
then he turned the knob and reentered the classroom. ". . . about the
working conditions of the poor.* David Copperfield *doesn't object to children working in dark, squalid, unhealthy factories. What seems wrong to
David is that such a situation should befall himself, a bright, sensitive
child. Dickens's hero was no crusader after social justice, and neither was
his creator, though he didn't object when he was confused with such cru-
saders." And he was off. My father focused on a point midway up the tall
seminar-room windows, considerably above the heads of even his tallest
students, trusting that, from where they were sitting, he would appear to*

be looking not so much "up" as "back," into nineteenth-century London. From the depths of the blacking factory where David Copperfield was employed, my father could hardly be expected to notice a twentieth-century hand raised in question or objection.

As my father talked, he was full of inner marveling that the remedy to his affliction should be so simple, that it could have evaded him for so long. All he needed to do was not take roll or stare directly at the expectant faces of his students. Miss Wainwright had dropped the class the same day he cooed at her nose, and he felt bad about that, but he was back and functioning, and that was the important thing. William Henry Devereaux, Sr., was back.

There.

I hope the above will satisfy my readers' curiosity about the doings of William Henry Devereaux, Sr., subsequent to the events of my last column. It is, I'm sure everyone will agree, a happier story than the last, which had a dead dog in it and which caused more than one reader of this newspaper to stop and consider the whole issue of mortality, never a pleasant thing to do. The above tale is more optimistic in every way, and I hope readers of this column will take heart from the understanding that even complex problems like the one faced by my father often have simple solutions if we keep our minds open. An open mind, I need not remind readers, is the key to a successful university life, and may even have indirect applications to those living and working outside the Academy.

CHAPTER

21

When the telephone rings early Monday morning, I decide to let Julie answer it. She's been on the phone all weekend, so it's probably for her. I've not wanted to listen in on her conversations, so I don't really know who she's been talking to or what she's been saying. But I'm pretty sure she hasn't made any of the phone calls she *should* make. She hasn't called a realtor, for instance, to put their house on the market. And I don't think she's talked to Russell, though in fairness that may be because she doesn't know where he is. What she seems to have done is talk *about* Russell, to everyone she knows. "It's called a support system, Daddy," she explained yesterday afternoon. "When bad things happen, it's not smart to try to be the Lone Ranger."

"Well, sure," I concede. "A Tonto or two, but . . ."

But my daughter belongs to a talk show generation that seems to be losing the ability to discriminate between public and private woes. She sees no reason she shouldn't tell her friends about her marriage, even encourage them to take sides, pass judgment. It's not even the knee-jerk confession mode that worries me most. It's my daughter's fear of silence and solitude that seems unnatural. If she weren't talking to her friends, she might be listening to other voices in her own head, voices she might benefit from hearing out. Instead, she telephones. When she runs out of people to call, she opts for electronic company, the television in one room, the stereo in the next. She may even consider these part of her support group, for all I know.

I know without looking that the large suitcase she's brought with her, which contains what she imagined she'd need to survive a weekend at her parents' house, does not contain a single book. My daughter has never found a moment's comfort in a book, and this provokes in me a complex reaction. She has done, without apparent thought or effort, what I myself once intended to do. The offspring of two bookish parents, I made up my mind as a boy that I would be as unlike them as I could. I was determined not, as an adult, to look up from a book with that confused, abstracted, disappointed expression that my parents shared when jolted out of book life into real life. I may even have thought that becoming a *writer* of books would be a kind of ironic revenge on people like my parents. *They'd* be taken in by my tale spinning, whereas I would not. I'd know how the dream was made, how the trick was done, and so it would have no power over me. The joke, of course, was on me. For three years during the writing of *Off the Road* I lived between worlds, not really in either, perhaps to the detriment of both. My father read the book in the hospital the night before he was to have a kidney stone surgically removed, and he confessed afterward that my novel had not distracted him as thoroughly as he might have wished. He kept noting how it was put together, he said. At the time I was wounded, although now, at nearly fifty, I realize how a stone can focus a man's attention, how it may even diminish the power of literature.

This morning, like every morning for a week, I have awakened needing urgently to pee. There's no use denying it. I have inherited from my father most of what I had hoped to avoid. When all is said and done, I'm an English professor, like my father. The most striking difference between him and me is that he's been a successful one. Karen, our older daughter, is another apple that hasn't fallen far from the tree of academic knowledge. She tried a few nonacademic things after college, but then suddenly she decided to go back to graduate school, where she's recently concluded both her dissertation, on Matthew Arnold, and an unwise affair with her dissertation director, though I learned of this only recently, the same way I learn so many things. From Lily. After the fact.

No, it's Julie who's the wonder. A child who's made good on her childhood oath not to become a fool of books. *People* magazine perhaps, but not *Moby-Dick*. Her ambition I understand, but how has she been able to pull it off? Also, why isn't she picking up the ringing phone?

I almost recognize the voice on the other end of the line when it asks for Dr. Devereaux. It's thick and slow and dogged sounding, the voice of a man who thinks he knows something you don't. It sounds a little like Lou Steinmetz, of campus security. Since I can't imagine why Lou Steinmetz would be calling me at—I peer over at the alarm clock on the nightstand—six-thirty on a Monday morning, I try to think who else I know who sounds like Lou Steinmetz that might have a reason for calling me.

"This is Lou Steinmetz," the voice says. "I was wondering if you'd be willing to come in to campus."

Something about the way he says this makes it sound as if I'm being asked to surrender to the authorities. Like he wants to know whether I'm going to give myself up peacefully or whether he's going to have to come get me. I can almost imagine him saying we can do this the easy way or the hard way, it's all up to me. "Lou," I say. "I come in every morning, just like you." This is not precisely true, of course, but pretty close, since I took up the reins of abusive power in the English department.

"We've got ourselves a little campus incident is why," Lou explains.

"An incident?"

"I'm not authorized to say more at this time."

"I'll be in."

"When would that be?"

"I'm not authorized to say, but soon."

The phone rings again before I've even had a chance to put my feet into my slippers. This time it's Teddy. "I can't believe it," he says. "You really did it. I can't believe it."

"It's six-thirty in the morning," I remind him. "I haven't even had my coffee. What have I done?"

"Are you saying it wasn't you?"

I hang up on him and sit there on the edge of the bed trying to clear the NyQuil cobwebs. I've spent the entire weekend in bed, watching television and dozing and trying to draft on my laptop computer a short piece for the *Railton Mirror* about my father at Columbia, and discovering as I did so that a strict diet of broth, cold remedies, and nasal spray is not especially conducive to good prose. This morning, I don't feel too bad, considering. If the phone would just stop ringing, I'd be fine.

"Don't hang up," Teddy pleads.

"Okay," I agree easily. It's a promise I won't mind breaking if I need to.

"Somebody killed a goose and hung it from a tree branch on campus. Lou Steinmetz thinks it was you."

"How would you know what Lou Steinmetz thinks? How can you be sure *that* he thinks?"

"You know Randy over in security? He was the one on the desk. He called Lou, and the first words out of Lou's mouth were, 'I bet it was that beatnik English professor.' "

"Beatnik?" I say, though I recognize Lou from his word choice.

"You want me to come over?" Teddy offers.

"Why?"

"We could drive in to campus together?"

"Why?"

Silence. No doubt he's still miffed by my refusing to engage in his proposed council of war yesterday afternoon after I promised I would. "Okay. Just tell me. I won't breathe a word. Even to June. Did you do it?"

I'm pretty tempted to tell him I did. I can tell how badly he wants to believe it. "I'm not saying another word until I speak to my lawyer."

"This could be just the thing you need today," Teddy says. I search for sarcasm in these words, but I don't find any. "This could put everybody back on your side in the department meeting."

"What department meeting?" I say, and hang up.

I put on coffee, then shave, shower, and get dressed. I pour myself a cup of coffee and am about to knock on the guest room door and tell Julie I have to go in to school when I hear a car drive up outside and see that it's my daughter. She comes in carrying a cardboard box, which she sets down in the middle of the island.

"He's been there," she says, a variation on the more traditional 'good morning.' "

She takes her sunglasses off, slings them onto the counter, and turns to face me. Her eye doesn't look as bad today. The swelling has gone down, the purple and blue metamorphosed into less angry look-ing yellow-green. Julie herself, on the other hand, is no less angry. "He picked up some clothes and some of his other stuff. He showered, too." This last seems to have particularly galled her.

"Did he use the toilet?"

She ignores this question and the man who spoke it. "Today the locks get changed." Though her eye looks better, the tuck at the corner is heavy this morning, dragging the lid down.

"Julie—" I begin.

"And don't try to talk me out of it."

"Okay," I say, taking my coffee cup over to the sink and rinsing it out.

"See?" she says when I turn around. "That's a simple enough thing. I can never even get him to do that."

I'm lost. "Do what?"

"Rinse out a damn coffee cup."

Actually, the way she's glaring at me suggests that she'd trade the two of us, husband and father, for a one-legged Puerto Rican maid.

At the foot of the hill I turn left instead of right and head out toward Allegheny Wells instead of Railton. I'm not anxious to get in to cam-pus. If indeed a goose has been killed, there's no telling what manner of shit awaits me. Admittedly, the idea of being interrogated by Lou Steinmetz is appealing. Under normal circumstances the William Henry Devereaux, Jr., who is accused of cleverness by his mother might enjoy twisting Lou Steinmetz into rhetorical knots, but today Lucky Hank's heart is not in the enterprise. In fact, he's reminded as he drives along the two-lane blacktop of a famous experiment performed on children to gauge—what?—their ambition? self-confidence? self-esteem? In the test each child is given a beanbag and shown a circle, then invited to toss the beanbag into the circle from behind a line, something even the clumsiest child finds easy to do. Next the child is moved back to a second line, so that the toss to the circle is farther and more difficult. After each toss the child is moved back a few feet, so that each toss becomes more difficult, failure more probable. Finally the child is given the beanbag and told he can have one more toss, from anywhere he chooses. A few kids opt for the most difficult toss, sensing, without being able to articulate why, that glory is lurking somewhere along the back line. But far more kids go right back to the spot of the first toss, where success is assured. Doing battle with Lou Steinmetz, it occurs to me, is a little like tossing the beanbag from the front stripe. This morning, at least, I have little taste for it.

In the village of Allegheny Wells I head up the hill, and at Russell and Julie's mailbox I pull into their drive. It's occurred to me that maybe Russell is watching the house. If so he's seen Julie leave and may himself have returned in the interim. There's no sign of him or his car, however, just the sad, unfinished house that Julie, no matter how stubborn she wants to be, will have to sell now. She and Lily will decide all that. My job will be to keep my mouth shut until it's a done deal. Then it will fall to me to figure out how best to sell an unfinished house. As is? Or do we—Lily and I—spend the money to finish it, then sell it, hoping to make the money back? I make a mental list of things that would be necessary. Shutters for the windows. At least minimal landscaping. Fill up the hole dug for the swimming pool and resod the lawn. And even then the house won't be easy to sell. There are eight or ten houses for sale in our own development.

Our work—Lily's and mine—is cut out for us, and not just this stuff with Julie and Russell. We have spoken over the weekend. Not for long, partly because I was hazy and stupid with NyQuil, and partly because Angelo—her father—is a subject I tread lightly around. But at least I've been given a vague outline of the events Lily did not want to share with me on Friday. The reason that Angelo was not home last week when I called, it turns out, is that he was in jail. Apparently he's been there for over a week, either too stubborn or too embarrassed to inform anyone of his whereabouts. He was arrested on several charges, ranging from public endangerment to discharging a weapon in the city. And despite Lily's spending most of Friday trying to arrange for her father's bail, he remained in the county lockup over the weekend.

According to Lily, who pieced the incident together from a police report and a neighbor's account, a young black man made the mistake of going up onto Angelo's porch, ringing the bell, and then refusing to go away when Angelo, who met him at the door with a pump-action shotgun, advised him to. Clearly, there's more to the story than this, but I've been reluctant to press for the kind of detail that would make such a narrative spring to life. As I said, Lily and I agreed long ago never to allow each other's fathers to become the cause of serious conflict between us. The necessity of this arrangement became clear to us when we realized that we were each fond of the other's parent. Lily found William Henry Devereaux, Sr., charming (which he is), while I found Angelo hilarious (which I still maintain that he is, though I admit he has never threatened me with a loaded shotgun). My father's charm and Angelo's ability to keep me (however unintentionally) in stitches were, of course, beside the point of these men, or at least beside what we, their more vested offspring, considered to be the point. It's possible to overlook character flaws of in-laws for the simple reason that you feel neither responsible for them nor genetically implicated.

Lily's situation is far worse than my own. Her relationship with her father is complicated by the fact that she just can't quit loving him, even though his rank bigotry both shames her and makes her crazy. But she cannot forget that after her mother's death, which occurred when she was still a girl, Angelo's devotion to "his little girl" was complete, and this devotion, more than anything else, got her through, finally, her mother's loss. They were a team until she went away to the university, which changed their relationship overnight. In a matter of months she was no longer his little girl. Suddenly it was as if they spoke different languages. Every time she came home on vacation she'd learned more words that excluded him. Worse, she asked him not to use a lot of his favorite old ones in her presence. Where once father and daughter had been inseparable, they now found themselves strangers. Lily started dating the kinds of men Angelo had no use for and eventually married the worst of the lot. Me.

I sympathize. It's the dilemma of the lower middle class when it sends its children off to be educated, often at great expense. Their naive hope (they don't see it as unreasonable) is that the kids they send off will return more affluent but otherwise unchanged. Certainly not contemptuous. Angelo now regards his little girl's chosen mate, listens to her learned speech, witnesses the way she's raised her own kids, as well as her devotion to what he considers society's dangerous youthful dregs, and cannot help but feel the complete repudiation of himself as a man and a father. Shortly before we were married, Angelo visited us at the dingy apartment where we were living and trying to save money. He took us out to dinner and encouraged me to tell him my plans. I don't remember what I told him, but when I finished he turned to his daughter and said, "Where did I go wrong, little girl? Can you at least tell me that much, because I'd really like to know."

Of course, Angelo is not the first parent ever to ask this question, it occurs to me as I sit in the rutted dirt driveway that leads to my own daughter's house. Lily, who agrees with my mother that I am unprepared for my father's return, considers my own relationship with William Henry Devereaux, Sr., unnatural, but I think our emotional distance is both sensible and admirable. Our disappointments in each other are deep and probably irrevocable. That we don't give voice to them, that we don't try to change each other or ask what the other cannot give, is both wise and prudent. Angelo could get away with asking his daughter where he went wrong because he knew she loved him far too much to answer. My father and I not only understand clearly where we've failed in each other's estimation but also know that a full, detailed explanation awaits the one who is unwise enough to ask the wrong question.

I head to campus over the mountain so I can sneak in via the back gate. People may be waving signs with my picture on them at the front entrance.

I stop at the intersection across from The Circle Bar and Grill, and though I'm not hungry, it's tempting to pull in and have breakfast in the company of men like Mr. Purty. That is, I'm tempted even before I see a pickup truck that looks like Mr. Purty's towing a U-Haul trailer pull in, and a man who looks like Mr. Purty, dressed in jeans and cowboy boots and a western shirt, get out of the truck. I pull into the parking lot and I have to toot twice before he looks up, and until he recognizes the tooter, he looks like he'd like nothing better than to kick the tooter's ass. The pointed toes on his cowboy boots appear particularly lethal, so I stay in my car and roll down the window. On second observation, Mr. Purty looks like a man who's been stomped by a man wearing boots similar to his own.

"Henry," he sighs.

"Hi, Mr. Purty," I say. "What've you done with my mother?"

"She's back at her place," he shrugs. "Her and your dad. You know how much a hotel room costs in New York City?"

"Let me park, Mr. Purty," I tell him. "I'll buy breakfast."

"Okay," he says. "Beats me why people live in a place like that, what with the price of everything."

I pull in next to his truck, which looks different, somehow. It's still bright and shiny, but it seems altered in ways I don't immediately identify.

"They done some job on it, didn't they?" Mr. Purty says when I get out and he sees me inspecting it. "Took my hubcaps. Stereo. Speakers. Mirrors."

I glance inside the cab, and sure enough, wires are dangling from the dash.

"They stole my tark, too," he says, indicating the bare bed of the pickup. "Why would anybody want to live in a place like that? We wasn't gone no more than twenty minutes."

"You insured, Mr. Purty?"

"Yeah, it ain't that," he sighs meaningfully. "We made it back in one piece, anyhow. That trailer's full of your dad's books. They put the furniture in storage. Couple nice pieces, too. Worth more than all these books. Not that anybody wanted my opinion."

We contemplate the U-Haul.

"They're two peas in a pop, them two," he remarks.

Over more scrapple and eggs I get the story. More than anything it's a tale of Mr. Purty's finally understanding the true folly of his long courtship of my mother, something he has suspected for a long time, though even when my mother announced my father's return, he apparently still held out some kind of hope. Only when he saw the two of them together—realized they were two peas in a pop—did he finally grasp who this woman was. It must have been a long weekend.

My father, according to Mr. Purty, was exactly no help, which I could have told him in advance. The only real work I ever saw William Henry Devereaux, Sr., do when I was growing up was dig the grave for Red, and he complained of blisters on his palms for a week afterward.

"He don't look too good," Mr. Purty admits, "so I didn't want to ask him to help out. How comes he cries like that?"

Cry? William Henry Devereaux, Sr.? It's hard to imagine this. Crying is not an ironic stance. "What are you talking about?" I ask, a little sharply perhaps.

"He cries all the while," Mr. Purty explains, minimally.

"He cries?"

"Damnedest thing you ever saw. One minute he's sitting there smiling, then all of sudden he's bawling like a little kid. Then, bam! he stops again. Grins at you again like he don't remember he's just been blubbering."

"You witnessed this yourself?"

"I guess you ain't seen him in a while."

In the literal sense it hasn't been so long. A couple of months or thereabouts. My mother and I went to New York when we heard about his collapse, but he was in the hospital then and pretty heavily sedated, so in the truest sense Mr. Purty is right. It's been a long time, probably five years, since I've seen my father, a fact that doesn't seem so strange to me until I think about how I might explain it to a man like Mr. Purty, who may have concluded from talking to my mother that my father and I are on the outs.

"Your ma said just ignore him," Mr. Purty's explaining. "Just let him cry. He'll quit it eventually. She was right, I guess." He shakes his head, remembering. "The way he cries you'd swear he meant to keep it up forever. Then he'll just stop and grin at you. You'll see," he adds.

I try to imagine this, and, failing, I consider for the first time the possibility that my mother may be right, that I'm not prepared for my father's return.

"*You* aren't going to start blubbering, are you?" Mr. Purty asks. He's staring at me suspiciously.

I assure him that I'm not.

He looks unconvinced but hopeful. "I was going to come by your place after breakfast," he explains, wiping his eggy mouth with a napkin. "Your ma said to put everything in your garage for now."

"She did?"

"Didn't tell you, I guess."

I can't help it. Suddenly, I'm furious with her, and not over her presumption that Lily and I would be pleased to give over the better part of our garage to William Henry Devereaux, Sr.'s private library. "Did she even say thank you, Mr. Purty?"

He shrugs, pushes his plate away. "Not yet," he admits. "Course the job ain't done yet. She's probably waiting, so she don't have to say it twice. Aren't you going to eat?"

It's true. I've eaten only a couple forkfuls of eggs. My stomach is churning, and I'm not sure it'd be wise to fill my intestines with other intestines.

"That plate of eggs right there would cost you thirteen, fourteen dollars in New York City. Why would people live in a place like that?"

I slide my plate of eggs over to Mr. Purty. "Doesn't it bother you when people take advantage of your good nature?" I ask him.

He shovels my bleeding eggs into his mouth and chews thoughtfully, as if paying such an exorbitant price for eggs has deepened his respect for them. "I'm glad if she's happy, I guess. But this whole deal didn't turn out the way I'd hoped, I gotta admit."

"You think she's happy?" I wonder, genuinely curious about Mr. Purty's opinion on this subject.

He shrugs. "They talk just alike, the two of them."

I consider this prescription for happiness.

"So do you," he adds. I can tell it's not his intention to hurt my feelings.

"I have to go pee, Mr. Purty," I tell him.

"Go ahead," he says.

"And then I have to go in to campus for a while."

"Go ahead."

"Just unhitch the U-Haul and leave it in the drive."

"Your ma won't like that."

"So what? Just walk away from it, Mr. Purty. It's not your problem."

"She'll have to pay a late fee if the trailer don't come back today."

"Let her."

He considers this course of action. "Actually, I'm the one put down the deposit."

"I'll try to get back at noon," I sigh. "Leave it till then, okay? You know where I live?"

He nods. "Your ma give me directions."

I leave some money on the table for our breakfasts.

"Your pa says he read every one of them books out there," Mr. Purty says, and he considers this for a moment. "But I don't believe him."

"How come, Mr. Purty?"

"Because it ain't possible," he says. "There's too many of them."

"You calling my father a liar, Mr. Purty?" I grin at him.

"I guess I am, Henry," he admits, grinning back at me.

At the trough at the men's room of The Circle Bar and Grill I try to imagine William Henry Devereaux, Sr.—a man whose greatest gift in life had always been his ability to see to his own needs—in the condition Mr. Purty just described. Having swilled larger than recommended dosages of NyQuil all weekend, I feel detached. My head cold symptoms have vanished, but so has my equilibrium. The graffiti on the men's room wall swims before my eyes like my father's lecture notes. I am dazed, unable to comprehend the simple messages that previous pilgrims to this spot have left for me on the wall. "Eat shit," I am advised.

The William Henry Devereaux, Sr., of my adolescence would see nothing amusing in such witless vulgarity. Is that why these two words strike me, at this moment, as the funniest in the English language? And who knows? This new William Henry Devereaux, Sr., the one Mr. Purty has just described to me, might find them funny too. Maybe he'd laugh like a lunatic. Then again, it could be they'd strike him as infinitely sad, so damn sad the tears would streak his old, spotted, hollowed-out cheeks, making him unrecognizable to himself.

CHAPTER

23

From the faculty parking lot I can see that the TV van is again parked in one of the VIP spaces close to the pond, and once again protesters have gathered. In fact, it looks like there are twice as many of them. Not nearly as many people as used to protest the Vietnam War, but then again these people are protesting *me*. They are protesting the demise of a single goose. Still, they are chanting loud enough that I can hear them in the car with the windows rolled up.

April, I remember from my own days as a sign carrier, is the best month for high moral dudgeon. Spring break is already over, so there's no danger of having to interrupt the protest. The warming weather makes it seem right and natural to be outdoors. With finals a mere two weeks away, a good moral protest offers the requisite rationale for forsaking the dorm, the classroom, the library stacks. Lily and I courted through a series of protests—more worthy ones, I can't help thinking— and I still remember the way my wife looked carrying a sign. Fierce. Beautiful. Strong. Good. I wonder if there's some young woman like her in this gaggle of protesters, disturbing the moral focus of some young Hal with a sign.

From where I sit in the faculty lot, I can see that in the distance several large steel girders have sprung from the ground over the weekend, the framework of Technical Careers. I'm reminded of my dream last week, the one of my suddenly Brobdingnagian house. That dream makes a different kind of sense to me this morning, my head still full of NyQuil cobwebs, a jailed Angelo, a weeping William Henry Devereaux, Sr., and a separated Julie and Russell. I guess I've been sitting there awhile when someone raps on my driver's side door, causing me to jump about a foot. I see it's Meg Quigley and that she's mightily pleased to have caused me to jump. When I roll down my window, she says, "Are you going to sit there all morning?"

"You have a better plan?"

When she just grins at me, I roll up my window and get out, ashamed to have been caught in a reverie, something that seems to happen to me more and more. I check my watch, try to gauge how long I've been there, how much time has elapsed during this particular ellipsis. "You're not afraid to be seen with me?" I say when she falls into step with me on the way to Modern Languages.

"I'm seen with dubious characters all the time," she informs me. "They should all be so harmless."

I'm not sure I like the idea of being thought harmless by a young woman as beautiful as Meg Quigley, but I let it go. "I hear you're off to graduate school again next year."

"That's the plan," she admits. "My father's, not mine."

"You could do worse," I hear myself say, taking Billy's part. Is this advice so wrong?

"I'm not sure I want a Ph.D.," she says, more thoughtfully, less combatively, than I expect. "If you were to hand me one right now, I'm not sure I'd want it."

"Get out of the profession altogether then," I suggest. "You're young. Do something else."

"If I do that, then I've wasted all his hard-earned money. An M.A. isn't worth the paper it's printed on."

"Then get the Ph.D."

"And waste even more of his money on something I don't even want? Beggar him completely, so he can die happy?"

"*Somebody* should be happy," I point out.

"Are you?"

"Ecstatic. Can't you tell? And I don't even have a Ph.D."

She looks me over. "Your nose looks better, anyway."

I look her over too. God, this is one beautiful young woman. "Thanks."

We've arrived at Modern Languages. Meg's office is located one floor below the rest of the English department, in a huge room with a dozen desks shared by twenty-four adjunct faculty.

"I think I'm going to wait and see if *he* has a job next year."

I can hear the question in this statement.

"I don't see how your old man could be fired, Meg," I tell her. "He's been here since Christ was a corporal."

"He's not on your list then?"

This week, it occurs to me, is beginning just like the last one ended. Only worse. Now, instead of being offered a bite of juicy peach, I'm being accused. I'm Judas Peckerwood not only to Meg's father but to Meg herself.

"Did you know that he wanted to be a writer when he was young? Did you know he wrote a novel?"

"Billy?" I say, genuinely surprised, though I don't know why I should be. Virtually everybody in the English department has a half-written novel squirreled away in a desk drawer. I know this to be a fact because before they all started filing grievances against me, I was asked to read them. Sad little vessels all. Scuffy the Tugboat, lost and scared on the open sea. All elegantly written, all with the same artistic goal—to evidence a superior sensibility. Maybe I'm surprised about Billy because he hasn't asked me to read his. I've always liked Billy, and now I like him even more. It's a hell of a fine man who'll write a novel and keep it to himself.

"Tell Julie I'll call her tonight."

"Julie who?" I say, genuinely confused.

"You have a daughter named Julie?" she reminds me. "I was gone this weekend. She left messages on my machine."

"I didn't know you two knew each other."

Meg just looks at me. Like the list of things I don't know is pretty comprehensive.

"So you didn't talk to her?" I say.

"I know about her and Russell, if that's what you mean."

I start to ask, then realize I don't want to know Meg's take on these events. "Russell seems to have disappeared," I venture.

"Not really," she says. "He's around."

"If you see him, tell him I'd like a word."

"Oh boy, a fight."

"Don't be an idiot."

"Okay, I'll tell him," she says. "If I see him."

The English department office has a window with a view of the duck pond. June Barnes and Orshee are watching the protest rally from the open window, and Rachel glances up at me when I enter. Rachel is always a frightened-looking woman, and she's got her reasons, but this morning she looks genuinely terrified. Exhausted, too. There's more gray in her hair than I've noticed before, more than there probably should be for a woman in her—what?—late thirties. Her eyes are darkly circled and puffy. Her whole face is puffy now that I look at it.

"Come look," June says, noticing me. "This is delicious. Dickie's at the microphone."

I study the two of them standing there at the window. Something about their proximity, their posture, suggests that Orshee is about to slip his hand up under the back of June's sweater. No doubt this is projection on my part. A minute ago, as I held the door for Meg Quigley, my own fantasy hand made this same journey up the small of Meg's back to where her bra strap would be if she wore one. Which she doesn't.

"He's standing on a box," June continues. "Apparently, they couldn't adjust the mike stand. God, he's a tiny little toad."

Orshee titters nervously at this remark. He's only a couple inches taller than Dickie, and as an untenured member of the faculty he's not sure of the wisdom of laughing at a joke made at the expense of the

CEO. Of course, *not* laughing could be unwise as well. "We're on the third floor," he reminds June. "We're looking down on him."

As I said, the serious competition in an English department is for the role of straight man.

"I look down on him no matter what floor I'm on," June responds, giving it a whack, since it's all teed up.

Rachel hands me a fistful of message slips and mouths, "We need to talk?"

"Why don't you two go someplace else," I suggest. "I need some quality time with my secretary."

"Our offices face the wrong way," June explains. Neither moves from the window. There are many advantages to being the chair of an English department, but giving orders isn't one of them. Actually, you can give all the orders you want, as long as you don't mind them being ignored.

"Let's go in here," I suggest, and Rachel follows me to my inner office, closing the door behind her. I riffle quickly through my messages. One from the dean, apparently back from his job interview, who would appreciate an audience. So would Finny. Herbert Schonberg wonders if I would return his call at my earliest convenience. My mother would like me to call her at *her* earliest convenience. "You must be holding back all the ones with the good news," I tell Rachel.

When I look up, I see that Rachel is in genuine distress. "I think I'm going to puke?" she says, surprising me with the word. I've learned a good deal about Rachel from reading her stories. I know about her lower-class roots, how hard she's worked to learn manners, polite behavior. Her diction will still betray her, but only rarely. Her clothes, her posture, her gestures—all learned and practiced—are flawlessly mimicked middle class.

"Sit," I tell her. "If I had a window, I'd open it."

She sits, leans forward, her head between her knees, trying not to hyperventilate. Seeing her in this intimate posture inspires in me a set of complex emotional responses, foremost among them, irrationally, guilt. I lock the door so we won't be interrupted. Whatever this is about, it can't be good, I conclude.

Finally, swallowing hard, she looks up and breathes deeply. When she speaks, though, her voice is a barely audible whisper. "Wendy called me this morning? Your agent?"

Now the guilt I feel is no longer irrational. Seeing Rachel's distress makes me understand how wrong I've been to send her stories to someone without her permission. Wendy is not a cruel woman, just busy and tactless and honest. She believes, not unreasonably, that any writer who can be discouraged should be discouraged. I've failed to imagine the effect such a woman would have on Rachel.

"Look—" I begin.

"She wants to represent me?" Rachel blurts, bug-eyed with horror. "What should I do?"

"Rachel," I say. "This is wonderful. What's wrong with you?"

"I'm . . . scared?" she says, like she's not sure this is an emotion she's entitled to.

"What did she say?"

If anything, this question induces even greater fright. "She said the stories were . . . terrific?"

Wendy has said a lot more than this, I can tell. She's praised Rachel just this side of catatonia.

"Hell, *I* told you they were terrific. I've been telling you that for over a year."

"Yes, but . . ."

I can't help grinning at her. What I'm recalling is our previous conversation on this same subject. "What makes *her* the final arbiter?" I ask again.

"Who is?"

"I am. I keep telling you, but you won't pay attention."

"She said some of the stories are rough? What does that mean?"

"That they need work."

"Is that bad?"

"Only if you don't want to do the work."

"I *do* want to do the work?"

I can't help wondering if, after publishing a book of stories, Rachel's personality will become more declarative, whether she'll learn to let her voice drop. "Rachel," I tell her. "Enjoy this. Brag about it. Call up that jerk you were married to. Say I told you so. They're the four most satis-

fying words in the English language. You could rupture something trying to keep them inside you."

There's a commotion in the hall, and someone tries the inner door
I've locked. I go over to the other door, the one that opens onto the hall,
open it a crack, and peek out. The camera crew has arrived and they're
setting up lights and a couple umbrellas.

"They called earlier?" Rachel says. "They want to interview you?"

"Trapped like a bug," I declare.

"I should have told you about that first?" Rachel laments.

"Don't be silly," I say. "Aren't you going to ask me if I killed the
duck?"

"No?"

"How come?"

"Because you didn't? Because it wouldn't be a very good joke?"

It's a wonderful thing to be perfectly understood, especially by a
woman you could fall in love with under the right circumstances.
Especially when the circumstances aren't so terribly wrong. "Do you
realize, Rachel, that if you published a book, our department secretary
would be more distinguished than the faculty she serves?"

I really should stop terrifying this poor woman, but I can't help
myself. Besides. Only part of her is terrified. Rachel's fine secret heart
is singing, because it has to be. My own is humming backup.

"Will they hate me?" she wants to know.

"They already hate you. For helping me."

"That reminds me?" she says, opening the three-ring binder she's
brought in with her, and extracting from it a thick booklet that I see
is a copy of the English department's operating paper. She hands it to
me open to the page that describes the procedure for the recall of a
department chair. She's highlighted in yellow the passage she wants
me to consider, which states that a three-fourths majority vote is
required.

"Huh," I say. "I thought it was two-thirds."

"So does Finny? I heard him talking?"

"It would be unusual for Finny to be wrong about something like
this," I say, checking the date on the front of the booklet.

"It hasn't been two-thirds since 1971, when Professor Quarry was
recalled?"

I vaguely remember this. It was Jim Quarry who hired Jacob Rose and me. No wonder they recalled him. What I can't remember is how I voted. "How many voting members of the department are there?"

"Twenty-eight?"

"Make thirty copies," I suggest. "Don't tell anyone."

She hands them to me. Thirty copies. Amazing.

When she's gone, I peek out the door again, and I see that the crowd has swollen. Missy Blaylock has arrived and is doing her endless sound check. "You're sure he's in there?" I hear someone ask. "That office right there," somebody else says, and everybody turns and looks right at the door I'm peeking from behind.

I take a deep breath and step into the hall and the lights. Quickly Missy has me by the elbow and draws me toward the camera. Down the hall, placards are bouncing up and down and last Friday's chant is raised again. "Stop Devereaux! Stop the slaughter!" My colleagues, the ones who aren't in class, have come out into the hallway to witness this spectacle.

"We're here at the Railton Campus of West Central Pennsylvania University talking to Professor Henry Devereaux, chair of the English department. Professor, last Friday you threatened to kill a duck a day unless you got a budget. Early this morning a duck was found hanging from a tree limb here on campus." ("Goose," somebody corrects.) "Do you have any knowledge of the incident?"

"No comment," I tell her, and there's a groan from the gallery.

"He did it," somebody shouts. "Look at him."

"Have you received the budget you demanded?"

I confess that I have received no budget.

"Is there a causal link between that fact and the dead duck?"

"*Goose!*" somebody yells, exasperated. I search the crowd for Tony Coniglia.

"No comment."

"We've just spoken with Richard Pope, the campus executive officer. Dr. Pope says he feels certain you are innocent of this crime."

"How could he know that?" I point out. "Unless he did it himself."

This wild inference throws Missy completely off stride. "Are you saying he's involved?" Incredulity.

"He doesn't have a budget either," I point out.

"Do you think there will be further killings?"

"Do you think I'll get my budget?"

When the light goes off on the camera, someone shouts, "Murderer!" and a new chant goes up. Lou Steinmetz makes his way through the crowd. Somebody yells, "Bust him!"

Lou turns on the demonstrators, tells them to disperse, which they do, somewhat reluctantly. To me, Lou Steinmetz is beginning to look old, like a man who knows he isn't going to have many more opportunities to crush a student revolt. Turning the key on a radical English professor might offer slender compensation. "A moment of your time, Professor?"

"Not now, Lou. I'm busy."

"I could insist."

"You could try."

"Yes, I could."

"Except I'm connected all the way to the governor," I tell him. "You could bust me and throw me in the slammer, but I'd be back on the streets with all the other scum before you completed the paperwork."

Lou studies me seriously. He's almost sure I'm joking, but not quite.

"How about I come by and see you this afternoon after my class?"

When he's gone, Missy comes over. "I still have to talk to you about that friend of yours," she tells me.

Actually, I don't like the fact that Missy wants to talk to me about Tony Coniglia. I left them, two happily naked, consenting adults in Tony's hot tub. If Missy Blaylock has regrets—and I can't imagine she wouldn't—I hope she doesn't express them to me, especially if she's trolling for sympathy. "This really weird thing happened after you left?"

"It was all pretty weird before I left, thanks."

But she's too serious to be diverted. "Get him to tell you about it," she says. "If he doesn't, I will."

"Okay," I say, though I have no intention of following through. Tony and I are scheduled for another of our racquetball matches this afternoon. If he brings up the subject of what transpired, or didn't transpire, after I left, fine. Otherwise, I don't want to know.

"Between us," Missy says, her voice lowered, "did you off this duck?"

"Goose," I remind her.

"Goose."

"No comment."

CHAPTER

24

It's almost noon before I can kick free and pay a visit to Jacob Rose. In the interim, half the department has traipsed through my office. Finny has stopped to determine my intentions with regard to this afternoon's meeting. I've asked him to remind me what meeting we're talking about just to watch him flinch. The meeting that will remove me from this office and from the chairmanship of the department, he wants me to understand. Will I be attending, is what he'd like to know. Of course, I have every *right* to attend. Charges will be leveled and discussed, and of course I'll have the *opportunity* to respond, perhaps even the *obligation*. Still, I'm to understand that, in this present circumstance, even my staunch political allies have aligned themselves against me. It is unlikely that I will get much support, and I may be uncomfortable listening to so many low opinions of my performance as chair, the detailing of so many grievances. If I attend, I should expect to be charged with giving aid and comfort to the administration, of misinforming and betraying the department I'm charged with notifying and nurturing. Finny would also like me to understand that while he hopes, officially, that I'll attend the meeting, he privately would prefer I didn't. He's anxious that I not reduce the proceedings to farce. In Finny's opinion today's meeting is serious business, and English has been a joke department in the eyes of the university community long enough. He actually says this. I repeat: in an English department the serious competition is for the role of straight man. We leave it that I will not attend the meeting. I will be permitted to vote by proxy, assuming I can find someone to bear one.

I have also been visited by Teddy and June, separately, each wanting to urge me one last time not to take this lying down. It chills their blood to vote with Rourke and Finny, and they see my behavior as perverse. All I have to do is attend the meeting, announce that I've not provided Dickie Pope with a list, assure my colleagues that I would never do such a thing, and once again our house will divide against itself, return to the gridlock we've lived with so long it's begun to seem natural. Teddy reminds me that the last time our department ever agreed on anything we hired Gracie. Consensus is unnatural for us, is his argument. We're an English department. Let's act like one.

Just before heading over to see the dean, I'm visited by Orshee. He's been thinking about our department all weekend, he confesses, and the more he's thought about it, the less reason he can see for the sorry state we're in. "I mean, we're all reasonable people," he says. ("Who?" I can't help responding. "Name one reasonable person in our department.") What's really troubling Orshee, of course, is not so much the sad state of our department as his own place in it. He's had the weekend to consider his rash position at the last personnel committee meeting, where he urged us not only to disqualify all male candidates from our search but to vote against him when he comes up for tenure next year. It's not that he fears someone may have taken his admonition seriously. As he explained to June over the weekend, his contempt for the pervasive sexism of our culture is so powerful, so profound, that he wouldn't mind being sacrificed to further the cause of gender equality. Still, he's afraid that his position may have been misunderstood and possibly misstated. What if, in paraphrase, it sounded like he just didn't *want* tenure? What if his deepest convictions were misinterpreted as personal dissatisfaction, which was the way June herself, he was horrified to discover, had taken them.

What he would like the chair to understand is that, as a white male, he isn't sure he *deserves* tenure, but he does *want* it. Actually, he's seriously thinking about making an offer on a house in Allegheny Wells. His realtor keeps insisting it's a buyer's market, and June agrees. The problem is, how can you even *look* at houses, how can you contemplate the future, in such a climate of rancor and antagonism? Take today's meeting. How he votes will be remembered. He hasn't decided how he is going to vote yet, I'm to understand, but he knows that no matter which way he votes he's going to make enemies. Even June says so. What did *I* do when I was in his position? he wonders. "It's so hard to be moral," he laments.

If William Henry Devereaux, Jr., were a more honest man, he'd confess to his young colleague that he's not going to think much of him no matter how he votes. Instead, my advice to Orshee is to listen to his realtor. I tell him I believe he will be tenured, that he will be chair before he's through, which in fact I do believe. If he suspects he's been insulted, he gives no sign.

Jacob Rose's secretary, Marjory Brownlow, has been at the university longer than anyone I know. A former secretary in English, she followed Jacob over to Liberal Arts when he was made dean. Since that time, she's been offered half a dozen positions in the administration and turned them all down, out of loyalty to Jacob, I've always assumed, or contempt for the new regime of Dickie Pope. I don't get over to this end of campus that often, and seeing Marjory reminds me of something I'm surprised to have forgotten. Back in late November she called me, wanting to know whether there was any chance of her returning to English. If Rachel was planning to leave, would I keep her in mind? I assured her that if Rachel were ever to give notice I'd pick up the phone, but that, as far as I knew, Rachel was enjoying her job, the fact that I was her boss notwithstanding. "Is this something you want to talk about?" I recall asking. "It sure is," Marjory replied. "But it's not something I can. Not a word to Jacob, Hank. Promise me." So I promised and kept my promise in the same fashion Lily always accuses me of keeping such promises. By forgetting entirely whatever it is I'm not supposed to tell anyone.

Seeing Marjory now, however, brings the conversation back in its entirety, and with it comes a suspicion—that whatever is happening or is about to happen on campus is something Marjory knew or suspected in the fall. Secretaries to the deans always know all the dirt, and only gender and class bias keeps department chairs from dealing directly with them and bypassing their bosses altogether.

"Marjory," I say from the doorway. "Tell me everything. Don't leave anything out. I can take it."

Marjory has been around, and been around me, too long to be taken aback by much, but this smart-ass hello seems to have caught her like a good left jab. She looks me over long and critically before observing, "You're limping."

I plop down in one of the chairs reserved for people begging an audience of the dean. Actually, this is the inner of two offices, where people like department chairs and union representatives wait. The outer office is for students, several of whom I've made my way past already. They stare at me maliciously. "No cuts," they'd like to tell me, and who can blame them? Not me, and I'm a cutter. I recognize a couple of them from Finny's morning comp class, poor devils. They're probably here to complain to Jacob about Finny's dullness. This errand would be a waste of their time, even if people like me weren't cutting in line ahead of them. Jacob Rose himself was no fireball in the classroom, and he's been hearing the same complaints about Finny for a decade. There are lots of dull teachers. You can't make them all deans.

What Marjory says is true. I am limping. "Old pal-o'-mine," I say, "let me see your phone book."

She hands it over. I find the number of my doctor, Philip Watson, which I read out loud to Marjory, who dials it, then hands me the receiver. In the next room I hear Jacob is also on the phone.

After several rings, the phone is answered. I identify myself and ask if I can speak to the doctor. I'm asked if I can hold. My problem is the exact opposite, I explain. Muzak, by way of response.

"Ah, Marjory, we're getting old, you and I," I say, studying her. She's in her early sixties, but still a vigorous woman. Her body, instead of growing slack, has become compact, as if she's reducing everything to essentials. Nearly a decade ago I played golf with her and her husband, Harold, Lily's colleague at the high school. Marjory had one of the sweetest swings I ever saw. One-eighty from the tee with a three wood, right down the center of the fairway every time. You could set yardage markers by where her ball dropped. "But we still have our memories. Those hot August nights, lying naked on the beach, the sand still warm, our skin cool, nothing but stars above. Remember?"

"No," she admits. "But I like your description."

"Watson," I say, when Phil comes on the line. "I need you."

"Hank," he recognizes the voice of his left fielder. "I need you, too. At first base this season. I talked my nephew into trying out this year, and I want him in left."

Most people who don't call their doctors when they should, have perfectly good reasons. They don't want their medical fears confirmed. But when your doctor doubles as the captain of your summer softball team, there are additional reasons to steer clear of him in the off-season. I had hoped not to see Phil until June, at which point I intended to just trot out to left field and thereby avoid discussion.

"And the reason you need me is that I never see you *until* you need me," he went on. "Regular checkups and you wouldn't have these emergencies."

"Fine. Punish me."

"What is it this time?"

"I'm trying to pass a stone," I tell him, winking at Marjory. "It won't."

Marjory starts to rise. "Maybe I could go somewhere?"

"No," I say. "Stay here. Hold my hand."

"What?" Phil says.

"Not you," I tell him. "From you I want an X ray."

"Do you *know* you're trying to pass a stone, or is this something you suspect? You always come in knowing what's wrong with you, and you're always wrong."

"I know I can't pee," I tell him. "My father is a certified stone for-mer. You should see all his citations."

Marjory pushes back her chair. "Back in a few minutes." She smiles, and leaves.

"And you've waited until you're in serious pain before calling," he intuits.

"Pain was last week," I tell him. "Discomfort, the week before that. This week my back teeth are floating."

"Idiot."

"I'd hoped to get through the semester."

"And now you can't get through the lunch hour."

"See? You *do* understand."

"One hour."

"I'll be there."

When I hang up, I hear Jacob do the same thing in the inner office. I take advantage of Marjory's absence by ringing him. "Hello, Numb Nuts," I greet him.

"Marjory," he says. "You always did do a terrific Hank Devereaux."

I go in, take a seat in one of Jacob's plush leather chairs. He's got a nice office, my pal the dean. Much nicer than mine. "So. How was California?" I inquire.

"Texas," he corrects me. "Hot. In the nineties already. Also, there are no Jews in Texas."

"I've heard they're very strict."

"Good tacos, though."

"I bet."

We're grinning at each other now.

"So," I say. "Who do you figure snuffed this goose?"

Jacob shrugs. "Lou Steinmetz thinks it was you. I told him I didn't think you could take a goose in a fair fight."

"You're in an awfully good mood," I observe. "Things must have gone well."

Jacob takes a moment to consider his response, as if precision were important. "I *did* receive a job offer this morning."

"Congratulations. Where in Texas?"

"This particular offer didn't come from Texas. It came from out of the blue."

In truth, I'm surprised. Jacob is a fine fellow, but not a distinguished one. I wouldn't have thought even a lateral move would be all that easy.

"How come you were on the market to begin with?" I ask, since this has been puzzling me. Most of us who came to the university twenty years ago continued to make applications for years after we arrived, but then tenure and promotion locked us in place and we gave up.

"Because Dickie shit-canned me back in October," he says, smiling at the effect that this intelligence has on me. He's enjoying himself, it occurs to me, and I can understand why. He's taken a fall and landed on his feet. My unflattering view of his marketability was probably a view he himself shared. He's as surprised as I am. Also, he's kept his firing a secret, something nobody who knew him would have suspected he was capable of doing. His reward is that he can announce his firing and triumph over adversity in the same breath.

"How come you didn't tell your friends?" I ask, realizing too late that this is a straight line.

"I did," he assures me. I can see that his spirits are absolutely irrepressible. This must be one hell of an offer he's just received, from the kind of institution that will make all of us jealous when we hear. I can't imagine how such a thing has transpired, but apparently it has. "But enough about me," he grins. "Let's talk about you. I understand you had your talk with Dickie last Friday?"

"You might have told me what was coming."

"I thought you knew. It's been going on for weeks. You were the last one," he admits.

"That kind of hurts my feelings," I admit.

"Lots of reasons though," he says. "You're a lame-duck—pardon the term—interim chair. Also, the Vatican views you as a genuine loose cannon. Unpredictable and therefore dangerous. Anyhow, don't feel bad about being last. I was first, and now you know why."

"So you think it's going to happen? The twenty percent?"

"I got news for you. Twenty percent is what everybody's hoping. What not many people know is that there's also a thirty percent scenario, depending on what the legislature does."

I shake my head. "Even as the concrete is being poured on a new Tech Complex?"

"That's right. I'd be careful, too. Another duck dies, and you could end up in one of the footers."

"Does any of this make sense to you?"

"Sure. Think about it."

Actually, although my public posture is incredulity, a picture has been forming in my head over the weekend. The whole university is being reorganized, duplicate programs eliminated, the academic missions of each campus redefined. Technical Careers will be the center of our particular campus.

"You must be relieved to be shut of the whole mess."

Again Jacob appears to consider his response carefully. "I'm not shut of it quite yet," he says. "What I'm hearing is that you will be shut of it before I will. This afternoon, is what I'm hearing."

"My troops are in mutiny," I concede. "I could maybe rally them. I'm told it's still possible. The question is, should I?"

Jacob meets my eye and shrugs. "Honest Injun? I don't see how it matters."

I nod. "Once again, you've failed to cheer me up."

What's really depressing is the idea of Jacob leaving. He's been a reasonably well-intentioned, lazy, honorable, mildly incompetent dean, and that's about the best you can hope for. And he's been a friend I'll miss. Worse, I have to admit to feeling the jealousy of one crab for another that has managed to climb out of the barrel.

"I doubt this will cheer you up either," Jacob says, "but what the hell, I'll ask. How would you feel about being my best man?"

I blink at him, thinking, What an odd metaphor. I recall Jacob saying last week that if he got the job, he'd take me with him, but he couldn't have been serious. Then it occurs to me, it's no metaphor. Jacob is getting married.

He risks a weak smile. "Gracie will kick, but she'll get over it."

I must look stupid, staring at him as I am. He seems to have forgotten that I know nothing about the woman, whoever she is, that he intends to marry. I had no idea he was dating, much less serious about anyone. And why would Gracie have been commissioned to arrange his wedding? It's true she's often consulted about putting on the various festivities at the university, and Dickie Pope purportedly conferred with her in the matter of books for his empty shelves. Still. The whole thing comes into focus a split second after I hear myself ask, "What's Gracie got to do with it?"

"Well, it's her wedding too," Jacob says. The bride chooses the bridesmaids, the groom his groomsmen, but neither chooses parties who are anathema to the other, is his point.

Even though the penny has dropped, I'm still confused. "Gracie's already married," I feel compelled to point out.

"Her divorce becomes final next month," he says. This is the first I've heard about any divorce. True, Mike Law has been looking especially depressed lately, but I took this to be the result of his *union* to Gracie, not of the dissolution of that union. "We're thinking maybe a June wedding."

I try to think of something to say.

"That's a very unnatural way for a man to hold his jaw," Jacob remarks.

Perhaps. "Did you get a good look at my nose last week?"

He's grinning again. "Admit it," he says. "You had that coming. Besides. I know everything there is to know about her. Her flaws. Her insecurities. We've been fighting for twenty years. Also fucking. My wife kicked me out over Gracie, you recall. Gracie married Mike to piss me off when I wouldn't marry her before."

"And these strike you as compelling reasons for matrimony?"

"There *are* no compelling reasons for matrimony," Jacob admits. "Getting married is something you do despite compelling reasons."

"Have you mentioned you'll be taking her to Texas?"

"If that's what we decide, she's okay with it. Actually, I doubt we'll be going to Texas. This other offer looks better."

Again, I'm speechless.

"Anyway. We'll work things out. Marriage is about working things out."

"Have you ever noticed that it's only divorced people who ever say that?"

"Don't be a smart ass, always," Jacob advises me. "You and Lily always work things out. It's time for me to make something work. Seriously. You live by yourself out in West Railton for eight or ten years, you look at things differently. I don't look forward to dying alone."

I bite my tongue. Jacob was wise to leave the English department. The competition is stiff, but he's a straight man extraordinaire. "Marry this woman and you'll learn to," is the punch line I bite off the tip of my tongue. "Marry Gracie and you'll look back on your terrible loneliness as the good old days."

But these are not things for me to say to an old friend, even one who's been keeping secrets. I know that. No, my role in this is the offered one. I'll be best man and make a toast. It looks like I've got a couple months to come up with one.

"Well, I'll mark June on my calendar then," I tell him.

We're standing now, facing each other. Suddenly, Jacob looks inexpressibly sad, and to my way of thinking, he's got his reasons. Another baser thought tracks warily across the nether regions of my consciousness, stopping to gnaw, like a rat through a rope. I could be dean. A phone call to Dickie Pope. A verbal list of the most egregiously incompetent and burnt-out members of the English department, a promise to cease and desist killing geese (an easy pledge, given my innocence in the matter of the first goose). As Dickie Pope himself has said, those who are fired will deserve to be fired, and everyone else—the institution and its students—comes out a winner. And *I* would come out a winner. I do not, I think, covet Jacob Rose's job or his office, but there is the matter of karma, and I'm greatly attracted to the idea of my English department colleagues impeaching me as their chair today, only to discover me reborn as their dean tomorrow.

Still. I would trade it all for a good pee.

"Anyway, thanks," Jacob is saying as we shake hands. He seems to think this a particularly poignant moment, and perhaps it is.

"What for?"

"For not ridiculing my decision. For not telling me I'm a fool."

"Would I do that?"

He gives me a look. We let our hands drop.

"You're sure the wedding can't happen before June?" I ask.

"I don't see how," he says seriously, our poignant moment clouding his vision. "Why?"

"I was just thinking that maybe you could do it during halftime of the donkey basketball game," I tell him.

Suddenly there's such a braying behind me that I half-believe a donkey has materialized to complete the joke. But it's only Marjory, who returned while I was inside. It takes her a moment to compose herself, and when she does, she looks like a woman who'd willingly slit her own throat if someone would only loan her a knife. There are tears of sheer mortification in her eyes. "Oh, Jacob," she says. "I'm *so* sorry."

Truth be told, I'm almost as ashamed as she is, and I can't look at Jacob, who hasn't moved. I should have looked at him, though, because then I wouldn't be looking at Marjory, who has started braying all over again.

CHAPTER

25

"Then where is it?" Phil Watson wants to know.

We're studying the hanging X ray, looking for the stone I'm convinced is there for the simple reason that it has to be. Phil has tried his best to cover his reaction upon seeing me, but without much success. He's also seen no reason to order this X ray. He's done it to humor me, I know. I'm the one who wanted the X ray, and I wanted it to prove him wrong, to prove that there is a stone. Something's got me all backed up, and I've been both imagining and dreading this stone for a week. It's become too real to give up without a fight. Phil Watson, who has the advantage of not being tormented by an imagination, and whose father is not William Henry Devereaux, Sr., stone former extraordinaire, has not jumped to my conclusions but rather retreated lamely into standard medical procedure. Before agreeing to X-ray me, he's done a urinalysis and, despite my protest that he's going about things ass backwards, given me a rectal examination that was remarkable, it seemed to me, for its thoroughness. He's also done something called an IVP, results available tomorrow, and ordered blood work, results due by the end of the week. Meanwhile, if there's a stone, it's invisible, and Watson, to his credit, has not said I told you so, at least not in those words. If there had been a stone, he's explained, there'd be blood in my urine. Calculi are not like beach pebbles, worn smooth by tidal motion. They're sharp, jagged, ugly little monsters. He's shown me photographs. No, the problem, I'm told, is that my prostate is enlarged, my bladder slightly distended, though neither quite enough to cause the extreme symptoms I'm claiming. And I do, Phil admits, look like hell. What the hell's wrong with me? is what he'd like to know. At least we agree about the question.

"Maybe it's hiding somewhere?" I suggest, still unwilling to surrender the stone. "Maybe it's behind something."

Phil makes a face to let me know that this isn't much of an explanation. "Calculi don't hide. One large enough to cause an obstruction will show up every time."

I study the X ray. "According to this I don't even have a dick," I point out, though this is not precisely true. It's kind of an outline, a shadow, a ghost dick.

"Look," Phil explains again. "There are two kinds of calculi that are germane to the urinary tract. A kidney stone, here, could obstruct the ureter. They're tiny and very painful. Could conceivably not show up on the X ray even. Problem is that kidney stones don't restrict the flow of urine. What you'd have would be lower back pain. And you'd be peeing like a racehorse."

In fact, now that he says this, I do have a distant memory of my father doubled over in pain, getting my mother to massage his back. And he was always in the bathroom. "Not with that dick," I point out. "I've seen racehorses."

Watson ignores this. "Now a bladder stone, up here, can shut you right down. Back the urine right up to your eyeballs. Unless they're removed or broken up, the kidneys fail, then the patient fails. Trouble is, a stone large enough to do that is huge. It'd show up like a Susan B. Anthony dollar."

"So there's no stone."

"Other scenarios make more sense. Three I can think of." He shuts off the screen with an air of finality. I and my ghost dick disappear in a beat. "Enlarged prostate, as I said. You're the right age, unfortunately. Maybe a little young, but it happens."

"What do we do about that?"

"Long term? Possible removal of prostate gland. Short term? Catheterization to relieve the pressure may be warranted. Let's wait for the results of the IVP on that though."

I try not to wince. "What's scenario two?"

He hesitates. "We won't worry about that until we get the blood work back."

"Cancer?"

More hesitation. "A tumor is a possibility. Remember though. Not all tumors are cancerous."

"Wouldn't a tumor show up on the X ray?" I say, suddenly aware that Phil has turned off the screen before beginning this discussion of scenarios.

"Not always."

"Let's look again," I suggest.

He shakes his head. "We'll wait for the blood work."

"Just flip it on." I lean forward to do it myself.

"No," he says, preventing me. "In the rectal exam I felt an asymmetry that concerns me. Not large. Probably nothing."

How to explain this? How to describe the strange exhilaration at this information? Fear? Surely. But more than this, and it's the "more" that I can't explain. Because surely fear, given the circumstance, would be a perfectly adequate emotion. Unalloyed fear of death would satisfy William of Occam, and it should satisfy me. It's my mortality we're discussing. There's no need for complexity, no need to multiply entities, no need to court anticipation. But there it is, regardless. I can feel the exhilaration where it begins in my groin and radiates outward and upward like my backed-up urine. "What's scenario three?" I wonder. "I'm already dead, and this is all your dream?"

"The third scenario is more remote, more rare," he admits. "There have been cases where anxiety and tension have resulted in the symptoms you describe."

"This doesn't feel psychological to me," I tell him.

"Frankly, you don't seem like the type, Hank," Phil admits. "You aren't experiencing big money problems right now?"

I shake my head. "Not that I know of. Lily writes the checks."

"She and the girls okay?"

I've anticipated this question, so I don't hesitate. "Fine."

"You haven't taken up with some young graduate student or something?"

I blink at him. I've told Phil Watson about my father's propensity for forming stones but not, unless I've suffered another ellipsis, about his penchant for bedding female graduate students. How has he intuited that I may possess this infidelity gene? "No," I say, trying to sound convincing, which should be easy. I have, after all, declined to share a peach with Meg Quigley. "Should I?"

He ignores this. "Any other symptoms?"

"Of what?"

"Of anything."

I figure what the hell. "Time is slipping."

He blinks. "You mean it's slipping away?"

"Not exactly." I explain the phenomenon of what I've come to think of as my ellipses. How suddenly I'll be aware that a small chunk of time has passed without my being able to account for it. I explain what happened in Bodie Pie's office last Friday, how one second she was sitting there trying not to light a cigarette, and a second later she was asking me where I'd been, a half-smoked cigarette dangling from her lips.

"Sounds like simple abstraction to me." Phil shrugs when I finish. "But it's interesting. How old are you?"

"Fifty this summer," I confess.

He nods, studying me. "Rough age."

"I'm having a ball," I tell him, vaguely pissed off at the direction the conversation has taken. The thrilling glow of anticipation I felt while we were discussing the hypothetical tumor has dissipated.

"The fifties make first basemen of us all, Hank."

"Let me understand this," I say. "You think I can't pee because I don't want to play first base? *That's* your diagnosis?"

At this he surrenders a reluctant grin. "I haven't made a diagnosis. For that we await the blood work."

There's a knock on the door then, and a nurse appears. Phil follows her into the corridor, leaving me to dress. When I hear their voices receding down the hallway, I find the switch on the X-ray screen and flip it on. The screen is full of shapes and shadows, and I can't be sure which is the asymmetry that troubles Phil Watson. As I study the image, I can feel the warm glow of anticipation return and radiate all the way to my fingertips. I confront the question: Is it even remotely possible that I *want* to die?

When Phil Watson returns, he looks like he suspects what I've been up to. "I'll call you tomorrow with results of the IVP," he says. "Meantime, try not to worry."

"Can't help it," I say, though it's not precisely worry I'm feeling. "This is my favorite organ we're talking about. And I'm an intellectual."

Phil snorts at this. "It's the favorite organ of all intellectuals," he assures me. And he's never even met my father.

When I drive back out to Allegheny Wells to help Mr. Purty, I find he's ignored my advice to walk away. The U-Haul trailer itself is nowhere in evidence, and when I hit the remote for the garage door opener, I see that the boxes containing my father's books have been neatly stacked along the back wall of the garage. There must be a hundred of them. Can Mr. Purty have done this job all by himself? It's possible that Julie helped, I suppose, but I've worked with Julie before, and I know that having her help you do something is a lot like doing it alone. The boxes are stacked three deep, six feet high, and they completely block the door from the garage into the kitchen. Which is okay, I guess, since there's no longer room in the garage for my Lincoln, a car that barely fits when I inch it right up against the wall. I try not to think about the symbolism of all this—that my father's books, the physical manifestation of his intellect—have cut me off from my own house.

Julie is off somewhere, which leaves me alone with Occam, who is strangely subdued, as if he too were present during my visit to Phil Watson and is now contemplating the meaning of the "asymmetry" discovered during my rectal exam. When I let him out onto the back deck, instead of doing his usual frantic laps he goes over to the railing, gives the external world a leery sniff, returns to the sliding glass door, lies down with his head on his paws, and sighs. I pour myself a small glass of iced tea, hit the play button on the answering machine, and settle onto a barstool at the kitchen island, sipping the tea cautiously, aware that any liquid I ingest will have to be expelled.

When the machine stops rewinding I'm treated to my mother's voice, vexed as always when she speaks to our machine, an experience she so detests that she will usually hang up rather than utter a syllable. "Henry?" she says. "Are you there?" A pause, five full beats. "Are you there? If you're there, pick up. It's me." Another pause, then a muttered, "Damnation . . ." Followed by the sound of irritated hanging up. Then she's back. This time no hello. "Once again you disappoint me, Henry. If you're well enough to leave home, you're well enough to stop and say hello to your father. Don't call back. I'll be out most of the afternoon and I don't want your father disturbed. He's not well . . ." Again, a hang-up. Then back again. "He's not ill, just exhausted from the move. . . . I can't do all of this myself, you know. . . ." There's more to say, I can tell, but not to a damn machine.

I try to imagine William Henry Devereaux, Sr., left alone in her flat. Will it occur to him there, or has it already, that he's been delivered at last to retribution? He's too keen an observer of life to believe in anything like earthly justice, but it must look like something pretty close to that. All morning I've been haunted by Mr. Purty's description of my father bursting into tears. It may be that he has lost his mind, which would mean that destiny has played another cruel trick on my mother, allowing her to reclaim the mere shell of the man she'd been married to.

When the telephone rings, I stay right where I am, empty iced tea glass in hand, numbed by a melancholy that's easier understood than dispelled, a sadness that my daughter's voice deepens instead of lifting. "I'm out at the house," she informs me, "waiting for the fucking locksmith. Nobody can, like, tell you what time they're coming anymore. You get a morning appointment or an afternoon appointment. . . ."

Her voice falls tentatively, like she knows I'm here in the kitchen and is offering me the opportunity to pick up, to admit my own presence. "I thought that funny little man in the cowboy boots was going to have a stroke unloading those cartons. I figured he was a mover, but he said he was just a friend of Grandma's. Anyway, he was too old to do all that work by himself."

The answering machine has heard enough. It cuts her off and dutifully goes through its series of clicks and whirs, finishing up just as the phone rings again.

"Rude machine," my daughter continues. "I'll be back later, after the locksmith. Maybe we . . . well, I'll talk to you then, I guess."

But she's not finished. Her voice feels nearer now, more intimate, than when she was talking about Mr. Purty. "There's something you should know about Russell, Daddy," she says. "This isn't all his fault. He didn't . . . shove me, exactly. You probably already know that. Like, who am I kidding, right? There's something not . . . right with me . . . I've known it forever. I just get so . . ."

I'm standing at the counter now with my hand on the phone. I don't remember getting up or crossing the room, but I must have, because here I am.

"I thought it was a secret, but I guess it's not . . ."

"Julie," I say, my throat so constricted I can barely choke out the word. I still have not picked up the receiver, and I know I won't.

"Anyhow, don't blame Russell, okay?"

Again the machine hangs up, and while it whirs and clicks, I stand, hand still on the receiver, staring out the kitchen window. Occam has slunk off somewhere, as if listening to Julie's voice was more than he could bear. Besides, it's spring and there are new gardens to root in. Over the weekend, the trees have come into full leaf, insulating us once again. From where I stand, it's no longer possible to see Allegheny Estates II on the other side of the road, not even Paul Rourke's satellite dish. In fact, even Finny's ex-wife, our closest neighbor, has all but disappeared into the lush green foliage. Still, this feels, right now, like the blighted side of the road.

CHAPTER

26

For twenty-five years I've driven through the university's main gate and parked in the faculty lot nearest Modern Languages, but apparently I'm becoming a sneak, because for the fourth time in as many trips, I head over the mountain to campus, so that I may slip in unobserved through the rear gate. Judas Peckerwood, Back Door Man. Earlier today, if only for a fleeting moment, I entertained the idea of becoming dean via a back door phone call to Dickie Pope. What next? As I approach the campus's rear gate, it begins raining gently, and the surface of the road becomes slippery. Just how slippery I realize only when some lunatic woman in a car with a Century 21 logo on its side panel, parked facing the wrong way, opens the passenger side door without warning and steps out into the street in front of me.

This is, however, no ordinary lunatic, it turns out when I get a good look. It's my mother, and I slide to a stop a foot in front of her. The look of horror on the face of the realtor, her companion, testifies that she would hate like hell to lose this client. My mother, unimpressed by my screeching tires, remains unimpressed when she looks up and sees who made them screech. She's waited forty years for William Henry Devereaux, Sr.'s return, and she knows that God lacks the temerity to claim her in the very midst of her triumph. He's just toying with her, through me, and she's having no part of it. She slams the car door shut and opens her umbrella with a defiant flourish. Then she points at the two-story, gabled Victorian she's about to enter.

By the time I park farther down the block, both women have disappeared into the house in question. I'd know which one they went in even if my mother hadn't pointed it out to me, even if it didn't have a For Sale sign angled crazily on the front lawn. I'd know because it's a dead ringer for every house I lived in with my parents when I was a child. I don't even have to go in to know what it will look like inside, or to know that it will smell damp and feel clammy.

My mother and her realtor are waiting in the foyer next to their dripping umbrellas. The realtor still looks shaken by my mother's near miss, evidence that she's only just met my mother if she thinks Mrs. William Henry Devereaux can be killed when she's on a mission. In fact, Mrs. W.H.D. observes my slow, limping approach critically. "You might have helped poor Charles with all those boxes," she observes. "Especially since he's such a favorite of yours."

"The abuse of Mr. Purty is not a subject I should think you'd want to open, Mother," I warn her, introducing myself to the Century 21 lady, whose name tag identifies her as Marge.

"I hope you aren't going to blame me for that poor man's deluded affections," my mother says abstractedly, attempting to peer through the inner door's ornamental stained glass. "I may be their object, but I'm certainly not their cause."

"You play him like a violin."

"Nonsense," my mother says. "We had a very pleasant weekend in New York. We ate in restaurants of Charles's choosing. Even a truck stop on the way home. You should have seen your father trying to eat barbecued ribs, if you want to feel sorry for somebody."

"I do feel sorry for him," I assure her.

"He needs a new denture, and it's one of the first things we're going to attend to as soon as we're ensconced."

i

Marge can't seem to find the right key to the inner door, which delay affords my mother the opportunity to observe me more closely. "Your eyes are all puffy. Have you been weeping?" She reaches up to touch my right eye.

I deflect her index finger. "Don't be asinine. And speaking of weeping, what's this I hear about Dad bursting into tears?"

"I'll wait inside," Marge volunteers, feeling, no doubt, peripheral to this strange conversation.

When she's found the key and gone in, my mother says, in a voice intended to convey confidentiality without being actually confidential, "Your father is not in the best shape. That last woman—the Virginia Woolf one—really did a number on him."

My mother identifies all the women my father has aligned himself with according to their academic specialties. The young woman he left her for was in his D. H. Lawrence seminar, and since then he's taken up with a Brontë woman and a Joseph Conrad woman, before finally coming a cropper with Virginia Woolf.

"I'm convinced she was responsible for his collapse. Did you know she cleaned out both his checking and savings before abandoning him? Your father is a virtual pauper."

She pauses to let me contemplate a world in which such a thing can happen.

"And I don't care what they say at the hospital. He's not over it. Not that it would do him the slightest good to remain there. What he needs is normalcy. He needs familiar surroundings. He needs his books and someone to talk to about the things that matter to him. It's a shame he can't resume teaching until the fall, but the timing can't be helped."

I blink at her. "Teach where?" I ask before I think.

"Right here, of course," my mother explains, as if to a child. "One course per semester is not too much to expect, I think. Who's that little man with the ridiculous name who runs everything?"

"Dickie Pope?"

"I've an appointment to discuss the matter with him next week."

"I wouldn't mention my name."

"There shouldn't be any need," she assures me. "Your father's own name carries considerable weight, as you know. And the chancellor is an old friend. He's promised to instruct the little papal fellow to give your father the one course. They're fortunate to have a man of your father's stature. He'll have to have a designation, of course, but all that can be worked out later."

On this note we move from the foyer into the house, where the excellent Marge awaits us.

"Ah, well, yes," my mother says when we enter the formal dining room through two French doors. The room is lined with bookcases, floor to ceiling, and what she imagines, I suspect, is the room full not only of books but of people—the best graduate students (of which there are none on our campus), the occasional visiting poet or other dignitary (for which there is no budget), an adoring English department faculty to hang on my father's ideas (Finny?). What she's looking at is her own faith, and the smile that blossoms on her old face is pure vindication.

"Mother," I can't help but say, "you take my breath away."

At the rear gate to the university I encounter three idling Railton police cars, as well as a campus security vehicle. My first irrational thought is that they're waiting there to prevent my entrance, but apparently they have other business, because after I turn in, the lead car pulls out into traffic and the other three follow. In the last of these, a young woman occupies the rear seat reserved for miscreants, and as the two vehicles pass I catch a quick glimpse of her face, which is familiar, though I can't place it. Was she among the throng of animal rights protesters this morning? Even more bizarre, that split second in which I register the young woman's features, she seems to take me in as well, perhaps even to recognize me. Do I imagine it, or does her head turn to follow me?

I park in the far lot behind Modern Languages. There's a red Camaro idling in the no parking zone at the rear door. Rourke's wife is at the wheel, apparently waiting for her husband to emerge. Even with the Camaro's windows rolled up, I can hear music pounding inside as I approach. Barefoot as usual, the second Mrs. R. has one foot up on the dash and is wiggling her toes. Another person caught in this posture might conceivably suffer a misgiving or two, but not the second Mrs. R., who smiles at me dreamily when I wave, as if she suspects I might wish to join her, take off my loafers, and compare toes.

Her husband comes out through the back door just then, studies me for a moment, and observes, "You look like shit."

I tell him thanks, then, to my surprise, hear myself say, "Listen. Don't misunderstand this, because I'm not after your vote. But I didn't give Dickie Pope any list." Why I tell him this, I have no idea, since I haven't even given this assurance to my friends.

Rourke nods. He seems almost disappointed. "Funny thing. I believe you."

"Okay," I say, and for some reason I feel absurd pleasure at being able to arrive at this simple understanding with an old enemy. I feel better about it, in fact, than I've felt about anything for days.

"That still leaves the fact that you're an asshole though," he points out, a thin smile creasing his lips.

"Well, sure," I tell him. "There's still that."

Could it be that Rourke is also feeling the strange, momentary camaraderie? Because otherwise this is where our conversation would end. Instead he says, "You missed the fireworks upstairs."

"Which?"

"Juney and Orshee. She called him a hypocritical little putz. Shouted at him, actually, out in the hallway."

I'm not sure how to feel about this news. "Was Teddy there?"

"No, he was hiding in his office. Too scared to come out, probably. Now Orshee's hiding in *his* office."

"Thanks for warning me. I think I'll go hide in mine."

He nods, as if to suggest this would be a good tactic for a man like me.

"So," he continues. "How does it feel to be in your final hours as chair of this pathetic department?"

"You sound sure."

He snorts at this, starts for the Camaro. "I can count. And don't worry. I'll be back for the meeting."

"Tell me something," I call after him. "How come you never drive anymore?" It's just occurred to me that the last half dozen times I've seen the Camaro, a car Rourke never used to let anyone drive, it's been the second Mrs. R. at the wheel.

He turns back toward me, apparently considering how, perhaps whether, to answer. His hesitation makes me realize that the question is more personal than I intended. "I'm not really supposed to," he finally says. "I started having dizzy spells around the first of the year. Blacked out once."

"I had no idea."

"It's not common knowledge."

"I won't say anything."

"Don't." Not a request. A warning.

I've got half a mind to tell him what my own doctor suspects is wrong with me, just so the words could be spoken.

"They're running some tests. In the meantime she drives, so I don't hurt anybody."

"And here I always thought you wanted to hurt everybody," I say.

He snorts at this but doesn't appear to take particular offense. "No fun hurting somebody if you aren't even awake to watch."

"Right."

He's grinning again. He seems as aware as I that this is the longest, pleasantest conversation we've had in fifteen years. What can it mean? we both seem to be wondering. "We should round up the gang and play one more Sunday afternoon game of football. Before half of us get canned."

"Remember how Gracie played for a while after we hired her?" I ask. "Jacob would take the snap, hand her the ball, and then tackle her himself?"

"Fucking Jacob. I'd like to snap that little prick in two," he says, like he means it. So much for nostalgia.

I shake my head. "Reverend," I tell him. "You've cheered me up. As usual."

"I never mean to."

"I know it," I assure him.

A campus security cruiser glides by, its driver peering into the illegally parked Camaro at the second Mrs. R. "Go ahead. Stop," her husband mutters beneath his breath. "Get out of the car and say something. I'll feed you your revolver."

The cruiser continues on its way. Which reminds me. "What was going on with all the Railton cops earlier?"

"Some lunatic townie crashed a class. Took all her clothes off and started speaking in tongues, is what I heard."

"Whose class?"

"That I didn't hear," he says. "Women ever take their clothes off in your classes?"

"Never," I admit.

"Mine either. How about in your office?"

"Not there either. Yours?"

"Just once. Her." He nods in the direction of the second Mrs. R., who's now watching us thoughtfully and chewing on her hair. "I should have been prepared, but I wasn't."

CHAPTER

27

My afternoon comp class is not persuaded. In fact, they feel ill-treated. I've asked their advice, in essay form, then apparently gone ahead and killed a goose before they've even handed their papers in. A couple of the students in this class were present for my on-camera interview this morning, at which time I did not deny that I was the perpetrator. Worse, they have heard my implied threat to continue the carnage unless I get my budget. And so they are upset with me, despite the fact that I have apparently followed the explicit advice of the majority of their essays, which I have glanced through after collecting them and separated into two unequal piles. From the larger "kill a duck" stack, I've read three short essays aloud, anonymously, for the purpose of inspiring discussion or, failing discussion, private misgiving. It's my hope that if the majority of these intellectually addled young folk actually hear their words aloud, if they are forced to digest not only their advice to me but the logic that led to this advice, they will, if not change their minds, at least become acquainted with doubt.

The three essays I have read aloud, authored by two young men and a young woman, proceed along similar lines. I should kill a duck, they argue, because I have threatened to, and if I don't follow through, no one will ever again take my threats seriously. The writers draw foreign policy parallels. They hate it when America threatens third world nations and then, in the words of Bobo, the student I have threatened with failure if he misses another class, "pussy out." The great thing about Desert Storm was that we said we were going to kick butt and then we kicked it. If we made a mistake, it was that we stopped kicking butt too soon. We should have kicked it all the way to Baghdad. Same way with World War II. When we were done kicking German butt, we should have kicked Russian butt and saved ourselves the necessity of kicking it later. All three writers seem to be under the impression that we did kick it later.

I don't need to ask my class whether they find these arguments persuasive. The more outrageous, the more historically inaccurate and fallacious the analogies, the further the essays drift from the assigned topic, the more the authors are cheered. Apparently, *some* form of persuasion has taken place here. The majority of my students have persuaded each other and themselves, and they've done so in such an enthusiastic and raucous fashion that they've effectively smothered dissent. Among my twenty-three comp students, I have a half dozen or so who are daring to frown disagreement, but that's all they're daring. My best student, Blair, who is pale and thin and has impossibly delicate hands with veins that are large and blue, is actually squirming in her seat, but I know from experience that she's paralytically shy, and, perhaps because of this, she thinks it's my job to show these louts the error of their ways. I'm the one who's paid to be here, after all. Everyone else pays. There is some merit to this argument, though I disagree with it. Still, it probably *is* my job to start the process.

"I'm not persuaded," I finally tell my unworthy majority, eliciting a massive groan. They've suspected as much. They know me. They know that if they think one thing, I'll think another. Their parents have agreed to pay their tuition on the condition that they major in something sensible and pay no attention to people like me, who are, they warn their kids, intent on transforming their values and undermining their religious principles. If Angelo were here, he'd assure them they're right to be wary. Look what happened to *his* daughter.

And of course the fact that I am not persuaded can mean only one practical thing—more bad grades. My handful of thoughtful students perk up a bit when I say I'm not persuaded, but they are aware that they are a small minority. Also, the majority is espousing violence, even more reason to be cautious. Blair starts to raise her hand, then lowers it again, which, for some reason, makes me angrier than the essays I've just read aloud. "Is there anyone besides me who is not persuaded that I should kill a duck?" I say, looking directly at Blair and letting her know that I've caught her gesture. The look she gives me in return could not be more eloquent. "Don't do this to me," she's pleading silently. "Just read my essay at home. You'll see what I think."

"Blair?" I say. Another communal groan. Not only do Bobo and company know me, they know this Blair girl. They know that she gets good grades. They know that she can spell and everything. They are convinced that if she were not in this particular class, their own grades would go up dramatically. She invites invidious comparison, and they wish to hell she'd quit it.

Blair draws a deep breath, the kind of breath you take when you fear it's the last you'll get before the anesthesia brings you down, down, down. "I saw it," she says in a voice so quiet I can barely hear it.

"What?" says Bobo from the back row.

"I saw it," Blair repeats. "The goose. Hanging from the tree branch this morning. It made me sick."

She's embarrassed to say this last, I suspect, not because she'll be derided, which she will, but because the person who hung it is perhaps her instructor.

"I bet you've eaten goose for Christmas dinner." Bobo goes on the attack, to the delight of his compatriots in the back row. "I bet you went back for seconds."

Although Blair looks like she's never gone back for seconds of anything, she does not dispute her adversary's claim, or even acknowledge him. I can tell that she's conceded defeat, surrendered the field. If she's angry with anyone, she's angry with me. Or she would be if she thought she had a right to be.

"Blair," I say.

"Please," she whispers, but she's pleading with the wrong man.

"It made you sick," I repeat, noting that she looks more than a little ill right now. "But tell me. Did it surprise you, seeing that goose hanging there from a tree?"

At first she seems not to understand my question. Am I trying to trick her? I'm not above tricking students, as they all well know. If she says yes she was surprised, isn't she accusing me of being all talk? If she says no, she wasn't surprised, isn't she suggesting that, sure, she thought me capable of violence? There seems to be no way out of this without insulting her instructor.

"Be honest," I suggest.

"Yes," she says, I hope, honestly. "I was surprised."

"Why?"

Another deep, painful breath. She's already taken several since the one she feared would be her last before passing out in dread.

"I didn't think you'd do it."

At this point I could help her with my inflection. What is there that prevents me? Why not help my best student off the hook? Why let her twist? There's another pretty good student next to her who has raised his hand. I could turn to him. "Why? Why did you think I wouldn't? I threatened to, didn't I?"

She's in the front row, and I've come out from behind my desk to stand over her, loom over her. She reminds me a little of Lily when she was young, when we were wielding signs together, except Blair lacks Lily's steely combativeness. This girl's mortification is tangible, which has the effect of taking me outside myself, seeing the whole scene as an objective observer would. I imagine Finny standing outside my door the way I stood outside his, even more aghast at my classroom behavior than I was at his.

When I begin again, I try to lower and soften my voice, but what comes out is little more than a croak. I'm seeing through the eyes of Finny the Man, speaking through the constricted larynx of Finny the Goose. "Didn't I?"

Blair neither speaks nor moves, and who can blame her?

I can. "Blair," I say, as calmly as I'm able. "You're right. But it doesn't do any good to be right if you won't *speak*."

"Then I'll be wrong," she says, gathering her things from beneath her chair, shoving everything hurriedly into her backpack. Everyone is watching her now. No one has paid the slightest attention to my question. When I step back to give her room, she's out the door with breathtaking speed and grace.

I'm the next to speak, but it takes me a while. "Anyone," I say. "Why was Blair right to be surprised, given my public threats?"

No one moves or speaks, not even the boy whose hand had been in the air and ignored for so long. In the end it's the bell ending class that breaks the silence.

"Because," I explain to them, without conviction, "it was a comic, not a serious, threat. Because the man who threatened to kill a duck a day until he got a budget was wearing a fake nose and glasses. Because it makes no sense to carry out a comic threat to serious consequence."

Needless to say, we end where we began, unpersuaded. My argument, that comedy and tragedy don't mix, that they must remain discrete, runs contrary to their experience. Indeed, it may run contrary to my own. These students have watched this very class begin in low comedy and end in something, if not serious, at least no longer funny. They file out, sullen, confused. Bobo is last. He stops at my desk as I'm stuffing the essays into my satchel. "You can flunk me if you want," he says, "but that was a shitty thing to do to her."

"Congratulations, Bobo," I say, looking up. "You've just articulated a persuasive ethical position."

Back in the halls of the English department, people have begun to cluster outside their offices in anticipation of the department meeting that's twenty minutes away. Paul Rourke has come back, as promised, and is caucusing with Finny and Gracie at the far end of the hall. Teddy, returning from class, head down, disappears quickly into his office, pulling the door closed behind him. There's no sign of June or Orshee.

Rachel, to my deep regret, has gone to pick up her son at school. She's left a swatch of messages and a personal note in her elegant hand: "Good luck? Call me tonight? Let me know how it turns out?" I can't help smiling. Question marks even in her Post-it notes. Perhaps it's not all insecurity though. Rachel knows ambiguity when she sees it, knows that good luck in this instance may mean my opponents win. She may even suspect that I'm considering not distributing the guidelines for the recall of a department chair that she's located and reproduced for me. "Sorry about the ceiling mess?" the note continues. "I've called the physical plant? They'll replace the tile tomorrow?"

Sure enough, there's a large rectangular tile missing from the ceiling directly over my desk where one of the asbestos removal workers charged with detoxing Modern Languages apparently stepped through. The jagged shards of the tile are sticking up out of my wastebasket. It's actually a relief to see both the hole in the ceiling and the tile in the wastebasket because I'd been puzzling over why the air in the room seemed full of suspended dust. What I can't help wondering is if there's anybody still up there. When I stand on my desk I can almost see up into the dark cavity in the ceiling. All seems to be quiet. Apparently asbestos removal workers keep sensible hours.

I'm still standing on my desk staring into the darkness, when the phone at my right heel rings. I can see that it's Rachel's outside line that's blinking, but I climb down off my desk and answer anyway. If it's for me, I can always pretend to be somebody else. "I was hoping to reach Rachel Williams," says a vaguely familiar voice.

"Wendy?" I say, placing it.

"Hank Devereaux?" my agent wants to know.

I admit it.

"Well, I guess you've become a celebrity after all," she says. "I can't believe the play that duck story is getting. There may be a TV movie of the week in it if we play our cards right."

I can't tell if she's joking. "Wendy,". I say. "You know how fond I am of you, but how about I just give you Rachel's home phone?"

"Long day?"

"This day is already the worst month of my life," I assure her, "and it's not over yet."

"Actually, I just called her at home."

"Try again. You probably caught her in transit. She picks up her kid at school about now."

"I'm on my way out myself. I may have to call her tomorrow."

"I'm glad you decided to take her on," I say, fishing a little, maybe. "She said you liked the stories."

She pauses before responding. "I not only liked them, I sold them."

"When?"

"About twenty minutes ago." When I don't say anything right away, she says, "That's a very unprofessional thing I just did. Telling you before the author. Except I know you helped her. I thought you'd be thrilled."

"I am, Wendy," I assure her.

"You sound funny about it, is why I mention it."

If I sound a little funny, the explanation isn't one I'm sure I can share with her. In fact, her news has taken me back more than twenty years, to the afternoon this same woman called with the news that *Off the Road* had been bought by a trade publisher, news that ultimately resulted in Julie's conception, our buying the land in Allegheny Wells that started the faculty stampede, my refusal to sell to Paul Rourke, my promotion to full professor, which deepened our roots in a place we never planned to live for very long. All from one phone call. What her call is going to mean to Rachel I don't know, but I do know her life is about to change.

"It's not much money," Wendy says, as if this will make me feel better. "It won't be a big seller. There's a lot of grunge fiction out there since Ray Carver."

"There's a lot of grunge out there in real life," I feel compelled to point out.

"Is her husband like the guy in the stories?"

"They're separated, but yeah," I say. "Call her now, okay?"

"What time does she get in to work in the morning?"

"Call her now, Wendy. You've no idea what this is going to mean to her."

"Okay, I'll call until I reach her."

"Listen, while I've got you on the phone . . . do you suppose this has ever happened before?"

"What?"

"A guy gets a call from his agent, who informs him she's just sold his secretary's book?"

There's a beat, and then she says, "I can't sell books you don't write, Hank. Are you working on a book?"

I have in my hand a sheet of Xerox paper I've been absently folding and refolding into half a dozen different shapes. When I unfold it again and flatten it out on my new blotter with the palm of my hand, I realize it's one of the thirty copies of the department's operating paper detailing the rules governing my ouster. I have been hoping that my old agent and friend would ask this very question, so that I could tell her I was thinking of maybe having another go. If the piece of paper I've just been worrying into various shapes were the first page, however wretched, of a new book, I might be able to tell her that. But it's not the first page of anything, and so I feel compelled to give her the simple truth, unadorned. "No," I tell her. "Call Rachel."

When we've both hung up, I refold the sheet of paper in half, lengthwise, and slip it into the inside pocket of my coat. Outside the frosted glass of my office door, shadows are moving, migrating down the hall toward the English department conference room. Intellectually, I know the purpose of this shadow movement is to determine the immediate administrative future of one William Henry Devereaux, Jr., Department of English Interim Chair. But let's be frank. It's a future that doesn't interest me much.

CHAPTER

28

During my sophomore year in high school, I fell in love with a beautiful black-haired girl named Eliza, and on the night of our third date, at the homecoming dance, she broke up with me, offering not a word of explanation and leaving me to drown my sorrows in one cream soda after another in the dark, strangely unlocked school cafeteria. Having that big, dark, familiar room all to myself suited my sense of tragic loss, especially with the sound of the Everly Brothers leaking in from the gym next door. Whenever I want you all I have to do is dream. Dream, dream, dream. I couldn't bring myself to leave the cafeteria until I heard the announcement for the last dance, whereupon I got up, collected my armload of Fanta bottles, deposited them in the rack next to the soda machine, and sloshed back into the gym to retrieve my coat where I'd left it on the bleachers. The lights were always turned down low for the last dance, and my plan was to get my coat and slip out into the tragic night unobserved, but suddenly she was there, my Eliza, and she wanted to know if I would dance with her, even though she was terrible, would I dance with her, please. She touched my elbow bewitchingly.

Well, I could and did dance with her, and when we came together on the dance floor, her small breasts on either side of my jutting, adolescent breastbone, explanation was unnecessary, though I listened to how she'd suddenly realized what she had in me, how she didn't want to lose me. Even in the dark gym I could see her eyes were full of tears, and it made me a little misty-eyed myself to think how much she loved me after all. The next day I heard the truth from her girlfriend—that Eliza had broken up with me so she could be available for another boy who, she heard, was about to break up with his girlfriend of many months. When this did not happen, she'd come back to me. Even as I'd listened to Eliza's tearful epiphany, part of me suspected something like the friend's version, but it must be said that I preferred the tale told by the little minx who nuzzled herself so sweetly against me. What is truth, anyway?

The truth is I am dreaming. I realize this without completely waking up. The truth is I don't want to wake up. In my dream I'm in bed with my wife, and the bed is in the middle of an empty high school gymnasium. The Everly Brothers are crooning dreamily in the background about all I have to do, and it ain't much. My wife is contrite. In fact, Lily is offering an act of contrition, her eyes full of tears. I've been reluctant to believe she has anything to feel guilty about, and so she's explaining just how wrong I am. She's spent the weekend in Philadelphia with a man she met on our honeymoon in Puerto Vallarta over twenty-five years ago. She's not sure I'd remember him. He sat all alone at the table next to ours, and she fell in love with him then and there, and he with her. They've kept in touch over the years, and now after loving each other from afar they've spent the weekend together, consummating their faith and devotion. What my wife wants to know is if there is any way I can forgive her.

I would like to believe my wife because this is one beautiful love story she's telling me, and I've got a meaty dramatic role in it myself. I mean, this is truly heroic forgiveness that's being asked of me. I'm a hell of a guy in this story. And so I forgive my wife despite the fact that there are parts of her story that simply can't be true. We didn't honeymoon in Puerto Vallarta, for instance, and she may be lying about other things as well. Still, my dream logic goes, if I could forgive the lying little Eliza, whose memory seems to have furnished the props for my dream, can I do less for my own wife?

Well, it's true there are other inducements to Christian forgiveness. My dream-Lily is naked beneath the covers, and apparently she has not lost all fondness for her husband. When she moves on·top of me, I feel a terrible, wonderful release. We make love with almost unbelievable gentleness. In fact, there seems to be precious little friction, which may be why my dream orgasm is curiously devoid of, well, sensation. Even so, I don't want it to end, and it doesn't. I'm amazed. It's the longest orgasm of my life, and wouldn't you know, I can't feel a thing. Still, if this is what I'm offered, I'll take it. I'm that delighted to see Lily, that moved she'd confide in me about this other guy she's been in love with all these years.

There may be no harder admission for a man of my years to make than that he has wet his pants, but this, to my horror, is what I have done. By the time I jolt fully awake, my chinos have gone from tan to dark brown in the crotch and all down one leg. I also have a wet sock and shoe. My whole office smells like the doorway to a lower Manhattan bank at eight in the morning in mid-August. I call Phil Watson, make his receptionist put him on the phone.

"Watson," I tell him. "I fell asleep and wet my pants."

"Significantly?"

I notice a shadow go by outside the frosted glass, so I lower my voice. "I'm going to need a new office chair."

"Huh."

"I must have passed the stone."

"There's no stone, Hank."

The certainty in his voice is more annoying than I let on. I remember falling asleep with one foot up on my desk, and my logic is that this gravity-shifting posture has caused the stone to move, unlocking my urine. This explanation makes such immediate sense that I can give it up only reluctantly, a necessary concession to my physician's expertise. This is the way my students feel, I realize, when I suggest stylistic revision. They *like* the sentence the way they wrote it. They defer to my greater knowledge and experience because they must, but they still like the way the original sentence sounded when it had a dangling modifier, and they secretly suspect that my judgment, while generally sound, may be flawed in this instance. And they're a little miffed at my insistence, just as I'm now miffed at Phil Watson.

"You think it's cancer, don't you?" I accuse him.

"I don't think it's a stone," he admits. "Actually, this emission may be good news."

"Not from where I'm sitting," I tell him.

I hang up, examine my situation more closely. This morning it took me a half hour to fill a thimble with urine, barely enough to do a urinalysis. Now, in the half hour or so I've been asleep, I've voided my bladder enough to soak a pant leg, a wool sock, a size ten shoe, and a deep office chair.

What I require now, I realize, is an escape plan. I've talked to the only person in the world who is likely to understand my predicament. Now my duty is to avoid all the others until I can clean up. It's five-twenty and still light outside, which means I'm going to have to walk halfway across campus in dripping, reeking chinos. Either that or wait until it's dark and my pants have dried. The good news is that at this hour the faculty (except for those meeting to recall me as chair) have gone home, and most of the students have adjourned to their dining halls. The other good news is that having voided my bladder I feel wonderful, better than I have felt in days. I feel like I could do the quarter mile from Modern Languages to the back lot where I left the Lincoln at a dead sprint. In fact, this is the plan I've about decided on when I hear the double doors grind open down the hall and voices heading in my direction. I recognize Billy Quigley's voice immediately, and I'm grateful that it's Billy. If I had to choose someone on this campus to find me in my present condition, it would be Billy, who, like all drunks, knows humiliation. If he were alone, I'd go out into the hall and demand his pants, and, knowing Billy, he'd hand them over.

But Billy is not alone. Recognizing his daughter's voice, I'm filled with blind panic. There are many things I would spare Billy's beautiful daughter, and the fact that she has been flirting with an incontinent man is one of them. The footsteps and voices stop outside my door. There's a tap on the frosted glass.

"He was just in there," I hear Meg tell her father. "I heard him talking on the phone."

"Come out of there, you peckerwood," Billy Quigley demands. He's got a late afternoon load on, I can tell. "Our dimwit colleagues are still at it. Let's go down there and raise hell. We'll save your worthless peckerwood bacon."

"Maybe he went to the men's room," Meg suggests. It may be the scent of urine seeping from beneath the door that suggests this possibility.

"Nah, he's in there hiding." Billy pounds on the doorframe with his fist, rattling the glass.

"Maybe he's . . ." She stops. I can almost hear her thinking. "Are you all right, Hank?"

I hold my breath.

"I know where Rachel keeps the key," I hear Meg say. "Let me into the office."

They go next door, and I hear Billy use his key to get them inside. He's not supposed to have one of these, but most of the faculty do, so they can sneak inflammatory anonymous memos into the mailboxes in the dead of night. A light goes on in the outer office.

"Somebody's in there," I hear Billy say. "I can hear him."

"Here," Meg says, and a key is inserted into the lock.

They both enter, look around the office for a hiding space large enough to conceal a man my size. Meg checks the cavity under my desk. "It smells like he's been keeping cats in here," she observes.

Billy is looking up at the hole in the ceiling. She sees where he's looking and follows his glance. "You don't suppose . . . ," she says.

I withdraw farther into the shadows. My eyes are beginning to adjust to the darkness, but there's a thick, slanting oak beam overhead that keeps me from rising.

"Nah," Billy says. "He ducked out the other door when we came in through the office. I heard him." But he's still looking up into the ceiling suspiciously. It's *possible,* he's thinking. I'm just crazy enough. "Well, screw him," he concludes. "I'm going to go disrupt that meeting. They must be about ready to vote. They've had their hour to posture."

"I'll wait here a few minutes," Meg says, "in case he comes back."

When her father's gone and out of earshot, I hear Meg pick up the phone, dial a number. After a moment she says, "Hi, it's me. He's still here at school if you want to see him . . . I don't know . . . suit yourself."

When she hangs up, I lean forward, sneak a peek below at Meg, who's begun to pace. Next to finding me in my hiding place, the thing I fear worst is that she'll decide to see what it feels like to sit in the chair's chair. Perhaps she suspects what it will feel like, because she doesn't. She stays on her side of my desk, and I've just decided that Meg is a good, respectful Catholic girl when she pauses and turns her head at an odd angle so she can read what's sitting in the middle of my desk, which happen to be the Xeroxes of the department operating paper that Rachel gave me this morning. Meg reads part of the text upside down, then sensibly turns the papers around, rotating the neck of my desk lamp and bending over the small print in earnest. She's wearing a shirt with a scoop neckline, no bra on underneath.

My behavior at this moment, it occurs to me, is undignified. I lean back into my self-imposed darkness to contemplate the position I find myself in, though the privileged view I have just been afforded is of precisely the sort that muscles out abstract thought. It's not entirely dark up here among the rafters, I realize, now that my eyes have adjusted. By the light coming from the office below I'm able to examine the close, low space I've folded myself into so unnaturally. Directly above me, inches above both my head and knees, is the slanted ceiling. I have difficulty turning around, but when I do I see, off in the distance, other shafts of light shooting up from below like lasers, and I hear, though just barely, Billy Quigley greeting our colleagues as he enters the meeting. Also, now that I'm paying attention, other distant voices.

There's an urgency to these murmurs that reminds me of the distant arguments I listened to as a boy. The old university houses we lived in transmitted sounds through heat registers in the walls and floors, and some nights, when I wasn't sleepy, I'd crawl out of bed and put an ear to the cold register and learn what I could before the heat clicked on about what was on the minds of my parents. Once I heard them discussing what they were going to get me for Christmas, which was good to know, since it was something I didn't want. Knowing their plan so far in advance meant I'd have many natural opportunities to subvert it. On another occasion, I heard a man's raised voice say the words, "You bet your ass," which caused me to conclude we had a visitor downstairs. The only other time I'd heard the same expression was outside a restaurant where my mother had taken me. There, propped up against a parking meter, a man dressed in dark, shabby clothing seemed to be waiting for us when we came out. He looked right at us from beneath hooded eyes and said, "You bet your ass." My mother whispered that I was to pay no attention, the man was drunk, but it was hard for me to understand that his words were not meant specifically for us. What in the world, I now wondered, my ear to the cold register, was this same man doing as a visitor in our house? The heat clicked on before I could discover.

The next morning the question was still fresh in my mind when I came down to the breakfast table, and I was about to inquire when I saw something in my father's expression that stopped me. My mother and father hadn't said a word to each other since I came in, and suddenly I knew it was my father who had uttered those strange words, that he spoke them in anger to my mother, and I believe this may have been the first time I intuited that adults had secret lives, that there were things about my parents I didn't know, things they didn't want me to know, maybe ever. Moreover, there was apparently some common emotional denominator between my elegant father and the shabby, leering drunk outside the restaurant. I felt strange all that day when I thought about it, and I remember it was scary at first. But by the end of the day I felt the thrill of knowledge, and when I arrived home and my mother asked if I'd had a good day at school, I very nearly said the words that I'd been practicing in my head all afternoon. You bet your ass.

I'm thinking these words when the light goes out below, plunging me into near total darkness. Meg has apparently grown tired of waiting for me to return and switched off the desk lamp. I hear my office door open and shut. Only the light from the other side of the frosted glass keeps the darkness from being complete. I can barely see the outline of the hole in the ceiling I've climbed up through, and it occurs to me that if I tried to lower myself through it, blind, I might very well end up in the hospital, as Lily predicted. But never mind. I have no intention of returning to my office just yet. Many inspired plans are hatched in darkness. And once dignity is surrendered, there are plenty of options.

.   .   .

"Let's vote and go home, for Chrissake," Billy Quigley is saying, directly below me.

"You weren't even here for the discussion," Finny, who's chairing the meeting in the absence of the chair, points out.

"I've been listening to you people for thirty years," Billy reminds his colleagues. "Don't tell *me* I haven't been here for the discussion."

"That doesn't mean you can stroll in an hour late, reeking of whiskey, and call the question," Finny says, not unreasonably.

"Better whiskey than hypocrisy," Billy says before putting his head down on the table and falling asleep.

"We do seem to be all talked out." I recognize this voice as belonging to Jacob Rose. His attendance surprises me until I remember that either the dean or the dean's representative must be present during proceedings initiated against a department chair. Jacob is also, technically, still a member of the English department.

My perch is far from ideal. I'm right above the long conference table, having been drawn to this spot by a thin crease of light. I don't dare move around for fear of making noise that will result in my discovery. Still, I can't see much. Billy Quigley's balding head is directly below. Paul Rourke, doodling geometric designs on a notepad, is across from him. Gracie is somewhere nearby. I can smell her perfume wafting up. I try jimmying the ceiling tile with the point of a pen to give me another half inch or so, but I have to give up when fine particles of the pressed tile begin to float down like pollen onto Billy Quigley's scalp.

"We appear to have a motion before us to call the question." Finny sighs. "Do we have a second?"

"I second," Jacob Rose says.

"You're ex officio," Finny, ever the parliamentarian, points out. "The rules permit you neither to move nor to second."

The motion dies for lack of a second.

"Further discussion?"

Silence. This is my department, all right. A motion to call the question dies for lack of a second, and the discussion dies right along with it. We do understand irony though. I detect nervous tittering below.

"Look," Jacob says. "By all means. Talk as long as you want, but when you finish there are still two issues. If you want to recall Hank as chair, do it. But you will then have to elect a chair."

"You're certain our search is dead?" Gracie wants to know.

"Yes," Jacob says. "I know you all were counting on going outside. But the funding didn't come through. What can I tell you? You knew that was a possibility."

"Do you know how many hours the personnel committee has worked to arrive at a final list?" Gracie wants to know of the man she's planning to marry.

"No," Jacob admits, "but I know all of you. This is a department that can't agree to call a question, regardless of the question. So my guess is, many hours. The fact remains. If you recall the chair, you'll have to elect another. Do you want one election or two? Do you really want another interim chair for the last two weeks of the spring term? Then yet another election in August for the fall? My advice is that you resolve this procedural issue first. Don't recall your chair before you decide how and when you're going to elect another."

"How long have you known all this?" Paul Rourke stops doodling long enough to ask.

"About the outside search?" Jacob says. "Since late Friday morning. I heard just before I had to leave town. I got back this morning, and now I've informed you."

"How long has Hank known?" Rourke again.

"Since he's not here, I have to assume he doesn't know even now."

"You and he haven't discussed this?"

"I've been out of town. I told you."

Rourke smiles, bored. "Since you didn't answer my question, I'll ask it again. Have you and Hank discussed the fact that our search was canceled?"

"No," Jacob says, and if I didn't know better, I'd believe him.

Rourke, I can tell, does not, though he goes back to doodling. "Sorry," he says. "I always feel better after I've made you tell an outright lie."

"Why would I lie to you?" Jacob wants to know. The aggrieved innocent is one of his better roles.

"Because that's what deans do?" Rourke suggests. "Because you and Hank are friends?"

"Hey," Jacob says. "We're all friends here, aren't we?"

Rourke lip-farts.

"That's a motion somebody *should* make." Orshee's voice. "In fact, I will. I move that we all try to be friends here."

Silence. This motion too dies for lack of a second, though it may not have been taken seriously. I hear June Barnes, somewhere below, mutter, "Grow up, friend."

And hearing these words I believe, perhaps for the first time, that there has been something between Teddy's wife and Orshee. Maybe it's just the silence that her muttered words engender, as if to acknowledge that somehow life—something real—has wormed its way into this living parliamentarian death, something no one quite knows how to deal with. How many meetings like this one have we sat through in the last twenty years? How many hours, weeks, months would they total if measured out in Prufrock's coffee spoons? How many good books have gone unread, essays unwritten, research discontinued, in order to make room for brain-scalding meetings like this one? How many books might I myself have authored? I know what William of Occam would say. He'd say it doesn't matter. Had I been meant to write books instead of sit in English department meetings, I'd have written them. I made my choice, the fact that I can't remember making it, to the contrary, notwithstanding.

I am now literally above all this, a posture I have long attempted to suggest from my seat at the table. For years Lily has been urging me to stand up and testify. Either I'm one of these people or I'm not. To her way of thinking I should either throw in my lot with them, live among them, my friends and colleagues, or take my respectful leave and find out where I *do* belong. Other people make their peace with who they are, what they've become. Why can't I? Why live the life of a contortionist, scrunched in among the rafters? So that I can maintain the costly illusion that I am not what my father is? Is this pretense worth the effort? To this reasonable argument I offer my father's own words. You bet your ass.

Below, the procedural issue has been decided. The Finny-Rourke contingent, having seen through Jacob's strategy, has forced a vote on the recall issue today and scheduled another meeting for Friday to enter nominations, the election itself to follow the Friday after. I'm grateful things have speeded up. It has to be ninety degrees up here among the rafters. I'm sweating profusely, and when I lean forward, a drop of perspiration from the tip of my nose finds the crevice I'm peering down through and lands with an almost audible plink in the center of the long conference table. Finny is distributing the ballots, explaining that a yes will be construed as a vote *for* impeachment, a no as a vote of confidence in the chair. Several of my colleagues are confused by this. Billy Quigley is awakened to vote, though he cannot be made to comprehend the significance of the yes and no. When he marks the yes box, someone, June, I think, angrily snatches the ballot from him and fills in the no.

"I'm *for* him," Billy protests.

"Then you vote no, against the recall," she sighs.

Billy shrugs and passes in the ballot.

"How do you live with this bossy bitch?" he wants to know. Which means Teddy must be down there somewhere. I recall the way he looked returning from class earlier in the afternoon, head down, unwilling to meet his colleagues' eyes. How long has he known? I try to put myself in his place, imagine what he must be feeling. His and June's marriage has always appeared to be one of professional and political convenience, and what romantic yearnings Teddy allows himself are safely vested in Lily, a woman he knows he can't have. Still it can't be pleasant for any man to swallow the fact that his wife is consorting with the likes of Orshee. In the end it all comes down to horse trading, and being traded breaks, if not the heart, then some mechanism in the heart necessary to its proper functioning. You don't believe me, ask my mother.

The counting of ballots is under way below. Chairs are scraped back, and a dozen private conversations begin. The dramatic moment I've been waiting for approaches, so I shunt Teddy's problems aside. A clever contortionist like William Henry Devereaux, Jr., *can* have it both ways, I've decided, as I prepare, after a fashion, to join my colleagues. I remove the folded sheet of paper from my jacket pocket and fit it into the crease between the ceiling tiles. There is just enough room. Released into the atmosphere, it catches a draft and skitters into one of Billy Quigley's hairy knuckles, startling him. He stares at it, confused. He looks around at the people nearest him for a sign as to where it came from.

Gracie and Jacob come into view below, and I hear Gracie whisper, "What's that smell?" I can't help smiling. This is the first time I've ever used scent to overpower her.

Jacob ignores this, having noticed the sheet of folded paper in front of Billy Quigley. "You might as well count them all," he suggests to Finny, having apparently concluded that it's another ballot.

Billy, I can tell, has come to the same conclusion and is about to pass it on, but then he opens it and begins to read. When he's finished, he wads it up and makes as if to fire it across the room at the wastebasket in the corner. To prevent this, I send him a telepathic thought. I see him receive it, clutch in midstroke, then unwad the sheet, as Finny announces the results of the vote: eighteen yes votes, favoring my recall, nine nos.

"The chair is recalled by the necessary two-thirds majority," Finny declares.

My colleagues have begun to file out of the room when I hear Billy Quigley clear his throat.

CHAPTER

29

Many things will occur to a man like me when trapped in a filthy crawl space, separated from light and camaraderie by asbestos-contaminated ceiling tiles and insulation. During the half hour since the vote, thirty long, hot minutes spent on my hands and knees, scuttling about in the dark, looking for a place to alight, I've reluctantly been forced to confront a dark reality. I appear to be a man in trouble. I have hated to admit to this, but facts are facts, and I know what William of Occam would conclude on the basis of these facts. As recently as late last week I was able to view Teddy Barnes's concern for my well-being as alarmist. The consensus view of my friends and enemies alike, that I am out of control, a genuine loose cannon, is a view that, stubborn as I am, I would still like to contest. But here are the facts. I am nearly fifty years old. When I woke up today, I put on chinos, a blue button-down oxford shirt, a cloth tie, scuffed but serviceable loafers, the threadbare, tasteful tweed coat of my profession. I was then and I still remain, however temporarily, the chairperson of a large academic department in an institution of higher learn-

ing. I have written and published a book that was favorably reviewed
in *The New York Times*. And I should not be trapped in urine-soaked
trousers in the ceiling of Modern Languages, afraid to alight.

Descending into my own office is no longer an option, even if I were
willing to risk it in the dark. The corridor is full of my excited colleagues, flying into and out of their offices, and every few minutes one
of them checks my office to see if I've returned. The dramatic developments of the department meeting have my colleagues all abuzz. They
remind me of the wasps on Russell and Julie's deck after Russell doused
their hive with Raid. With the whole wide world to travel in, they persist in circling the hive. Agitated, they seek each other's company and
reassurance. They try every conceivable configuration.

So. The men's room being occupied, I descend into the women's
and quickly lock the door in order to prevent having to share with those
persons who have a more legitimate claim. There I discover my condition is even worse than I have imagined. My pants have mostly dried in
the forty-five minutes since I wet them, but they have also served as a
magnet for all the dust, dirt, grime, asbestos fibers, and mouse drop-
pings of the crawl space I've been confined in. In the long, fiercely lit
wall mirror of the women's room, I am a genuine sight. I have no idea
how many women have studied themselves in this same mirror in the
years since the building was constructed, but I'm certain it has never
reflected a reality like this one. Even Lily, who predicted I was going to
have a rough few days in her absence, could not have imagined this. I
look like a B-movie commando, my face smudged darkly with perspiration and grime, my clothing grayed with fibrous muck, my hair mat-
ted with sweat. I have a candy wrapper stuck to my elbow. I could be
convicted of murder, looking like this, and I'm not talking about killing
ducks. I'm visited by an insight not unlike the one I entertained last
week when I saw myself on TV holding Finny (the goose, not the man)
up to the cameras. This isn't funny.

I've cleaned up a little when someone tries the door, and I hear
Gracie curse mildly. Then the door rattles more violently, and I hear
Jacob remark that it seems to be locked from the inside. I'm tempted to
let them in and be done with it. Having admitted to myself the possibility that I am a man in trouble, I know only one thing for sure: I'm
not going back up into that ceiling.

"Why would it be locked from the inside?" Gracie wonders.

"How should I know?" Jacob says. "Maybe June Barnes is dealing crack again."

"June, are you in there?" Gracie raises her voice to the door.

"No, I'm right here." I hear June's voice down the hall. A door closes, June coming out of her office, locking the door behind her. "And I heard that crack crack, Jacob."

"Crack crack? Who who? Me me?"

"Come away from there, Teddy," I hear June say. "We're going home." I can picture this. Teddy, keeping a vigil outside my office door, awaiting my return. Somebody's gone inside, reported that my satchel is still there, which means that I must be around.

"I can't understand it," he says. "Where can he have gone?"

Apparently all the commotion has distracted Teddy from his own problems.

"He's probably playing handball with that defiler of young womanhood."

"Racquetball," her husband clarifies.

"I'm telling you," Gracie says. "He was up in the ceiling."

"Jesus," Jacob says.

"That piece of paper dropped out of the ceiling."

Silence.

"It came *out* of the ceiling," Gracie repeats. "I saw it drop. It fell right past me."

"You people are all certifiable," Jacob says.

"I really need to use the little girls' room," Gracie says. "I'm not kidding."

"Oy," June says. "I knew that somewhere in this country there had to be a woman who still uses the term 'little girls' room.' "

"Use the little boys'," Jacob suggests. "There's nobody in there. We'll stand guard."

"Check for me," Gracie says. "Make sure."

I hear the men's room door creak open and then shut again. "All clear," Jacob says.

Then the door opens, shuts, and opens again more violently. "God-damn you, Jacob," Gracie says. There's a soft thud, as of a purse making contact with a dean. "Finny's in there with his dick in his hand, as you well know."

"I didn't think you'd mind Finny," Jacob says, aggrieved innocent again.

"Damn," Gracie says, jiggling the women's room door one more time, just in case she was hallucinating before. "All right. I'm going to use the one downstairs."

I hear the men's room door open again. Finny exiting.

"I'm sorry, Finny," Gracie says. "I didn't see anything."

"Now you've really hurt his feelings," Jacob says.

It's the double doors I hear swinging open now, signaling Gracie's exit.

"I can't understand where he can have gone to," Teddy says again.

"He's insane," Finny says. "Last week I caught him outside my class-room door, making faces at my students."

"He certainly seems to have captured your imaginations," Jacob says. They're all moving down the hall now. "Gracie believes he's in the ceiling. You're seeing him outside your classroom."

"If we had a dean who took things seriously . . . ," Finny begins.

"He'd have killed himself years ago," Jacob finishes.

"Maybe I should drive out to Allegheny Wells and check on him," Teddy proposes halfheartedly.

I hear an office door open and close somewhere down the hall.

"Jacob," Billy Quigley says. "Are you aware that Gracie is going around telling people that you two are getting married?"

"I asked our pal Hank to be best man," Jacob tells him by way of rebuttal. "But if he's going to kill ducks and crawl around in the ceiling, I may need to rethink my options."

"I don't think he killed that goose," Teddy says, with what sounds like real regret.

"Surely you don't think he's too squared away? Too emotionally stable?" Paul Rourke's voice.

"What are these pink spots that go all up your sleeve?" Jacob wants to know, apparently of Finny.

"You can see them?" Finny says, clearly alarmed.

"Not really. Only in a certain light," Jacob assures him.

"Isn't Gracie still married?" Billy Quigley says, reassuring me, since this was my first question too. Their voices are growing distant.

"Only in the legal sense," Jacob assures him, and then the double doors at the end of the corridor open and close on their conversation.

I cautiously unlock the women's room door and peek out. The corridor is deserted, quiet. I study the double doors at the end of the corridor through which my colleagues have passed. Each of these doors contains a small rectangular window, but they're too far away and the lighting is too dim for me to see whether these windows contain faces. I take a chance, slip out of the women's room and quickly down the hall and into my office, where I gather my satchel and my workshop stories for tomorrow. Then down the back stairs.

Outside, darkness is falling, for which I'm grateful. I sneak out of Modern Languages and cut across the lawn toward the back lot where my Lincoln awaits. This late in the evening there are only a half dozen cars in the two-acre lot, and maybe it's odd that there should be another car parked right next to mine, but I don't pay any attention. It's been too long a day to confront minor riddles, slight statistical anomalies. There's nobody in either car anyway. I can see that from fifty yards away. I unlock mine, get in, insert the key in the ignition. In my peripheral vision, I see the car next to me rock gently and a head pop up. I draw the conclusion that William of Occam would draw. Surely William was once a young man, subject to the impulses of spring, especially a late-arriving one. No doubt I've interrupted a young couple who thought they would be safe way out here in the back lot. They wish now they'd waited for it to be completely dark. I find reverse and start to back out. When a horn toots, I can't help looking over at the car next to mine, and in it I see my son-in-law Russell's bristly head framed in the window. I put the Lincoln in park, and Russell gets out, stretching and yawning. I lean over, unlock the passenger door. He gets in, still rubbing his eyes.

It's the smell that wakes him up. "Whoa!" he says, looking over at me, startled. He hasn't closed the door yet, so the dome light is on and he can get a good look. "Jesus, Hank. What the hell happened to you? Don't tell me another poet."

"Teaching English isn't the clean work it used to be," I explain. "Most people don't realize."

He's leaning out, gulping air. "Sorry," he says, and he sounds genuinely sorry too. "I've got a hair-trigger gag reflex. I lose it if I smell cabbage cooking."

"How about oral sex?" It occurs to me to ask this.

"Oh, God, Hank." He's still hanging out the door, this fastidious son-in-law of mine, who may or may not have given my daughter a shiner. "Have a heart."

"I mean in general. I'm not talking about you and me."

He gets out of the car again. He really does look sick.

"What are you doing here, Russell?"

"Waiting for you. I have been for over an hour. I thought we could go have a beer someplace. Talk."

"Okay. Let's."

He peers in at me to see if I'm serious.

"If you don't mind, I'd like to shower and change my clothes first though."

"I insist."

"You want to follow me out to the house?"

He hesitates. "Will Julie be there?"

"Could be. I doubt it though. I think she's back in hers. Yours. Now that the locks have been changed."

"I don't think I'm ready to see her," he says.

"You're married to her, Russell. You may have to see her again." I doubt he even registered the information about the locks.

He's still peering in at me, grimacing. "You really got like that *teaching*?"

Russell follows me out to Allegheny Wells. It's fifteen minutes of solitude for each of us. He probably uses his fifteen minutes to consider the implications of the fact that he plans to seek marital advice from a fifty-year-old man who kills ducks and wets his pants. I use my own solitude to consider what may well be my worst character flaw, the fact that in the face of life's seriousness, its pettiness, its tragedy, its lack of coherent meaning, my spirits are far too easily restored. Darkness is very nearly complete by the time we arrive in Allegheny Wells. Our headlights do little more than pierce the epidermis of the Pennsylvania woods that border the narrow blacktop. In their deep, dark interior, it's easy to imagine wolves roaming, gathering into packs, circling, closing in, howling and slathering. They may even be close enough to hear me chuckling.

When I've showered and dressed, I find Russell outside, camped in a deck chair, Occam snoring peacefully alongside. The tape on my message machine looks pretty close to full, its green light blinking in rapid-fire bursts. I consider it, but I hate to ruin my good mood by pressing play and allowing my colleagues to share their thoughts with me. Most of them just want to tell me what happened in the department meeting, but hell, I was there. It'll be interesting to compare their versions with each other and with the truth but, frankly, not that interesting, so I put on a jacket and join my son-in-law on the deck. The wolves I imagined closing in earlier seem to have found other distractions. I sniff the air for evidence of lupine presence, find none. Perhaps in the shower I've removed the scent they've been following.

Russell informs me that the phone has rung several times since I was in the shower. I ignore this, pull up a chaise longue. "There's beer in the fridge," I tell him.

"Like hell," he says. "I looked."

"Really?"

"Really."

I consider this. "Does Julie drink beer?"

"Sure."

"Since when?"

"Since she was sixteen, like everybody else," Russell assures me. Sons-in-law like knowing things their fathers-in-law don't. They like sharing what they know.

The evening is surprisingly warm. Still too cool to sit outside without a jacket, but warm enough to imagine summer. On such nights as this Lily and I have, over the years since we built the house, welcomed the approach of summer this way, by enduring the mild discomfort of a reluctant spring, substituting promise for reality, knowing our days are headed in the right direction. Tonight, a fast-moving cold front is forecast to pass through central Pennsylvania. Temperatures are predicted to plunge, though by tomorrow warmer weather will return.

Russell observes me stroking the arms of my chaise longue fondly. "Deck furniture was one of the things we were going to buy before the money ran out," he tells me.

When I don't say anything to that, he continues tentatively, "Tell me honestly. Do you like your house?"

"I don't think much about it, Russell. I guess I like it well enough. We've had a comfortable existence since we built." If Lily were here, she'd explain that I'm like most men, oblivious to my surroundings. But I do like the fact that the house we built has lots of windows, plenty of light. And I like being far enough away from the university that I can't be called in to campus every time somebody leaves the lights on.

"I ask," Russell says, "because I've never hated anything so much in my life."

"You hate my house, Russell?"

He looks over at me in the dark. "My house," he clarifies.

"But they're identical," I remind him. "I can't help feeling you've insulted my house."

Russell wisely ignores this. "I hate the house itself," he continues. "I hate the furniture. I even hate all the things we'd have if the money hadn't run out."

"Next you'll be saying you hate my daughter."

I expect a quick denial, and I don't get it. "Here's what I don't understand," he says. He's choosing his words very carefully, as well he might. He knows I'm fond of him but doesn't know how much this will count for in the overall scheme of things. He'd like my fondness for him to be trump in this game, but he suspects it isn't. Or maybe it's just that what he has to say is hard. "You and Lily aren't . . . acquisitive," he says finally.

Again, I'm not sure how to respond to this. His compliment trails an insult, as he well knows. How did two people like Lily and me manage to raise such an acquisitive daughter? is what he wants to understand. He actually seems to want me to explain it to him. What I'd like to explain is that I don't think Julie in her heart of hearts is all that acquisitive either. She's just unhappy and frustrated and she hasn't yet discovered how to "be" in the world. Unsure what to desire, she simply wants. Or this is the conclusion I've come to. A father's too generous theory, perhaps. Applied evenly, it might be a rationale for acquisitiveness in general, not just in my daughter. Who *is* truly at home in the world? Who *is* sure what to desire? Well, lots of people, I answer my own question. Lots of people know exactly what they want. I just can't believe Julie is one of them. I can't believe my daughter's soul is so easily purchased.

"You want to tell me how she got that shiner, Russell?" I ask, before our discussion becomes too abstract.

"She didn't tell you?"

"Last Friday she said you shoved her," I tell him. "This morning she suggested maybe that wasn't the full story." These are approximate statements I'm making to him actually. Julie neither told nor suggested anything to me this morning. She told my machine, while I stood by, paralyzed, and listened.

Russell nods, gets to his feet, and leans over the railing of the deck, peering down in the dark, at I can't imagine what. When the breeze shifts, I catch a distinct whiff of lupine presence. I'm expecting Russell to speak when I see his body heave violently, and he begins to retch off the side of the deck. Occam awakens, gets quickly to his feet, goes over to survey the situation, then turns and looks at me expectantly. Humans have a more complex response to regurgitation than animals do, and I'd like Occam to understand this. I'd like for him to understand that we people do feel natural sympathy for someone in this sort of distress, even as we choose to limit our personal involvement. I try to convey all this to my dog in a look, but he's having none of it, I can tell. He'd like to *do* something. If he could think what, he wouldn't mind getting his paws wet. He can always lick them dry later. Wet paws are a small thing when weighed against suffering. What's wrong with me? is what he'd like to know. Well, I've just showered, for one thing. Still, he's right. I *should* do something. So I go inside and get a swatch of paper towels and return with them when it feels safe. Russell is still standing at the rail, but his body has stopped heaving. I hand him the paper towels, which he accepts gratefully. "I warned you about my gag reflex," he says. "I've felt like doing that all day. I wonder if I'm coming down with something."

He collapses back into his deck chair. Occam sniffs the paper towels. There's no aspect of this entire proceeding he doesn't want to understand.

"What's down there anyway?" Russell wants to know, indicating whatever is below the spot where he lost the contents of his stomach. I haven't turned on the exterior lights, so beyond the deck, which is illuminated by the kitchen light, it's pitch black.

"Don't worry about it," I tell him.

He uses a clean paper towel to wipe his forehead. "I feel better," he confesses.

"I bet."

He looks over at me and offers up a weak grin. "Do you realize that during the last hour we've managed to entirely gross each other out?"

"Male bonding, they call it."

"It works," he shrugs.

This is a funny, touching thing for Russell to say, and I *am* touched, though the emotion is complicated by the fact that I too have a hair-trigger gag reflex.

"I appreciate the fact that you haven't gone ballistic over all this, Hank. All weekend I've been thinking you probably wanted to kill me. I guess that's why I had to see you. To find out."

"I harbored a violent thought or two," I assure him. Now that we've bonded, I wouldn't want him to get the idea that I'm incapable of righteous fury, that my daughter can be knocked about with impunity, just because her father's an English professor and in theory a pacifist. Not that I ever really believed that Russell knocked Julie around. Some damn thing has happened though, and apparently he's going to tell me what. Whether what he'll tell me is true, whether I'd recognize the truth if I heard it, these are other questions. I can tell one thing. Whatever Russell means to tell me is either a difficult truth or a difficult lie. He doesn't launch right in. He's scratching behind Occam's ears, and the animal's limbs are palsied with pleasure.

"She came home with this chair," Russell finally says, his words small in the dark, and again I imagine wolves gathering in the woods behind the house. "For the guest room. As if we could afford to have guests. She's telling me she got this great deal because the store is going into bankruptcy. Sixty percent off. Only three hundred dollars."

He stops scratching Occam to rub his own temples with the thumb and index finger of his left hand. His right hand contains the wadded up paper towels. I can tell he'd like to toss them over the railing, but he doesn't.

"The idea of buying something at a bankruptcy sale . . . ," he begins, then stops and laughs bitterly. "I mean, you've got no idea how strapped we are, Hank."

He shakes his head, a lost man. "Actually, that's a dumb thing to say, after all the money you guys have loaned us."

I nod, agreeing about something, I'm not sure what. "How much money have we loaned you?" I ask, genuinely curious.

"Too much," he says, leaving me in the dark, where, if Lily were here, she would say I belong. "Anyhow, I felt something in me snap," he explains, staring out over the tops of the trees. The darkness is so complete that the trees and the sky blend into each other.

"I looked at her and that chair and I *did* hate her, Hank. I'm ashamed to admit it, but right that second, I did. Lately, I've mostly hated myself for being out of work when she was working, but right then I hated her worse, and God it felt good to hate her more, that look on her face when she brought in the chair."

He'll allude to her face, but not her eye, I think, and for this I am grateful. I know the expression he's referring to, and I know the way that old injury drags the one side of Julie's face down, making her look like a stroke victim. It's a thing she can't help, so Russell won't mention it. He's too decent to enter that detail in evidence before her father, even though it's the thing that contains and represents what he most wants me to understand. What he wants me to understand is how, under the right circumstances, a person you love can be ugly, repulsive.

"Anyhow," he continues. "I knew I couldn't stay in any house that contained that chair. That sounds ridiculous, I know, but it was the one thing I was most sure of." He chuckles, like a man who knows that what he's chuckling at isn't funny. "You'll appreciate this, Hank. A man and his wife. Faced off. Ultimatum time. It's either me or the chair, he says with a straight face. Not, it's either me or him. Your husband or this other man you're in love with. That would be a tough one, right? No, I tell her to choose between me and a chair she bought on sale, sixty percent off."

"Well, it may have been on sale, but it wasn't cheap," I tell Russell. "Three hundred bucks is not a cheap chair."

"I'm not sure you're grasping my point," Russell admits. "My point is that, when she had a choice between her husband and an inanimate object, she chose the chair."

"I understand that, Russell, I do. And I can see where it would hurt your feelings."

"She didn't even hesitate, Hank."

"Except it doesn't prove that she doesn't love you," I tell him.

"She just loves the chair more? Is that what you're telling me?"

"Actually, I was going to say it proves she knows where to plant the knife. She doesn't really prefer the chair. She just knows how much it will hurt you if she acts like she does."

He hangs his head. "I know," he admits. "By the time I packed my bag and came back downstairs, I could see everything had changed. She'd put the chair off to the side. She had tears in her eyes, and she was standing in front of the door. We could have made it all up right there. It was my inch to give, and I couldn't give it. I didn't hate her anymore. In fact, I wanted to take her and make love to her right then."

"Careful, Russell," I warn him. I know he'd like me to understand, to chart his emotional trajectory, but this is my daughter we're talking about.

"I wanted my marriage and I wanted my wife. Hell, I even liked the damn chair. It's not a bad-looking chair or anything."

"She's got her mother's good taste," I admit.

"But like you said, she'd hurt my feelings, and I wanted to hurt her back. And I felt this strange . . . rush. She'd tried to run this bluff, see, and I'd called it. She'd lost, and now it was time for her to learn her lesson. So instead of . . ."

I wait awhile for him to finish, but he doesn't. "Right," I say, because I hate to see him struggling for something I understand already. Hell, I could finish this story for him.

"So I went over to where she was standing in front of the door and told her to get out of the way. I remember it didn't even sound like my voice. I kept wondering, who are these people? And I was still thinking, I can stop all this right now."

"But you didn't."

"No," he says. "When she wouldn't get out of the way, I set the bag down and took her by the shoulders."

He held his hands out before him in the dark, seeing her there.

"Then . . . I don't know. She must have tripped over the bag. I heard a crash, and when I turned she was on the floor. She'd fallen into . . ."

He stops, unable to continue.

"The chair," I say.

He stares over at me through moist, confused eyes. "No, the stereo cabinet."

"Oh, sorry," I say. In my writing workshop I'd have explained to my students why, for symmetry, it had to be the chair.

Russell isn't interested in symmetry. "I kept thinking, this isn't right. She can't have fallen. All I'd done was move her aside. Maybe I was a little rough, but I didn't push or shove her. What was she doing down there on the floor?"

Again, I wait for him to continue, until I realize that this is the end of his story. He hasn't reached any conclusions about these events because he hasn't moved past the moment when he turned and saw Julie on the floor and imagined himself responsible, even though he didn't quite see how he could be. As I've listened to him relate what happened, the thing that's puzzled me is that he hasn't asked how Julie is, and the deeper he's plunged into his story, the more I've feared the reason for this was that he didn't care. Now I suspect it's something else. The image of Julie on the floor has burned onto the retina of his mind's eye. It hasn't occurred to him that she might be okay, because every time he thinks of her, he sees her there, on the floor, one hand clutching the already damaged eye. There simply is no *after.* If I asked him where he thought Julie was right now, the question would confuse him. Intellectually, he knows that days have passed, but where Julie *is* for Russell is right where he left her. Probably he went to her, tried to see how bad she was hurt, tried to take the hand away from her eye, but by then the dramatic focus of the scene would have shifted. A few minutes earlier it was *his* scene, and he could have altered its course had he chosen. Now it was *her* scene to play out as she chose. Her decision, to exclude him, was the same as his own decision to punish her.

And now his life has turned mysterious. Because it can't go forward, he can only keep going over and over how he got where he is. "Anyway," he says. "I wanted you to hear my side. I know you have to believe Julie, but . . ."

"Listen, Russell," I begin, without the vaguest idea how I'll continue.

"I want you and Lily to know that I'm going to pay you back every nickel of the money you loaned us. I mean, even if Julie and I don't make it."

"Russell."

"It may be a while," he admits ruefully, this son-in-law of mine who's been out of work since last fall. "I mean, maybe this has gotten me jump-started, finally. I've got to do something, even if it's wrong."

"People often say that before they do the wrong thing, Russell."

"I called this guy in Atlanta today," he says. "Last summer he offered me this great job there, terrific money. But we were building the house, so I said no."

"This is a story I've heard before."

"I don't think so, Hank," he says. "I never even told Julie."

I just grin at him in the dark.

"Oh, I get it," he says. "It's a familiar story, you mean. How does it turn out?"

"I forget," I tell him. I and the majority of my colleagues in the English department are how it ends. There's no need to depress him further.

"The job he wanted me to take before is gone, of course," he continues. "But he says he thinks he can scare something up."

"In Atlanta."

"That's where the company is, Hank. Atlanta. If the company were in Railton, this whole story would be different." Now that he's got Julie out of his mind's eye, Russell is his mischievous, slightly mocking self again.

"I understand that, Russell."

"Good. I thought maybe you'd nodded off there for a minute."

I assure him I've been hanging on every word.

"Anyway. If this guy calls back, I guess I'll take the job. If I can scrape together plane fare."

The phone rings inside. "That must be Lily," I tell him, "calling to offer you the money."

"She's always right there," he admits. "You lucked out."

We listen to the phone ring.

"Aren't you going to answer that?" Russell wants to know, as the machine picks up.

After a few seconds we hear a voice leaving a message. With the closed patio door between us and the machine, I can't tell who it is.

Russell gets to his feet. "I guess I'll let you go back to your life. I'd appreciate it if you didn't mention Atlanta to Julie."

I promise him I won't.

"And thanks for everything," he says, looking around the deck. "I always feel right at home here for some reason." He surveys my house with more affection than I've ever seen him view his own. "You lied about the wasps though," he says, pointing at the eaves where a nest would hang if we had truly identical houses.

We shake hands. "Promise me you won't leave without seeing Julie," I tell him, because I suspect that this is his plan.

"I'll call her," he says. "I don't think she wants to see me."

"You should go see her anyway," I tell him. He needs to see that she's all right. That she isn't on the floor anymore. That she won't be going around for the rest of her life with one hand over her eye. "Lily will be back tomorrow, sometime. You can meet over here if you want."

"I'll think about it."

"Where are you staying?"

"With a friend."

I hand him a slip of paper and a pen. "Leave me a number where I can reach you if I have to."

He's reluctant, but he does as he's told.

"Aren't you going to tell me how you managed to fall in the sewer earlier?"

I consult the stars for dramatic effect. "I fell asleep and wet my pants. Then I got embarrassed and hid in the ceiling above my office."

He shrugs. "You don't want to tell me, just say so, Hank."

"Maybe some other time," I suggest. Later, I'm sure I'll be able to come up with something more plausible than the truth. Sure, I'm out of practice, but *The New York Times* once said of young William Henry Devereaux, Jr., son of the famous literary critic, that his stories had "taken firm root in the garden of realistic fictions."

"My feelings are kind of hurt," Russell admits. "I mean, I told you everything."

"Not everything, Russell," I say. "We never tell everything."

He looks surprised to learn that I know this. Like maybe it's his secret. What does he think a man like me *does* for a living?

Russell has been gone maybe twenty minutes when a car pulls in at the foot of our road. I track its headlights through the trees as it snakes up the incline past my neighbors' houses. When it passes the driveway of the last of these, it can mean only one thing. I am to have a visitor.

I momentarily hope it's Lily, returning early to surprise me, but I know it isn't. You're married to a woman as long as I've been married to Lily, you get to know not only the sound of her vehicle but the sound that vehicle makes with her at the wheel. I've watched my wife come up this hill hundreds of times, and I know this is not she. It's not Lily's car, not her speed, not her headlight pattern. This is someone who's been here before, but not for a while, at least not at night, who remembers how sharp the turns in the road are without remembering exactly where they are, who has to go slow enough to really watch. I fear it's Teddy Barnes come to celebrate my victory, to ask if it's true, what Gracie said about my being in the ceiling, to plan further strategy, to find out if Lily's returned and bring her up to date on her husband's lunacy. Or, worse, he may want to talk about his wife and Orshee.

Telling Occam to stay, a command he occasionally obeys, I get up and turn on the outside lights, then go over to the railing in time to see Tony Coniglia, one of the very few people in the world whose companionship I might actually enjoy tonight, get out of his car. "*You* are not answering your phone," he observes. "And you're not returning calls, as that lying machine of yours promises."

He's carrying a bottle. Occam woofs down at him.

"I myself have had a dozen calls for you tonight," Tony informs me. "Your colleagues say you disappeared after the department meeting. They seem to think you might be hiding out at my place."

"You know the kind of company I keep. If it weren't for erroneous conclusions, these people would never arrive at any at all."

He hasn't made any move to join me on the deck. Instead he's leaning against the grille of his car. The night has grown quiet, and I can hear the ticking of his engine as it cools. The temperature has fallen since Russell left. Occam circles himself twice, collapses onto the deck, sighs, and puts his head back down on his paws.

"Come on up."

"I will," Tony says, without showing any such inclination. "I'm trying to solve a mystery first."

"Okay, I'll bite," I tell him. "What mystery?"

"There's vomit on the hood of your car," he points out.

He's parked right next to me, and now that I look, I see he's right. This, it occurs to me, is my father's fault. But for his books taking up space in the garage, my car would have been safely inside.

Tony goes over to examine the mess. "Fresh, I'd say. A good forensic team would put the time within the hour."

I can't help grinning.

Tony trots up the deck stairs, goes in through the sliding door to the kitchen, and returns with two glasses, handing me one. "Alcohol," he says conspiratorially, holding up the bottle for my inspection. It's a fifth of very expensive Kentucky sour mash, about two-thirds full. Even in the poor light of the deck I can see that Tony's eyes are bloodshot, that he's started on this bottle without me. "When this bottle is gone, I know a place where we can score another."

He sets the bottle down, leans forward, hands on the railing, peers down at the hood of my car. "Whoever was sick," he says, "was sitting in this chair." He examines his hands for further evidence, brushes them off on his pants legs before pouring two heavy shots of whiskey. I take a sip, and it's everything you could hope for. Billy Quigley, were he here, would weep religious tears.

Tony is studying me, deadpan. "He was a small man. Left-handed. He walked with a limp. He served in India. So much is obvious, but beyond this I can tell you nothing except that he may have recently eaten asparagus."

While Tony has been investigating this mystery, I've solved one that's been on the periphery of my thoughts all afternoon. Seeing Tony has somehow caused the penny to drop. The girl I saw in the back of the police car this afternoon is the same one I saw last Thursday night when I left Tony's, the big girl who wasn't afraid when I came out of the trees at three in the morning, who told me I wasn't him. The "him" she referred to, I now realize, is Tony, and I also comprehend that it was to his house that she was heading. I remember the phone calls that kept getting Tony out of the hot tub, as well as the fact that after the last one he left the phone off the hook, which must have made her decide to come see him. And I remember Missy Blaylock's insisting, this afternoon, that I ask Tony about what happened at his house after I left. My final intuition is that it must have been Tony's class the girl crashed this afternoon, causing the police to remove her from campus, the ramifications of which caused Tony to cancel our scheduled racquetball match. William of Occam would be pleased with my deduction, which accounts for the major facts, is contradicted by none of them, and is not unnecessarily complex. All my theory lacks is reasons, human motives, the truth behind the known facts. The former novelist in me wonders this: How close could I get to the deeper truths, proceeding from the factual outline?

Not very, probably. Tony's mock investigation of the vomit on the hood of my car suggests how wide is the gap between known facts and a genuine understanding of their meaning. How could he be expected to intuit Russell and Julie, the breakup of their marriage, the failure of their love. What ails people is never simple, and William of Occam, who provided mankind with a beacon of rationality by which to view the world of physical circumstance, knew better than to apply his razor to the irrational, where entities multiply like strands of a virus under a microscope. Russell is not a small man, he's not left-handed, he hasn't served in India, he doesn't walk with a limp, and he probably hasn't eaten asparagus recently, but past a certain point, almost any set of random details stand about as good a chance of being true as any other.

The limitations of intuition, of imagination, are what make one-book authors of men like William Henry Devereaux, Jr., I fear, and perhaps this is why I am envious of Rachel tonight. For though I told my agent that I was not jealous, the truth is that I am. Not of her success. The envy I feel has less to do with accomplishment or validation than with the necessary artistic arrogance that these breed. Usually all questions, Rachel, tonight, will feel like she got some of the answers right, saw some of the patterns clearly enough to detail them convincingly. She will consider the possibility that the leaky vessel of her talent may be seaworthy after all. Instead of being dictated to by the waves of doubt that threaten to swamp all navigators, she'll turn bravely into the wind. The moment she does is the moment I envy.

Tony is peering at me strangely, and I realize I've just suffered another ellipsis. As I usually do when this happens, I consult my watch to see if I can ascertain how long I've been away. And as usual I'm prevented from arriving at a valid conclusion by not having noted when the ellipsis began.

"Pay attention," Tony says, "because we're about to embark on an intricate topic."

I'm glad to hear this. Nothing could please me more than to be assured that Tony has come armed with a subject, prepared to hold forth.

"I've been considering the mystery of human affection," he says, by way of preamble.

I nod. "You've moved on. Last week you were thinking about fornication."

"I'm thinking of giving up fornication," he says, deadpan, as always.

"The act or the subject?"

"Both. There wasn't much point in discussing the subject with you, and I've concluded that the act may be coming between me and my true vocation, which is religious. . . . You laugh."

"Now you're saying you have a lot to offer God?"

"I happen to have the loftiest spiritual dimension of any person you know," Tony insists. "Are you aware that I attend Mass every day of the week?"

I tell him the truth, that I was not aware of this. In fact, from the way he's informed me, I can't tell whether it's true or not.

"I *do* have a lot to offer when it comes to spiritual matters. The mystery of human affection, especially as it pertains to desire, is a spiritual matter, though not everyone understands this."

I settle deeper into my deck chair. We're rolling now.

"Take men like us," he suggests. "We are, in the end, true men of faith."

"We are?"

"I shit you not."

"Good," I say. "Great."

"For instance. I believe it would not be inaccurate to say that you feel considerable affection for your wife. A lovely woman, if I may say so, well worthy of your highest regard."

"According to Teddy I don't love her enough," I tell him.

"Aha!" Tony exclaims. "Teddy also bears the burden of human affection for the very same woman. Whose affection is greater? Yours by virtue of knowing the beloved, or his by virtue of *not* knowing her?"

"We're talking biblical knowing here?"

"We're talking knowledge with a capital *N*. We're talking epistemology. We're no longer talking fornication except insofar as fornication helps us to know our spiritual world. I thought that was clear. You feel affection for your wife but also, if I'm not mistaken, for other women?"

I don't respond right away, having concluded that this question, like most of Tony's questions, is rhetorical. Apparently not. "What are we talking about here, love?"

"Affection," Tony says. "Human affection. Oh, all right, love. You're in love with your wife."

I do not deny this.

"And yet you feel affection for other women?"

"I feel"—I search for the word—"crushes."

"Ah," he sounds sad, disappointed. "This unfortunately supports the consensus view that you are a case of arrested adolescent development. But let's not be hasty. Let's assume that a crush is intuitive knowledge of the virtue of another human being. And that our attraction to virtue, in the final analysis, is our desire to know God."

"By all means," I say, though I can think of no reason why we should assume any such thing. I recall looking down the front of Meg Quigley's shirt this afternoon, and the undeniable attraction I felt was pretty much devoid of theological dimension.

"But is it love? Are you in love with other women?"

"Maybe half in love."

Tony squints at this, but there's no stopping him. "You're half in love with other women who are not your wife," he sums up, nodding, as if this is a perfectly reasonable position. "Half is okay. Half is legitimate. There's nothing wrong with the fiftieth percentile. No *more* than half is the rule. You're sure it's not fifty-one percent?"

I take another sip of whiskey and track its warm glow all the way down into my belly. "Teddy thinks I only half-love my wife though. If true, that would mean I love these women equally, those who are my wife and those who are not."

"*If* true," Tony says, noting the utmost importance of the subjunctive. "More than half is the rule for a wife," he concedes. "I loved Judy right up there in the high ninetieth percentile."

Tony was one of the first of our generation of Railton professors to be divorced—what?—twenty-some years ago now. Either the year of or the year after our arrival in Railton. He's been chasing young women so long that many people remember him as a philanderer in his marriage, which was not the case. His wife's leaving him was the cause, not the result, of his having so much to offer other women.

"Comfortably in the exceptional range," he continues, clearly pleased to have found a metaphor to apply to his topic.

"A tiny sliver on your pie chart. Right up there at the top on your graph. And for most of our marriage her affection for me was considerable. Not in the exceptional range, but well within acceptable boundaries. Seventieth percentile or thereabouts. Not bad. Satisfactory. 'Fond' would be a good way to describe her feelings for me. Back then, I was always trying to push her into the low eighties, which I thought was a realistic goal for her. Out of the satisfactory and into the good range. I mean, when you yourself are exceptional, you aren't all that keen on 'satisfactory.' But the more I urged her into the low eighties, affection-wise, the more she slipped in the other direction. Before long she was mired in the midsixties. Barely a passing grade. Marginal effort. I was still exceptional, mind you. Day in, day out. Ninety-five, ninety-six, ninety-seven was routine for me. In the end she finally slipped below the fifty percent you speak of, where she was less than half in love, at least with me."

As I suspected, Tony is just the man for me tonight. Listening to him talk, I can't help but smile. At least I think I'm smiling. My face is doing something in the dark, I can feel it.

"In the end her leaving was a good thing. Long term, it's not healthy to love up there in the exceptional range when your beloved is struggling to achieve a modest showing in the seventies. You keep that up too long, and somebody goes out and buys a gun."

He leans over and pours more whiskey in my glass, not much, though, because I haven't made much headway with what he gave me before.

"How come I can drink twice as much as you even when I'm doing all the talking?"

In truth, I'm afraid to start really drinking. Afraid I won't be able to stop with this wonderful stuff Tony has brought. If I could be sure we'd stop when we got to the end of this one bottle, I'd race him to the bottom, but Tony has warned me that he knows a place where we can score another, and I know about twenty such places, the nearest being the kitchen cabinet, where I've stashed, unopened, a bottle of Irish whiskey even more expensive than the stuff we're drinking.

"For a long time after she left, I stayed right up there. Very little slippage, affection-wise, but I have to tell you it's true what they say. It's lonely at the top. And after a while, you feel a little foolish, too. You begin to consider that you have a lot to offer women, if you could just be a little less exceptional."

"You forget I know how this story ends," I remind him. "I know how much you've offered other women. You brag about it in the locker room twice a week."

"And *you* forget Joe Namath," he says. "It ain't bragging if you can do it."

The whiskey that was in my glass has mysteriously disappeared. I hold it out for some more.

"But here's the thing," Tony adds thoughtfully. "Most of the time, since I have so much to offer women, I'm comfortably down in the lower sixties where my ex-wife is concerned, sometimes the midfifties even. Last week, in the hot tub with the local press, I'm in the low to midfifties tops, which is where I like to be, because in the fifties you got options. You can zig, you can zag. There's the possibility of dignity. And you know my motto."

I smile. "Dignity first?"

"I've told you this before?"

"A lucky guess."

"But here's the thing," he says again. I can't tell if it's the same thing or a different thing than the one he was getting at before. "You're cruising along in the midfifties, you're in the hot tub with the local press, which has terrific knockers, and suddenly, for no reason that makes any sense, you're back in the exceptional range, affection-wise, for a woman you haven't even seen in over a decade and who's probably gotten sloppy fat, for all you know, this woman you meant to spend the rest of your life with—you even said so, at some point, in front of witnesses—and what you'd like to know is, Why now? I mean, you're in the middle of an important interview here, and you don't want to be so exceptional anymore. You like it down in the fifties, the sixties, modestly above average, nothing to be ashamed of."

"So what are you advising here?"

He looks at me like I'm stupid but fills our glasses again. "Who said anything about advice? Pay attention. The subject is the mystery of human affection. I'm talking statistics. I'm talking fine calibrations of the human heart, done scientifically. You, personally, I have no idea about. You said you were half in love. I'm just trying to clarify your statistical thinking. I don't even know who you're half in love with."

"Would that matter? Statistically?"

"No," he admits. "But I'm curious what kind of woman a man like you might be half in love with."

"You know Billy Quigley's daughter Meg," I hear myself say.

"And who could blame a man like you for this?"

"And there's my secretary, Rachel."

"A fine woman for a man like you to be half in love with. I understand."

"And there's Bodie Pie, over in Women's Studies."

"A lesbian," Tony remarks. "You know she's a lesbian?"

"That means she can't be half in love with me, not that I can't be half in love with her."

"True," Tony concedes the logic of my distinction. "But this is where dignity comes in."

I glance over at him.

"It's the futility I object to, not the lifestyle," he explains. "I'd say the same if you told me you were half in love with a socket wrench. I think your problem may be that you're right at fifty percent. That's neither fish nor fowl. Speaking of which, have you had dinner?"

I confess that I have not.

"I know a little place in town that has good food. And here's something that may interest you," he adds, holding up the bottle, now empty, except for half a finger of murky liquid sloshing at the bottom. "If you know how to ask, they'll serve you alcohol."

"We're too drunk to drive."

"It's too far to walk. Besides, there's nothing between here and the restaurant but trees."

"It's trees I'm worried about," I tell him. "They don't move when you hit them."

"Just follow me," Tony suggests.

"I bet they aren't even serving. It's going on nine o'clock."

"You've lived in Pennsylvania too long. In New York, civilized people are only now beginning to think about dinner. Only fundamentalist Christians have eaten their evening meal."

"They too have a lot to offer God."

"Nonsense. They believe God has a lot to offer them. Get your coat. Maybe we'll run into one of the women you're half in love with."

We take both cars. Our speedometers do not break the twenty-five-mile-per-hour barrier all the way to Evergreen's, which by Railton standards is a pretty decent restaurant. There aren't many, which accounts for why on any given night you always run into people you know. From the foyer on this given night I see June and Teddy eating dinner in the third booth. I'm surprised to see them out in public together, given the scene that took place between June and Orshee in the hallway of Modern Languages, and even more surprised to see

Teddy quietly reach across the table and take June's hand. On the other side of the room, Paul Rourke and the second Mrs. R. appear to be waiting for their check, the second Mrs. R. dangling her sandal from her big toe beneath the table. In the middle of the dining room I see Bodie Pie with a good-looking young woman.

"Just your luck," Tony says, too loudly. "The lesbian."

I have sobered up a little on the drive. Tony, I would guess, is in far worse shape than I. Now that we're here, it's good that we're going to eat.

Teddy and June spot us in the doorway, so I wave. Their heads go together, and we don't have to be there to follow the discussion. Teddy wants to ask us to join them. June, who has no use for Tony, says absolutely not.

"What are all these people doing eating out on a Monday night?" is what I want to know.

"Two-for-one night," Tony says.

"One of our meals is free?" I say.

"Mine," Tony clarifies. "I paid for fifty-five dollars' worth of clams last week."

"I wondered who paid for all that," I tell him. "I'm glad it was you, since you're the one who ate them all."

We get the last table in the place, though in about two minutes Rourke and the second Mrs. R. stop by our table on the way out. The second Mrs. R. is not a woman I'm even half in love with. What I can't help wondering is how it's possible for a woman to go through life with the same bored look on her face all the time. I wouldn't want to be married to Paul Rourke, but I doubt boredom would be the emotion he'd inspire. "Hello, Reverend," I say.

"Lucky Hank," he observes. "You must be celebrating the fact that you've got one more week as chair."

"I think I'll have the lobster," I tell him.

"You should have been here ten minutes ago. Juney actually leaned across the table and kissed her husband. I'd been about ready to order dessert until I saw that." He's about to leave when he remembers something. "How long have you known that our chair search was going to be canceled?"

Even drunk as I am, I recognize this trap. Rourke would like nothing better than to catch Jacob Rose in an outright lie. "Has our search been canceled?" I ask. I'm prejudiced, of course, but I think I play the innocent every bit as convincingly as my dean. Which may even be a reason to believe I'd make a good dean. Maybe it's the influence of a fifth of fine whiskey or the proximity of my longtime enemy, but the idea of becoming his dean has grown on me. Judas Peckerwood. I can almost see the nameplate on the door.

"I should know better than to ask," Rourke says. "Twenty years I've known you and Jacob, and you've never told the truth yet. Enjoy your lobster."

"You drive carefully," I tell the second Mrs. R. Her husband flinches but does not turn around.

"*That* used to be one wild woman," Tony observes when they're gone.

"Don't tell me you had a lot to offer her too," I sigh.

He doesn't look up from his menu. "You think all my knowledge is carnal, but it's not."

In the middle of the room the young woman with Bodie Pie gets up to go to the women's. She's tall and athletic-looking, vaguely familiar. A coach of one of the women's teams perhaps. Something about the expression on Bodie's face suggests to me that this dinner they're having is good-bye. Bodie takes out her cigarettes, starts to light one, then remembers she's in nonsmoking and puts them away again. When I catch her eye, I give her the kind of loopy smile that's supposed to convey understanding and sympathy but that probably conveys only how drunk I am. The look I get back suggests that she's confusing me with her ex-husband, the man who convinced her to be a lesbian.

When the waiter comes, I order a large cut of prime rib, which causes my companion to look at me with disgust. "You wouldn't."

"What do you mean I wouldn't?"

"Do you know how bad that is for you?" Since his heart bypass, Tony is death on red meat. "Do you know how many pounds of undigested animal fat the average American carries around in his body?"

Given the amount of sour mash Tony has consumed tonight, I'm in no mood to listen. When I see that the waiter has hesitated before writing down my order, I repeat it. "Rare," I add.

Tony orders the brook trout.

When the waiter leaves us, and when June Barnes gets up to go to the women's room, Teddy comes over, his face flushed with excitement, and pulls up a chair. "What'd Rourke want?" he asks eagerly. "He broke a lamp in his office after the meeting. Threw it against the wall."

"He was just wondering if I thought you'd stand for chair again," I tell him. "He didn't want to nominate you unless he was sure you'd accept."

Teddy knows better than to entertain this possibility. Paul Rourke was the power behind his ouster from the chair I now temporarily occupy. Still, I can see the hope in his eyes. In the ever-changing world of departmental politics, it's just possible that things have changed enough for Teddy to become acceptable to Rourke. Perhaps my even more abusive reign has made his own look democratic by comparison. Maybe his tenure as chair looks like the good old days now. Maybe, compared with me, he looks sane. Not once during his six years as chair did he ever threaten to kill ducks.

You don't have to be Teddy to know these thoughts are flickering through his mind, rendered plausible, as even the most ridiculous scenarios are, by desire. It's a crazy world, he's telling himself. If Jacob Rose and Gracie DuBois can marry in it, if his wife of twenty-some years can have a fling with a man whose academic specialty is sitcoms, is there really any reason to believe he shouldn't be chair again? Well, yes, but it takes Teddy far too long to realize it.

"You're joking, right?" he finally says, and his attempt to disguise his disappointment stirs in me a powerful desire to be cruel to this man who has been my friend for a long time. As I've said before, I share with my dog many deep thoughts and feelings, and at this moment I understand completely his desire last week to groin Teddy, and I'm no more capable of resisting the temptation than he was.

"Don't be pathetic, Teddy," I advise.

I can see from his expression how badly I've hurt his feelings. This low blow is indeed Occam-like, a pointed snout to the gonads, and it's either Teddy's fundamental generosity of spirit or our long friendship that drives him to find an excuse for my boorish behavior. "Boy, you're really drunk," he says.

"Immaterial, but true," I admit.

He shrugs. "I just came over to congratulate you—"

"Like hell," I tell him, unmoved by the beginnings of tears forming in Teddy's eyes. He looks like he did the night he confessed his love for my wife, the night he told me I didn't love her enough, back when we were both young men. "You came over to gossip."

I'm half-expecting a reprimand from Tony, but my companion has unaccountably lapsed into an almost comatose silence. When the waiter arrives with our salads, I look over at him and am surprised to discover on his face an expression like menace. He stabs, off center, the cherry tomato in the middle of his salad with such violence that it jumps off the plate and skitters across the table. Since it's closest to Teddy, he reaches out to pick the tomato up and return it to its owner, only to discover that Tony has risen from his seat and lunged after it with a second thrust of his fork, skewering it this time with all three tines, pinning it to the tablecloth, where it oozes juice and seeds. He's missed Teddy's fingers so narrowly that Teddy, startled, jumps back. Bodie Pie is watching all this, and so is half the restaurant. Like the drunks we are, at least tonight, we've been talking too loud, and of course no sound travels in a restaurant quite as clearly as anger.

"Cripes. All right," Teddy says, pushing his chair back. "I'll go away."

"Oh, sit still," I tell him, unnecessarily, since Teddy has made no real move to get up. All Teddy's threats are academic, especially his threats to leave. And maybe he can sense that I'm belatedly ashamed of myself. In driver's manuals they say that only time can make a drunk man sober, but in my experience shame is also sobering. "Really. Sit."

He scoots his chair back in, eager, Occam-like. "How come you're so pissed off at me?" he wants to know. "I voted for you."

"Maybe that's the reason. Did you ever think of that?" When he doesn't say anything, I continue. "Maybe it's the fact that you can't even go out to dinner on a Monday night in this town without running into half the Railton Campus."

This observation has not made things better, I can tell. I meant it to refer to the Rourkes' presence, but of course it includes Teddy and June as well. And Bodie Pie, who has also overheard it, no doubt.

"Anyway, forget I said anything," I tell him. "It's been a long day. What's going on with you?"

Teddy's face brightens, and I realize he's been waiting for me to ask something like this. "June and I are going on a cruise," he says, beaming. "We just decided. We really need to get away for a while. It's going to cost a lot, but . . ."

Tony, I see, has miraculously finished his salad while I've been twirling a strip of lettuce on my fork as if it were pasta. He still hasn't said a word to Teddy, and his expression of malice has, if anything, intensified at the mention of Teddy's wife. It's as though he's tapped into my own surge of inexplicable anger and is surfing this borrowed emotion at its crest, unaware that its owner has slipped mercifully down into the trough. He reaches over, uninvited, and furiously stabs at my cherry tomato, nailing it on the third try, though most of its ruptured insides leak out onto my lettuce. This is too much for Teddy, who slides his chair back for real this time and stands.

"Do me a favor," Tony says unexpectedly, his mouth full of my salad, acknowledging Teddy directly for the first time. We all wait until Tony has finished chewing. "Tell that fucking bitch you're married to that I never laid a finger on that girl."

There's no reason, of course, for Teddy to do this favor. Everyone in the restaurant, including June, who's just returned from the women's room, has heard the request. Bodie Pie is trying to attract the attention of a waiter with her credit card. Her companion has not returned to the table.

Tony now has my entire salad in front of him, and he's devouring it with startling ferocity. I can't help but watch, and Teddy, who's been given every imaginable permission and encouragement to leave, seems rooted to the floor. Only when he looks over at me and our eyes meet and I give him a shrug does he take a wordless leave. The last piece of my romaine lettuce is huge, but rather than stop to cut it, Tony stuffs it into his mouth whole, using his fingers to accomplish his design. This from a man who has the most meticulous, indeed the fussiest manners of any man I know except Finny. This from Tony Coniglia, who accuses me of being a cretin because I doctor clams with cocktail sauce. At the moment, there's no danger of my exhibiting bad manners. My companion has eaten his own salad, plus mine, and now he's finishing the bread. Which leaves nothing for me but the condiments, and I'm not even sure I'm entitled to these.

There's only one person I can think of who might be able to defuse the present situation, and that's Jacob Rose. I wish he were here, despite the fact that I know he'd defuse it at my expense. The first thing he'd observe is that I have piss poor luck in restaurants. Most of the time I'm ignored, and even on those occasions that I'm actually served food, I still don't get to eat it. And I've already been warned that I'm going to pay for this dinner.

When he finishes the bread, Tony looks around for a waiter, but they've all made themselves scarce. Both his water and his whiskey glass are empty, and I notice that Tony is sweating profusely, though it's not warm in the restaurant. Given his history of heart problems, it occurs to me that he might be having an attack, but when I ask him if he's all right, he gets up from the table, wipes his face, his forehead, and the back of his neck with his cloth napkin, and tosses it onto the chair. "I'll be right back," he assures me.

Since it's the men's room I assume he's heading toward, I don't try to stop him, but instead he goes over to Teddy and June's table, where they too have been unsuccessful in getting their waiter to bring them their check. There isn't a single waiter in the dining room, and I make a mental note not to overtip this evening. Courage isn't something you normally require in a waiter, but this entire crew is far too timid to prosper.

June tries to get up when she sees Tony approaching, but she's too late, and anyway Tony is holding up his hands in surrender. At least I think it's surrender. He doesn't have anything in either hand. He slides into the booth next to June.

Suddenly Bodie Pie is at my elbow. "Is this scene going to get better or worse?" she wants to know.

I gesture for her to sit down, but she declines. "I have no idea what's got into him," I confess.

She nods. "I warned you about this last Friday."

"When?"

"When you were out picking daisies. He hasn't told you about it?"

"Nope," I tell her. "He's working up to it though." It's when I say this that I realize it's true. This is precisely where we've been heading all night. "If he doesn't pass out first. If *I* don't pass out first."

"You aren't driving, are you?"

"Hell no."

She shakes her head. "That damn Jesuit is right. You *never* tell the truth, do you?"

"Well . . ."

"Call me if you need a lift," she says. "Here he comes again."

Tony is indeed weaving his way toward us, hangdog now, no longer dangerous, though the other diners are not sure of this, and the dining room is full of the sound of people scraping in their chairs to give him plenty of room. I see he's picked up Teddy and June's check, which is a good way of saying you're sorry to Teddy. There may be no good way of saying you're sorry to June.

"Professor Coniglia," Bodie says. "How lovely to see you this evening."

"Professor Pie," Tony says, taking her hand gallantly, kissing it. "May I call you Sweetie?"

In the few minutes he's been gone, he's located his old self. Mock-charming, outrageous, impossible to take seriously.

"It's my night to offend everyone," he explains.

"Between us," Bodie says, taking her hand back as soon as she's decently able, "you're right about Juney. She's a bitch on wheels. And she won't forget."

"Well, then," Tony says, raising my water glass in a toast to good fellowship, "she'll just have to remember."

Our dinners arrive then, all the waiters having returned to the dining room at once, and Bodie takes her leave. "I have to admit," Tony says. "That's one classy lesbian."

I'm astonished to discover that I have an excellent appetite for my prime rib, which has arrived sweet and bloody. Tony picks at his trout, then finally asks if he can have a taste of my dinner. When I start to carve off a portion, he stops me. "Just the fat," he explains, leaning over to take the piece he wants from the tail. He chews it with something akin to religious ecstasy.

We do not want what's good for us.

CHAPTER

31

Her name was Yolanda Ackles, and she'd been a longtime resident at the nearby Hereford Clinic until it was decided that she should be main-streamed. One of the first things Yolanda did after she settled into her new apartment at the Railton Towers was sign up for classes on campus. She was encouraged to do this by her counselor, who assured her that the state would pay. The counselor's only other advice was for her to stay on her medication: "Don't forget what happens to you when you start skipping."

The problem with the medication was that it made everything fuzzy and abstract and gray. Still, Yolanda appreciated the fact that her meds allowed her to go among other people, who would treat her, when she was medicated, much like they would treat any other big-boned, over-weight girl with straight, mouse-brown hair, who lumbered across floors so heavily that objects rattled and the surfaces of liquid in glasses boiled. It was a relief not to be viewed as someone with special problems. She sat in the rear or off to the side in her classes, and she took lots of notes, though these often did not make sense to her later. She studied her professors meticulously for signs of kindness, and she was often more interested in these signs than in what her teachers had to say about cell division. She did not sign up for any classes with women professors.

Despite her difficulty in processing information, her inability to differentiate between important and less important facts, her tendency to mishear, to get sidetracked, to mistake irony for its opposite, she managed to do comparatively well, earning mostly C's and the occasional B in her course work. As long as she stayed on her medication, she could compete with the hungover, the lazy, the drug-addled, the terminally bored.

There was no need for her counselor to remind Yolanda about what happened when she started skipping her meds. She had not forgotten. In fact, she remembered fondly. It was like there was suddenly wind for her sails after months of breathless calm. Properly medicated, Yolanda felt becalmed on a flat lake where others nearby were sailing about merrily, wind snapping in their sails, and she could hear the sound of their laughter and catch, every now and then, a scrap of joyous conversation. Was it fair that there should be wind on one part of the lake and not on the other?

Skipping her medication caused the sails of her own small craft to billow like the others, allowed her to join in the merriment, tacking in and out among the other revelers, the wind in her hair and her clothing. The low gray sky went high and blue, the air so clear that Yolanda could almost see in the high cirrus clouds the face of a benevolent God. She was still alone, of course, but it was exhilarating to move, and the laughing people from nearby boats waved to her in a manner that made her feel welcome, even though it was impossible in such a wind to do much more than wave and smile.

This was what it felt like to Yolanda on days when she skipped her medication, and this was why there was no danger of her forgetting her counselor's warning. And she knew he was right. If she stayed off her meds too long, the warming winds grew too strong, ripping her fragile sails to shreds and driving her onto the rocks of the Hereford Clinic, a thing Yolanda did not want. Still, even that was not so much worse than the return of the dreaded calm of the medication, of seeing the other boats sail merrily off, of realizing that the other revelers had been waving not to her but to each other.

This much I compose in my head as Tony talks. We now have coffee and the whole restaurant to ourselves. The sailing metaphor is my own invention, the omniscient telling merely an exercise. These last few years, having limited my creative endeavors to the op-ed page of *The Rear View,* I've had little opportunity to indulge omniscience, though I continue to teach it, out of duty, to my fiction writers, even as I warn them against it. Omniscience requires a combination of worldly experience and chutzpah, in more or less equal measures, a technique I'm drawn to now in advancing middle age, perhaps because, as my wife and daughter never tire of reminding me, I tumble to the truth of things late and would prefer to give the impression that I've known all along. By making use of omniscience I may be able to explain to myself life's mysteries, which I'm not even close to grasping in the first person, a more modest form, even when you're William Henry Devereaux, Jr.

"So this girl's in love with you?" I say.

"Obsessed," Tony corrects me. "She claims to hear my voice coming out of the walls at night. She thinks I'm God. She says she's carrying God's child."

"Jesus," I say. It slips out before I can think. "So she's claiming you've had sex?"

"Great sex," he says sadly, with only the most distant hint of his usual braggadocio. "Sex like nobody's ever had before. Sex on a whole 'nuther plane."

"I should think that the fact that she's hearing your voice come out of the walls would make her testimony in these matters suspect."

"Some people are apparently anxious to believe the worst. Juney's harassment and sexual misconduct committee is going into full-blown investigative mode. I suspect the whole thing will be on the front page of the newspaper tomorrow unless you kill another duck."

"Speaking of people anxious to believe," I say. "Can't the girl be placed under observation?"

"We're hoping. Today's was the third incident this term. Twice she's had to be forcibly removed from campus. Usually, though, they just call her therapist, get her back on her meds, and let her go. And there has to be an opening back at Hereford before she can be readmitted."

"Thank heaven we're almost to the end of the term."

"That'll keep her off campus," Tony concedes, "but she shows up at the house now too. If you'd stayed twenty minutes longer the other night, you'd have met her. One minute the local press and I were alone, and the next there she was, taking off her clothes, about to get in the tub with us. Naturally, the press freaked."

"Take a long vacation," I suggest. "Rent the house to a graduate student for the summer and go somewhere."

"I'd probably be better off to sell it and just go. This is going to put me right at the top of Dickie's list. Everybody in bio has tenure, and what I'm hearing is that one of us is going to have to go anyway."

"You really think they can just start sacking people with tenure?"

"I think *they* think they can."

"I'm not so sure."

"Well, here's an interesting item," he says. "Remember how all of us who were coming up on our sixtieth birthdays this year were offered early retirement incentives last summer?"

I do vaguely recall. If memory serves, Billy Quigley had briefly considered the offer.

"Well, last week I called personnel to say I might be interested. Guess what I found out?"

"The offer's been withdrawn?"

He nods.

"For everyone in that situation?"

"I don't know. But for me, the offer is no longer on the table."

"So you think they're considering even more economical methods now?"

"That's what I think. Also, I'm not sure I have the unqualified support of my dean. He's wished for a long time that I didn't have quite so much to offer women."

Which makes me wonder if Tony would have my unqualified support if I were dean. "And you think your department has a list?"

He's looking me in the eye now. "I think every department has a list. I think English has a list. I've heard for a fact that English has a list."

"And you heard I drew up this list?"

"I heard there was a list."

At the register I pay for my dinner and Tony's. He pays for June's and Teddy's. I tell him I'm going to make a stop at the men's room. He offers to wait, but he looks exhausted, bottomed out, and since I may be a while, I tell him to go on home. On a night like this, a man like me fears the truth before he knows it. After my soul-cleansing, chino-soiling pee this afternoon, I've returned to dribble mode. I had hoped, of course, that a man who could fill an office swivel chair with urine at five o'clock in the afternoon might be able to relieve himself sensibly at midnight, but I find that I am again backed up, painfully, angrily.

Outside, snow. As predicted. Even so, amazing.

It has only just started when I emerge from the restaurant, but it's coming down heavy in wet, thick flakes. The spot where Tony's car was parked is already white. Chances are, if it's snowing like this here in Railton, it's coming down even harder in Allegheny Wells, which is higher up.

At the bottom of Pleasant Street Hill I pull off to the side at the gravel entrance to the railyard and watch another car, the only one I've seen since leaving the restaurant, make the long, steep ascent. Halfway up, the car begins to lose traction and the rear end drifts sideways as the wheels spin, but it makes the first plateau, where it stops, as if to summon courage and steel resolve, its brake lights glowing anxious red. It remains there too long though, and I begin to suspect that the car's driver and I are soul mates. "Now what?" I say out loud, and only when I hear the words spoken does the left blinker come on. Then the car turns into the intersection, inching slowly away from further confrontation. My soul mate gone, I turn my attention to the dark railyard, its flat landscape interrupted here and there by the black silhouettes of boxcars. What they remind me of, strangely, is an urban skyline, except that would mean that the entire city was belowground, only the very tops of its rectangular buildings poking up through the snow. Seen so fancifully, the world tilts and with it my stomach. I close my eyes, and my mother's words find me across the long decades. "We will forget this," she assures me.

Somehow we, or at least I, have managed to remain faithful to that promise. How long was it after my father left before it became clear to me, if not to my mother, that he wasn't coming back? A year or so in my memory, but it may have been far less. We were still in the same rented university house, which means the year's lease had not run out. So, perhaps only a few months. With him gone, the house had become engulfed in silence. Strange, since my father was a reader and a writer, and the house was always kept quiet for these sensible pursuits. My mother was a reader too, but I always had the impression that it was my father we were keeping quiet for. But apparently not, because now, with no William Henry Devereaux, Sr., to consider, the house was more deeply, eerily silent than before. After school I became the denizen of its dark, dank cellar, from which my mother always had to call me for dinner. What did I do down there? she always wanted to know. I remember there was no way to explain.

The house, situated at the outer edge of the campus, had recently been purchased by the university, which was buying adjacent property to ensure the possibility of future expansion. In fact, the house we lived in then would be leveled a few years after we moved out, along with all the others on that block, to make room for a medical school annex. The house's previous owner, also a professor, had apparently been a different order of being from William Henry Devereaux, Sr., because his basement was full of tools. There was a huge workbench, complete with a heavy, cast-iron vice at one end and a jigsaw I discovered how to turn on at the other. There were also a sander and several drills and a special tin case containing dozens of drill bits. One whole wall sported hooks from which hung hammers, planers, handsaws and hacksaws, and the grips on all of these were worn smooth with use. Off in an unlit corner stood a cluster of yard tools: two or three rakes, a snow shovel, a hoe, a spade. I remember thinking when I discovered the spade that there'd been no reason to borrow one from our neighbor when my father dug the hole to bury Red. To my knowledge, my father never ventured down into the dark cellar, so he never knew what tools were at his disposal. When the furnace went out, he called for help, and when the repairman arrived my father showed him to what he understood to be the door to the cellar where the furnace was located. That was about as much information as he could furnish.

His tools were nearly all I knew about the man who'd occupied the house before it became ours, except that he had lived there for many years. We'd heard he never married, and therefore had no children. Which seemed to me a shame, because when I handled his tools, I always pictured a man who wouldn't have minded the company of a boy like me as he worked. I'd concluded he might even have enjoyed it.

The afternoon my mother crept noiselessly down the cellar stairs instead of calling to me as she usually did, I had taken a coil of rope, climbed onto a chair, and tied a knot onto one of the pipes that formed a complex grid running along the ceiling of the cellar. The moment before I turned around and saw her, I had been testing the rope by yanking on it with both hands, to see if the knot would stay tied, if the pipe would hold my weight. To another kid, I would have looked like I was about to swing, Tarzan-like, from one imaginary tree to another, but at the moment our eyes met, I knew this was not the conclusion my mother had come to, and I let loose an explosion of violent grief I had not known until that very moment I possessed.

How did I get from the chair I was standing on and into her arms? How did I know to go there, know that she would not be angry? There was no way to explain to my mother what I didn't fully comprehend myself—that I didn't want my life to end, rather just to know that the pipe would hold me if I needed it to later, if things got worse, if they became unbearable.

And how did she know the right words to whisper as she clutched me to her, her fingers digging in beneath my jutting boyish shoulder blades? How did she know to say that we—she and I—were going to forget this? How did she know to whisper these words so fiercely that I would have no choice but to believe her? Did she recognize the ambiguity of her message to me? Was it the pain of his abandonment we would eventually forget? Was that what she meant? Or was it the fact that she had come down into the cellar and found me standing on a chair? Both, I felt certain. What I didn't know was how we'd manage to do this necessary thing. *How* would we forget? Was it time we would put our faith in? God's grace? Each other? It didn't matter. Only her certainty mattered. It simply would be done. I had her word. I was to trust her, and I did.

By the time I open my eyes, the world has tilted back again, and the boxcars are merely boxcars, not the skyline of some lost, submerged city. Not even squinting at them, blurring the edges of my vision, can make them into anything but what they are. Which is just as well. It is a mistake, I feel certain, to be sentimental about a boy visited by a fleeting thought, a passing sorrow. After all, not far from where I sit, a man my age, a man named William Cherry, has recently surrendered his life by lying down on the track and allowing something larger and more powerful than himself to bear away and out of the world some pain I will never know. What I wonder is this: Did this world tilt for William Cherry, as it just did momentarily for me? Had he forgotten that the world could do such a thing? Did the visible world become infinitely alien just before his leaving it? Or did the world *fail* to tilt? Did it remain mundane and true to his trained, melancholy expectation right to the end, its boxcars merely boxcars, all lined up along the seemingly endless track, as far as William Cherry's eye could see?

I do not want to die. I'm as sure of this, I think, as a man can reasonably be. I do not want to learn, when I speak to Phil Watson tomorrow, that the asymmetry he thought he felt in my prostate is a tumor, and yet, there is a part of me that would thrill to receive such news. Why that should be I cannot imagine. Nor do I want the woman that I'm married to and that I love to leave me, but the thought of her doing so moves me in a way that our growing old together and contentedly slipping, in affectionate tandem, toward the grave does not. The thought of Lily's having found someone to replace me is not welcome, but an urgent new love—and what makes the world stranger than love?—is a thing that I could half-wish for her. For me.

Half. I can hear Tony Coniglia whispering to me that I'm permitted half.

The more immediate question is what I'll be permitted by the young uniformed officer I see approaching through the snow on foot in my rearview mirror. How long has the revolving blue and red light of his cruiser been flashing back there? When the cop taps on my window, I roll it down and provide my license. He studies this with his flashlight, then shines the light in my face to see if I'm the same guy. Would I mind stepping out of the vehicle? he wonders. Hell, no. Have I been drinking? Hell, yes. Where am I headed? Good question. Would I mind answering it? Allegheny Wells, I tell him. That's what you think, he replies. Where I'm headed is the backseat of his cruiser. He takes me by the elbow, the big, helpful lug.

On the short drive to the station I notice him studying me in the rearview mirror. "Tell the truth," he grins when we pull into the lot,

and for a second I think he's going to accuse me of indulging sui-
cidal thoughts out there in the dark railyard. "You're that duck guy,
aren't you?"

With my one phone call, I try Tony Coniglia. He's responsible for this
mess, is my reasoning. But there's no answer at Tony's. He was
drunker than I, though. If he's passed out, it'll take more than a ringing phone to rouse him. I consider calling Teddy. Getting me out of jail
in the middle of the night is the kind of duty that would appeal to him.
He's always on the lookout for a new Hank story for his repertoire. But
he'll tell this one badly, just like all the others, and besides, I've been too
mean to him at the restaurant to call him now.

"Your wife ain't home?" the old cop says, eyebrow raised, when I
hang up. I can read his thoughts. Going on two o'clock and this poor
bastard's wife isn't home. No wonder he's drinking. "I tell you what,"
he says. "We have lovely accommodations right here."

Fine with me, at this point. "There are lots of other people I could
call," I tell my escort as he leads me down a corridor to the drunk tank.
I don't want him to think I'm alone in the world, a man without
friends or colleagues. I mean, hell, there are academic deans I could call
who'd come and get me if I asked. The only reason I'm here is to fulfill
a prophecy.

"Monday night. You got the place practically to yourself," I'm told,
and it's true. The cell's got a half dozen cots, only one of which is occupied. "You'll like your roommate too. We're pretty upscale tonight."

Truth underlies all reality. I believe this. Often there are several
explanations for observable phenomena that make varying degrees of
sense, but the correct interpretation of the facts is always recognizable
for its beauty, its simplicity. Tony Coniglia did not answer his telephone for the simple reason that he wasn't there to answer it. He
wasn't there to answer it because he can't be in two places at once. If
he's here, he can't be there. And he's here. I see this.

I decide not to wake him to say hello, though I'm tempted. I don't
because it would rob him of tomorrow morning's mystical moment
when he awakes and finds me in the same cell and cannot for the life of
him account for my being there, with or without the application of

Occam's Razor. He will not rest easy until everything is explained to him, until the rich possibility of a world different from the one we know is thoroughly dispelled, though it is this *other* world we yearn for.

I lie down on a cot across the cell from Tony's and consider the future. By the time William of Occam was my age, he'd been excommunicated and was on the run, ecclesiastically speaking, from a vengeful pope, whose authority he continued to question in a series of inflammatory pamphlets, sort of op-ed pieces, with a distribution smaller than that of the Railton *Rear View*. There was, of course, no middle class to write for, and William, long banished from the university, would in any case have perceived a different academic mission from mine at West Central Pennsylvania University. He'd probably have felt a greater kinship with William Henry Devereaux, Sr., who always imagined himself speaking to an elite few colleagues and graduate students, the modern-day equivalent of the medieval scholastics, bearers of learning and arbiters of secular taste. At my age, fifty, William of Occam still had fourteen more years to live, and sixty-four was a ripe old age in the fourteenth century. Best of all, his life didn't leak out of him gradually, like a tire with a tiny puncture. He died of the Black Death, and he never saw it coming until it was upon him, a dirty, brutish, democratic foe who argued with William in precise, elegant syllogisms, defeating all the philosopher's logic and unifying in swift death, as life never could, the conflicting impulses of reason and faith that had shaped his life.

These are strange thoughts for a man to have in a Railton, Pennsylvania, jail cell at two in the morning, and if what's written on the ceiling above me is any indication of the intellectual tenor of my cell's former inhabitants, I'm the only one to concern myself with such issues. As I stare at the ceiling it occurs to me that this is the second time today I've been advised to eat shit. I close my eyes and fall asleep counting boxcars.

When I awake Tony Coniglia is standing over me. He looks like he might be having the kind of transcendent moment I foresaw last night.

"What I asked you to do was come and get me, not come and join me," he gives me to understand.

"What are you talking about?" I say, propping myself up on one elbow.

"I used my one phone call last night to leave a message on your machine," he explains.

I can't help grinning at this. "I called you too," I admit. "You weren't in either." I hand him the bottle of aspirin I always keep in the glove compartment of the Lincoln and was wise enough to bring in with me last night. He chews several tablets thoughtfully. When we compare notes, it turns out that we've been run in by the same young cop, that neither of us has been charged.

"He wanted to book me until I told him I was a professor," Tony says. "Until I told him my name was Hank Devereaux."

"He must have been pretty surprised to run into another one half an hour later."

"Did you tell him your father was back in town?" Tony says. "Because that would explain it."

I can't remember mentioning my father's return to Tony, but I must have, because he knows. I'm going to have to go see W.H.D., Sr., today, a duty I've been putting off. "When do you suppose they'll let us out?" I wonder, swinging my feet onto the floor. Though today promises to be no more fun than yesterday, I would like, for some reason, to get on with it.

"When do you suppose they'll serve breakfast?" is what the other Hank Devereaux in the cell would like to know.

CHAPTER

32

After I retrieve my car from the railyard, I drive out to Allegheny Wells behind a news van that sports the logo of a Pittsburgh television station. When I ask myself what sort of story can have attracted a news team from so far away to this two-lane macadam blacktop that leads from Railton to Allegheny Wells, I don't like the conclusion I come to. I like it even less when I get to Allegheny Estates, where there's a cop directing traffic at the turnoff. Instead of turning left into Estates I, I turn right between the tilting stone pillars of Estates II and follow the road that leads up through the trees to Paul Rourke's house, where I pull in and turn off the ignition. The second Mrs. R., in furry slippers, a flannel nightgown, and a winter coat, is seated in a deck chair eating Sugar Pops from a tall box. It's still early. Twenty minutes to eight. Sunny and warming but still cold.

"Permission to come aboard?" I call up.

She's looking down at me. "Wow," she says dully. "I actually know something nobody else knows."

Her husband's voice, from somewhere inside the house, is heard. "Mark the calendar."

I climb the stairs and join her. There are two folding chairs on the deck, which means we're fine if her husband doesn't join us. When she hands me the box of cereal, I take a handful. "Sugar Pops are tops," I tell her, this slogan returning to me across the decades. If I'm not mistaken, the woman I'm speaking to may be hearing it for the first time. "What is it that you know that nobody else knows?" I ask her.

"Your whereabouts," says her husband, coming out through the sliding glass door. He's got two cups of coffee, one of which he hands to me. The second Mrs. R. looks at her husband to see if the other one might be for her. When he drinks from it, she gets up and goes inside. Rourke settles into the vacated chair. His hair is still shiny and wet from the shower. "I knew you'd come over to my side eventually," he says, putting his feet up on the rail. They haven't taken very good care of their deck. The wood is dry and splintering. Two or three boards have buckled, and some of the nails used to keep the others in place have begun to inch up dangerously.

"Pretty nice view," I tell him. "No leaves to obstruct it."

Actually, the trees over on this side of the road are budding, at least some of them. Whereas on the other side they are so thick we can see only occasional glints of metal and glass. Still, it's clear that cars and vans line the entire winding road up through the trees, and if I'm not mistaken there's a mobile satellite hookup being assembled atop a truck.

"A wild guess," I say. "Another duck has died."

"You just missed an interview with Lou Steinmetz on the local news. He claims they know the identity of the perpetrator."

"He used the word *perpetrator?*"

Rourke nods. "He didn't mention you by name though."

What's occurred to me is that the second Mrs. R. has not returned with her coffee. I've been prepared to offer her my chair. Rourke notices me glancing over at the sliding door. "Don't worry about her," he says. "She's off smoking her first joint of the day."

"No kidding?"

"She hasn't been anything but stoned since we got married."

"Huh."

He nods. "I've pretty much had to quit. I think it may be responsible for my blackouts."

"I never knew you smoked."

"How do you think I've kept from coming after you with a baseball bat?"

"Then you shouldn't stop," I say.

He snorts. "Just do me a favor. Don't tell anybody you came over here. I've been promising people for years that if you ever did I'd throw you off this deck for the pleasure of watching you roll all the way down to the road."

I know my role in this drama. I stand up halfway and peer over the side, showing the requisite respect for his fantasy. It's a hell of a drop, too. Unless he hit a tree head-on, a tumbling man wouldn't stop until he reached the pavement.

"Not that you're interested, but I got a call from that schmuck Herbert this morning," Rourke says. "The union's managed to get its hands on a copy of the list."

I study him for a moment before I say anything. "I was under the impression you believed me when I told you there wasn't one."

"Not exactly," he corrects me. "You told me you didn't make one. That I believed."

"But now you say there's a list."

"For every department."

"Including English?"

"Including English."

I consider this. "I'm touched, Reverend," I tell him, and it's the truth, I am.

Now it's his turn to study me. "Why, for Christ's sake?"

"You're always accusing me of lying."

"You always are."

"And yet you believe me now."

He shrugs. "Just this once."

We're quiet for a minute. "I guess you better tell me who. I'll go see Jacob."

"Fucking Jacob."

In fact, when I said Jacob's name, I was myself visited by an ugly thought.

"Call Herbert," Rourke says wearily. "Let him tell you. Or Teddy. I'm sure that little gossipmonger knows by now. Three of the four were predictable anyway."

"Orshee?"

"That's one."

"Finny?"

"Two."

I take a deep breath. "Don't tell me Billy Quigley?"

"You're three for three."

"And someone I wouldn't guess?"

He shrugs, studying me. "You might. I wouldn't have."

The glass door slides open then, and the second Mrs. R. comes back out with a third deck chair. Her face is beet red, and she emits the kind of snorting sound pot smokers make when they can't hold it in any longer. Rourke studies his wife impassively while she sets up her chair on the other side of the deck. "Life always pays you back," he remarks. And you don't have to know him all that well to know he's thinking about his first wife, a lovely, unintellectual woman he belittled into leaving him, thus creating space for the second Mrs. R. I slide back my deck chair and stand.

"By the way, is that mutt of yours loose?"

"Occam? No. He's in the house."

"I thought I saw him in Charlene's garden earlier. There must be another white shepherd around. How the hell did you slip past all the reporters?"

"You know me, Reverend," I tell him. "Just when you think I'm cornered . . ."

He nods, as if to suggest he knows all too well how slippery I can be. "Herbert's calling for a strike vote this afternoon."

"With a week left in the term?"

"To prevent the seniors from graduating," he explains. "That's as close to real political clout as we can muster."

"Herbert on his department's list?"

"So he says."

I nod, risk a grin. "Not a bad list, sounds like."

I'm standing next to the railing, the long drop to the road behind me, so I'm glad when he smiles back. "I thought it was excellent, top to bottom. I could almost vote for it, in fact."

Another snort from the second Mrs. R. A thin trail of marijuana smoke is tracking upward from her corner of the deck.

When I get to the bottom of the stairs, I call back up. "Hey?" From where I stand, I can see only my colleague's feet up on the railing. "I have this idea that maybe the fourth is one of us two?"

"I wouldn't worry about it too much," the voice of my old enemy condescends. "You'll luck out some way."

"What are you in such a good mood about?" my daughter wants to know when I turn up at her kitchen door as she's about to leave for work.

"Who?"

"You," she explains. "You're grinning."

"I've been excommunicated. The pope and his Vatican goons are hot on my trail. Find me a fast horse and saddle it up. Meanwhile, I need to borrow your shower," I tell her, pausing to look her over, this kid whose diapers I used to change. She looks like she's passed a dark, thoughtful night and emerged from the experience in better shape than she'd have predicted.

"Go ahead," she says. "You paid for it."

"I did?"

Julie nods sheepishly. "The money you and Mom loaned us? So we could finish the kitchen and master bath? Don't tell me you've forgotten."

"I'm not sure I ever knew."

She studies me knowingly. If she's spent the night trying to figure things out, at least she's succeeded in pegging me. "That's one of your great fictions, isn't it? That Mom never tells you anything. That way you can pretend there are things going on behind your back, things you don't approve of."

"There *are* things going on I don't approve of," I tell her.

"Right," she says. "Like you wouldn't have loaned us the money when we needed it. Like you're too reasonable, too logical. Like Mom's the one with the heart and you're the one with the brain. That's your public posture. Except everybody knows better. Remember the day I fell off my bike when I was little? Remember how you cried?"

"How *you* cried, you mean."

She shakes her head. "This is exactly what I'm talking about. Why can't you admit you cried? You *cried,* Daddy."

"Well," I admit.

"I only cried until it stopped hurting," she reminds me. "*You* couldn't stop. I was afraid to look in the mirror when I got home. I thought it must be horrible. I expected to see half my face gone. I kept looking in the mirror for the part that made you cry."

"You were my daughter," I remind her.

"I know," she says. "I understand. It's just . . ."

I wait for her, wishing I could help out, but in truth I feel as helpless now as I felt then when her back wheel slid in the gravel, then caught, and she flew over her handlebars. Was that how my mother felt there on the cellar stairs, when she pulled me to her and told me we would forget? At the time it felt like the opposite, to me. Until now it hasn't occurred to me to imagine what it felt like to her.

"I left you a message yesterday."

"I got it," I tell my daughter. It's not easy, but I meet her eyes. "You left it for the wrong person, though. Russell's ready to shoulder most of the blame, you know. Why not talk to him?"

"Because I'm too much like you. I have a public posture to preserve. I changed the locks. Now *I'm* the one who can't get *out.* Funny how that works, huh?"

"Maybe if somebody explained that to him?"

"Will you see him?"

"I might." I still have the number he gave me, though for some reason I don't tell her this.

"So how come you need to shower over here?" it finally occurs to her to ask, and I can't help smiling at her. Even as a child, Julie was essentially uncurious. You could walk in the door with an aardvark on a leash and she wouldn't ask why, and I suspect this lack of curiosity was, more than anything else, the reason Julie was never much of a student. Ninety percent of answering questions is anticipating which ones will be asked, having a sense of what's important, being interested enough in something to pose the questions for yourself in advance. Julie, I would guess, has never guessed a test question in her life.

And I know what Lily would say if she were here. She would remind me that Julie is a product of her experience. In the world we provided her, she felt safe and protected. She knew we wouldn't ask her any trick questions or make unreasonable demands. She didn't have to peer nervously around corners, or check constantly over her shoulder. If her mother or I came in with an aardvark on a leash, she could rest assured there was a reason, and this certainty made the explanation unnecessary. Julie, my wife would insist, is living evidence of our skill in parenting, that rare adult who doesn't see the world as a dangerous, treacherous place. She expects to be loved, to be rewarded for her efforts, to be treated generously. She had tenure as a child and now expects it as an adult. Until this thing with Russell, she's been optimistic. Her optimism has been tested of late, by their not having enough money and probably by other things too, but it hasn't occurred to her until recently that things might not work out.

"Julie," I say. To this little girl. To this novice adult.

When I've showered, I locate a pair of Russell's undershorts and some socks. I also swipe his one blue, button-down oxford dress shirt. It's a bit big in the torso, short in the sleeve, but it will look fine beneath my tweed coat. I also find a new disposable razor, forgotten in the back of the medicine cabinet, and a bottle of Christmas gift aftershave. I have always liked Russell and sometimes even felt more instinctive understanding of him than of my own daughter. We're a lot alike, is what I'm thinking, dressed as I am in his clothes.

Using the telephone in his kitchen, I dial the number he left me in case I needed to reach him. It's a woman who answers, and when I recognize her voice I hang up without even saying hello. It's only then that I remember the telephone call she made from my office, the intimacy in her voice, reporting my whereabouts, to Russell, who was waiting for me in the parking lot. I look up her number in the phone book, compare it with the one Russell gave me. Why shouldn't Meg Quigley answer? It's her number I just dialed.

I make a note of the address. It's in the student ghetto, a neighborhood full of big, old houses that have been subdivided into seedy flats. This late in the spring term, the sidewalks, even on weekday mornings, are strewn with beer cans, and every third sloping porch sports a dented silver tub large enough to hold a full keg of beer. Student life is no different, my Ivy League colleagues tell me, at Dartmouth and Princeton.

I pull into the driveway next to the house Meg's living in and just sit there for a few minutes, hoping one or the other of them will look out the window, see me there, and come down so I won't have to go up. But the windows are shaded and still, and I know this plan is doomed. When the screen door of the house next to Meg's swings open, a young man dressed in jeans and a baseball cap and no shirt emerges, scratching his stomach and yawning. I recognize him as Bobo from my comp class. It's probably not a good thing that I can't remember Bobo's real name. It suggests that I may have been unfair to him in other ways. I've just about decided that this must be the case when Bobo ambles over to the side of the porch, turns his baseball cap around backwards, yanks himself out of his fly, and arcs an impressive stream over the porch railing and onto the door of the car parked in the drive below, the one I've pulled in next to. I'm pleased to observe that when I get out of my car Bobo soils himself getting back into his jeans.

"Dr. Devereaux," he says nervously. "I didn't see you sitting there."

He really is stunned by my sudden appearance, I can tell. He hugs his bare chest, as if somebody's just this second whispered into his ear that it's cold outside. What he'd like to know, and what he's too hungover to figure out, is how much power I might wield over him in the present circumstance. He knows I have the authority to grade his compositions and make these grades stand despite his protests, and for all he knows I may have other powers too. I can see the wheels turning in Bobo's slow brain. I've caught him with his dick in his hand in broad daylight peeing on somebody's car. On the other hand we're not on campus, which means I may be outside my legal jurisdiction. What the hell am I *doing* here? is what he'd love to know. He's trying to think of a way to ask.

"I'm curious," I tell him, because I am. "Why is it necessary to turn your hat around backwards in order to pee forwards?"

Bobo entertains this question with high seriousness, as if I'd just asked him to explain the disappearance of the Fool after Act Three of *King Lear*. "It isn't," he finally explains, without much confidence, it seems to me.

"Kind of a precaution?" I suggest, confusing him further, though he agrees that this is what it must be. "You have a nice day, Bobo," I tell him.

"You too, Dr. Devereaux."

Meg's flat is on the second floor, and I meet her on the stairs. Her hair is wet, and normally I would find this intimate detail attractive in Meg, but today she stirs little in me besides misgiving.

"You the cowardly person who called and hung up fifteen minutes ago?" she wants to know, suggesting that I'm not the only person on this staircase suffering misgivings.

"I wasn't expecting to hear your voice," I explain.

"I can't believe he gave you my number. He must have forgot you and I knew each other."

"Must have."

We both become aware at the same moment how awkward it is for us to be talking on the landing of a dark hallway. "Look," she says, not meeting my eyes now. "I've got the feeling he'd like to stay. And I really need him to go, okay?"

"He'll be gone within the hour," I assure her.

"He's a sweet man, but I'm friends with Julie too."

"Right."

"I mean, it's not like the sex is a big thing," she explains, "but I feel weird about the deception part."

"I can understand how you would."

"Well, the door's unlocked," she says, turning away and heading down the stairs. She stops suddenly, as if she's just realized something. "You're *really* pissed, arcn't you?"

"Maybe sex is a bigger thing with me," I say. What I don't say is that right now I'm very glad I didn't share that peach with her.

She seems to understand this without my saying it. "You're just like my old man," she says, shaking her head on the way out, "only sober."

Meg's flat, at least the living room, is typical graduate student chic, decorated as if to suggest that she still hasn't made up her mind whether to drink or read. Everywhere there are candles, half burned, dripping colorful wax down the necks of wine and liquor bottles. There are about two tons of books stacked on boards spaced atop concrete blocks. A quick scan of the books' spines reveals that many of her favorite authors are ones who also couldn't decide whether to drink or write. Her copy of William Henry Devereaux, Jr. (funny the way it leaps off the shelf) is wedged in between a Frederick Exley and a Scott Fitzgerald.

Finding Russell fast asleep in the tangle of Meg's sheets, I jiggle the bed with my foot until he wakes up. He's even more surprised to see me than Bobo was. He's so surprised, in fact, that he looks around to make sure of his whereabouts. It would be strange enough to wake up in his own bed and see his father-in-law standing over him, but in Meg Quigley's bedroom, with him in Meg's bed, my presence makes no kind of sense.

"See what I meant last night?" I say. "Nobody tells everything."

This is definitely anger I'm feeling right now, and I'd like it to be righteous anger, but it's hard to feel that toward a man whose undershorts you're wearing.

"Get dressed," I suggest. "Take a shower first."

He makes no immediate move to do as he's told, despite the clarity and simplicity of my directions. "Are you going to leave," he finally asks, "so I can?"

Unbelievable. "What, are you shy, Russell?"

He's sitting up in bed now, covers pulled up to his waist. "This isn't anything, Hank," he says. "Meg doesn't mean anything to me."

I nod my understanding. "At least your stories are consistent. She just assured me you mean nothing to her either."

Russell looks a little hurt to hear this, but he covers it quickly. "It's just . . ."

"It's kind of like a support system," I suggest, recalling Julie's explanation for all the phone calls she made over the weekend. "You shouldn't try to be the Lone Ranger when you're hurting."

He's squinting at me now, unsure whether this New Age, talk-show language of mine constitutes mockery. "You look funny," he says finally.

"Funny how?"

"Violent funny," he acknowledges nervously. "Like you wouldn't mind killing somebody you were sure deserved it."

"Get dressed, Russell," I tell him again. "Shower first. Then dress. Then pack everything you'll need in Atlanta for a week or so. Maybe longer."

I go back into the living room so he can begin. It's a tiny apartment with thin walls, and I can't help hearing his powerful postcoital stream in the toilet bowl. It's only fair, I suppose. I've mocked him, so now he's mocking me. First Bobo, now Russell.

I consult my watch, try to gauge how long it will take to drive to the airport and back. I've got a lot to do before my workshop at two in the afternoon. I call the office to get Rachel to schedule an appointment with the dean, but instead of Rachel I get her voice mail. Hard to believe, but she seems to have followed a direct order and not reported for duty today. Which means I'm on my own. Thankfully, when I call the dean's number I get Marjory, not Jacob.

"I need to see him late this afternoon," I tell her.

"I think he wants to talk to you right now," Marjory informs me.

"Well, I don't want to talk to him," I tell her, but I hear a muffled sound on her end, and then Jacob is on the line.

"Goddamn it, Hank," he says before I can hang up on him.

To pass the time, I count the William Henry Devereaux books on Meg's bookcase. The final tally is four—three of my father's, the one of mine. When I hear the shower thunk off, I call Marjory back.

"Boy, is he pissed at you," she informs me.

"Good," I tell her. "I've been having bad thoughts about him all morning. One right after another."

"He's doing the best he can, Hank."

So I tell her the joke about the priest who hires an old woman to play the organ at services. Nine o'clock Mass on Sunday morning, the church is full. Everyone stands for the processional hymn, and the organ thunders to life, but the notes are completely random. Nothing like this has ever been heard in a church before. All through Mass it's like this, as if a small child has been allowed to experiment on the instrument. After Mass is over, the priest is pretty steamed. Clearly the old woman has lied about knowing how to play the organ. Furious, the priest wants to know what she has to say for herself. "Guess what the old woman replies," I ask Marjory.

"I'm doing the best I can?" she guesses, confirming what I and others have long suspected, that *she* should be dean. "How's three-thirty this afternoon?"

I tell her three-thirty is perfection.

"So," Russell says when we've driven halfway to the airport in silence. "You're, like, running me out of town?"

"I think you need to look into this job opportunity in Atlanta, Russell," I tell him.

He nods, his hair newly moussed and prickly. "I forgot all about your old man," he tells me. When I glance over at him and frown, he continues. "Julie told me he was, like, this Olympic adulterer. He left you and your mother and ran off with a grad student, right? In that context I guess I can see why you're so upset with me."

"Shut up, Russell."

He ignores this friendly, heartfelt advice. "Still, it's pretty amazing you think you can just run me out of town like this. I mean, a man in your condition."

"What condition is that?"

He studies me. "You look awful," he confesses reluctantly. "I could easily overpower you. I could wrest the wheel from your control. I could toss you out and leave you by the side of the road and take your car. You know I could."

"Overpower?" I say. "Wrest the wheel?" What kind of language is this?

"I could," he says. "You want to know the reason I don't?"

"Because you feel guilty and humiliated, a failure in marriage and life?"

"Ah," he says, staring straight ahead now. "You *do* understand why."

What I understand is that a bad thing is beginning to happen, one I might have predicted. Now that he's not in Meg Quigley's bed anymore, all my affection for Russell is returning at a gallop. I haven't liked him this much since the day I thrashed him at basketball, since he made that wild, awkward, desperate hook shot and the ball landed on the roof, wedged in behind the backboard so that I had to climb up and get it, his new wife, my daughter, looking on.

"I hope you don't think my running you out of town means that I don't like you, Russell," I tell him. "This isn't forever. I just think everything will be better if you leave town for a while. I know *I'm* going to feel a lot better."

"I just hope you don't imagine I have plane fare to Atlanta."

I glance over at him and raise an eyebrow, as if to ask just how dumb he thinks I am.

"Or money to live on when I get there," he adds, sheepishly.

"Don't try to talk me out of this, Russell," I warn him.

We make the airport in record time. Russell puts up exactly no fuss. His only visible resentment of his father-in-law is manifested by his refusal to let me carry either of his bags.

"I hate commuter flights," he tells me after I've booked him on one to Pittsburgh, where he will connect with a direct flight to Atlanta. We've left the return open-ended. I write him a check for expenses. He studies it dubiously. "Stay someplace cheap," I advise. "Call Julie when you get in."

"Really?"

"Take my advice," I say. "Tell her this was your idea. She'll like you better."

"What are *you* going to tell her?"

"I haven't decided," I say, though I have.

Russell notices his flight is boarding, and he takes a deep breath. "I'm really scared of these little planes," he confides, and I can see he's not kidding.

"You're not going to die on this flight, Russell. You came closer to dying in bed this morning before you even woke up."

"Knowing how scared I am, you're still going to make me do this?"

"That's right."

He shrugs, as if to say he's not surprised. "Well, good-bye then."

We shake hands like two men who may never see each other again.

"Meg told me she'd been flirting with you for a long time."

"She did, huh."

"She said you wanted to fuck her. She could tell."

"Really."

"She said you wanted to, bad."

"Not bad enough."

He nods. "That kind of hurt her feelings. I told her about your father, so she'd understand."

"So she wouldn't misunderstand my stubbornness for virtue?"

"Hey," he says. "I never thought of it that way."

"Good luck in Atlanta," I tell him, and I wish it for him, too. I wish for it with a hard, determined, childlike intensity. A prayer, almost.

When he's on the plane and the stewardess pulls up the stairs and locks the aircraft's door, I immediately regret having done this. Russell is always good company, and I wish I had some for the trip home.

CHAPTER

33

By noon, when I pull up to the curb in front of my mother's place, she and Mr. Purty are just backing out of the driveway in his truck. Which means I've narrowly missed witnessing her climbing into it, something I feel sure would have cheered me up.

"Hi, Mr. Purty," I say, addressing the person who is nearest, who is also, I judge, the person gladdest to see me and most likely to be civil regardless. My mother's stony expression conveys eloquently and with great economy several things: that she is put out with me, that she is frustrated, that she has been trying to call me, both at home and at the office, getting only my machine, which she hates.

"Henry," Mr. Purty says flatly. I understand his position. He can't afford to appear too pleased to see a man in my mother's dog-house.

"Henry"—my mother leans across the seat—"I'd appreciate a word with you."

"I'm right here," I tell her, since I am. But I know what she means. She doesn't want to speak across Mr. Purty, given what she has to say. She wants me to come around to her side.

"I'm crazy," Patsy Cline tells the three of us. "Crazy for lovin' you." I go around to my mother's side of the truck.

"Do you have any idea how many times I tried to call you last night?"

"I'm sorry," I tell her. "I didn't mean to worry you."

She frowns at me. "I wasn't worried. I needed your help."

What I'd like to ask her is if she remembers after all these years what she promised we'd forget. My having at last disinterred the memory will seem doubly strange if it turns out my mother is unable or unwilling to dig it up herself. It's the sort of knowledge I ought to be able to see in her eyes, but I can't. Her frustration and annoyance with me is clear enough though.

"The boxes that wouldn't fit in the U-Haul have arrived at the post office. We're going down to pick them up."

"Is he inside?" I ask.

"Who?" she wants to know. "Are you acknowledging that you have a father? You're actually deigning to pay him a visit?"

"I wasn't deigning, actually. Just stopping by. Maybe when the semester's over there'll be time for deigning."

She ignores this too. "He's been wondering where you were since yesterday," she informs me, which may or may not be true.

"And here I am to satisfy his curiosity," I point out. "We wondered where *he* was for close to a decade. Or have you forgotten."

Our eyes meet then, in earnest, for the first time in years, and yes there *is* something. "I have *not* forgotten," she assures me. "I have merely forgiven. You should, too."

"How many times do we have to go through this, Mother?" I ask. "I told you, I bear the man no ill will."

"But that's not the same as forgiving, is it?" She gives me her "significant" look, to indicate that I'd do well to chew on this distinction for a while.

I sigh. "What is it that you want from me exactly?"

"For now, I want to store the boxes in your garage," she tells me. "Is that permissible?"

"Sure," I say, stepping back from the truck. "I wouldn't go out there right now though. The house is surrounded by the media."

My mother closes her eyes slowly, then opens them again. "What will he make of you? I wonder," she says.

I wave good-bye to Mr. Purty, who puts the truck in gear. "Charles knows a great place for lunch," I call after my mother before the window gets rolled up all the way. "Try the scrapple."

Inside, there's a home renovation show on television. At first, my father appears to be watching it intently, but then I see that he's dozed off in my mother's reading chair. His repose has a ferocious quality to it, as if in his dream he's anticipating some scholarly objection to his line of thinking and is preparing to make short work of it.

Truth be told, it's a little shocking to see him again. Especially in this context. The last few years have not been kind. For a long time my father's aristocratic features were immune to the assault of time, but now everything seems to have caught up to him at once. A cursory glance tells you he's had his last young lover, and I can't help wondering if he feels relief in this knowledge. Since the late sixties he's worn his hair long, a bright mane of flowing silver, though it's gone a little yellow now, like stained teeth. What strikes me most is how womanish my father's features have become, which makes me wonder if he looks a little like an old woman to my mother too.

He awakens under my none-too-sympathetic gaze. "Henry," he says, getting slowly to his feet, extending his hand.

"Henry," I reply. When we shake, his palm is dry, mine moist, though he seems not to notice.

And then silence. This meeting of the two William Henry Devereauxs, the first in nearly a decade, not counting the one in the hospital after his collapse, when he was heavily sedated, must be rather like the fabled encounter between Joyce and Proust, when each professed ignorance of the other's work and, that established, could think of nothing further to say. We both look at the television, as if for help.

"They were talking about you earlier," he says vaguely, no doubt referring to a morning news show. "Something to do with . . ." He shakes his head vigorously, as if the agitation will float what he's searching for to the surface of his liquid memory. When it does, he can hardly believe it. "Ducks?" he says. Did he dream this?

I concede that the subject could very well have been ducks, which seems to satisfy him. At least he knows he's not going crazy. "Would you object to some fresh air?" he wonders, peeking at the sunny day outside my mother's front windows. "She keeps it so dark in here," he says, looking around at my mother's world.

He locates a cowl-necked sweater, and we go out onto the porch. "Is this a safe neighborhood?" he wonders, peering up and down both sides of the wide street.

"You're in small-town Pennsylvania, Dad," I remind him.

He's got ahold of the porch railing for support and is staring off down the street in the direction of the old amusement park. The top of the Ferris wheel is just visible among the trees. "What's that?" he wants to know, standing up straight.

"The old midway," I tell him.

"Let's go," he says, and he starts down the steps before I can object, his silver mane all astir in the breeze. I can't tell if he means to walk over and have a look at things or if he means to go on the rides when he gets there. For a man who's suffered a major collapse, he's still got a hell of a purpose to his stride. My own would normally be longer, but it's shortened by what I'm now doubly convinced, here in the presence of William Henry Devereaux, Sr., X ray or no X ray, is a stone the size of a pearl, blocking the entryway to my ureter. I have all I can do to keep up with him. I keep thinking he's going to tire, but he doesn't, and five minutes at our brisk pace brings us near the shore of the lake. Or rather to what was once a lake and is now a muddy, foul-smelling declivity. From here we can see all of what was once the midway: its Ferris wheel, the abandoned building that once housed the carousel, the weed-infested go-cart track. This is about as far as it makes sense to go, but my father has already started off around the lake.

"It's gated, Dad," I call after him, wondering what in the world he has in mind. To look at him, you'd swear he intended to drive a bumper car. "It's all locked up to keep the kids out."

But around the lake we go, stopping only when we come to the chain-link fence. My father goes right up to it, puts his slender fingers through the wire links, and pulls the fence toward him. It looks for all the world like he intends to climb. "This is a terrible thing," he says, staring at the empty carousel building. "Something like this should never be abandoned. What possesses people?"

"Before the amusement park this was all public gardens," I tell him. "They were famous. People rode the trains in from New York and Philadelphia to see them."

He studies my face to see if this can be true, then looks back at the midway, perhaps converting the present scene to gardens. "Beautiful women strolling everywhere, I imagine. Dressed to the nines. Young men trying to make an impression. Wonderful. Just wonderful. Are there books on the subject?"

"On all this?" I say, scanning the lake, the midway. "No idea."

"There should be," he says, letting go of the fence. Then again, "Wonderful."

I can see that he's suddenly tired now, and when I suggest we rest before heading back, he's all too glad. There's a bench nearby.

"Your mother says you're going through a midlife crisis," he observes. "You don't look at all well."

"I'm terrific, Dad," I assure him. "Never better, in fact."

He gives no indication of having heard, much less digested or believed this. "*I* had a turning point of my own when I was your age," he says. "It was a true crisis of the soul, as I now conceive it."

I'm not surprised when he launches into the story of his lost voice the year he went to Columbia. It's sweet, I suppose, for him to concede that I'm going through some kind of crisis worthy of comment by him. Perhaps his intention in telling the story of his early humiliation at Columbia is to make me feel less alone in my own predicament. "Crises of soul," he means to suggest, are not uncommon to men like William Henry Devereaux, Senior and Junior. But before he gets very far into the story he's lost his thesis, and his crisis-of-the-soul story starts getting illustrated with details that undermine his intention. He reminds me that his salary was enormous, unheard of at the time, that it paved the way for the salaries of today's academic superstars, an entirely inferior breed. What would he be worth, in his prime, on today's market? No English department in the country could afford him. Eventually, he does return to his story, but by the time he gets to his triumphal Dickens lecture, his scathing attack on *Bleak House,* it's become nothing more than a story of personal triumph over adversity, of mind over body, intellect over larynx, scholarship over art. A story of vindication, of William Henry Devereaux, Sr., and his salary. I'm only half-listening to all of it, so I'm not entirely prepared when his narrative takes an unexpected turn. "You may find this strange," he says, "but I've recently started rereading Dickens."

Clearly he imagines he's paying the author a compliment by returning in his final years to a writer whose mawkishness he's derided over a long career. "Much of the work is appalling, of course. Simply appalling," my father concedes, genuflecting before his previous wisdom on the subject. "Most of it, probably. But there is something *there,* isn't there. Some power . . . something"—he searches for the right word here—"transcendent, really."

It would be pointless for me to offer an observation, I know. This conversation he's ostensibly having with me he's really having with himself, and the truth is I can never remember having a conversation with him that wasn't this way.

"I feel almost," he says, "as though I had *sinned* against that man."

This statement, it must be said, brings me to the brink of powerful emotion. It must be a hybrid of some sort, since sorrow and hilarity seem equally justifiable in this circumstance. "Dad," I finally say, when I locate my voice. "*This* is what you feel guilty about? You feel guilty about the way you treated *Dickens?*"

He nods without hesitation. "Yes," he says, then again, "yes."

I think it's me he's looking at as he says this until I realize his focus is somewhere behind me, on the abandoned carousel, perhaps, or maybe he's with Pip and Joe Gargery at the forge. At which point something happens to his face. It seems almost to come apart, and then tears are streaming down his cheeks, exactly as Mr. Purty described. "I wish . . . ," he begins, but he's unable to continue. He's too overcome with grief.

CHAPTER

34

My fiction writers seem to have remembered the morose silence that ended our last workshop, and then to have concluded that we should pick up where we left off, despite Leo's surprising absence. Not only does Leo never miss class, he usually arrives early and paces in the hallway, hoping to have a few words with me beforehand, a strategy I defeat by arriving exactly one minute after the bell and pointing at the clock face at the end of the hall. And after he's had a story workshopped, he always arrives at the next class loaded for bear. I'd have thought that would be especially true today, since a story of Solange's is up for discussion.

Perhaps Leo's taken Hemingway's advice. Earlier in the term he explained to me why Hemingway would have disapproved of our workshop. Hem advised young writers to live. He derided the whole idea of writing groups and talking about writing. He certainly wouldn't have approved of the contemporary workshop concept. When Leo explained all this to me, I seriously considered agreeing with him, since that would have implied that he'd be better off to drop the class and move into a log cabin in the mountains with an old typewriter and a couple reams of paper. Instead I reminded Leo that when the young Hemingway was living in Paris, he wrote in the morning and spent his afternoons talking writing with Gertrude Stein and Sherwood Anderson in what may have been the world's first and best workshop. My reward for setting Leo straight was, of course, another semester's worth of his slasher stories.

It may be that today's workshop is less impeded by Leo's absence than by my presence. William Henry Devereaux, Jr., appears to have taken over today's workshop at several levels. Not only am I seated at the head of the table, but I'm also beneath it. Whereas yesterday I was above things, peeking down at my colleagues from the gap between the ceiling tiles, today literally nothing is beneath me. When I entered the classroom, several of my students hastily folded up their campus newspapers, dropping them to the floor so that their professor could stare up at them from shoe level. I am pictured on the front page, and unless I'm mistaken several of my apprentice writers are dealing with the oppressive classroom silence by grinding their heels into my wry, smiling countenance. It occurs to me that I'm experiencing my father's classroom dilemma in reverse. It's my students who are speechless.

After returning a weeping William Henry Devereaux, Sr., to my mother's flat, I've arrived on campus with just enough time before my workshop to skim the newspaper in the relative privacy of the men's room stall on the first floor of Modern Languages. Thanks to the demise of yesterday's duck and my growing celebrity, the story detailing the incident in Tony Coniglia's classroom has been pushed back to page two below the fold. Thankfully, there's no photo of Tony, or of Yolanda Ackles. Unfortunately, the paper did print the young woman's claim that she and her former professor were lovers, that in her belief Professor Coniglia was God, that he spoke to her through dreams and fevers. June Barnes, as chair of the sexual harassment–professional conduct committee, assured the campus reporter that the incident was under investigation, though she noted that the young woman in question had a history of mental illness. What did June think of the young woman's allegations? Well, she had known Professor Coniglia for twenty years and could say with confidence that he was not God. When asked if she considered Professor Coniglia to be one of those professors who regarded undergraduate women as a "pool of potential sexual partners," a reference to an opinion piece printed in the campus magazine June edits, she offered a damning no comment. Still, given the standards of the campus newspaper, this is relatively high-road coverage.

There's also a late-entry, boxed story on the bottom of the front page announcing the strike vote meeting set for late afternoon, urging all faculty to attend.

Just when I've concluded that no one's going to speak today, one of my seniors says, "I know this is kind of off the subject, but is it true we may not graduate?"

"Is it true you've been fired for killing ducks?" asks another student, who seems to have concluded that if off-the-subject stuff is allowed, then there's plenty to talk about. I can't quite tell from her tone whether my being fired for killing ducks would be a good or a bad thing.

"I heard the donkey basketball game's been canceled," observes another student. Now, *this* I hadn't heard.

Suddenly the whole class is talking at once. We're alive and on the move, albeit in the wrong direction.

"The subject of today's workshop is Solange's story," I remind them, causing everyone, even Solange, to sulk. The events of the real world, dramatically ratcheted up as they happen to be at this moment, seem infinitely more interesting to my novice writers than a bad made-up story. I'd like to remind them that it doesn't have to be this way, that we've come together so that they might learn how to make up stories that are *more* compelling than real life. The fact that this particular work of fiction makes reality look enchanting does not prove that life is inherently more fascinating than art.

Solange's story is titled "The Clouds of August," and it's as full of vapor as Leo's was of misogyny. Every time something threatens to happen in the story, the sky clouds over and the young woman protagonist stops whatever she's doing to contemplate the clouds. These become progressively darker and more ominous, until by the end of the story they positively rain significance.

"I like the clouds," somebody offers. If we're going to have to talk about the story, this is as good a place as any to begin. "They're, like, a metaphor."

This comment deeply satisfies Solange, everyone can tell.

"They *are* a metaphor," I point out. "If they were *like* a metaphor, they'd be, like, a simile."

"I liked the clouds too," somebody else offers. "Good writing."

"Are metaphors good?" I ask.

"Sure. Yeah." General agreement on this point. "You said so yourself."

I decide to take a different tack. "Okay, but what are all these clouds obscuring? And don't say the sky."

"I don't understand your question," someone makes the mistake of admitting.

"What happens in this story?" I ask this person. "Give me a plot summary. You remember plot. A causes B causes C causes D. Start with A."

Lots of frowns, and not just on the face of the person I've asked the question. There is no B, they've come to realize. Maybe not even an A. I give them a while, but nobody can find anything that causes anything else. Finally, I turn to Solange. "Okay, kiddo," I tell her. "It's your story. Tell us what happens. Literally. Leave out the metaphors."

Solange runs her long, artistic fingers through her streaked hair, then tosses it back. "She falls in love. Then she falls out of love. It's like what happens in real life."

The other students have all turned to look at Solange now. This is clearly news to them.

"Who does she fall in love with?" somebody wants to know.

"Am I allowed to answer?" Solange inquires, since I normally don't encourage authorial participation in workshop discussion, except for points of clarification.

"I insist."

"It's unspecified," she says. "Love doesn't require an object. It's like clouds. When you're flying through them. You're just in them, and then you're not."

I've just about come to the conclusion that this class can't get any worse when I look out our ground-level window and see how it can.

Leo, head down, is cutting across the lawn, making for the door of the building we're in, his red hair all aflame.

"Can this be true?" I ask the others. "Does this square with your experience of love?"

No one wants to testify on this subject, and who can blame them? They're all afraid that their experience of love may be too narrow, too limited, and that their testimony will reveal this. Love is one of the many things they're confused about, and they're not even talking about being half in love. About finding themselves 61 percent in love, or 77 percent or higher, as Tony Coniglia calibrates these things.

"Is good fiction more likely to be about clouds or stones?" I ask.

"I still like the clouds," one student who senses where I'm headed insists.

"Is good fiction more likely to be about the air we breathe or the nose we breathe it through?" I ask.

"What?"

"Last week I had a nose the size of two noses," I remind them. "I was breathing air through it. Which are you tempted to make use of in a story?"

"I've already used your nose," one student admits. "It's in my next story."

"You used *my* nose?"

"Sorry," the student shrugs.

"Don't be," I say.

As Leo enters the building, I see a campus security car pull up. Lou Steinmetz and an officer I've seen around campus quickly get out and trot across the lawn. Which would make a better starting place for a story, I'd like to ask, a frustrated old cop or the need for a safe campus community?

Leo enters, and by the time he's apologized and taken a seat, the penny has dropped and my heart along with it. He seems to know that everybody in the class is looking at him, a sad, shunned, pimple-encrusted, red-haired boy, more real than you could possibly make any allegorical figure designed to represent low self-esteem.

"We're discussing Solange's story," I tell him.

It takes him a minute to find the story in his backpack, to catch his breath. "I liked the clouds," he says, having located the manuscript. I see that he's tugged another hangnail back from its cuticle and that he leaves a bead of bright red blood on the title page. Seeing this, he quickly smudges it with his wrist, then blots the offending finger on his jeans. "I think that's the sort of thing my story needed."

This is Leo's conclusion. He needs to cloud his necrophilia.

Solange is not one to recognize an offered olive branch. Her mean streak hangs down in front of her nose, and she's examining several long, silver strands through crossed eyes. "What you need is counseling," she observes.

The classroom door opens at this moment to reveal Lou Steinmetz and the uniformed officer. Another campus cop, I see, has stationed himself outside our classroom windows. "I'm conducting a class here, Lou," I tell him.

"I just need to speak to one of your students, Professor," he says. "That one there."

Leo starts to gather his things.

"You can wait until we're finished though," I say. "I'm sure of it."

Apparently Lou Steinmetz can hear the warning in my voice, because he stands quietly, for a moment, calculating. He knows he has no business in my classroom, no business opening the door, no business even knocking on it, which he hasn't done. He's got the mentality of all bad cops. Exceed your authority until you're questioned, then back off, regroup, attack again from a different angle.

"Okay, Professor," he says. "I guess we can wait out here in the hall. We get paid the same either way. Mind if we take a couple chairs?"

"Yes, I do mind."

He nods. "Thanks for your cooperation."

When the door closes again, I realize that, having marked my territory, I have no further use for it. If there's a way to return to Solange's story now, I don't know it. Perhaps sensing this, Leo has resumed gathering his things. "May I be excused?" he wants to know. He seems aware only of the immediate application of his question.

I should say no. I should keep him, on principle, right where he is. But Leo wants to get on with things. I know the feeling. We all watch him shoulder his backpack and make his way to the door. In a story he'd pause there, turn, and leave us with a memorable line, some honest observation, something truer than anything he's managed to write all year, but this isn't a story, and he exits our company quietly, undramatically. A moment later we see him again, hands cuffed behind his back, being led across the lawn to the waiting cruiser.

"Could we all go now?" asks the student who says he's already used my nose.

"Solange?" I ask, since it's her story we're discussing.

"Please," she says, wearily.

The others file out. Solange is last, and she stops at my desk. "I know the clouds were bullshit," she informs me. "I'm not, like, stupid."

"Nobody said you were, Solange."

"Professor Rourke says I should forget fiction writing and concentrate on literature," she says. "Go for my Ph.D. He says I'm smart and mean-spirited."

"I'm sure he meant it as a compliment."

"It's not that I *want* to be mean," she shrugs. "It's just that I'm good at it. My dad always says you should do what you're good at. He's mean too."

"Come by during office hours tomorrow," I suggest. "You got cheated today."

"I didn't deserve anything," she says. "It was shit."

"Maybe we can get you started on something that isn't."

"The story started out to be about this boy? This shit-heel, beautiful boy I have no chance with. Then I thought, why should I give him the satisfaction?"

"I guess you showed him."

"Yeah, well," she says, watching out the window as the police car pulls away from the curb. "What will they do to him?"

"Kick him out, probably."

"First interesting thing he's done all year and he gets tossed out of school for it."

The police car is out of sight now.

"What do you think he was trying to prove?" She's remembering, I suspect, that she called him a wimp last Friday, called his manhood into question. Could she have caused all this? is what she'd like to know.

I half-expect Lou Steinmetz to be waiting for me out in the hall, but he isn't. He's got his perp. He's restored order, put things right. If there were something he could do about me, he would, but there isn't.

CHAPTER

35

By letting my class out early, I have a half hour to kill before my appointment with the dean, someone who *can* do something about me and apparently has. What I should do is go back to my office and call Phil Watson, as I promised I would. But the halls of the English department will be bedlam with the most recent political news, and the truth is I'm up to meeting neither friend nor foe. If Rourke is right and there's an English list, half of my colleagues will be anxious to berate me for composing it, and the other half will want me to explain to them who composed it if I didn't. I could find a pay phone somewhere, but the more I think about it, the more I want to do things in their proper dramatic order. If I'm to be told I have a malignant tumor, I want to learn of it after I've been fired, not before.

It's turned out to be a stunningly beautiful day, the sun high in a sky of robin's egg blue, so I make my leisurely way over to the dean's office, find a park bench with a view of the back parking lot, take off my jacket, roll up my sleeves, and let the warmth rain down upon my

bare forearms. Today, I realize, is the end bracket to a now recognizable segment of my life. This winter, when I attempted to climb Pleasant Street Hill and ended up slaloming, out of control, from top to
bottom, I lost my faith in consequence. Fearing I was forever tenured
on drab "Pleasant," where nothing dramatically good or bad could
happen, where I was fully insured against catastrophe, I began to doubt
the power of either "unpleasantness" or ecstasy to touch me. What
remained to William Henry Devereaux, Jr., was the gradual day, the
inevitable transition from left field to first base, and finally to designated hitter, that misbegotten invention designed to convince the
washed up that they're still in the game. Today is the day I'm to learn
how wrong I was. Today, I learn the lesson of those who live on Pleasant Street and grouse at being moved out of left field. Those who complain don't even get to play first. I wanted consequence? Here it is.
How do I like them apples? *That*'ll teach me.

The problem is, I'm not sure I've learned my lesson. Right now,
unless I'm mistaken, Lou Steinmetz is explaining to young Leo where he
went wrong, explaining the terrible thing he's done, how foolish he was
to do it, how inevitable that he'd get caught. As a result, he'll be kicked
out of school, Lou will explain, and it will be nobody's fault but Leo's
own. Let this be a lesson to you, the chief of campus security will conclude. And then he'll study Leo to see if the lesson has sunk in. And be
disappointed. I've seen that look on Leo's face more than once, and it
expresses, more eloquently than Leo himself could ever express in words,
his conviction that he was not put here in this world to learn other people's lessons. He'll accept his punishment because he has no choice, but
he'll pass when it comes to the education, thanks just the same. Leo has
only to look at Lou Steinmetz to know that Lou is not God. The problem is that if Leo were privileged to look directly at the face of God, he'd
probably arrive at the same conclusion, and I suspect that, in this respect,
he and I are the same. If we were capable of learning our lessons, we'd
become obedient. Sensing this, we're dead set against moral instruction.

In the center of the parking lot stands a trailer with slatted sides
from which a long line of tethered donkeys are being led down a
makeshift ramp. They are the scrawniest, saddest-looking animals I've
ever seen, and that includes geese in neck braces. Lethargic and docile,
they appear blind as they descend the ramp, though this may be a tem-

porary condition caused by their removal from the dark, comfortable trailer into the bright afternoon sunlight. Pathetic as they appear, consider this: their dignity has not yet been assaulted. Tonight their hooves will be bound in cloth and foam, their hindquarters diapered to protect the floor of the women's gym. (They would never be permitted near the men's gym.) I can't imagine anyone would want to pit faculty against administration, even in a humorous fashion, in the current political context, but if tonight's game has been canceled, nobody's told the men in charge of these docile beasts.

"Every time I see you, you look worse," Marjory observes when I limp in.

"I should come over more often," I tell her. "That way my decline wouldn't seem so pronounced."

"See this?" she says, indicating her large blotter calendar. She turns April over so I can see May. The fifteenth is circled in bold red. On the sixteenth a small note in Marjory's neat hand: "Happy days are here again."

"You're taking your retirement?"

"With a vengeance. Thanks to Jacob, I was made a nice offer. Harold and I are looking at condos in the Chapel Hill area."

"Harold really enjoys golf, doesn't he?"

"More than sex. It's one of the things we have in common. I like it more than sex too." She's been studying me all this time. And it occurs to me to wonder if this is Marjory's way of suggesting that after I'm fired my life may actually improve. Surely I would prefer golf to academe, if not to sex.

"You've known about all this shit for a long time, haven't you?"

Her guilty expression makes me regret pinning her down this way. "Since last fall when Jacob was fired."

"And that's why you were thinking about coming back to the English department."

"This early-retirement golf package is even better."

The door opens then, and Jacob Rose emerges, to my surprise, in the company of Terence Watters, the university's counsel, whose face is the same blank mask he was wearing when I saw him last week coming out of Dickie Pope's office. Henry Kissinger was emotive by comparison. What he's doing talking to Jacob Rose I can't imagine.

"You know Hank Devereaux?" Jacob asks.

Terence Watters surrenders the slightest of nods, as if to suggest that it may be necessary to disavow all knowledge of me later. By tomorrow this whole meeting may not have taken place. It may be necessary to send someone to rub out Marjory, because she too is a witness. For now, it's too soon to tell.

"All right, get in there and drop your pants," Jacob tells me when Terence Watters has taken his leave. "Marjory, bring the switch."

We go into Jacob's office. He closes the door behind us.

"Sit there," he instructs me. "And keep your hands where I can see 'em."

This is some good mood he's in. I can't for the life of me figure out why, and I need to. A liberal arts dean in a good mood is a potentially dangerous thing. It suggests a world different from the one we know. One where any damn thing can happen. Which is exactly what this present circumstance feels like. I mean, this is a *really* good mood that Jacob Rose is in. Not just the kind of good mood that may descend upon a man when he's gotten a couple of job offers and asked a woman to marry him and she's said yes. A *really* good mood. He looks like a man convinced not just of his own inherent goodness but that virtue is destined to prevail, evil predestined to failure. In other words, he looks nothing like a liberal arts dean, especially one who's just compiled, for the purposes of termination, a list of four names, one of which is that of his best man.

"Let's start small, shall we?" Jacob suggests. "How come you're terrorizing my niece in class?"

"Your niece?"

"Blair," he explains. "I'm her uncle."

"You are? I had no idea."

"She didn't want any special treatment."

"She won't stand up for her convictions," I explain. "I didn't realize the problem was genetic until now. I wouldn't have been so hard on her."

This is one of my better jabs, but Jacob doesn't even flinch. He just chuckles. "God, you are *such* an arrogant prick. You remember when we came here?"

"Black September, 1971? Sure."

"Remember old Rudy Byers? Even twenty years ago people were saying what an arrogant prick you were. Rudy said, Don't worry, he'll grow up. Pups are supposed to mess themselves. Swat him on the ass with a rolled-up newspaper a couple times and he'll get the message."

"Now *there* was a dean," I say nostalgically.

"The thing is, you're worse now than you were then. And you think you're just being frisky. Fifty years old and you're still shitting on the carpet and thinking it's clever."

"Well," I say, "at least one of us got trained. Somebody says 'heel' and you heel. Somebody says make out a list, you make out a list."

I study him carefully, because this is where he'll start denying, if he's going to. I guess I'm surprised when he doesn't. Jacob and I go back a long time, and it's time that makes you think you know people. But instead of looking guilty, Jacob appears even more full of himself.

"That other job offer was from right here, wasn't it?" I say. "That's why you didn't have to worry about what Gracie would say about Texas."

"I think she would have gone with me," Jacob says.

"So now, finally, you're a player," I say. "And all you had to do was write down four names."

"Wrong again," he says. "It wasn't all I had to do. It was the easy part of what I had to do."

"That's the first thing you've said I don't believe," I tell him. "I refuse to believe that writing down those names was easy." What I don't tell him is that I know how hard it must have been because I considered doing it.

He raises his hands in the air like he's going to surrender. "Dee-fee-cult for you, easy for me." Still grinning.

"Jacob," I say.

"It's a rough break for Orshee," he admits, "but he'll be given a year to find something else. He's publishing that trendy cultural theory crap, and he's sufficiently smarmy. Somebody will hire him."

"I wasn't thinking about Orshee," I tell him.

"Who then? Finny?" Jacob says. "Finny will be given a year's sabbatical at half pay to finish his dissertation at Penn. He won't, but that's his problem. After his sabbatical, we'll keep him on to teach comp as an adjunct if he wants. That's more than he deserves."

"And Billy Quigley?"

"Walter is retiring over in university publications. Billy will be offered his job. He can nip in private all day. I know for a fact he's wanted Walter's job for a long time." Jacob is having all he can do to contain himself now. I half-expect him to leap up on his desk and do a jig. The expression of pure delight on his face makes him look like a Jewish leprechaun. "Which leaves only William Henry Devereaux, Jr. What's to be done with *that* asshole?"

Until this moment I've felt myself to be a match for Jacob, even though he's had the advantage of playing a concealed hand while most of my cards are face up on the table. But now I have a sinking feeling. Jacob knows he's got me beat on the board. It doesn't matter to him what I'm holding. And when I realize the card he's about to turn over, a wave of pure nausea passes over me, and I feel the weight of my backed up urine pressing down hard on my groin.

"You're wrong," I say, a little desperately. "It doesn't leave just me. It also leaves you." And I'm about to ask him what his price was, what sort of carrot Dickie had to dangle in front of him in order to get Jacob to play ball, when the penny drops. Terence Watters doesn't waste his time talking to liberal arts deans.

"My God," I say. "Dickie's out, isn't he?"

Jacob chortles. "Big tidal wave came and washed him clean away."

"And you're in. Congratulations."

"Thanks," he says, and it's only now that his grin disappears. It was at this point, no doubt, that he expected me to be happy for him. And maybe I am.

"Is it what you want, Jacob?"

"It is," he admits, a little sadly, it seems to me. Perhaps he's remembering that when we were hired, we were *both* loose cannons. With this move, it's official: the revolution has become an institution. "I don't expect you to understand . . ."

But of course I do, or I think I do. Jacob is a decent man of sound, thoughtful principles and educational values, who's been subservient throughout most of his career to lesser men. He'd like to see what he can do while he can still do it. He won't get another chance, and I can't find it in my heart to blame him for seizing this one.

"Listen," I say, getting to my feet. "I'm sorry. Since I came in here, I've been trying to hurt your feelings. I really have no idea why."

He waves this off. "Forget it. I've known you for twenty years. I know you've got no idea why you do what you do."

"I'm sure you'll make a good CEO."

"Hey," he grins. "I'm sure you'll be a good dean of liberal arts."

I go over to the window, to *my* window if I want it to be, just in time to see the last of the tethered donkeys being led up a ramp into the women's gym. Truth? I'm tempted. The same thing has occurred to me that no doubt occurred to Jacob. Just imagine the two of *us* in power. What fun we'd have. And, for a man like me, who's so enjoyed rattling the English department's cage, a promotion represents a wider field of play. Sure, I've always taken pride in my ability to wreak havoc from any position on the game board, but from this one . . .

I indulge the fantasy for a long moment, then put it away. Even if I wanted this job, and I don't, I can't let Jacob do it. Of all the moves he's made, appointing me dean is the only one that would cost him, and it would cost more than he can afford. No one will miss Orshee. No one will deny the justice of his decision concerning Finny, except possibly Finny himself. And Billy Quigley's reassignment will be seen as an act of kindness. On the other hand, making me dean would be seen as an act of arrogance and defiance, a plum given a friend. He couldn't do a worse thing without appointing Gracie.

"Of course nothing is free," Jacob is saying. He's apparently read my temptation in my hesitation. "This is going to cost you your secretary. Marjory's going to hit the links, and I'm going to need someone to make me look competent. Since Rachel damn near made *you* look competent, I'm going to have to steal her. I figure we get our department colleagues to elect Paul Rourke chair, then we take turns abusing him. What do you say?"

What does William Henry Devereaux, Jr., say? Nothing for a long moment, then, "Listen, Jacob. Thanks anyway."

Jacob just stares at me for several beats before exploding. "I knew it." He's gotten up from his desk now and is pacing behind it. "I knew you'd do this. What's *wrong* with you?" he wants to know, and he's not the only one. Another wave of nausea has crashed over me. I have all I can do not to double over. "What kind of man goes through life content to be a fly in other people's ointment? What kind of pleasure do you derive from that? How old are you?"

All these questions mix dangerously with my nausea, and I have to sit down, certain that I will pass out if I don't. I try to remember if I've ever felt worse in my life. The tips of my fingers are tingling, the edges of my vision blurring. Jacob appears blissfully unaware of my plight.

"You know who I feel sorry for?" he's saying. "Your wife. Women are always telling me I can't see anything from a woman's point of view. But I'll tell you, my heart fucking bleeds for any woman—much less a woman as bright and kind as Lily—who has to spend a lifetime with a bonehead like you."

At the mention of Lily I break into a cold sweat. I can feel four distinct tracks of perspiration moving down my trunk and into the waistband of my shorts. Waves of nausea are rolling over me like contractions. Like Jacob—like every man our age—I have been accused of not being able to imagine anything from a woman's point of view, but sitting here, paralyzed with something very much like fear, I feel like I've just crossed into the final stage of labor. Transition!—the term for it suddenly returns to me. I feel fully dilated, like it's now okay for me to push. Except that this is not the place. I know the place. It's just outside the dean's office and down the hall a couple of doors. Time? At a dead run, ten seconds, if I were capable of a dead run. In my current cramped condition, limping tenderly, grabbing onto the backs of chairs and doorframes, three times that, at least. I wait for a monster contraction to subside and struggle to my feet.

"You know what you are?" Jacob asks me. He's got a good, righteous head of steam up, and I envy him this. He's saying things that friendship has kept him from saying for twenty years, and their release at this late date is orgasmic. Asking him to stop would be like asking him to pull out. "You are the physical embodiment of the perversity principle," he gives me to understand. "Fake left, go right. Fake right, go left. Keep everybody in suspense, right? What's Hank going to do? If you have to fuck yourself over to surprise them, so be it."

Somehow, I've made it out into Marjory's office, and Marjory, who prefers golf to sex, and who is not, like Jacob, in the throes of an intense rhetorical orgasm, is looking at me with such alarm that it's clear she's intuited my distress. I'm tempted to tell her I'm in labor, the contractions are coming one right after the other. Instead I fix her with a homicidal glare and say, "Get him away from me!"

But this merely encourages Jacob. "There he is, Marjory," he addresses her. "Hank Devereaux. The man who fucked himself and claimed it was the best lay he ever had."

"Jacob," Marjory says sharply. "I think Hank is sick."

I've made it as far as the door that leads to the outer office where the students who have come to petition the dean are required to wait. They too look alarmed when they see me.

"They don't come much sicker," Jacob agrees.

My palm is so slick with sweat that I can't get a grip on the stainless steel doorknob. It keeps slipping. I wipe off my palm on my tweed coat and try again.

"Just answer me one thing before you go," Jacob says, leaning against the door so it stays shut. "I'll ask you the simplest question I know, and I bet it stumps you."

I try to bring him into focus, but I can't. I swear to God if I had a forty-five I'd blow him across the room and into eternity.

"Just answer me this," he insists, blind, apparently to the fact that perspiration is now pouring off me. There's a bead of ice cold sweat on the tip of my nose. "Just one simple question. It's one your wife and your kids and all your friends would like you to answer." He's close enough to whisper now, so he does. It's a nice, short question, but he pauses between its elements for emphasis. "What . . . the fuck . . . do you . . . *want?*"

This is the question with which he expects to stump William Henry Devereaux, Jr.? Even Marjory, telephone to her ear, looks like she could answer it on my behalf. But there's nothing for me to do but gird, as they say, my loins, summon what strength remains, grab my dean by his lapels, lift him onto his tiptoes, and draw him to me. This I do.

"I want," I tell him as solemnly as I know how, because I don't want this to be mistaken for irony or any other literary device, "to *pee.*"

Something—the seriousness of my demeanor, or the simplicity of my text—gets through to Jacob. "Okay, I was wrong," he shrugs so I'll let him down. "You *do* know what you want."

And I'm out the door and into the corridor, hobbling at full throttle, unzipping as I go for the sake of efficiency, toward the door marked MEN. A minute or so later, Jacob follows, either sent by Marjory to check on me or summoned by the sound of my laughter. The look on his face as he watches me is a mixture of embarrassment and concern and perplexity. I cannot for the life of me stop laughing, and I certainly don't expect him to understand the meaning of what he's bearing witness to. But the fact is that no fifteen-year-old boy standing barefoot on an icy tile floor after awakening from a ten-hour sleep in a cold bedroom has ever hit porcelain with a more powerful, confident, thankful stream than mine. It is heaven. "Dear God," somebody moans. Probably me. It's the last thing I remember.

In my dream I am the star of the donkey basketball game. I have never been more light and graceful, never less encumbered by gravity or age. My shots, every one of them, leave my fingertips with perfect backspin and arc toward the hoop with a precision that is pure poetry, its refrain the sweet ripping of twine. And remember: I'm doing all this on a donkey. I have chosen an excellent beast—honest, bright, generous, and kind—to bear me up and down the court, and we have established between us a deep rapport. I have whispered into his ear that when the game is over I will not give him up, he will have his freedom, and this news—that he will no longer be indentured to the foolish master who keeps him in diapers—has made a young ass of him again. He is so ennobled by the prospect of his freedom that he sees in the occasion of his last game the opportunity for glory. Together we steal the ball and fast-break at every opportunity, thundering down the court to the wild cheers of the capacity crowd. I *love* this game.

"I love you, too," Lily assures me.

Lily? How did she get here?

She got here, I conclude solipsistically, in the usual way, by my opening my eyes.

"I was having a dream," I tell my wife, looking around at the hospital room she's brought with her. I appear to be lying in its bed, though why is a mystery. This is one beautiful woman, my wife, and I'm very glad to see her except for her bad timing. I was about to achieve glory, and now I never will. Someone left a cake out in the rain, I think, my dream sliding away on greased skids, and I'll never have that recipe again. I've always feared the day would come when that lyric made sense, and now that day is apparently here.

"How do you feel?" Lily wants to know.

"Great," I say. "A little sleepy."

The door to the hospital room is open, and out in the hall there's a large man sitting, looking in at us. There's something wrong with his face. It's sectioned off, like a chart of a cow, the kind of diagram butchers display in supermarkets, telling you where the various cuts of beef come from. Despite this, he looks familiar.

"Phil said you'd feel pretty good. They've got you shot full of painkillers."

"My head hurts a little," I admit, studying the large man out in the hall, who has not moved a muscle. I wonder if he might be an allegorical figure. Maybe if I look at Lily and then look back he'll be replaced by another shape whose significance I'm supposed to decode.

"You hit your head when you blacked out," she explains, taking my hand. "You've had a busy few days."

"It wasn't easy making all your predictions come true," I tell her. "Jail was easy enough, but how to get into the hospital had me stumped."

The large man with the diagrammed face is still there, immobile.

"I think you're about to go back to sleep," Lily says.

I think she's right, as usual. I can feel my eyes closing. Maybe I'll be reunited with my donkey, finish the game, and make good on my promise to give the poor beast his freedom, though none of this seems quite as appealing as it did before. Now that I've awakened, the dream emotion, once powerfully felt, too closely resembles my father's sorrow at the thought of having once wronged Charles Dickens. And speaking of fathers, I motion to Lily to come closer so I can whisper to her. "Is that Angelo out there?"

She nods sadly. "We're going to have a houseguest for a while."

"That's okay," I whisper. "Don't worry about it. Welcome home."

As I drift back into sleep, I can't help thinking that it's a wonderful thing to be right about the world. To weigh the evidence, always incomplete, and correctly intuit the whole, to see the world in a grain of sand, to recognize its beauty, its simplicity, its truth. It's as close as we get to God in this life, and we reside in the glow of such brief flashes of understanding, fully awake, sometimes, for two or three seconds, at peace with our existence. And then back to sleep we go.

"So what's he doing sending his brother, is what I want to know," Angelo explains. "Like I'm supposed to know this seven-foot-tall Negro is Raschid's brother? Angelo, the goddamn mind reader. I mean, here's a kid who looks like he's got all he can do to read the headline of the goddamn paper he's delivering—but me?—I'm supposed to be able to read his mind. I'm supposed to know this seven-foot-tall Negro and his two eight-foot-tall pals mean me no harm. Here they are on my stoop, giving me the look, right? I've never seen them before, and I don't know them from a bag of assholes, but I'm very polite. I explain how it's my policy not to give money to strangers, whether or not they happen to be giant Negroes. I tell them my paper boy's name is Raschid, and whether he has a brother or not I myself have no fucking idea. Again, I'm no mind reader. I tell them if Raschid has mononucleosis like they say, I'm sorry. I like Raschid. He's a nice, polite Negro boy. One of the few. He don't go around giving white people the look. When he gets better, he can come by my house any time he wants and I'll pay him what I owe him. But I don't give money to giant Negroes I've never seen before and that's that. It's too bad, but that's the way it is. And I don't really care if they happen to be holding Raschid's collection book. This they could have taken off his body for all I know. It's always the nice, polite Negro boys that get it in the neck. You don't believe me, watch the news. See 'em come filing out of church, all dressed up and wanting to know why some Negro kid had to be shot down crossing the street when all he was was an honor roll student who sang in the church choir. Like the rest of us are supposed to have an explanation for why things happen to these people. But they're right. It's the polite ones that get it in the neck every time. That much I do know. That much I've figured out."

It's eight-thirty in the morning. I've slept through the night, and Phil Watson's confident prediction has come to pass. I don't feel nearly as good as I felt coming off the triumph of my donkey basketball game and the news that my blood work has come back negative. No tumor. The painkillers I've been given have worn off, though I have a prescription for Tylenol 3s in my pocket. I refused one at the hospital, and I regret it now, listening to Angelo explain why he was in jail and had to be bailed out by my wife, who is driving the three of us out to Allegheny Wells. As soon as I get home I'm going to have to pop a pill and look for Occam, who's gone missing. I should have believed Paul Rourke when he told me he'd seen the dog in a neighbor's garden, but I didn't. How he got out of the house is a mystery, but my guess is that some member of the media, not believing that I wasn't home, and finding a door unlocked, must have poked his head inside to call my name. My sincere hope is that this person got a good groining.

The other mystery is why our money was required to get Angelo out of jail. I suspect he probably could have made his own bail, but he's too stubborn to spend money this way. He's lonely at home, and residing at the courthouse gave him people to talk to. Retired from the force for almost a decade, he still knows half the cops in Philadelphia. It was probably old home week in the slammer. Now it appears he's going to live with us until his court date later in the summer. Lily has already impressed upon him that our rural life will be very different from what he's used to in Philly. Very few people will come knocking on our door in Allegheny Wells, and there should be no need to shoot them. Any of them.

"But they insist, right?" Angelo continues. "Raschid has come by a couple times when I was hither, or maybe yon, so I'm a little in arrears, payment-wise. Just give us the fuckin' money, they say, which makes me think I'm right, this seven-foot Negro is no brother of Raschid's, who is always a polite boy, like I said. So I tell them, fine, wait right here a second, like I'm going to get the money. I go get something all right, but it ain't the money. My pump action is what I get. I keep it right in the hall closet for unforeseen circumstances like this one. I'm gone maybe five seconds, and when I get back I show them what I've brought with me. I explain to them again, still polite, about my lifelong policy of not giving money in either large or small amounts to seven-foot-tall Negroes I've never seen before. This time the two eight-foot Negroes, they seem to understand this practice whereas they didn't before, but the one who claims to be Raschid's brother, he's still giving me the look, like he hasn't noticed what I'm holding. He wants to know where do I get off pointing such a thing at him when all he's trying to do is collect money I owe. I say to myself, This fuckin' kid was born without ears. Maybe I should feel sorry for him, going through life deaf. But, so there's no misunderstanding, I go through the whole thing again, except louder this time so I'm sure he can hear me.

"I tell him that I have this pump action in my hands because, though it breaks my heart to admit it, this is now a necessary thing where I live. I even take the time to give him some historical perspective on the situation. I explain how when my daughter was little we used to let her ride all over the neighborhood on her bicycle, because back then it was safe. This was before the days when seven-foot-tall Negroes you've never seen before showed up on your stoop demanding money. This was before there was prostitutes and crack dealers on every other corner and every fourth or fifth car was a pimpmobile with dark windows. I tell them the reason I'm taking time to explain all this is because they're too young to remember. Back then, I was the only guy in a ten-block radius who had a gun in his house, and the only reason *I* had one was because I was a cop. Now everybody on the block's armed to the teeth. I tell them it ain't none of my business, but I wouldn't go up on any more porches if I was them. I describe some of the advanced weaponry that resides behind some of the doors we can see from my porch.

"The two eight-foot Negroes, they're backing down the porch steps slow. They started backing up as soon as they saw the pump action, so there's at least some intelligence there. But Raschid's brother, he stands his ground. He tells me to lower the shotgun and he'll go, like he's talking to some moron. Lower the shotgun and he'll go, my ass. But this is what he actually says to me. If I don't lower the shotgun, he ain't going nowhere. He tells me this like *he's* the one holding the shotgun on me. Which I do not fucking believe. I think to myself, This poor fucking giant Negro is not only born without ears, he's confused in his head. He can't tell the difference between a shotgun pointed at his middle and one hanging on the wall above the fireplace, but he's about to learn. I tell him I'll count to three and I'll do it nice and loud on account of he was born without ears. I know everybody understands this situation because the two eight-foot Negroes have backed all the way down the steps and out through the gate and they're calling to their friend to come on before I do this thing I've promised to do. They keep calling to him, even while I'm counting, Come *on*, nigger—a word they use on each other which my own daughter don't allow me to say in her presence—what's wrong wit you? they want to know. This crazy old bastard's gonna cut you in half.

"Now, normally I don't like being called a crazy old bastard by giant Negroes, but in this instance here I figure, fine. At least the two eight-footers are in touch with the reality of the situation, and anyway I've called them some names too, so we're even. What's fair is fair, and they are trying to help, right? They keep calling to the seven-footer while I'm counting, saying, Come *on*, man, this crazy old bastard, et cetera, et cetera. They call him by his name, which is another screwball name like Raschid, which took me forever and a fucking day to remember. Le-Something, they call him. You know how they do? They take a real name and add *Le?* LeRon. LeBill. LeBob. LeBruce. Some goddamn thing like that. LaFonso. That's my favorite. Al-phonso, a name that already exists, they don't want no part of. LaFonso. That's an improvement, right? But I figure, it's their name. Call him LePutz for all I care. Personally, I think LaFonso's not a very nice thing to do to a kid. Like he's not going to have enough problems in life if his name's Harry, right? No, let's name him LeHarry. Any-way, I've just got the hang of Raschid, and here comes LeBig-Brother."

I glance over at Lily, who I can tell would pay cash money for this story to be over. She's heard it before. How many times I don't know. I reach over and give her hand a squeeze. I try not to be too cheered by all this, though I know that Angelo's presence is a good thing for me. Every time my wife spends time with her father, my own stock rises. I hate to think of him staying with us for an entire summer, but by the time he leaves, I'm going to look pretty good to Lily. In a few short days my wife will be burying her face in my neck and choking back tears of frustration and guilt and terrible love.

I feel for her, but I also wish my fiction-writing students were here. Angelo could teach them something about the nature of suspense. He's had this narrative shotgun cocked, safety off, for a long time, but he's a patient storyteller. He's got time slowed down, and even though we've known from the beginning of the story that he's going to pull the trigger, we're still waiting to find out if he will. Real time, on the other hand, is moving along briskly. We're already halfway home to Allegheny Wells, the Pennsylvania countryside sliding by gracefully, well outside the field of Angelo's narrative vision.

"So finally I get to three, which I say loud enough for even a seven-foot Negro with no ears to hear. And here's LeBrother. He hasn't moved a goddamn inch. And I'm thinking, What's wrong with this kid? Does he have a fucking death wish? Because if he does, he's come to the right place. But I'm also thinking, You've got to admire the kid's balls, even if he is confused in his head. And the more I look at him, the more I see he does look like Raschid, and I think maybe he *is* the kid's brother after all. I mean, he could be, right? I don't know if Raschid has a brother, but he could have, and if he does, this could be the kid. He might just be an exceptionally tall, impolite, confused, deaf, big Negro brother. How the hell do I know? Right this second I almost wish I didn't have the shotgun in my hands, because I've got this weird feeling that it's holding me instead of me holding it. Stupid, I know, but that's how it felt."

"I bet," I say, because his voice has fallen and he seems to be inviting comment.

But something about the way I say this pisses Angelo off. The very sight of me has mildly pissed Angelo off for about twenty-five years, so I'm not surprised. He doesn't much care for educated, professional people of any stripe, and my particular stripe elicits in Angelo his deepest misgivings. On his misgivings meter, I'm right up there with seven-foot-tall Negroes.

"*You* bet," he repeats. "Let me tell you something, pally. You live where I live, nine times out of ten, you're glad you've got the shotgun. You only regret *not* having the shotgun once. After that, no more regrets for you. You've already had your last regret."

Lily's grip on the steering wheel has tightened, and in her white knuckles I see a truth I've long known—that the world is divided between kids who grow up wanting to be their parents and those like us, who grow up wanting to be anything but. Neither group ever succeeds.

"Where was I?" Angelo wants to know.

"Three," I remind him.

"Right," he continues. "So here's big LeBrother and here's me, and neither of us back off an inch. This much I learned as a cop. If you aren't going to use a gun, don't even take it out. You aren't going to use it, it's worse than useless. I know better, but this is the situation I've got myself into with this seven-foot Negro. Truth?" Angelo pauses here, as if to suggest he's about to reveal something shameful about himself. He can barely bring himself to say it. "I don't want to shoot this kid. I don't know what he's doing still standing there, but there he is, big as life, after I've said three. The two eight-footers are now flat on their bellies on the sidewalk with their hands over their ears, praying out loud. They've gone from give-us-the-money-you-crazy-old-bastard to Sweet-Jesus-Sweet-Jesus-Sweet-Jesus in the amount of time it took me to say a Hail Mary after confession during baseball season, and I'm thinking, There's two things I can't do here. I cannot cut this stubborn, confused LeBrother in half. Don't ask me why. I just can't. I'm taking my life in my hands if I don't, but I figure, so be it. I mean, maybe the world won't stop if there's one less giant Negro kid in it, but on the other hand, I don't see it slowing down all that much if Angelo Caprice stops breathing all of a sudden. The same thing applies to me as to him, the difference being that I'm seventy three next year and this kid is what?—twenty? I mean, if I'm twenty or thirty years younger, maybe I look at it differently, right? Even if I'm fifty, I got good, useful years left. At fifty, I'm still strapping on a forty-five and going out in the morning and coming home at night if I'm lucky. But I'm seventy-three and I'm kidding myself if I think I'm still useful. Most days I get up, I don't even shave. Her mother would be ashamed, but I figure, Who the hell's gonna see me? If I go out, I shave, if I don't, fuck it."

"Finish your story, Dad," Lily says quietly. "We're almost home and we're not bringing this story into the house, okay?"

"Whatever you say, little girl," Angelo agrees. "The judge says I gotta do as I'm told or go back to jail, so boss your old man around all you want. Go ahead. Only not too much, okay? Jail wasn't so bad. Anyhow. On the one hand, I can't shoot this kid. On the other, I know I can't *not* shoot this gun. I've said I'm going to shoot it, I've gone back into the house to get it, I've brought it out and showed it to them, I've stressed its importance. Not shooting this gun is no longer an option. You tell somebody you're going to count to three, by the time you get to three, you better be prepared to do something very like what you said you'd do, or the next time you say you're going to count to three, you're going to have a hard fucking time getting anyone to take you seriously. So I don't have a lot of room to wiggle here. Maybe I never should have counted to three. I don't know. But now that I'm here, now that I'm at three, I no longer have what you'd call a wide range of options. Also not a lot of time to consider the ones I do have, because after you say three, you got exactly one beat, the same amount of time it took you to get from two to three is the time you now got. The next sound you hear after three is not supposed to be four. It's supposed to be bang. You don't hear bang, all bets are off."

We have arrived at Allegheny Estates now, and Lily makes the turn up our hill. There's no cop directing traffic, no traffic to direct, no sign of the media. The William Henry Devereaux, Jr., story has run out of gas, now that the true duck slayer has been identified. "Go slow," I say to Lily. There are several newly planted spring gardens in our neighbors' yards. Maybe I'll spot Occam excavating one of them.

"So," Angelo says, winding down now. "In the time I was given, I arrived at an imperfect solution."

"Oh, God," I hear Lily say, and at first I think it's in response to her father's characterizing as "imperfect" his lunatic compromise—his raising the shotgun and discharging it into the porch roof, bringing the whole decrepit structure down on himself and LeBrother, so that the neighbors had to dig the two of them out from under the rubble. But then I see a man seated on the steps of our deck, it appears, crying. I don't immediately recognize him as Finny, because he's dressed in simple slacks and a button-down shirt, not his usual white suit.

My first thought is that Finny must be weeping over his own academic fate. Lily has told me this morning that according to *The Rear View,* the faculty, after learning that Dickie Pope had been canned and that Jacob Rose, a man they'd known and respected for years, would be the new CEO, voted overwhelmingly not to strike, a decision that defeated the position urged by their own union, not to mention the interests of those faculty like Finny who would be directly affected by next year's budget cuts. In this context I am not surprised to see Finny awaiting the return of his longtime adversary. No doubt he's concluded, in the naive way of career academics, that a shifting wind will have caused a realignment, that we are now made allies by our shared reversal of fortune. But then I see there's a white bundle, like a sack of dirty laundry, only flatter, at Finny's feet. As we draw closer I see that it's a white sheet, darkly spotted.

"Anyhow," Angelo is saying, "to make a long story short—"

But I have already gotten out of the car and so has Lily. When we arrive at the bottom of the step, I lift up the sheet, though I already know what I will see.

"I never saw him," Finny says, struggling to his feet like a very old man, his eyes red, anguished, swollen. "He ran right in front of me."

God, as always, is in the details, and I see that Occam's legs are crusted with mud, which means that he spent his night of freedom miles away at the lake, returning just in time to encounter Finny's car.

"I'd come to see Marie," Finny explains, referring to his ex-wife, who still lives at the bottom of the hill. "She gave me the sheet."

I let the sheet fall back. Lily has turned away rather than look. Angelo takes her in his arms, and she lets him, and the sight of this has me right up there in the high ninetieth percentile, affection-wise, for this wonderful woman I have too long taken for granted, as Teddy warned me years ago I was doing.

"You probably think I did it on purpose . . . ," Finny croaks.

"Don't be an ass," I tell him. For in fact I have never been more convinced of the string of cause and effect, of the sequence and consequence that is destiny, than I am at this moment. It begins with a comic threat to kill a duck and ends here at my feet. Finny doesn't know it, but he's merely acting as the agent of Chance, the nameless footman of the drama. "Another man would have driven away. *I* might have driven away, Finny," I feel compelled to add.

Because the truth is, we never know for sure about ourselves. Who we'll sleep with if given the opportunity, who we'll betray in the right circumstance, whose faith and love we will reward with our own.

Angelo has no more idea what his own story means than he knew what he would do until he did it. How was he to know that he would be visited by such a strange emotion in the very doorway to the home he had guarded for so long? How could he have predicted its consequence? When my poor mother came down into the cellar that afternoon and saw her son standing on a chair, how could she have had any idea that by drawing me to her so fiercely, by saving her son she set in motion our mutual estrangement, for how could we forget such a moment without distancing ourselves from each other, who shared its anguish? Only after we've done a thing do we know what we'll do, and by then whatever we've done has already begun to sever itself from clear significance, at least for the doer.

Which is why we have spouses and children and parents and colleagues and friends, because someone has to know us better than we know ourselves. We need them to tell us. We need them to say, "I know you, Al. You're not the kind of man who."

EPILOGUE

For every complex problem there is a
simple solution. And it's always wrong.
—H. L. Mencken

By the third week of August I notice the leaves beginning to turn on the doomed side of the macadam in Allegheny Wells. Lily and I, without ever speaking of the matter, have taken to jogging in the early morning to avoid the worst of the summer's heat. Sometimes we run toward Railton, other times out toward the village of Allegheny Wells, though we avoid the right turn at the Presbyterian church that would lead us past the house that used to be Julie and Russell's. A new family moved in last week, renting with an option to buy, a flexible arrangement for all concerned. Last month Julie joined Russell in Atlanta, where, I have it on excellent authority, they are doing well. Julie has found work, and Russell has been promoted already, and I'm told they are thinking about buying a house. What they are planning to use for money I don't know. From little things Lily says I gather that she and Julie speak almost every day. I'm not allowed to see the phone bills.

But the leaves. Yesterday, returning from our morning run, we encountered Paul Rourke pulling out from between the tilting stone pillars of Allegheny Estates II, on his way in to campus, which is gearing up for fall semester. Since being made dean, Rourke is working longer hours, which, according to him, is fine under the circumstances. He and his wife have separated, and the second Mrs. R. disappeared clean, like her predecessor, taking with her little more than the clothes on her back. A large contingent of divorced academic men in Railton would love to know how Rourke always manages this. Some have joked that somebody should sneak into his house some night when he's away and dig in the basement. Personally, I don't find the disappearance of the second Mrs. R. all that mysterious. The wife of a dean of liberal arts has few responsibilities, but there are occasions upon which she cannot be stoned and barefoot. My own best guess was the second Mrs. R. liked being stoned and barefoot. She liked wearing jeans and being braless beneath her thick sweatshirts. She liked to smoke a joint and hold her breath and wiggle her toes and stare at them, none of which you can do when you're entertaining the chancellor.

In any event their house is for sale along with half the others in the two Allegheny Estates, though I heard Rourke has rented it for the upcoming school year and himself plans to move over Labor Day into Jacob Rose's town house in West Railton, which has also been on the market since his wedding. Jacob and Gracie have begun building on the lot I sold them in May. The house is going up fast, and sometimes when Lily and I are deck sitting, I catch a whiff of Gracie's cloying perfume born upwards on a breeze. Lily, of course, insists that I'm imagining this.

I feared that selling to Jacob what I refused to sell to Paul Rourke might enrage my old enemy further, but, strange as it seems, I'm apparently no longer on his shit list. Jacob says that this is because the job always makes the man, a line I've often used on Jacob himself when he's done what struck me as a cowardly thing. According to Jacob, Rourke has simply realized that as dean he cannot afford to have personal animosities, and so he's had to give me up. My own feeling is— and I've always maintained this—that most people have a finite amount of meanness in them, and Rourke used his up with me back in June when a group of us (Jacob, Teddy, Rourke, a couple guys from biology, and me) started playing basketball again on Sunday afternoons. I may have suggested it. Basketball is a beautiful game for a tall, graceful man like me. At times I'm so overwhelmed by its beauty that I lose touch with reality. When my shot is falling, when I'm moving across the lane and back out to the perimeter for my jumper, I forget my age and position in life. I feel like my dream self in the donkey basketball game, and in the throes of such emotion I'm prone to acts of foolishness. One Sunday afternoon in late June I made the mistake after a missed shot of crashing the boards, where I caught one of Paul Rourke's big, churning elbows. The fractured cheekbone and black eye that resulted seem to have satisfied my old enemy. Also he seems cheered to be driving the Camaro again, his fainting spells having ceased now that he no longer has to breathe the second Mrs. R.'s secondhand smoke. At any rate, yesterday, when Lily and I encountered him at the end of our run and I pointed up at the sickly yellowing leaves on his side of the road, he merely rolled down the window, nodded at me knowingly, and said, almost affectionately, "Lucky Hank."

He's right, of course, I am lucky. As a result of the series of events that landed me first in jail and then in the hospital, I've followed my mother's somber advice, taken stock, and made a list of things a man like me might be thankful for if he were so inclined, and here they are:

1. I have my health. My dick (or rather my prostate gland and my entire urinary tract) has been put through the metaphorical wringer of what Phil Watson referred to as a full battery of tests. In fact, I think he would have hooked me *up* to a battery if I'd let him. There is nothing wrong, I am reassured to know, with either me or it. Certainly, there is no tumor. Subsequent rectal searches by several educated and lubricated index fingers have found neither asymmetry nor enlargement of my prostate gland. More important, to me at least, I am again peeing freely, regularly, and without discomfort. I am, in all respects penile, as other men. Which leaves only the mystery of my temporary affliction. According to Phil I most likely suffered from a condition known as hysterical prostate, a phrase itself calculated to induce hysteria, at least in a man like me. According to Watson, who I suspect may have invented this condition to entertain me and explain my otherwise inexplicable symptoms, it's a rare circumstance that is in part physical and in part psychological, induced by stress, aided and abetted by antihistamines, which I'd been overusing all spring to combat allergies and colds.

Anyway, this explanation accounted for all the known facts of my case. What the diagnosis lacked, I decided when Phil Watson shared it with me, was poetry, and for that reason I told him why it was that Jacob Rose found me laughing like a madman before the commode when he followed me into the men's room. For with the first blast of urine against porcelain I'd heard a distinct plink, as of a small pebble on china, evidence, it seemed to me, that I had been right all along. I had just passed a stone. Watson, a man not easily taken in by poetry, merely smiled and reminded me that this simply could not be, that it would be impossible to pass through a human ureter a stone large enough to make an audible plink. Further, a stone that large would have caused considerable bleeding before, during, and after the event, and I had experienced none. He did have enough poetry in him to concede that my decision to turn down the position of dean and relinquish my tenure at the university may have been the symbolic equivalent of passing a stone, but he maintained that the worlds of symbol and matter, of meaning and substance, remain discrete. This from a Roman Catholic who extends his tongue every Sunday morning to receive the Body and Blood of Christ.

2. I am still married. Here I must be circumspect. Forgive me. You may believe that a man willing to share candidly the intimacies of his urinary tract has waived his right to circumspection, but I claim it, nevertheless. I will report little more than the facts. The first is that I'm no longer pestered by fantasies of my wife making love to my friends. Affection-wise, I find myself hovering in the high nineties regarding Lily, and though Angelo's presence may be a factor, I believe she has been fonder of me this summer than in some time, though she resists representing her affection for me in percentiles. I get the distinct impression that despite managing to fulfill all of my wife's dire prophecies about how I would fare in her absence last April, I passed some sort of test, though I have no idea how, nor is she telling. Perhaps no man should possess the key to his wife's affections, what makes and keeps him worthy in her eyes. That would be like gaining unauthorized access to God's grace. We would not use such knowledge wisely.

What is it that we want from women? To be understood? I've heard men say this—I may even have said it myself—but I have my doubts. Not long after Lily returned with Angelo, she took some things to the dry cleaner's, including my tweed jacket. In one of its pockets she found the Polaroid Tony had taken of Missy Blaylock and me in his hot tub, which I'd forgotten. This she presented to me for explanation, and who could blame her? Except that she seemed less troubled than puzzled by the fact that her husband had been photographed in a hot tub with a naked woman. "Isn't that the girl from 'The People Beat'?" she wanted to know.

3. I have friends and loved ones. In fact, our house has been full to overflowing most of the summer. Angelo spent over two months, returning to Philadelphia in early August for his trial, which ended, as expected, with his conviction, though it now appears he may get a suspended sentence if he agrees to sell his house and move out of the neighborhood, which the judge seems to have concluded directly impacts his ability to cope. He will pay LeBrother's reasonable medical expenses.

Julie moved in with us temporarily after their house rented, before joining Russell in Atlanta, and Russell visited twice during that period. Our daughter Karen also paid a visit, bringing with her a young music professor and the news that she will be having their child around Christmas. They hope to marry in the spring. ("*You* hope," her father remarked.) On Memorial Day weekend it required two Weber kettles to barbecue for the crowd, which included my mother, my father, Mr. Purty, Angelo, Julie and Russell, Karen and her young music professor, Tony Coniglia and an ex-student now in her late thirties, Jacob and Gracie (who bickered), and Teddy and June (just back from their cruise). June got drunk, followed me out back to my stand beside the two Weber kettles, and confided she wasn't sure how much longer she could do it, how much longer she could stay married to Teddy, how much longer she could allow all the brightness to leak out of her life. Her sordid affair with "that little turd" Orshee, she now understood, was nothing but a measure of her growing desperation. The good news was that their pussy research (my term, not hers) was beginning to pay dividends. The Emily Dickinson article had been accepted for publication by a good academic journal, and the Virginia Woolf had gone to its third reader at an even better one. If that got accepted as well, and if I would write her a letter of recommendation, she might go on the job market in the fall. The week after that I had a beer with Teddy to celebrate his winning by one vote a runoff election for a three-year term as department chair. Though he was clearly elated, he played down the election, reminding me that he was going to have it a lot tougher than I ever did. In Paul Rourke he'd be dealing with a hostile dean, and the election gave him a less clear mandate than I had enjoyed as chair (I'd won by three votes). The best news was that he felt his marriage was back on track. The cruise had cost a hell of a lot of money, he admitted, but the chair's salary would make up for it. He also announced his intention to surrender his crush on Lily, which he'd begun to see as unhealthy, though he admitted he'd probably always be a little in love with her. There were tears in his eyes.

But the summer's nearly over now, and the crowds have pretty much departed. At night, when it's too warm to sleep, Lily and I are often drawn out onto the deck. There we watch the night sky and listen to the distant sound of our neighbors' nocturnal voices. Not words, just sounds. Old husbands and wives. Old husbands and new wives. Old wives and new husbands. By the time the sound of their lives reaches us, there is only tone and texture, no meaning, but at the end of a long summer day it's mostly affection, though I have no idea what percentile.

4. I have enough money.

I don't understand how this can be so, but Lily promises to explain it to me. Since there's no reason to be circumspect about money, I'll share what little I do know. First, the money Lily used to make Angelo's bail was returned when her father went back to Philadelphia to stand trial. We have loaned Julie and Russell what Lily refers to as substantial sums but not, she maintains, dramatically more than she's told me about, and certainly no more than we spent on Karen's education. Our portfolio, I'm to understand, is intact. This is good news. That we have a portfolio, I mean.

Nor have I severed all ties with the university as I originally intended. True, I tendered my resignation to Jacob Rose, but the letter got lost somehow, and now I find myself on some sort of half-year sabbatical, something I'd forgotten was owed me when I agreed to take on the position of temporary chair. I'll be teaching in the fall, on leave in the spring. I have more advisees than anyone in the department, and this fall they will include Blair and Bobo, who came in together to announce their decision to become English majors. I explained to Bobo, whose name is John and who had in his possession, incredibly, a García Márquez novel, the corner of a page turned down about halfway through, that "English Major" was not a military designation, but he was undeterred. I saw them together on campus once or twice after that, and Bobo was holding her hand tenderly and stroking the blue veins in her pale wrist that I had myself often admired. I don't get to count Leo among my advisees, but I got a letter from him a few weeks after the end of the term. He decided to take Hem's advice and go it alone. Well, not completely alone. His letter was accompanied by the first hundred pages of a new novel he'd written since moving into a cabin in the mountains. It appears to be the story of a young novelist who moves into the mountains after a disastrous semester at the university, where no one, not even his writing teacher, understood how revolutionary his writing was.

Also, Jacob Rose went into his files, resurrected a grant proposal Lily and I had written up nearly a decade ago, and without our permission pitched it to the chancellor. The idea had been that we'd track bright, disadvantaged high school kids in and around Railton, starting in their sophomore year, and guarantee them tuition and books at the Railton Campus for as long as they kept their grades up. Now that Lily's been promoted to principal at the high school, the proposal makes even more sense, we're told. Rourke got wind of the whole deal, including the fact that during the pilot program I'd be teaching part-time (number of classes to be negotiated) at the campus, part-time at the high school (ditto), and promptly labeled it a typical Devereaux boondoggle, but he didn't seem interested in opposing it.

Better still, Wendy, Rachel's agent, formerly and now again *my* agent, parlayed my fifteen minutes of media fame into a book sale. Later this fall my "Soul of the University" *Rear View* satires will be collected and issued by a trade publisher, which will offer them to an unsuspecting public under the title *The Goose Slayer*. The cover will be a still of me brandishing Finny (the goose, not the man) aloft for the television cameras, and I will provide a foreword explaining the event, as well as a personal essay on William Henry Devereaux, Sr., part of which I've already written and which Wendy claims is the best work she's ever seen from me. It's the only piece that isn't a satire, the only piece that doesn't contain, as far as I can tell, a single yuk, though I'm convinced it belongs in the collection. There can be little doubt that William Henry Devereaux, Sr., his life and works, embody the spirit of our increasingly demoralized profession. Which brings me to—

5. I am, as the last surviving William Henry Devereaux, my own man at last, though I must confess that my father's death in mid-July affected me more powerfully than I dreamed it would. William Henry Devereaux, Sr., died quietly and painlessly, sitting upright in his favorite reading chair, dressed as if for a faculty meeting in a tweed jacket, corduroy slacks, and button-down oxford shirt, reading *Our Mutual Friend,* his chin resting on his chest. My mother thought he was napping and went about her own business quietly, not wanting to disturb him. That was no longer possible, if indeed it ever had been.

We had little enough to say to each other, my father and I, before he died. His confidence to me on the day we visited the old midway— that he feared he might have once wronged Dickens—was as close to intimacy as we ever got, and I doubt we'd have improved upon that moment had he lived longer. That afternoon I came to understand that one of the deepest purposes of intellectual sophistication is to provide distance between us and our most disturbing personal truths and gnawing fears. The William Henry Devereaux, Sr., who returned to Railton with my mother and Mr. Purty still had access to the full range of human emotions, but after a lifetime of sophisticated manipulation they were no longer connected to anything real. They fired randomly, unexpectedly, like the passions of a newborn, urgent but without context or, in my father's case, appropriate context.

I suspect that my mother suffers from a similar affliction, though in a minor key, because my father's death, so soon after his return, did not shake her as I would have predicted. At some level she must have felt not only cheated but also the butt of some cosmic joke. However, instead of being devastated by losing him all over again, she seemed almost released from some weighty obligation by his passing. As if, having said before family and friends "till death do us part," she could now say with a clear conscience that she'd been good to her word. Shortly after the funeral I heard from her that she'd begun the task of going through his papers. She sounded almost excited, and I guess that would make a kind of sense. My father was probably more interesting and alive, more the man she knew, on the page than in life, and going through his notes must have represented some small recompense for all the actual conversations missed. She'd always claimed that she was my father's ideal companion and that, in betraying her, he'd betrayed his own best self, and reading through all his drafts and research notes and letters to famous colleagues must have made her feel vindicated in this belief.

A couple days after she'd begun the task, she called me, all excited, to say that she'd discovered two hundred pages of a novel in manuscript, dating back nearly twenty-five years. "Isn't it amazing?" she wanted to know, and I didn't have the heart to tell her that it would have been much more amazing if there *hadn't* been two hundred pages of a novel. He was an English professor. What did she expect? Well, what she expected was that I'd want to read it as soon as she finished, and I know I hurt her feelings when I politely declined, explaining to her that I'd already read it, that it had already been thrust into my hands by my English department colleagues. "You're comparing your father to the likes of William Quigley?" she wanted to know. She'd met Billy at some gathering earlier in the year. "Not at all," I truthfully assured her. I'd have much preferred to read two hundred pages of Billy's book.

After the midway, my father and I had only one other interesting conversation, and that took place in my imagination the day I got out of the hospital and returned home with Lily and Angelo. After we finally convinced Finny that nobody blamed him for Occam's death, and after I'd foolishly promised I'd read his dissertation when he finished it, *I gathered Occam up in the sheet and carried him around back of the house and down to the edge of the woods, where I dug the animal's grave. It took me about an hour, and cost a pair of loafers and my favorite chinos. I was standing thigh deep in the hole when I looked up and saw William Henry Devereaux, Sr., leaning forward heavily on the railing of the back deck, watching me work. Lily and Angelo (who'd wanted to help) and my mother were there too, but they might just as well not have been. This little vignette had clearly been arranged for the benefit of the two William Henry Devereauxs.*

We were some fifty yards apart, too far for him to see me clearly, and at that distance, to his aging eyes, I must have reminded my father very much of the man who buried my first dog forty years ago. In truth, as I have admitted, I've come to greatly resemble my father, and my soft professor's hands were now as blistered as his had become so long ago. He could not have failed to note the parallel events or to misread their significance. I had tried to be unlike him, but look at me. "This is my son," I heard my father think, in character as always, overestimating the importance of his own role in any proceeding, "in whom I am well pleased."

Well, it's easy to send thoughts downhill. He had the advantage of being stationed above, on the deck, whereas I was below at the edge of the woods, hip deep in a hole, my eyes stinging with salt. So I had to work harder to order a thought and power it up the sloping lawn. "Oh, yeah?" I replied. "Well, I didn't have to go borrow a shovel, old man."

But truly grateful people don't make lists of things to be grateful for, any more than happy people make lists of things to be happy about. Happy people have enough to do just being happy.

Growing old, as someone once remarked, is not for sissies, but age is not the issue so much as diminishment. This summer provided William Henry Devereaux, Jr., with two athletic milestones (I'm not counting the basketball game). Before leaving for Atlanta, Julie administered to her father a sound drubbing in tennis, an inevitable defeat I'd been postponing with smoke and mirrors for nearly a decade. One bright, warm Sunday afternoon, in a two set match that took just under an hour, Julie ran her fifty-year-old father back and forth from sideline to sideline, net to baseline, with a cruel efficiency that was entirely unlike her. I knew I was beat when I realized she wasn't listening to me, which is not the same thing as reminding herself not to listen to me, which is what she'd always done before. For ten years I'd been able to get her to double-fault by warning her not to, but that afternoon she found a way to tune me out on the tennis court as efficiently as she used to at the dinner table when I recommended books. Only when the match was over and she'd done what she hadn't quite dared to believe was possible did she finally break into the kind of radiant smile calculated to break a father's heart. "That's for what you did to Russell," she grinned at me on the way home, and for a moment, until I remembered the basketball game in which he put a hook shot up on the roof behind the backboard, I thought she was talking about my running him out of town after I found him at Meg Quigley's.

Worse than defeat is concession. This summer, after jogging all spring so that I might retain my spot in left field, I have voluntarily made the move to first base, a position I mastered so effortlessly that I reinforced Phil Watson's erroneous conclusion that I was born to play there. I was not. On first, the philosophical issues are competence, reliability, patience, and faith, but alas there is little poetry. There is satisfaction to be derived from digging an errant throw out of the dirt, but the heart doesn't leap when the hitter turns on a pitch and lifts the ball high and far enough for a man like me to feel awe and wonder. Watson's nephew has acquitted himself well enough in my left field. At the beginning of the season he had twice my speed and half my judgment, which meant the team was no better off, but as Watson correctly observed, his nephew's judgment would improve with experience, whereas I was all done getting faster.

Late one night on my deck, after Lily said good night, a bottle of good Irish whiskey between us, Tony Coniglia, who'd come over to say farewell before going to Pittsburgh for a year as a sabbatical leave replacement, tried to explain it all to me in what would have been another of his long, patented riffs, if I hadn't been in a quarrelsome mood. "We have entered," he explained, "the Season of Grace.

"Consider Beowulf," he went on. "There comes a time in every warrior's life when he realizes he doesn't have his best stuff anymore. He thinks he's the same guy that whupped Grendel, but he's not. If he were honest, he'd have to admit he could no longer take Grendel's mother in a fair fight."

"Beowulf *did* defeat Grendel's mother," I couldn't help reminding him. "And she was one tough broad, too."

"Huh," Tony said. "Beowulf defeated Grendel's mother?"

"It was a clear victory, as I recall."

"Ah!" he said, remembering now, pointing his finger at me as if I were to blame for his faulty memory. "It was the *dragon* he lost to."

Unfortunately, my own recollection of Beowulf was not much better than his. "I think he kills the dragon too, though he himself is mortally wounded."

"Then *that's* my point," Tony said, narrowing his eyes at me. "It's the dragon that's my point. Beowulf was a fool to fight the dragon. By then he was an old warrior."

"No," I assured him. "The point seems to have been that he was a hero for fighting the dragon."

He was glaring at me now. It actually seemed possible that we could have angry words over Beowulf. "But his skills were diminished. The time for deeds had passed. He had entered the Season of Grace but did not have the grace to admit it."

"He died a warrior's death. That *was* his grace."

Tony took a long swig from the bottle, considered my pigheaded views. "Okay, fuck Beowulf. There are no more warriors anyhow."

With this I could agree. "There are no more Grendels," I pointed out. "Men our age can't even find a good Grendel's mother. God knows what we'll do when we're the age to look for dragons."

"No dragons for me," Tony said. "I've entered the Season of Grace."

"You and Jacob," I nodded.

"He's merely entered Gracie. That's not the same thing," he said, before becoming philosophical again. "No, youth is the Season of Deeds. The question youth asks is: Who am I? In the Season of Grace we ask: What have I become?"

"And what have we become?"

"I have become very drunk."

"Then don't drive home," I insisted. "Stay here tonight. Drive back in the morning."

"I accept your invitation, for one reason and one reason only. Do you know what that reason is?"

"Because this is the Season of Grace?"

He grinned at me drunkenly. "You've always been my best student."

And so, I conclude, if William Henry Devereaux, Jr., is less than ecstatically happy, less grateful for his myriad blessings than he should be to the Bestower of Said Blessings, it must be because he has not fully accepted his good friend's invitation to join him and Nolan Ryan and Dr. J. and Nadia Comaneci, and all the others who have lost their best stuff, in entering the Season of Grace.

I am, however, relatively at peace with who and what I've become, thanks to a series of events that occurred back in May. One rainy Saturday morning Yolanda Ackles, Tony Coniglia's former student, attempted suicide by stepping in front of a car at the bottom of the steep hill that leads up to Tony's house. The driver, who owned a car identical in color and make to Tony's and who must have been preternaturally alert, saw her when she stepped out from behind a tree. He stood on the brakes, but even so he knocked her through the intersection. He later described for the police the way she had calmly stepped out into the street and turned to face his oncoming car, a beatific smile on her face, her arms out as if to embrace him, a sight more horrifying to him than her body when she finally came to rest in an unnatural position against the opposite curb. Everyone who saw the accident said it was a miracle that she had not been killed. Witnesses testified that at one point she sat up and smiled before passing out. At the hospital she was found to have sustained a fractured ankle, a broken collarbone, a severe concussion, and multiple lacerations. None of her injuries was life threatening.

Later that morning, however, Tony Coniglia was admitted to the same hospital with heart fibrillations, and because of his cardiac history he was kept overnight for observation. He returned home the next afternoon with a prescription for a mild tranquilizer and instructions not to play racquetball with me for the rest of the summer. That evening Jacob Rose called and suggested I join him in paying Tony a visit. Maybe he'd invite one or two of Tony's other friends. Together we'd cheer him up. Since Russell happened to be in town for the weekend, I invited him to come along. It had occurred to me that he might be able to get Tony's computer to function.

By the time we arrived, the house was full of men, and the atmosphere bordered, inappropriately enough, on festive. Jacob, acting as host, met us at the door with a glass of whiskey in his hand. "I thought I told you to bring the pizza," he said.

"I could go get some," Russell offered.

Jacob cocked his head at me. "I've got no idea who this kid is, but I like him." He turned to Russell then, extending his hand. "I've spent most of the day talking to the board of trustees, and you're the first person to take anything I've said seriously. I was joking about the pizza, but how were you to know?"

Inside, I introduced Russell around. There were a couple fellows from Tony's department, one each from Psych and Chemistry, as well as a few from English. Across the room I witnessed something I hadn't seen in years—Teddy Barnes and Paul Rourke in what appeared to be pleasant conversation. Or if not pleasant, at least nonadversarial. Mike Law, looking morose, but no more so than when he was married to Gracie, was also there.

There were no women, which was good. I would not have liked this convivial scene to be reported. If I understood correctly, we'd gathered to assure our friend and colleague that what happened to Yolanda Ackles was not his fault. This we might have managed to do if we had come one at a time, or even perhaps if the gathering had stayed small. But males who come together in numbers this large, without the civilizing presence of women, are genetically unable to sustain the solemnity of any occasion once the whiskey has been located. To look at us, you'd have sworn we didn't care a jot about what happened to poor Yolanda Ackles. It looked like we'd closed ranks around one of our own, and perhaps this *was* what we'd done, though I doubt it was what we meant to do. I could tell Russell was confused by the merriment. He suspected there was some aspect to the proceedings that I hadn't told him about, though he wasn't sure enough of himself just then to be critical. During the whole weekend Russell seemed more determined to get back into my good graces than Julie's, which was another reason I'd taken him along with me, to show him there were no hard feelings. He and Julie both seemed tremendously relieved to be back together again.

When Tony spotted us, he came over and I introduced him to Russell, explaining that my son-in-law was a computer guy and suggesting that Russell take a look at Tony's system while I got us a drink. Fifteen minutes later I poked my head into the spare bedroom, where I found Russell under the table, fiddling with the back of the computer, his bristly cranium just visible above the machine, the top of which he had removed. Tony himself I found outside on the back deck, sitting on the edge of the quiet hot tub, alone.

"I've been thinking about going back to Brooklyn," he said, raising his glass so we could clink. "The problem is, the Brooklyn I'd like to return to doesn't exist anymore."

"Should you be drinking?" I wondered.

"This is iced tea," he admitted. "Do you ever yearn to return to that horrible place in the Midwest where you were born?"

"Never," I told him, the simple, honest truth. Of course I had no recollection of it either. We'd moved by the time I was two, and by the time I was three we'd moved again.

"Most people are one way or the other," Tony explained. "They either want to confront the past or escape it."

I could feel one of Tony's long, scientific disquisitions, full of clinical observations and invented statistics, coming on, so I took a good, long pull of bourbon and settled in.

"I'd like to meet that woman again," he told me. "Did I tell you about her?"

"You came before she could get out of her brassiere."

He nodded sadly. "She must have touched me, though," he said. "I don't remember her touching me, but I think minimal physical contact would have been necessary."

"If you don't remember—" I began, though he wasn't really listening.

"I think I must have flirted with Yolanda Ackles," he said, staring out at the dark woods beyond his house. "I don't remember doing it, but you may have noticed I'm a flirtatious man. I have even flirted with your wife upon occasion."

"And you remember doing it," I pointed out, adding, "so do I."

"Well," he conceded. "Perhaps. But I can't help thinking that what happened to that young woman may be my fault."

"I know you," I told him with as much conviction as I could summon. "If you flirted with Yolanda Ackles, you did it to make her feel good about herself."

"You think so?" he said. "You think I did it to make her feel good? Not to make me feel good?"

"I'm sure of it," I told him. I know you, Al. You're not the kind of man who.

We looked each other in the eye then, both shrugging at the same instant. "I think that woman must have taken me in her hand," Tony says. "It stands to reason."

One of the things you never know for sure in life is whether a joke is the right thing. Sometimes even after you've offered one. I can only

say that I was too delighted to have caught Tony in an ambiguous pronoun reference to refrain. "I'm sure it was standing," I told my friend.
"But not to reason."

Back inside, the living room had been abandoned. We found
everyone crammed into the spare room, where Russell was watching
Tony's computer scroll, jammed to the margins of the screen with keyboard symbols that materialized below, inched upward line by line,
and disappeared into the top of the screen. You almost expected to see
the same lines appear, intact, in the air above the monitor, scrolling up
the wall and along the ceiling.

The small room was very crowded with men watching this bizarre
sight as if it were a feat of magic. Several more friends of Tony's had
arrived, and from out in the hall we could hear the doorbell. I saw that
Billy Quigley was there and had cornered his new dean and was reading him the drunken riot act. I overheard the word *peckerwood,* a term
I had always assumed Billy reserved for me.

To William Henry Devereaux, Jr., the whole scene took on a sur-
real quality. Dreams, it is said, are all meaning, and I couldn't help
thinking that that's what this scene must be, some form of concentrated
significance. I thought maybe if *I* concentrated I could figure it out. I
knew these men. I'd known most of them for twenty years. When we
met we were all married. A few of us still were. A few more were
divorced. A few more were remarried and trying again. Some of us
had betrayed fine women. Some of us had been ourselves betrayed. But
here we were, tonight at least, drawn together by some need, as if we
were waiting for a sign. And I was one of their number.

Russell pushed back his chair, confessing, "I don't understand this."

And then suddenly we were all chuckling, probably at the sight
gag that accompanied his words, the computer's packed screen still
scrolling upwards.

"No, I mean, this should work," Russell explained, having concluded perhaps that the laughter was directed at him.

"Maybe it *is* working," Jacob Rose suggested. "I think you've
hacked your way into God's mainframe. This is a list of our options.
All we need to do is break the code."

And maybe it was so much laughter, so many of us bewildered,
middle-aged men using up the oxygen in such a tiny room, but all at

once we seemed to realize how close it was in there, and just as suddenly we all wanted out. Only when we turned toward the exit did we
realize our predicament. The bedroom door opened inward, toward
us, but we'd moved too close to it. There wasn't room.

"Trapped," I heard a droll voice say. "Like rats."

"Everybody back up," another voice suggested, but those in the
back of the room either didn't hear the request or didn't understand its
necessity. Everyone knew where the door was and continued to press
toward it and imagined freedom. Suddenly, everyone was talking,
laughing, shouting panicky, desperate, half-joking obscenities. "Help!"
yelled someone near the center of the room, perhaps in jest.

Normally I'm subject to the kind of blind claustrophobic panic
that then filled the room, but I happened at that moment to catch the
eye of Paul Rourke across the room, and when I grinned, he tried
valiantly to smother a grin of his own. For twenty years he'd steadfastly
maintained that anything I thought was funny most assuredly was not,
and I could tell he felt his twenty-year resolve crumbling. I could see
him let it go, and his big, mean-spirited face broke into the widest
imaginable grin, and his shoulders began to bounce up and down.

Clearly, the only solution was for all of us to take one step backward so that the door could be pulled open. By this point a group of
plumbers, a group of bricklayers, a group of hookers, a group of chim-
panzees would have figured this out. But the room contained, unfortunately, a group of academics, and we couldn't quite believe what had
happened to us.